Along

the
Red Dirt Road

The uplifting historical novel rooted in the American Civil War/Great Depression era about secrecy, scandal, friendship, and truth

Jane Yearout

Copyright © 2020 Jane Yearout
All rights reserved.
ISBN:978-1-7348280-0-9

The characters and events portrayed in this book are fictitious. Any similarity to real persons, living or dead, is coincidental and not intended by the author.

No part of this book may be reproduced or stored in a retrieval system, or transmitted in any form or by any means, electronic, mechanical, photocopying, recording or otherwise, without express written permission of the author.

Cover design: Ashfoard Associates

Printed in the United States of America

ACKNOWLEDGMENTS

The story you are about to read is one that evolved over months and years. From the time I was a young girl, I loved reading and writing stories, but despite encouragement from family and teachers, my goal of writing a novel never progressed beyond a few long-forgotten chapters. By the time I reached my sixties, I knew I would never realize my goal unless I got my act together.

I have been asked what inspired this story. The answer is not simple. Some years ago, my family discovered the diary of a Confederate ancestor. In heart-rending detail, it described his escape from Union custody and arduous journey back to North Carolina. With that seed subconsciously planted in my brain, a song written and performed by Tim O'Brien one afternoon in a West Virginia field caused that seed to take root. For years, I had pondered the notion of weaving a tale around my maternal great-grandmother, whose pioneer spirit, spritely form, and given name had fascinated me since childhood. Numerous friends and family members, places and circumstances I have encountered on the "red dirt road of life" supplied the rest.

The red dirt and people of Oklahoma gave me my roots, my grounding. The people and lush hills of West Virginia gave me a love for their window to history. While all places and characters in *Along the Red Dirt Road* are fictitious, they are a compilation of bits and pieces pulled from my past and my imagination.

A posthumous thank you goes to my mother and aunt, who never stopped telling me to write. Thank you to my husband Bill, who encouraged me and was one of my first readers. Without his editing assistance, positive reinforcement, and much more, this book would not be what it is. Thank you to Judy Malone, who read the manuscript's first draft and provided plot/character suggestions and critiques. She and Bill gave me the confidence that this is a story that may touch the minds and hearts of others. Thank you to Joanne Brown, professional editor, who reinforced the belief that this story is a good one. A final thank you goes to all of my family and friends who provided love, insights into human nature, and an appreciation for truth. I hope you find this tale satisfying, inspirational, and worthy of passing forward.

Cover Image: Public Domain
(Federal Highway Administration)

All Other Illustrations: Jane Yearout

Table of Contents

PROLOGUE

The scene is an exact duplicate of the one her eyes first spied so long ago. Autumn's waning foliage allows objects hidden by summer's greenery to peer forth and become so distinct one wonders how they could stand unnoticed. The thigh-high rubble of the old stone wall, buried beneath a blanket of vines and brambles, is in its earliest stage of peek-a-boo. She knows it well.

She and the wall first met on a crisp fall day, much like today. The sun shone through the woodland canopy, casting ribbons of dappled light onto damp rocks glimmering beneath the undergrowth. Her mother had instructed her to stay within easy earshot of the house and away from the wooded thicket at the back of the property. Yet, as sure as her mother's warning, the forest beckoned, and she could not resist.

Her name is Anna Ruth. She is an old woman now. Her granddaughter, KT, has accompanied Anna Ruth here so she may see the location once again during her natural life. KT knows nothing of the scene or its story, nor of its permanent residence in her grandmother's heart. Besides being a physician, KT is a dutiful granddaughter with a penchant to indulge her eccentric grandmother with whom she feels an odd and unexplained connection.

At the property's entrance, a faded For Sale sign dangles from its post by a lone rusty wire. A once proud dwelling stands unoccupied, staring at them through dark and mournful windows. Littered with bird droppings and piles of yellowed newspapers, an overgrowth of trees and shrubs hides the once impressive front porch from worse disgrace. Rotted window frames, peeling paint, sagging gutters, and a weed-infested lawn tell of hard times but little else. An eerie sound catches Anna Ruth's attention. Branches of a cedar tree emit a soft squeak with each pass across filthy window panes that once peeked into a young girl's bedroom. She stops and remembers. Anna Ruth chuckles while poking her cane into a massive clump of twigs and leaves, flicking them aside.

As the women make their way through the overgrowth toward the property's rear boundary, KT is the first to speak. "This place gives me the creeps! I don't understand why on earth we're here."

"Help me, please, KT. These old legs are having trouble with this underbrush. Watch out for poison ivy. It's still out, and these briers will bite you."

KT supports her grandmother's elbow as they navigate rugged, uneven ground toward their primary destination, the stone wall. Anna Ruth spots a path that enables both to proceed with greater ease. Deer and other critters have worn the trail bare, and a gap in the wall provides wildlife easy passage down a rocky slope onto adjoining property. This break likewise allows the women to better view large homes now populating fields where an apple orchard stood long ago.

Stopping to gaze at the site, Anna Ruth snorts, "What a shame!" She remembers the orchard with the fragrance of ripening apples and sweet melodies sung by apple pickers wafting through the air this time of year.

The two women reach the wall, and Anna Ruth catches her breath. Although fatigued, she is eager to look around and remember. Anna Ruth wants to tell KT about the wall, her story, and secrets she has never shared.

"KT, set out these chairs. We'll have our picnic."

"Here?"

"Here. The ground is level, and underbrush has died back. This is the best spot we'll find. The fools who live in those monstrosities can't see us here. We're fine right here."

Annoyed and confused, KT removes her backpack containing their lunch and unfolds two camp chairs she has hauled through the woods. She sets them on the ground and sighs. She does not consider this a suitable picnic spot. KT assists her grandmother into one chair, tucks a plaid green and black fleece blanket around the woman's lap and legs, and takes a seat facing Anna Ruth.

"Nonnie, are you sure you're okay?" KT asks, addressing Anna Ruth by the name she has called her since childhood. "We can eat our lunch and go right back to the car. Chiggers, ticks, or . . . snakes may bite us."

"Oh, I'm fine." Anna Ruth ignores her granddaughter's question and concern. "I'm tired. Sitting a spell will do me good. I want to talk to you. Tell you of this place. You know nothing of it, do you?"

"No," concedes the reluctant diner with a roll of her warm, brown eyes.

KT is petite with chestnut ringlets scrunched under a baseball cap. Although she is in her early forties, her athletic build and freckled face make her appear much younger than her years. Focused and committed to her profession, she lives alone with two cats and neither seeks nor accepts companionship of male suitors. Marriage has never been in her plans. Since her mother's death from cancer, she spends more time with Anna Ruth, monitoring her health and venturing forth on excursions easy for the grandmother to tolerate.

While KT considers her grandmother an eccentric outsider, she perceives herself much the same. Her career is

3

not the prestigious one her parents and older brothers envisioned for her. KT's concerns are for the powerless, not the rich and powerful. Wealth and status do not motivate KT.

Anna Ruth views KT's professional choice through a different lens, one that evokes memories of her own physician father. She remembers his devotion to his patients, his fairness, thoughtfulness, and unwavering fidelity to truth. Anna Ruth understands KT's *outsiderness* because of her own experience here. She wants KT to know. She wants KT to understand . . . everything.

As she munches on her sandwich, KT directs a quizzical gaze toward her grandmother. Anna Ruth's behavior and this spot in the woods next to an old stone wall have piqued her curiosity.

"Tell me."

Thus begins an afternoon of revelation as KT learns the story her Nonnie has never divulged to anyone.

THE ARRIVAL

"**L**ook, Mama! Daddy! Daffodils! Oh, they are so pretty!" Anna Ruth's declaration radiated delight as her father urged the dusty, black Dodge up the gravel driveway of their new home.

"Yes, they are, Annie!" Ellen Young concurred.

The year was 1933. The Great Depression was in full swing when Anna Ruth, her parents, and a dog named Bitsy moved into the pristine wooden dwelling. Anna Ruth's father, Dr. Carter Young, had accepted an offer to move his family and medical practice. The new location was over a thousand miles east of the family's previous home on the plains, and its lush valley offered promise and opportunity.

Anna Ruth, or Annie, as everyone called her back then, was twelve years old, the age between childhood and young womanhood. It is a time when dolls perch on shelves, gathering dust and waiting for one more caress, but Annie was becoming absorbed in glamour and charm. She gazed at her collection of movie star photos and tried to imitate the women's poses. Annie Young practiced in her bedroom mirror, but the freckled face and light brown curls staring back bore a striking resemblance to Amelia Earhart, not the femme fatales she so admired.

Annie did not embrace the move from their home on the plains. She was a tall, shy, and solitary girl just emerging from her shell and gaining confidence. An only child, Annie felt comfortable in the company of adults. She enjoyed listening to their conversations, which ranged from politics to tales of a neighbor's gray cat whose preferred toilet was the closest flower bed. Annie pleaded with her father not to move, but the Great Depression and barren fields brought on by wind and drought had taken a toll on his livelihood. Patients could not pay for medical care. Their small town had trouble supporting the doctors they had, even in good times. As a family matter, Ellen Young's mother had proven to be intrusive and critical of her daughter's choice of a husband.

Carter and Ellen Young approached this move with trepidation. Their destination was a rural locale in the Shenandoah Valley where George Washington once roamed and Civil War battles raged. Carter's former medical school classmate practiced medicine there, and he reached out to his old friend to relocate to the town. Due to the death of an older, well-established physician, the region needed another doctor. Wind, drought, and dust did not torment this community, and it held the promise of a fresh beginning for Carter, Ellen, and Annie.

The move and the long drive east came with a high material and emotional price tag. Carter and Ellen sold or gave away furnishings. They kept necessities for the journey packed inside a wooden box Carter built and attached to the rear of the 1930 straight-six Dodge. Inside the sturdy, austere sedan, Carter's medical bag, books, clothing, plus a few tools and supplies took up every available cubic inch. They crammed items behind the rear seat, with the rear window kept free for visibility. More essentials needed for the journey sat beneath the feet of Annie and her mother, while other belongings consumed the space behind the driver's seat from floor to ceiling.

The Youngs left their old home empty. Sobs and pleas to stay from Ellen's distraught mother made their goodbyes painful and raw. Ellen lost her composure as she stared through the rear window of the packed automobile and saw her mother's hand wringing and ultimate collapse into her father's arms. Annie watched everything, overcome with grief, but her quiet whimpers and pleas for her father to turn around faded after a dozen or so dusty miles. Never having been in a car before, little Bitsy remained agitated. The black, white, and tan Wire-haired Fox Terrier panted, squirmed, and kept trying to jump over the back seat into the front for almost an hour. A stoic Carter Young steered the vehicle in silence, ignoring his wife's tears, the dog's incessant antics, and his daughter's indignant threats to run away.

Those first miles added to the journey's initial misery. Besides sobs and dog anxieties, continuous, swirling winds buffeted the Dodge, enveloping the car in a massive cloud of choking red dirt. This same red dirt kicked up from the unpaved road adhered to the car, painted the roadside landscape, and imbued the sky with an ominous orange-red hue. Although the car windows remained closed tight, gritty, red dust found its way inside the sedan, coating the dash and covering the travelers. Potholes and deep ruts made steering difficult and comfort impossible. Several times, Carter stopped the car so dust could subside and improve his vision. They passed no other vehicles, and their only encounter before hitting a graded surface was a scrawny coyote, a chicken dangling out of its mouth, ambling across the road.

As days wore on, they settled into a routine. Their new existence consisted of more bone-jarring roads, choking dust, and little or no access to bathrooms. Carter kept the radiator full and the speed moderate, which sometimes drew embarrassing honks from impatient motorists. A reliable vehicle with adequate power, the Dodge's plain exterior and interior matched the times.

7

The Great Depression was near its worst in 1933. Displaced Americans traveled roads and hopped freight trains in search of work. In the early stage of their journey, the Youngs' car chugged eastward past countless numbers headed west toward an uncertain future in California. Many traveled in old cars and trucks laden with precious remnants of better times. Some traveled by wagon, some on foot, often with livestock. At times, westbound refugees filled both lanes of the road, leaving little room for the black Dodge to pass. Other times, a lonesome soul hobbled along the shoulder. Blank faces looking downward and blank faces looking straight ahead comprised the norm. They offered a heart-rending nod or tipped hat, to which the Youngs replied in kind.

Carter did what he could to avoid crowding or covering them with a billowing cloud of dust. The Youngs began their journey with anticipation of a brighter future. The people they encountered along the way enriched the family with gratitude for their own circumstances and a deep and lasting empathy for others.

More than once, circumstances required Carter, Ellen, and Annie to camp along the road or in nearby clearings. Such encampments came with an abundance of unease due to noise from a passing car or truck, no privacy, worry of a malicious intruder, and whines from little Bitsy. At earliest light, the weary family rose to a gritty coat of red dirt and a painful urge to find relief.

On occasion, a resident along the way allowed them to camp in their yard or pasture. Such nights rewarded the travelers with a more restful sleep.

The Youngs did not look prosperous by any standard, but they attempted to stay clean and presentable. Whether it was their outward appearance or simple grace, Annie, Ellen, and Carter on two occasions received invitations to enjoy indoor bathrooms containing bathtubs filled with hot water. These baths were a rare and luxurious treat relished by Annie and her mother. Annie noted every person who offered hospitality also responded with wishes of good luck and a warm handshake or hug. Carter and Ellen expressed deep appreciation for each kindness that came their way. Ellen even took the addresses of three families and kept in touch with them for several years. When camping, their food was simple and boring, but no one complained, and Bitsy accepted with gusto any scraps offered.

When nature called, Annie learned how to follow her mother into the woods and relieve herself without making a mess. Ellen stopped fretting about her parents and the life left behind and began speaking of the unknown life awaiting them. Carter soon accepted rough roads and wrong turns with laughter instead of grim silence. Bitsy savored unfamiliar smells at each stop and gazed out the car window in eager anticipation as they bounced along toward their new home. For Bitsy, long naps with her head resting on Annie's lap followed window gazing.

The drive lasted over seven arduous days. The transition from red dirt roads and flat, drought-ravaged plains to green, rolling hills was in early spring. Smoother roads, clean air, and mild temperatures provided welcome relief to the stuffy quarters and endless bounces the four travelers endured during the beginning stage of their journey.

Carter had been in regular contact with the deceased physician's widow, Mrs. McCormick. Her home sat on four acres just three miles outside town, and she offered it to the Youngs at a reasonable rent. Mrs. McCormick had moved into town to live with her daughter and her son-in-law after her husband's recent passing. It was hard to sell real estate in 1933, so she left the house unoccupied and furnished, with each piece of furniture covered by white sheets to keep items free of dust. The house also came with a family of cats who lived beneath the floorboards and kept the dwelling free of mice. The acreage had been a wedding gift from Mrs. McCormick's father, carved out of his farm, when Dr. and Mrs. McCormick wed in the late 1800s. Embedded in the family's history, the land had been in her ancestors' hands since soon after the Revolutionary War. On that plot of earth and stone, Dr. and Mrs. McCormick built a respectable home and raised a family.

A cornfield bordered one side of the property, and a cow pasture bordered the other side. An apple orchard, blocked from view by dense woods on the McCormick property, occupied land beyond the rear boundary. A long, narrow gravel driveway gave access to the house from a dirt lane connecting to the macadam road into town. Ash, elm, oak, and walnut trees, along with several stands of sassafras and maple populated the outlying property. Two American chestnut trees, dead from the blight, stood alone in the back yard. Scattered throughout was an ample under story of chinquapins, ready to surrender bountiful crops of delicious little nuts that proved to be one of Annie's favorite snacks each autumn. Soon, ferns and may apples would blanket the most shaded areas near the home and in the woods.

The house was spacious but without extravagance. It faced west, so the front porch with its stone columns provided shade in the mornings and early afternoon for two rocking chairs. The covered back porch soon became a favored retreat to read and relax on warm afternoons because of its eastern exposure. Fresh paint, courtesy of Mrs. McCormick, made the house glisten in the sun. That early afternoon when Dr. Carter Young drove up the driveway on their journey's last day, the sight that greeted each of the travelers overcame them with boundless delight.

A field of daffodils blanketing the ground beneath two towering ash trees first caught Annie's eye, while the view of the house in which they were to live brought an audible gasp of approval from Ellen's lips. Carter sat without speaking, his chin and hands resting on the steering wheel as his dark brown eyes absorbed the peaceful sanctuary-like scene.

"Carter, this is more than I imagined! I can't wait to see it!" Ellen grabbed her door handle and jumped out of the car.

Wind caught her chestnut hair, and she brushed it from her smiling face.

Carter swung open the driver's side door and stepped from the vehicle, leaving the door open as he exclaimed, "Let's go!" Ellen and Annie's reactions brought relief to Carter because he had steeled himself for the possibility of substantial disappointment.

Bitsy sprang over the seat and took off barking as she leaped from the car. She spied one of the resident cats and chased it up a honeysuckle vine that clung to one of the back porch columns. The dog had not been so excited since spotting a fox while the family supped at a campsite in Indiana. Annie darted to the back of the house where she collared and clutched Bitsy as the pesky cat made a safe retreat. By this time, Bitsy was a wild and wiggling bundle, but Annie contained her squirms, and the little terrier returned to a lesser state of agitation.

Carter fetched a leash from the car. "Use this leash, Annie. Hang onto her in case other cats are around the house. We'd hate for Bitsy to harm one or get her eye scratched." Dr. Young's serene demeanor belied the inner turmoil he felt. This move was difficult, not just for Annie and her mother, but likewise for him. He was starting a new career far from anything familiar during a time of horrific and widespread economic hardship. Could he be successful in supporting his family? Could they be content in this unfamiliar environment? Concern for his beloved wife and daughter was paramount. He ran his fingers through his dark, wavy hair and drew his trim six-foot frame into a resolved stance.

"Well, my dear girls, Mrs. McCormick's daughter has left a key for us on the front porch. Shall we explore our new home?"

With a turn of the key and a swing of the door, they stepped inside the house. Ellen opened the parlor draperies, and her hazel eyes sparkled with delight at what she saw. Although sheets covered the furnishings, Ellen could tell Mrs. McCormick had decorated in excellent taste. Oak woodwork

11

stained to a walnut tone and floral wallpaper were elegant to Annie's brown eyes as she ran her hand along the smooth and polished woodwork framing the door between the parlor and dining room.

The family proceeded from room to room. Carter and Ellen removed protective coverings from furniture and piled them in corners. As Ellen opened draperies, her diminutive form and porcelain complexion glowed with the sunlight flooding each room, the sun's rays capturing red highlights in her hair. She envisioned herself cooking in the sunny kitchen, and it pleased her that a deep windowsill over the sink might one day house her favorite house plants, African violets.

Ellen noted the accouterments. "Carter, I think I shall love this house! Aren't we fortunate Mrs. McCormick will rent it to us? I believe we'll be happy here, don't you?" Her typical sunny disposition, muted throughout the entire journey, emerged, and its raucous quality shocked Annie.

"Mama! You're so excited! You're acting just like Bitsy!"

Carter started laughing so hard he stopped dead in his tracks. He gave Ellen a kiss on her cheek and pulled her close. The thought of Ellen Young twirling and leaping high in the air while barking as the little terrier was apt to do was hilarious in his mind. Bitsy was typical of her breed, and her stubby tail quivered with anticipation even when she sat still.

Ellen responded to her daughter's tease in a comic and mocking voice. "No, I do *not* think so!"

With a quick hug to the girl and a pat to Bitsy, Ellen Young took on a spirited, high stepping march as she led the group up the stairs.

Three bedrooms upstairs were large compared to most bedrooms of the day in which Dr. and Mrs. McCormick had built the house. A bathroom occupied a room off the short hallway, and it, too, was larger than one might have expected. It included a large linen closet and a door concealing narrow steps leading to the attic. Carter surmised the room had once been a bedroom, since indoor plumbing was not the norm at the time of the home's construction. The clawfoot bathtub reminded Annie of the one at her grandmother's house. One bedroom was larger than the other two, so Carter questioned his wife with a simple, "Ours?"

Ellen nodded. "This one will belong to Daddy and me. You may have either of the other two you wish, Annie."

Annie set Bitsy on the oak floor, still holding the leash in her left hand, and walked into each room. She examined the one at the end of the hall. The room was long and narrow. One window faced the front of the house, one faced the side, and the other faced the back of the property. Carter voiced the opinion that this room may have been a sleeping porch in past years. With drapes open, the sun shone in the west-facing window.

"I prefer this one, Mama. It's sunny."

"In summer, it may get hotter than the other room, Annie," Carter said. "The trees over here, though, once they leaf out, should help keep the sun out." He motioned toward the south-facing window.

Ellen concurred. "This room should be warmer during winter because it's right above the kitchen. Remember, Carter, it won't be as hot here in summer as back home."

"This room is now yours, Miss Anna Ruth Young." Carter bowed and flourished as if he was meeting the Queen of England, and Bitsy jumped up to lick his hand. Bitsy's action brought forth a giggle from Annie and a wide smile from her father.

Annie gazed at the room. Two beds sat close together with a small square table between them. Two dressers and one wardrobe closet provided space for clothing. A rolled-up rug rested on the floor against one wall.

"May I keep the second bed just in case I have a friend who wants to spend the night? I hope nice girls live here, and I'll make friends. The windows need prettier curtains than these brown ones. My movie star photographs can go on this wall next to the door. What color do you call this rug? Bitsy can sleep right next to this bed I want to be mine. Two dressers will give me lots of drawers! I love this, don't you?" The questions and declarations poured forth as Annie took in her new circumstances.

Her parents smiled and chuckled at each other, relieved their daughter appeared pleased. Carter and Ellen felt apprehension for the many changes confronting Annie. That she viewed the house and the room she had just claimed as her own with favor was a good first step toward contentment.

As rain clouds formed, Carter suggested they unpack the car and bring its contents inside before the rain. Annie tied Bitsy to a dogwood tree in the front yard, using the rope with which they had tied her while camping on their journey. Although Annie set the dog's water bowl within easy reach, Bitsy whined as everyone pitched in to empty the car.

Unloading did not take long. Most possessions they deposited in the middle of the parlor, with clothing dispatched upstairs to the bedrooms. Annie carried Bitsy's bed to her new room, placing the wicker basket next to the bed she planned to occupy. Ellen piled Carter's medical bag and books, along with dishes, utensils, and her pots and pans on the table in the kitchen. The few tools Carter brought found a temporary home on the covered back porch. Once they depleted the car of its contents, the three relaxed on the front porch with Carter and Ellen sitting in the two rockers while Annie and Bitsy rested on the front step. The afternoon was drawing to a close, and the trio was weary. Annie reminded her mother how much she loved lemonade as they shared a single glass of water.

"I plan to go to the market tomorrow, and lemons will be on my list. I hope they have lemons, but they may not be available. Lemons are a luxury, you know. I'm wondering where a suitable spot for our garden may be so we can plant seeds after danger of frost has passed. That decision can wait!"

The afternoon's tranquility ended with an abrupt roll of thunder and the sound of an automobile crunching and tossing gravel as it sped up the driveway.

The man behind the wheel leaned on the horn as he shouted, his head thrust out the driver's side window, "Yo, there, Youngs! Welcome!"

It was Dr. Jack Morrison, the friend who had convinced Carter to move. Dr. Morrison beamed as he bounded from his big, blue Buick sedan with its flashy white sidewall tires. A hearty, "You must be Annie!" followed a quick handshake for Carter and a peck on the cheek for Ellen. He folded his arms and smiled again, peering at the girl. Jack Morrison's rumpled, sandy hair and his too-large slacks presented a much different image from the one Annie had pictured. While Carter Young, with his dark brown eyes and wavy chocolate hair, exhibited a calm and deliberate demeanor, Jack Morrison's was the opposite, even boisterous. He was shorter than Carter, somewhat stocky, and his keen gray eyes danced when he spoke. Jack and Carter were exceptional friends in school and had kept in touch ever since that time.

Shy, pencil-thin Annie nodded with her eyes cast in a downward stare at the step where she sat. Bitsy lurched and pulled at the leash restraining her but didn't bark as Dr. Morrison leaned over and rubbed the dog's face.

"Carter, I knew you'd be here by now. Thanks for the telegram alerting me today was arrival day. Listen, Lou has prepared a scrumptious supper, and we want you to join us. How's that?"

Ellen protested, "Oh, I'm a mess!" yet she hoped her husband accepted the invitation.

"Mess? Mess? Look at me! I've been hanging new curtains for Lou. My wife always finds a chore for me! These are my work clothes. You are not a mess, Ellen! C'mon my friends." Jack's smiling eyes and enthusiastic welcome were so unbridled that Carter could not decline.

"Your invitation is too kind, Jack. We'll take you up on it, even if Ellen thinks she's a mess! Why, look at me!" Carter laughed and pointed to himself in his wrinkled shirt and dusty shoes. "If you don't mind three vagabonds invading your home, then we'd be most appreciative. We are tired and will welcome the respite. I know Lou is a grand cook, and a home-cooked meal sounds great."

"Terrific! Jump in my old jitney! Right this minute! I'll take you there and bring you back. Annie, your pup is welcome. We have a dog, too, and we fence our yard. Those dogs will play and enjoy a fine time of it."

A gathering of friends, a satisfying meal, and animated conversation brought Annie pleasure. Through the dining room window, she enjoyed watching Bitsy and the Morrison dog at play in the backyard. Everyone savored Lou Morrison's chicken and dumplings, and Annie emerged from her shell, taking part in conversations.

At supper's conclusion, the men retired to the parlor while the two women and Annie cleared the dinner table and washed dishes. Lou Morrison's chubby, buxom figure then stood in the parlor's doorway and announced, "Our guests are worn out, Jack. We will visit soon, but they must return to their new home and settle in for a good night's sleep."

Carter herded his two favorite girls and Bitsy toward Jack's blue Buick out front. Once everyone exchanged hugs, handshakes, and expressions of gratitude, Jack returned his guests to their new front door.

With quiet purpose, the recent arrivals made up the beds with fresh sheets and blankets left by Mrs. McCormick, collapsed under the covers, and drifted off to sleep. Even Bitsy stirred not a smidgen after snuggling into her wicker basket. Sleep in real beds instead of in bedrolls on the hard ground or rainy nights huddled inside the cramped Dodge sedan was sheer bliss.

SEEDS

arly spring gave way to early summer. Dogwood, redbud, and apple blossoms replaced daffodils and fading tulips. Winter's brown grass turned green, and the splendor surrounding them enthralled Ellen Young. From their new home in the Shenandoah Valley, Ellen could see the Blue Ridge Mountains to the east and the Alleghenies to the west. When she hung clothes on the clothesline, she often stopped and gazed at her surroundings for several moments, drinking in the sheer beauty, the likes of which she had never imagined.

The Dust Bowl had conquered the Youngs' original home. While a verdant landscape had never been part of that environment, drought turned a treeless, semi-arid landscape into one with no grass, where ever-present winds blew topsoil away, leaving everything with a coat of red grit. The dreaded red dirt crept into houses through cracks in window casings, down chimneys, and under doors. An open window invited an invasion of red that could ruin a home's interior within minutes. Thorough furniture dusting was an often-futile daily ritual aimed at keeping a home clean and livable. A whirling dust storm could strike a clothesline, staining clothes in an orange-red hue within seconds. The scene for farmers and ranchers was even more dire, as crops withered and died, and livestock perished from a lack of water to drink and grass to eat. As the 1930s advanced, drought, wind, and the Great Depression worsened, and the despair of their former home state became legendary.

The Youngs headed east just as the mass exodus to the west began. Times back east were difficult, but known opportunity awaited the Youngs, while a grim journey and unknown future faced the poor souls bound for California. It pleased Ellen to be in this setting, remembering her former home and its memories with fondness, missing her friends and family, but sensing a new promise.

Ellen's father was a druggist in the town from which they hailed, as was her older brother. Her younger brother was deceased, killed at the young age of thirteen when a buggy overturned after the horse pulling it bolted, frightened by a snake in the road. After the incident, Ellen's mother became more protective of her daughter. She monitored Ellen's every move, her friends, and anticipated her thoughts. The woman read her daughter's diary with regularity and pretended to know nothing of what Ellen had confessed to its pages.

Ellen longed to attend the state university back home, but her parents did not hold higher education for their daughter as a priority. As a result, Ellen sacrificed her dream and took employment with the local clothing and fabric mercantile. There, local ladies came to appreciate her exceptional talents as a seamstress.

In this store, with the pretentious title of Miss Madeleine's Fine Apparel and Accessories Shoppe, she met Carter Young. Carter was visiting an aunt and uncle who lived in town and had entered the shop to buy a pair of gloves for his aunt's birthday.

Carter Young was the oldest child of four. His family was from the same state but lived some fifty miles southwest of Ellen's hometown. Carter's father, a successful rancher, owned a large spread of close to a thousand acres. Carter's father desired his children to get higher education at the state university, and it thrilled him when his oldest expressed interest in a career in medicine. He assisted Carter with tuition. Carter helped with financial responsibilities, too, working in the college town's feed and seed store when he wasn't attending class. His room and board were gratis because he agreed to maintain the lawn of his elderly landlady and drive the widow in her brand-new Model T Ford wherever she needed to go. Although she had other boarders, the widow liked and trusted Carter. Ever considerate of the woman's distaste for noise and dirt, Carter removed his shoes inside the house and never allowed the screen door to slam shut. A cheerful Carter assisted her when she entered and exited the automobile and her home, engaging her in conversation.

During Carter's last year of medical school, tragedy struck. An ember escaped from the fireplace of his family's home and set the house ablaze. From what officials determined afterward, it appeared the sleeping family did not awake in time to escape. The remains of Carter's parents and those of his three younger siblings were discovered near the front door. Carter always hoped smoke inhalation overcame them before the flames did.

After the tragedy, Ellen and Carter's relationship flourished. Their decision to marry coincided with Carter's graduation and internship assignment to a large city hospital in a neighboring state. Jack and Lou Morrison attended Carter and Ellen's marriage ceremony at the courthouse, but Ellen's parents did not.

After Carter's internship ended, he and Ellen moved to her hometown, and Carter began his medical practice in their newly purchased residence. The primary reason for this move to Ellen's hometown came from pressure from Ellen's mother. Patients accessed Carter's office, located in two upstairs rooms of their home, by a side door. Ellen assisted him, serving as receptionist and helping with other duties.

Annie arrived on the scene one year later, and Ellen continued to help her husband with his practice. Because she possessed efficient organizational skills, she tended the baby in a small pen next to her desk and often zipped downstairs to do domestic chores between patient visits. The living quarters downstairs consisted of a living room, Carter and Ellen's bedroom, a kitchen, bathroom, and a dining room they converted into Annie's bedroom. The cozy arrangements were more than adequate for the threesome.

Nothing was good enough for Ellen's mother. She belittled her daughter's house, Carter's office, his patients, and the nature of his medical practice. Many patients could not pay, so they bartered for services. A few could neither pay nor barter. Dr. Young tended loose women of the locale, drunken old men, and others not blessed by station or good fortune. His clientele also included several of the town's more prominent citizens. His thoroughness in his examinations and continual study of medicine contributed to the perception he was more up to date than other physicians. A potpourri of humanity climbed the stairs to the cheery office for treatment, advice, and sometimes mere consolation.

Ellen's mother often dropped by without warning, her eyes scouring downstairs rooms for new and elegant accessories. There were none because frugal Ellen cared nothing for frivolities. The Youngs took Sunday dinner with Ellen's parents each week, and even Carter found these gatherings somewhat pleasant. Ellen's father admired Carter, but he never challenged his wife's treatment of their daughter and son-in-law, nor did he resist her intrusions upon Ellen and Carter's privacy. He remained silent, and his silence only bolstered her snubs and meddlesome ways.

After the horrific fire, Carter Young sold his family's cattle and two hundred acres of the ranch. Proceeds from the sale provided the couple with seed money to set up his practice and purchase a house. The attorney who handled the sale for the grief-stricken Carter advised him not to sell the remaining ranch land.

"Land will appreciate in value, Carter. The Lord isn't making more of it. You cannot see into the future, and this land might draw you back someday. You're selling two hundred acres now, but you have over seven hundred left. Keep it, please. Taxes are cheap. No upkeep is necessary. Land is a solid investment."

His attorney reminded Carter of another fact. Portions of the state were rich in the substance fueling America's automobiles. If a petroleum company discovered oil on a property, whoever owned the land with its mineral rights below the surface stood to reap financial rewards. Carter Young heeded his lawyer's advice and sold just two hundred acres and the cattle. Carter's decision at a time of unimaginable grief later proved to be a salvation.

In 1933, in this promising setting, Ellen and Carter Young hoped to make a brand-new life for their family, a content life filled not with material possessions, but with friends and fresh possibilities. While the couple revered their families and from where they came, they were ready for change.

Annie enrolled in school soon after the family moved into their rented home three miles from town, giving her two months to settle into a routine before summer recess. School was in the town, so on early weekday mornings, her father drove the Dodge to his office where Annie waited until time to walk the remaining few blocks to school. Most Thursdays, Ellen took her husband to work, delivered Annie to the school-house door, and kept the automobile for errands. Annie considered Thursdays a special treat.

Hillview was so named because it sat in a wide valley with one mountain ridge visible to the east and another to the west. At its conception, legend had it that the town was named for its founder, a supposed Revolutionary War officer claiming to have been a personal acquaintance of General George Washington. The fellow established a homestead in a small settlement/way station and oversaw building of a town center. Soon he purchased a fair chunk of land and seized property that he claimed lacked legal ownership. A cocksure, loud, and arrogant personality, he lured in more settlers with exaggerated advertising touting the town's potential as an up-and-coming metropolis. An honorable man he was not. His ruthless bullying, his disregard for financial obligations, and a tendency toward overindulgence of the drink created a climate of fear and distrust. Legal claims from his victims mounted, and rumors circulated that he was not an officer in the Revolution as he claimed but was instead the no-good son of a slave trader.

Early one morning, a citizen found the much-despised tyrant lying face-down in the middle of Main Street, bleeding from a severe head wound, perhaps the result of a nasty fall taken during another drunken stupor. Whether the victim of his own dereliction or of someone he cheated remained unspoken. Townspeople mulled their predicament and renamed the town. Residents held a vote (men only) and chose the name suggested by the Methodist minister's wife, that of Hillview. No one acknowledged the name of the town's founder by the time Anna Ruth Young and her parents arrived in 1933. It was just one more unpleasant secret locals attempted to hide in the murky recesses of historical truth and fiction.

Hillview never became the metropolis its founder promised, but it grew to thrive in its own way and became the county seat. Mercantile stores provided necessities. Farms provided income and sustenance. Textiles, apple processing, and the railroad became important to the town's growth.

After school or after spending time at the library, Annie took the short trek to her father's office and waited to ride home with her beloved daddy. She was a voracious reader, so the library became a home away from home to her. If she was not careful to keep track of the clock behind the counter, she was sometimes still reading when the library closed. On such occasions, she scampered to the office, arriving in a breathless state. An amused Dr. Young laughed aloud each time his daughter flung open the front door and rushed into his waiting room.

"I won't leave without you, Annie. I may need to make house calls on the way home, so it's important you be punctual." Patience was one of his most endearing traits, and Annie always recalled his manner and tried to emulate it when she became impatient.

One sun-soaked afternoon, Annie waited in a long line to check out a book she had removed from the fiction shelf. Annie liked mystery stories, and one aroused her interest. A petite, older lady not five feet tall standing in front of Annie wore an impeccable flowered dress, and the scent of rosewater encircled her presence. She leaned upon a cane and carried a large handbag slung over her left arm. As the line moved toward the counter, the woman dropped the book she was holding. Annie leaned forward, picked it up, and handed it to her. The girl noticed a brooch pinned underneath the collar of the dress the little lady wore, and Annie could not stop staring at the piece of jewelry. She had never seen a piece resembling it, and its charming ivory profile of a female face set upon a black stone entranced her.

The woman smiled at Annie, thanked her, and then stepped to the counter. Annie observed the lady's milk colored hair pulled back from her face into a bun. Annie continued to stare at her, thinking she was elegant yet different from other older ladies she had observed downtown.

"Good afternoon, Georgia." The woman with a slight southern drawl addressed the librarian.

The librarian, Mrs. Albright, beamed. "It's grand to see you again! How are you doing now?"

"Oh, I'm recovered, they tell me! That pneumonia is nasty, and I feared I might not recover. My age, you understand." Leaning into the counter, she whispered to Mrs. Albright as she adjusted her round horn-rimmed spectacles. "But here I am, Georgia!" The tiny woman appeared to dance as she addressed the librarian. Her bun even wiggled, Annie noted, and her voice rose above the whisper expected in the library.

"I'm glad you are better! It's nice to see you back," the librarian said.

"Thank you so much, Georgia. It's delightful to be out. Susie brought me here this lovely day so I can catch up on my reading. I haven't been able to do much, and now I must use this dreadful cane to keep my balance. Do you know I haven't even been able to meet the new doctor and his family? The ones who are renting my house? It's dreadful I haven't, and I plan to call on them this week. Susie says she will take me."

Mrs. Albright's eyes brightened, and she gestured toward Annie. "Why, their daughter is standing right behind you! This is Annie Young!"

Annie stiffened, stood as upright as she could, and stared ahead. The lady turned and gazed straight into Annie's soft brown eyes. With a cheery, high-pitched voice, she set the startled girl at ease. "Annie Young, it's so good to meet you, my dear. I am Mittie McCormick. You are renting my house, and I hope you enjoy living there. Welcome to Hillview!"

This introduction surprised Annie. She found it odd a woman of Mrs. McCormick's age introduced herself using her given name. Annie expected the woman to introduce herself in a more formal manner when addressing a minor.

Annie stuttered a moment and replied she was happy to meet the lady. Yes, she and her family liked the house.

"Annie is one of our best customers, Miz M. She loves to read just as you do. She spends many afternoons with us, and we have so enjoyed getting to know her in just this short time." Georgia Albright winked at Annie as she spoke.

"That is splendid! I cannot think of a better spot to spend an afternoon than in a library surrounded by volumes of literature and the sweet aroma of their leather bindings." Mrs. McCormick's blue eyes flashed as she spoke and beamed at Annie. This tiny woman did not resemble any older person

Annie had ever met. Her own stern grandmother seldom smiled. This lady with the bun and the exquisite brooch smiled and laughed in a lilting, melodious tone, and though she was frail, an aura of strength enthralled Annie.

"Annie, I intend to have my daughter Susie drive me to call on you and your parents this week. I have been ill. It is dreadful manners, and I hope you will inform your mother and father I shall see them soon. Please apologize for me for not coming sooner. Will you do that, dear?"

"Yes."

Mittie McCormick took her book, turned, and patted Annie on the shoulder. She more or less pranced out of the library, attempting to not lean on the cane for support, her two-inch heels clicking on the wood floor. Through the glass front door, Annie observed her on the front steps hailing a car parked in front of the building. A chic, blonde woman emerged from the driver's side of the fancy, new, beige and brown DeSoto Roadster, then assisted Mrs. McCormick as she navigated the steps and climbed inside the sporty car. The blonde woman toyed with her Marcel hairstyle, slid behind the wheel, and sped away.

Annie checked out her book as Georgia Albright addressed the girl with a smile, "Miz M is someone we love around here, Annie."

Annie walked with a quick pace toward the library's front door. She opened the door and bolted off the steps. Annie could not wait to tell her father she had met Mrs. McCormick. She wanted to tell him how pleasant she was, how petite she was, how she loved to read, and that she wore the most stunning piece of jewelry Annie had ever seen.

HOW DO YOU DO?

Carter Young knew Mrs. McCormick had been ill. Jack Morrison was her physician, and he had advised both Carter and Ellen before their arrival that it was possible the little lady might not survive her illness. When Carter first asked to visit her and introduce himself, Jack advised against it. Jack told him Mrs. McCormick's daughter was "difficult" and offered to convey best wishes to Mrs. McCormick until she improved.

Time and rest had brought noticeable improvement to Mrs. McCormick, and Carter looked forward to accompanying Jack on his next house call; therefore, he welcomed Annie's news she was improved and visiting the library. He wanted to thank the widow for renting her home and its contents to his family and to express his sympathy for her husband's death.

He wanted to tell her how much they enjoyed the home and express appreciation for the use of Dr. McCormick's former office. Carter's rental agreement with her not only applied to her home but likewise to the office space. She had agreed to provide the office with no rent for six months so Carter might build a practice and "salt money away" before having to face more expense. Rent for the house and office were both reasonable, and if the community accepted the new doctor in town, these expenses should not be burdensome.

"I will check with Jack on your news, Annie. It's possible Mrs. McCormick shouldn't be out taking bumpy car rides. From your description, it sounds as if she is doing well, though."

Annie described the woman. She detailed her bouncy hair bun, her piercing blue eyes, her horn-rimmed spectacles, her unique cane, the flowers on her dress, the title of the book she checked out, and the intriguing piece of jewelry she wore. The girl did not know what one called the brooch, but from her description, her father determined it was a cameo. He said this form of jewelry was old, dating back to the Middle Ages. He related that Queen Victoria of Great Britain had been a wearer of cameos, and this resulted in many American women in the 1800s coveting them.

"My mother possessed one and wore it often," he told his daughter. "Mother had a dark green dress she liked to wear with it." A faint smile crossed his lips as he remembered his mother seeming to float to the bottom of the front steps of their home, the hem of her skirt brushing along the steps. In bright sunlight, the cameo contrasted against the dress and glowed. "It was lost in the fire." A darkness appeared over his countenance, a darkness Annie saw when her father recalled the fire that took his beloved parents, two brothers, and sister.

"I'm glad you met Mrs. McCormick, Annie. She made quite the impression upon you! We'll tell your mother when we arrive home."

Animated conversation filled that evening's suppertime. Annie related her encounter with the woman to whom the family owed so much, and an amused Ellen reported how Bitsy turned over the clothes basket while Helen hung out laundry. Bitsy was chasing one of the resident cats and ran into the basket, knocking it on its side. The shock of hitting the basket forced the little dog to stop dead in her tracks and forget the cat. Ellen had to re-wash a few muddy items Bitsy's

28

paw prints had soiled. Carter chuckled as he mentioned Mrs. Blanton, the town gossip and matron of Hillview society, who saw him regarding a rash on her arms. She spent the entire appointment time spilling secrets of Hillview's citizens. The rash did not appear to have an adverse effect on her energy, as her arms flailed through the air with each tidbit she shared. Annie's father did not share any of those tidbits, but he imitated her gestures while convulsing with laughter. Her curiosity piqued, Annie pressed for more of what the patient said, but her father reminded her that conversation between a doctor and his patient was not to be shared. He allowed that poison ivy had caused the rash.

"Annie, I don't believe you know how to identify a poison ivy plant, do you?"

"I don't think so, Daddy." She took a bite of chocolate cake. "A poison plant? I won't eat any plants, I promise."

Ellen licked a trace of frosting from her fork. "No, it's a plant that gives you a dreadful rash if you touch it, Annie. I'm not sure I know how to spot it either, Carter. Is there any of it around here?"

"Oh, yes, there should be a significant crop this summer. It's emerging in the woods and at the edges. After supper, let's take a walk so I can show you examples. It contains an oil that will give you an itchy rash if you touch a leaf of the plant. It reminds me of gossip because it spreads so fast and creates misery. I'd hate for my girls to break out with such an itchy rash. We must watch Bitsy, too, because if she brushes against the plant, the oil can get on her fur. It is as if we touched the plant itself when we pet her."

The family finished dessert and left dishes on the dining room table while they roamed outdoors searching for signs of the plant that had caused Mrs. Blanton such agony. They fastened Bitsy to her leash so if they encountered a specimen, she could not brush against it. Darkness approached, so they were quick. Sure enough, Carter spotted the evil ivy at the edge of the woods.

"Ellen and Annie, remember the verse, 'leaflets three, let it be' and be mindful to avoid it, just as you should avoid gossip."

"Daddy, how will we know if Bitsy runs through it? She doesn't venture here often, though. I believe she's afraid of the trees and vines. It's spooky back here for her!"

"There isn't much we can do, I suppose," her father said, "but I'll pull it when I see it and discard it."

Annie was incredulous. "Pull it? Then you'll get the rash!"

Her father smiled and told her he was no longer affected by the plant. As a boy on his family's ranch, he had fallen victim to the unbearable itchiness many times. After so many years, he believed he was immune. He promised to wear gloves when handling the vine, however.

"Does this mean you're immune to gossip, too, Daddy?"

"I should hope so!"

With the botany lesson completed, the four Hillview newcomers strolled back to the kitchen door, Carter and Ellen arm in arm, while Annie instructed Bitsy how to avoid poison ivy. Bitsy did not appear interested. Her nose twitched with excitement as she caught a whiff of a kitty underneath the shed. After Carter installed fresh lattice around the porch so cats could no longer get underneath the house, they established new homes under the shed. The opening to the space was large enough to be cat accessible but not large enough for the feisty terrier. Bitsy retained her devotion to chasing cats, but she never seemed intent on catching any of them.

****

Soft breezes and cool nights continued for several days following Annie's meeting with Mittie McCormick, and the last day of the school session marked summer's arrival. On that first lazy Saturday afternoon of summer, the sound of a car crunching up the driveway disrupted the soothing melody of songbirds. Ellen was mending one of her husband's shirts while rocking on the front porch. Carter was at the rear of the property pulling poison ivy and clearing enough brush to expose a pathway to the rear boundary of the property. Annie sat near her mother in the other rocking chair, reading a book as Bitsy snored at her feet.

The flashy, beige and brown DeSoto approached the house before halting its forward movement. Annie put her arm around Bitsy because she did not want the dog to run out and frighten the car's occupants.

A blonde woman wearing a yellow linen suit and matching hat emerged and swept around the car to the passenger side. She opened the door with a noticeable air of impatience and assisted an elderly woman from the sporty roadster. Annie recognized the car, the spunky old woman, and the blonde driver she had seen at the library. Mrs. McCormick used her cane to navigate the gravel and grass, holding the arm of her driver as she waved her cane and shouted a big, "Hello there!" to Ellen and Annie. Ellen rose, hurried off the porch, and took Mrs. McCormick's hand.

"You must be Dr. Young's wife!" The perky little lady's voice was high and strong but held the faint quiver often heard in old ladies' voices. "I am Mittie McCormick. Allow me to introduce you to my daughter, Susie Rutledge. Please forgive me for not coming sooner to meet you, but I have been ill. You may know that, though! Oh, I see Annie there. Hello, dear!"

Annie wrapped Bitsy in her arms and joined her mother at the base of the steps. Bitsy was wiggling, but she didn't bark. This was unusual for the dog; she was a barker when a stranger approached.

"Hello, Mrs. McCormick," Annie said. She did not shake hands since her arms held the squirming pooch.

"I am Mrs. Henry Rutledge," the blonde woman corrected in a most dour tone as she nodded toward Ellen and Annie.

Ellen held Mrs. McCormick's arm in a gentle clutch. "The sun is hot. Please come inside and have a drink. Annie, go get your father and tell him Mrs. McCormick and Mrs. Rutledge are here. It will please him to meet both of you."

As Annie left to retrieve her father, Ellen helped Mrs. McCormick up the steps and into the house as the ever-so-stylish Mrs. Henry Rutledge followed.

Annie spied Carter in the woods and shouted to her father visitors had arrived. He emerged from the woods and removed his gloves, wiping his forehead with a handkerchief pulled from his shirt pocket. Perspiration soaked his brown hair, making it glisten in the sunshine.

"Who is it, Annie?"

"It's Mrs. McCormick and her daughter Mrs. Rutledge!" By this time Annie had set Bitsy on the ground, where the dog sat, its stubby tail quivering with excitement.

"Goodness, I'm dirty!" her father protested. But he began walking the distance back to the house in quick step, with Annie and Bitsy falling in behind.

Carter opened the screen door to the kitchen and entered the house. He went straight to the kitchen sink and washed his hands and face, drying both with a fresh towel Ellen had left on the counter. Annie gathered up Bitsy once again and entered the parlor with her father who addressed Mrs. McCormick.

"How do you do, Mrs. McCormick? Please excuse my appearance. I've been working in the back woods. Please allow me to shake your hand and excuse myself to change clothes."

Seated in a wing chair in a corner, Mittie McCormick emitted the lilting chuckle Annie had heard in the library.

"There is no need for you to change clothes, sir. You remind me of my father. He was outside every spare moment. How dirty he got! Please, sit, sit!"

Mrs. McCormick glanced toward her daughter. "This is my daughter, Susie Rutledge, Dr. Young. Susie, this is Dr. Carter Young." Carter reached out and shook Susie's hand.

With no hint of a smile, Mrs. Rutledge responded with a subdued, "How do you do?"

32

Ellen rose, opened a closet door in the entryway, and removed a sheet from a shelf. She spread it on the other wing chair and suggested to her husband he should sit there.

"Mrs. McCormick, I have kept the sheets that covered the furniture in this closet. How handy I did!"

The old woman smiled and chuckled at Ellen's attempt to keep the furniture clean. "There is no need for that, dear. Gracious!"

During this back-and-forth banter, Susie Rutledge's face showed no emotion. Not a muscle moved except for the blinking of her blue eyes.

Ellen told the visitors cold tea was in the icebox and offered it. Mrs. McCormick accepted the refreshment, but Susie declined. Ellen then withdrew to the kitchen and prepared a tray with tea for Mrs. McCormick, herself, and Carter, plus water for Annie. She set six oatmeal cookies on a plate and returned to the parlor.

Chit-chat between the Youngs and Mrs. McCormick was pleasant and informative. Mrs. McCormick asked many questions relating to their life before their arrival in Hillview. Carter's upbringing on a ranch out west fascinated her, as did his descriptions of the rich, red soil and stark terrain. Her upbringing had been right where they sat, on acres of orchards, crops, and farm animals. Mrs. McCormick's father had help from a few employees, but Carter, his brothers, and his father had provided the labor on their ranch.

Carter, Ellen, and Annie learned the big white house sitting on a ridge across the main road at the end of their lane was Mrs. McCormick's home as a girl. Her father not only engaged in farming, but he was a physician, too. She had been a child during the Civil War, but her memory of the times and both Union and Confederate soldiers was still vivid. As she began to tell a story involving Union horses kept in the stable underneath her family home, her daughter interrupted.

"Mother, we must go now. You are getting tired, and these people need to return to their chores." Susie stood, deposited her mother's now empty glass on the tray, and helped her mother as the old woman rose with reluctance from the chair.

"Mrs. Young, Dr. Young, thank you for your hospitality this afternoon. I know Mother appreciates it, as do I," Susie intoned as she glanced at the door.

Ellen's eyes caught Carter's as he returned a quizzical glance. Susie's abruptness and stoic persona puzzled both. Annie, sitting in a chair holding Bitsy, observed the four adults, her eyes darting from one to the other.

Mrs. McCormick grasped her cane and Susie's arm as they moved toward the front door.

"I enjoyed this visit so! I had no time to speak at length with Annie. That is disappointing." Mrs. McCormick turned toward Annie, who by this time was standing, still holding Bitsy.

"Annie, you must come visit me, do you hear? Now that school is not in session, please spend time with me. I enjoy your company, and we can discuss the latest book we are reading. Will you do that?" She smiled and cocked her head at Annie with a questioning gleam in her eye.

Annie stammered a response. "Yes. But, uh, I don't know where you live, Mrs. McCormick!"

"Ah, Susie, tell Annie and her parents your address. I never can remember." Mrs. McCormick waved her cane toward her daughter as she issued the instruction.

Susie Rutledge cleared her throat and complied in a monotone voice, "113 Clay."

"It's the gray two-story house with a scrawny cedar tree in the front yard," said Mrs. McCormick. "Now, Annie, I am serious, do you hear? I expect a visit from you and your mother, too! Soon!"

Ellen smiled and took Mrs. McCormick's hand, patting it. "I'll make sure Annie comes to visit you, and I will, too. We're so glad you came to visit today!"

"I look forward to seeing you! This was marvelous!" the little lady shouted as her daughter escorted her toward the car.

Carter sprang to open the car door for Mrs. McCormick. After he bade her goodbye, he turned to Susie and remarked that her vehicle's tan color was pleasing to the eye.

Susie Rutledge's eyes widened with pride as she ran her hand over the canvas top. "Yes, this is the new car my husband purchased for me. The color is Trouville Beige. It's not just a convertible, mine is the custom model with whitewall tires and chocolate fenders, a chrome grill, headlights, and dual horns. It has a rumble seat if I have over one passenger. I do love my automobile. It's quite the thing, don't you agree?"

Carter acknowledged her comments with a slight nod as he thought to himself Susie's infatuation with her new car was odd amid such troublesome times.

With a cool and contrived smile, Susie closed the door. She acknowledged Carter, Ellen, and Annie, walked to the driver's side of the roadster, and slid under the wheel. Mittie McCormick smiled and waved, and even as they turned around and rolled along the length of the driveway, she continued waving back at the three Youngs.

Annie set Bitsy on the ground, and the dog shook herself before running around in circles for a few seconds.

"Isn't Mrs. McCormick nice, Mama? I think she's so cute!"

"She's delightful, Annie. Jack and Lou told us she was a lovely lady. Daddy's correspondence with her was cordial and generous, too."

"I think you have made a new friend, Annie," said Carter Young. "I believe she is sincere when she says she wants you to visit her. She may be lonely there with only Mrs. Rutledge and her husband, not being able to live here in her own home any longer. I think you and your mother should pay her a visit."

The three headed back to the house. Bitsy, who had discovered a stick, stretched out in the grass and gnawed on her new treasure. Ellen and Carter muttered a few comments to each other regarding Susie Rutledge's bearing, being careful not to let Annie overhear.

Carter, through with brush clearing for the day, made his way upstairs to bathe. Ellen picked up the tray and carried it to the kitchen table. Annie folded the sheet upon which her father had sat and tried to fling it up on the closet shelf where they kept it with the other furniture protectors. It kept falling back to the floor as it was too high for Annie to reach. Ellen heard the girl's frustrated grumbles, walked back into the foyer, and landed the sheet on the shelf with an artful toss. Annie stretched out her slender arms and hugged her mother tight.

"Mama, I love you! I'm glad we're here!"

Ellen returned the embrace with a quick kiss to the girl's cheek. "Well, I love you, too, and I'm glad we are here, too!"

Animated chatter at dinner ensued that early summer evening. Ellen prepared a meal of leftover pot roast, green beans Lou Morrison had canned the preceding autumn, mashed potatoes, plus fresh peaches and cream for dessert.

Despite her age and recent illness, Mittie McCormick had enthralled Annie with her spirited air, her stories, her love of reading, and her keen interest in the members of Annie's family. She had even asked Annie to bring Bitsy to her so she could pet the dog. When Annie complied, Bitsy, who under ordinary circumstances may have squirmed and lunged at someone new to her world, put her head out and licked the old woman's hand. Mrs. McCormick responded by stroking and patting the dog, addressing Bitsy in a soft voice. During dinner, the girl bombarded her parents with questions relating to Mittie McCormick, but they offered a multitude of "I don't know" replies. This lack of knowledge and information only piqued her curiosity regarding the tiny lady.

The shy and reserved Annie had developed no school friendships. She related better to adults anyway because as an only child, she interacted with adults on a frequent basis. Her new peers thought her pleasant and bright, but to them she was an anomaly. Annie's accent differed from theirs. Her prior life experience and the geographical region from which she came differed from theirs, and unlike most of them, she had no brothers or sisters. Locals often viewed newcomers and differences with suspicion, so children, reacting upon what they heard at home, did not reach out to Annie or welcome her into their midst. As with earlier newcomers to Hillview, the Youngs found themselves the object of idle gossip and speculation among locals.

The Youngs lived a few miles outside the town limits, which limited Annie's social opportunities. Children living in Hillview congregated with ease and walked to and from friends' homes, the movies, the ice cream parlor, and a variety of other sites. Social interaction was difficult for Annie, especially during summer recess. This isolation did not concern Annie Young. The girl found contentment in the company of her parents, her Bitsy, and her books.

It was this lack of peer companionship that allowed summer's friendship between Annie and the spirited Mittie McCormick to blossom into one of mutual trust and love, one to withstand the turmoil that loomed on a peaceful horizon.

BLINK

"**B**itsy, stop! Come here! Come here! Bitsy!" Annie sprinted along the driveway, pursuing Bitsy as the dog chased a rabbit that made the mistake of entering Bitsy's domain. The rabbit was fast and far ahead of Bitsy, so the chase lasted longer than usual.

Annie lost sight of both animals as they careened into the woods across the lane from the house.

She could hear the dog barking, but from what direction the barks came was confusing. Annie continued running on the lane toward the main road, calling her dog's name. The woods, thick with underbrush alongside the road and a wire fence border beyond, made entering the thicket impossible for a person.

"Bitsy, please come here! Where are you?"

The barking became fainter and came from deep inside the wooded section, but Annie saw no sign of the dog. She was becoming frantic.

An opening Annie had never noticed in the woods stopped her in her tracks. Two rutted and dusty tire tracks led deep into canopy-covered darkness. Annie hesitated but started walking along the tracks toward the sound of Bitsy's barking. The barking stopped.

Annie began running once again and in a short while came upon a ramshackle cabin within a large cleared space. An old stake-body truck, a green REO Speed Wagon, rested in front of a barn, and the wide barn door opening allowed a view of two mules in their stalls. Clothes strung on a clothesline between the house and the barn swayed in a gentle breeze. And there, an exhausted and panting Bitsy sprawled on the grass underneath the clothesline.

A dark, brown-skinned boy skipped out of the barn. He looked at Annie and then looked over at Bitsy lying on the ground, panting.

"Hi, there! You looking for this pup? She j-just came up here and plopped right under my mama's sheets like she b-belongs here."

"Oh, yes! I've been chasing her from our front yard! She was after a rabbit! She refused to come to me."

"I heard you ye-yelling. Didn't see no rabbit."

Annie was unsure how she should continue. She was unaccustomed to interacting with people of color. This was 1933, and segregation and Jim Crow laws were still common throughout the South and Mid-Atlantic. It had been the same in her old surroundings, although she was naïve and unaware. Here, she was an intruder on a stranger's property, and she felt uncomfortable.

The farm boy put her at ease straight away. He was a head shorter than Annie and of sturdy build. He smiled and strolled over to Bitsy, kneeling and giving the dog a soft and long caress of her head. Bitsy, though exhausted, responded by wagging her stubby tail.

"I don't ha-have a dog any m-more. He died. She's cute." He continued to pat Bitsy's wiry head.

"My name is Annie Young. I live in the McCormick place. What's your name?"

"Everybody calls me Blink." The boy rose and strode toward Annie, grinning the entire time. "I've heard a b-bout you. New folks get talked about." He laughed and clapped his hands together.

Annie studied Blink's face and his physical presence. His pleasant expression and manner did not resemble that of other children she had met. She saw none of the wariness or hesitancy in expressing friendliness and openness she saw in others her age.

"Blink? That's a very. . . um. . . unusual name! Where did you get it?"

"That's just what they c-call me. My real name is Tobias. It's a long name, I guess. Nobody calls me Tobias. It's h-hard."

Annie noticed the boy's eyes blinked a good bit, perhaps because of a nervous habit. He stuttered over words. She thought Blink was not the kindest nickname one could have, and she felt sorry for him.

"How old are you, Blink?"

"I'm almost twelve." He clapped his hands. "How old are you?"

Annie's eyes twinkled. "Well, I'm twelve now! I haven't seen you at school. I'm new, though, so I haven't seen every student."

Blink screwed his face into a puzzled look. She could not have seen him at school because they attended different schools. Negro children attended school just outside Hillview's city limits.

"I go to the Negro school next to the ch-chapel over on Rock Howard Road. You go in town, don't cha?"

Blink's question surprised Annie. She had not considered the possibility of children attending schools based on their race. There were no Negro families where her family had lived. Her glaring naivete was obvious.

"Uh-huh. I must gather Bitsy and go home. Mama and I are headed into town. I'm glad to meet you, Blink."

Annie ambled over to where Bitsy was resting so she could pick up the dog and walk back home. As she did so, Blink began walking alongside her in a halting gait.

"Annie, if you need any v-vege . . . tables, my mam and pap grow 'em and they're so good! Pap planted the garden, and they sell what grows that we can't eat. Tell your mama. I like flowers, too. Do you like flowers? My mam's flowers are pretty. We have eggs, too. We have a chicken coop behind the barn. Mam sells eggs."

Just as they approached Bitsy, the little terrier got up, stretched, and trotted over to them in anticipation. "Chickens?" It relieved Annie that Bitsy had discovered no chickens.

"I'll tell Mama," Annie responded as she bent to pick up Bitsy. "She is planting a garden, but maybe she is planting different things from what your folks plant. I like flowers, too. My mother loves roses. She . . ."

Blink interrupted, nodding his head several times. "My p-pap fixes all kinds of things. If you need anything fixed, come get my pap, okay?"

"I will!"

Annie, with Bitsy snuggled in her arms, set off along Blink's driveway toward the lane that took them home.

"Bye, Annie!"

"Bye, Blink! I'll see you soon!"

****

Ellen was standing on their driveway when she spotted Annie and Bitsy coming back up the lane. Almost one hour had passed since Ellen had seen them.

"I'm relieved to see you two! I was becoming concerned, Annie."

"Mama, Bitsy took off after a rabbit, and I couldn't catch her! She ran through the woods and stopped at a little house near the corner. I didn't realize a house was there!"

"Oh, yes. You're speaking of a house near the main road with a driveway going a good way into the woods?"

41

Annie planted Bitsy on the ground and strolled beside her mother as they headed back toward the house.

"Yes. A boy lives in the house. He walked out from the barn when I found Bitsy. She was just lying under the clothesline! I lost sight of the rabbit. The boy's name is Blink, and he said his folks grow vegetables and you should get vegetables from them. Blink likes flowers. His father fixes things, so he says if something needs fixing, we should call him, his 'pap,' he called him. Oh, and they have eggs."

Ellen chuckled. "Well, you discovered lots of information! His name is what?"

"Blink."

"Blink? Such an odd name. Are you sure you understood him?"

"Yes, it's Blink. He said that's what everybody calls him. His proper name is Tobias. Mama, I believe they call him Blink because he blinks his eyes every few seconds. He stutters with words, and he's excitable. I wonder if I should call him Tobias because it sounds mean to call him Blink. What do you think?"

"If he told you his name was Blink, then I'm guessing that's what he goes by, and he doesn't consider it mean."

Annie hesitated. "Mama, he's colored."

Ellen did not flinch or otherwise show concern or surprise.

"Yes, I heard a colored family lived in a log cabin somewhere in the vicinity. I imagine that is Blink's family. Now that you mention it, someone told me they grow the best vegetables. How nice they are neighbors!"

It relieved Annie to see her mother had no issue with the fact their neighbors were not white. Blink appeared to be a nice but a simple boy, and since they were near the same age, maybe he could be a friend even though they did not attend the same school.

"Let's put Bitsy in the house and leave for town, Annie. We're late."

It was Thursday, the day Ellen had use of the family car so she could run errands and go wherever else she desired to go. Often, she and Lou had lunch at the Morrisons or went shopping. They purchased nothing, but the act of looking and dreaming brought them pleasure. She considered joining the garden club to which Lou belonged in order to broaden her circle of friendships. The club met on the third Thursday of each month at various ladies' homes. Sometimes she assisted Carter at his office on Thursday to give his nurse, Maude Renner, an afternoon off work. Maude had been Dr. McCormick's nurse, and she was proving to be an invaluable asset to Carter. Ellen enjoyed these substitution days because it reminded her of their early days together struggling to make ends meet.

A telephone call from Mrs. McCormick had implored Ellen to please come with Annie for lunch that day. Ellen accepted the invitation, which thrilled her daughter. During the meal, Susie remained cordial but distant. She answered questions put to her but did not contribute much to the conversation. As they concluded over cookies and tea, Mrs. McCormick suggested Annie visit Thursday afternoons for the duration of the summer. She was smitten with the girl, and the feeling was mutual. Ellen could see enthusiasm and connection between the two, so she agreed.

Before leaving, Ellen pulled Susie aside to ask if these visits were acceptable to her and might be of benefit to her mother. Susie, in her dour manner, assured Ellen visits were "fine."

"Mother does what she wants to do, Mrs. Young. Your daughter is invigorating to her, so I believe the company of such a lively child may be favorable."

"Susie, if you find the visits are not good for your mother, or if a particular Thursday is not convenient, please let me know. You will not hurt my feelings or Annie's. I will emphasize to Annie that she must not overtire your mother."

"But of course," said Susie as she escorted Ellen to the door.

****

On the following Thursday after lunch, Ellen delivered Annie to the Rutledge residence for her first solo afternoon visit with Mrs. McCormick. Ellen walked Annie, clutching her latest library book, to the front door and rang the doorbell. Susie answered, a pink and white apron covering her mid-length black and white polka-dot dress.

"Hello, Mrs. Young. Hello, Anna Ruth. Come in, please, won't you? Mother is on the sun porch, Anna Ruth. You may go back to see her." Susie pointed toward a room off to one side of the hallway.

Ellen remained on the porch for a moment. In an attempt at conversation with Susie, Ellen complimented Susie on the apron she wore.

"Thank you. I detest ugly aprons. They make one resemble a charwoman. My favorite one fell apart last week, and I discarded it. Too old, I suppose. This one is not large enough for my taste."

"Oh, that's too bad. I hope a new one comes your way soon. I will pick up Annie at five o'clock." Ellen stepped off the front porch and returned to the car with an idea planted in her head.

Ellen drove to the Piggly Wiggly to stock up on staples for the pantry. She had planned to visit the butcher next, but she detoured to the mercantile to peruse fabrics. She found cotton fabric with which to make a new sundress for Annie and a print fabric she fancied as a new blouse for herself. Then she spied a pale green and yellow-flowered remnant. Although the remnant contained enough fabric to produce a skirt for Annie, Ellen envisioned a large apron. She added it to her purchase along with a few lace remnants.

Ellen had adjusted to her new surroundings easier than she expected. Letters from home were frequent, and her replies faithful. Her mother's letters implored the couple to return, but Ellen's responses reiterated the same theme. This was their home now. Ellen suggested her parents consider visiting. Train travel was not as rigorous as traveling across country by automobile, she wrote. No response to Ellen's suggestions ever came. Ellen's sister-in-law wrote from time to time, and her letters expressed cautious optimism. She wrote that Ellen's brother was well, and the drugstore hummed along despite hard economic times.

Correspondence between Ellen and a few of her close friends was newsy and positive. These women understood why Ellen and Carter had left and undertaken an unknown life elsewhere. Their letters often expressed envy of their friend's new "adventure" as one put it. Ellen smiled as she read these letters, often showing them to Carter. She believed the positivity expressed by others validated their decision to move.

Annie was not standing on the porch of the Rutledge house when Ellen drove up, so Ellen tooted the horn to alert her daughter it was time to leave.

Within a few moments, Annie opened the front door and bounded toward the vehicle. She pushed her hair back behind one ear and fumbled with the book she was carrying as she opened the car door.

"Hi, Mama!"

"Hi, Annie! Did you have a pleasant visit with Mrs. McCormick today?"

"Oh, yes. She told me to call her Mittie! I told her you wouldn't approve because it isn't respectful for someone my age to call someone her age by her first name. I said you might be angry with me because that was poor manners. She said it could be 'just our little secret,' though, that she *insists* I call her Mittie. Are you mad at me?"

"Well, Annie, I believe it is disrespectful. If she *insists*, I suppose it's all right." Ellen's brow wrinkled as she considered this development in the friendship between a lonesome young girl and a lonesome old woman. "I have it! Miss Mittie! Call her Miss Mittie."

"Oh, good! I'll tell her next Thursday! Miss Mittie is such fun. She showed me how to play dominoes this afternoon. We didn't discuss my library book. Do you know that game? She said a lady named Thea who worked for her parents taught her the game of dominoes when she was a child."

Ellen confessed she did not understand the game of dominoes, and conversation between the two did not fill the drive home. Annie spent the time gazing out the window looking at the passing scenery, a smile on her face. Ellen mused in silence on the most unusual friendship she saw unfolding.

That afternoon, Dr. Morrison requested Carter accompany him to visit a patient who was experiencing heart difficulties because he hoped Carter could offer treatment advice. Afterward, Jack gave Carter a ride home, and the two doctors joined Ellen on the front veranda for iced tea.

Ellen briefed Jack and Carter on the day's events. She told them of Annie's introduction to Blink and of Annie's developing relationship with Mrs. McCormick. She also expressed bewilderment over Susie Rutledge's strange behavior.

Jack, sipping on his tea as he reclined in a rocking chair, attempted to explain Susie Rutledge as best he could.

"You may hear rumors concerning Mrs. McCormick's family. Susie is protective of her mother's history. Susie values her social standing more than genuine friendships and doesn't abide any gossip that may taint the image she promotes. She married a fellow who manages one of the textile mills, and she likes the status that goes with that. The mill is doing well, and Susie and her husband haven't suffered through these horrible times as others have. They have no children, and she doesn't appreciate children very much. I'm surprised she tolerates Annie, to tell the truth!"

"What history, Jack?" asked Carter, leaning against a porch column. "I've heard nothing other than Dr. McCormick was a superb doctor and his patients adored him. They tell me

46

themselves how much they loved him! You told me the entire region respected him, too."

Jack clarified, "Oh, not Dr. McCormick, but Mrs. McCormick's family. Folks considered her sister crazy or strange. I don't know details because it happened way before I was born, but the sister created trouble, I suppose. Mrs. McCormick had to handle the ramifications of that during her growing-up years. Turns out nobody forgets gossip. I have always held Mrs. McCormick in the highest regard, but whatever happened hung over her and affected Susie, in my opinion. Susie's brothers moved away and don't come around often. Susie was the only girl, so she has taken on the responsibility of her mother since Dr. McCormick died."

A somber Ellen shook her head. "My goodness, to make Mrs. McCormick's life difficult because of her sister is terrible. She is delightful."

Carter turned to his wife. "It's a small town, Ellen. Why are you surprised? We lived in a town such as this, remember? Gossip? Secrets? Suspicion of newcomers? Airs of importance?"

She nodded with a slight sigh and grimace.

Jack explained he left Hillview after high school graduation to follow his wanderlust and longing for new surroundings. He lived with his aunt and uncle in the college town where he and Carter met and stayed there throughout college and medical school. He always planned to return to Hillview to practice medicine.

"I felt it was my duty to return. I never paid attention to gossip or the odd goings-on around here. Adolescent boys are oblivious! I focused on my future, and I wanted to be a doctor. As to what Mrs. McCormick's sister did, who knows? Is it conceivable that events from years ago are still on people's minds? Maybe they aren't, and Susie is just . . . Susie is high society . . . she thinks . . . oh, I don't know."

"Well, it's too bad, Jack." Ellen began rocking in the chair, smoothing her skirt.

47

"I hope I've explained Susie to you as much as I can, Ellen. She's a complicated lady. But it's swell Annie has a friend and Mrs. McCormick has, too. There isn't a nicer human being around than Mrs. McCormick."

Jack rose from the chair and handed Ellen his empty glass.

"I need to get home for supper, friends! Lou told me we're having shepherd's pie tonight." He rubbed his stomach and licked his lips in anticipation, his gray eyes laughing.

As he leaped off the porch and sprinted toward his big, blue Buick, he turned to Carter and Ellen, now standing on the front steps.

"Oh, the Negro boy down the way. Blink. They're a good family, honest and always ready to help a neighbor. Last name is Hill. Their vegetables are the best, and their eggs are always fresh, so buy from them when you can. Lou does whenever they bring their truck to the Farmer's Market on Saturdays."

Ellen asked Jack why everyone called the boy Blink.

"Blink has a nervous condition. He blinks his eyes a lot and stutters. His mother, her name is Cora, started calling him that when he was small, and the condition became noticeable. Cora said other children would tease or bully him. If his nickname was Blink, and everyone called him that, teasing wouldn't be hurtful. I think she was right, because he is such a happy-go-lucky little fellow. There is just one child. Cora had such difficulties when he was born that she cannot have more children. Cora's husband is a good fix-it man, too. I swear he can fix everything. He drives an old Speed Wagon he keeps humming like a charm. His name is Ned. They're good folk."

"I'm off!" Jack opened the driver's door of his spacious sedan, slid in, fired up the powerful straight-eight, turned in the yard, and roared away with a farewell toot of the horn.

Carter and Ellen returned inside, where she put together the evening meal. The day had been satisfying. It saw Annie make a new friend and cement her friendship with another. The day brought news of good neighbors and a source of fresh vegetables and eggs. It supplied clues to the mystery of Susie's comportment, but it raised questions involving Mrs. McCormick's history, the answers to which would come in due time.

CONTENTED SUMMER

L azy summer days can fuel an adolescent girl's imagination as she becomes engrossed in the pages of books, magazines, and daydreams. Anna Ruth Young was no exception. Ellen delighted in the stories Annie concocted. The fantasies involved lords and ladies, a funny detective who solved crimes, a sea captain afraid of the ocean, and more. Ellen urged Annie to write her yarns, but the motivation to do so never materialized.

One of the first purchases Carter made after moving into their new home was a sewing machine for Ellen. Ordered from the Sears & Roebuck catalog, the machine came with a fine cabinet plus an assortment of useful attachments. Ellen broke into tears when she saw it because she had not wanted to leave behind her old one. In the week following Susie's comment regarding her discarded apron, Ellen began sewing. From the green and yellow fabric remnant, a full apron complete with ruffles at the shoulders and two pockets in front emerged from the sewing machine's shiny needle and Ellen's talented fingers.

Ellen finished the apron before Annie's next Thursday afternoon visit at the Rutledge home.

"Annie, I've made this apron for Mrs. Rutledge. When you visit Mrs. McCormick on Thursday, I want you to give it to her."

"Oh, Mama, it's so elegant! Don't you need a new apron?"

"I can always make myself one, but Mrs. Rutledge said she tossed her old one because it was showing wear. I thought it a nice gesture for you to take this to her."

Annie likewise wanted to establish a relationship with Susie Rutledge and smiled with approval.

Ellen draped the apron on the table by the front door and suggested they walk to Blink's house and buy eggs if available. Ellen was eager to meet their neighbors. Receptive to the suggestion, Annie jumped up from the chair in which she was sitting.

"We should leave Bitsy here. Other animals might be out, and we don't want Bitsy to make a scene," Ellen said, tossing a glance at the sleeping dog on the parlor rug. She picked up her handbag as she and Annie tiptoed out the front door.

Blink was outside when Annie and her mother strolled up the driveway. He jumped and clapped his hands, shouting, "Annie! Annie!" as a smallish woman peeked from behind the clothesline.

"Mam, it's my friend Annie I t-told you 'bout!"

Cora Hill was so petite she looked lost inside a baggy, gray dress that hung to the ankles. Her smooth, dark skin glistened with perspiration from working outside on a such a warm, muggy day. She hastened toward the two visitors, wiped her forehead with the sleeve of her dress, and stopped in front of Ellen.

"Hello, Mrs. Hill," said Ellen with a smile. "I'm Ellen Young from down the way in the McCormick house. This is my daughter Annie."

"Why, hello! Pleased to meet you! I've heard about Annie from Blink."

Blink stood next to his mother, nodding his head again and again, a toothy grin on his face.

51

"Where's your d-dog, Annie?"

"Oh, we left her at home. She can get into trouble sometimes."

Ellen addressed Cora. "Annie tells me you sell eggs and vegetables, Mrs. Hill. Do you have any eggs now? And please call me Ellen!"

Cora Hill acknowledged Ellen's question with a clap of her hands. "Yes, I do! Blink gathered a good many earlier, and they are next to my kitchen sink. I think I've a half dozen I can spare right now."

"Oh, that will be fine. I need a few for breakfast tomorrow." Ellen glanced around at the house and barn and noted how tidy and spotless everything looked despite the plainness of the surroundings. At first glance, the diminutive dwelling gave the impression of being dilapidated. It stood on blocks and appeared somewhat crooked with unpainted wooden slats covering its log exterior. Yet, to Ellen it was inviting. Zinnias splashed yellow, orange, purple, and scarlet throughout a flower bed in front of the porch, and a row of ivory-colored stones lined the bed. A rusty glider with multi-colored pillows across the back rested on the porch. The cabin's glossy red front door welcomed any visitor.

"Will you come on in the house and I'll fetch them for you?" asked Cora. "I've an extra basket you can have."

Cora's comment embarrassed Ellen, as she had neglected to bring a container for carrying eggs and was empty-handed except for her handbag. "Oh, I'm so sorry, Mrs. Hill! It slipped my mind!"

"Need not call me Mrs. Hill. Just call me Cora. Don't you worry! Just return the basket when you can."

Ellen followed her up the wooden steps into the cabin, leaving Annie and Blink in the yard chatting. The cabin's interior was small and dark with unpainted ship-lap walls and walnut stained pine floors. The walls, rough mortared logs around the fireplace, and a large blackened firebox added to the darkness Ellen found pleasant and peaceful. Bright white gauze curtains framed each window and fluttered in the slight breeze, adding light contrast and airiness to the room. A matching red rug at its base complemented the red front door. A vase of colorful zinnias adorned the dining room table, and just beyond was a cozy, well-equipped kitchen. There, Cora directed Ellen to the kitchen sink, where over a dozen eggs sat nestled in a bowl.

Cora lifted six eggs from the bowl and arranged them inside a small basket she took off a shelf. She then handed the basket to Ellen.

"How much do I owe you, Cora?"

Cora lowered her head. "Ten cents is fine."

"Well, that is very reasonable," said Ellen as she removed ten cents from her purse. "I've heard your eggs and vegetables are of the best quality, so I'll remember and come back for more. What vegetables will you have?"

"We plant onions, potatoes, carrots, squash, tomatoes, and beans. The garden is behind the house. My husband, Ned, says he's not making the garden any bigger, but each year he does and plants more! He's putting in cantaloupe this year. Ned's gone to town to get a new hoe because his other one broke. These rocks are hard on tools."

Ellen beamed. "I wish I had known you were close and had so many wonderful things to eat! We planted a garden, but the soil is not good. The rocks, though! They appeared everywhere I tried to turn the soil. I found rocks and more rocks! Our garden is tiny. Just one tomato plant and a smattering of lettuce have emerged, but the rock pile is growing!"

"Ned didn't plant lettuce, so maybe we can trade!" Cora laughed, a hearty, high-toned chuckle.

"I hope we can!" Ellen turned and headed toward the front door. "I think I may stick with sewing instead of farming, though!"

Cora followed and pushed the screen door open so Ellen could exit. "My Ned plants in the same garden plots his daddy and granddaddy did, so that ground is fertile and easy to plow.

It isn't easy in the plot he's putting his new crops in, though! I thought maybe when he broke his hoe he'd quit adding more!"

The two women laughed and sauntered to the front yard where Annie and Blink were tossing a ball back and forth. Seeing her daughter enjoy the company of one her own age gave Ellen pleasure. She wished Annie had made friends with girls at school in the time they had been in Hillview, but she held hope the new school year might bring new chums.

****

Uneventful days came and went that summer. Annie visited the Rutledge home each Thursday afternoon for her visit with Miss Mittie. She presented the apron Ellen had made to Susie, and the always dour woman's delight appeared genuine.

"My goodness, Anna Ruth! I had no idea your mother is such a talented seamstress. This is stylish! I will wear it starting right this minute!" After her proclamation, Susie removed the apron she was wearing and put on the new one. The apron's ruffled sleeves made Susie appear younger to Annie's eye. When Ellen arrived to gather Annie, Susie thanked Ellen for her thoughtfulness, and an actual smile crossed her face for a brief moment.

A less chilly Susie emerged after receipt of the apron, and she began referring to her mother's visitor as Annie instead of Anna Ruth. Susie even confessed that Annie's visits uplifted Mrs. McCormick. Smiles were still infrequent, and her general aloofness remained.

Meanwhile, the visits between Annie and Miss Mittie continued to strengthen the bond between them. Confidants, they shared countless conversations. Annie expressed her dreams for the future, and Miss Mittie shared her joys and regrets. Annie's youthful giggles and Miss Mittie's lilting laugh emanated from the sun porch each Thursday as they talked and talked and talked. Book discussions, dominoes, and

54

reactions to President Roosevelt's latest fireside chat filled the room with a vibrancy it had never known. Susie Rutledge and her husband seldom entered this sunny space or took pleasure in its ambiance. The sun porch served as Miss Mittie's private haven.

Ellen relished visiting with Lou on occasional Thursdays and accompanied her to more garden club meetings. The club ladies were not overt in their standoffish manner, and some even welcomed Ellen with genuine enthusiasm. It was obvious to Ellen, though, most considered her an outsider and viewed her with suspicion. She understood this, as she had grown up in a small town and had seen her mother's reaction to the rare "new person" in town. Undaunted, Ellen joined the group and looked forward to learning about the region's flora and experiencing any camaraderie the club offered. The ladies shared cuttings from their gardens, which Ellen accepted and planted at her home. She apologized for not having cuttings to share, but using more fabric remnants, she made garden aprons complete with pockets as gifts for each member. These were a hit with the women. Two of the ladies were friends with Susie Rutledge, and they had heard of Ellen's prowess with a sewing machine.

Annie and Blink enjoyed the company of each other. They played checkers and two-person baseball. Ellen became one of Cora Hill's best customers, and the two women, one black, one white, became fast friends, which was a rare circumstance for the region and time. Although Cora did not have much formal education, she kept up with world events by listening to the radio and reading the daily newspaper. Like Ellen, she expressed keen interest in political affairs and how people coped with the current economic disaster. The pair discussed everything imaginable around cups of coffee, either in Cora's kitchen or in Ellen's.

Ellen's mother shipped a box filled with fabrics to her daughter that summer. The Great Depression took a toll on Miss Madeleine's Fine Apparel and Accessories Shoppe, and it became impossible to stay open. Miss Madeleine held a final sale, and Ellen's mother purchased the remaining fabric at rock-bottom prices. She bought the remaining thread, too. The shipment elated Ellen. Imagine what she could create with these materials! New dresses for Annie and herself, shirts for Carter, and a handsome dress for Cora resulted from the fabric enclosed in the box. In her spare time, when she did not engage in the many activities required of a housewife and mother of the time, Ellen sewed.

Carter Young's medical practice continued to grow, although monetary rewards did not grow at the same rate. The region to which they moved was not the hardest hit by the Great Depression of the 1930s, but times were tough. The regional economy was tied to the railroad, two competing textile mills, and apple processing. Although few people in Hillview lost jobs during the Depression, ordinary people suffered from reduced hours and reduced pay forced upon them. Paying for rent or food always came ahead of paying the doctor. Both Carter and Ellen were frugal, though, and did not suffer hardships that affected many others. "We are blessed, Carter," Ellen repeated to her husband when he expressed concern over finances.

The lawn at the Youngs' rented home blossomed into a picture of serenity. Ellen positioned scattered stones with care, so they provided a noticeable border between grass and landscape. She tidied and weeded flower beds, trimmed shrubbery, and nurtured the cuttings she received from garden club ladies. On Ellen's birthday, Carter presented her with an American Beauty rose bush and planted it in a sunny spot where its profuse blooms graced the yard with a dazzling splash of red.

Carter engaged in weekend outdoor work on the property, which allowed him to enjoy the rigorous work he disliked during his youth on the ranch. Overgrown with vines and briers, wooded parts of the property became impenetrable fortresses accessible only to birds and small animals. His goal was to make a section of the apple orchard behind the property visible from the house and prevent wild grape and honeysuckle from overtaking majestic trees standing as forest sentries. This strenuous work of pulling, tugging, sawing, and digging up roots took longer than Carter wished, and it left him exhausted. The tranquility, however, mingled with the soft chatter of birds comforted him and provided a satisfying respite from concerns for ailing patients and the future of his family.

The family attended services at Hillview Presbyterian Church and often joined Jack and Lou Morrison afterward for a picnic lunch in Town Park. Their usual picnic spot was a quiet area just a few feet from Hanks Creek, in the shade of a giant sycamore. The picnickers sat on quilts spread on the ground, enjoying whatever goodies Lou and Ellen packed in picnic baskets. While the adults conversed, Annie gazed at the water tumbling over and among rocks in the stream or explored along the bank looking for crawdads and minnows.

When it was time to go, Annie helped the women fold the quilts and pack everything into the baskets. One afternoon as the group returned to their respective vehicles, Annie spotted a shabby and unkempt man sitting under a lone oak tree. He had a bedroll of sorts, and it appeared he had been riding one of the freight trains that came through town. Annie tugged at her mother's arm. "Mama, look, a hobo!"

"Shush, Annie!" whispered Ellen as she pressed her finger to her lips. Ellen motioned to Carter and Jack, who ambled over to where the man sat. It concerned Annie that they might try to shoo him away, but both addressed the gentleman in a kind and civil manner.

"Howdy, sir," said Jack. He leaned over, held out his hand, and shook the stranger's hand.

Carter knelt on one knee to the man's eye level and asked, "Are you hungry? We have food we'd be glad to share with you." He, too, shook the man's hand.

"Yes, I'm hungry. My name is Tom. I've been riding the rails a good many days and jumped off a few miles back hoping to find food. I forgot today was Sunday. Businesses in town are closed."

Lou and Ellen approached with their picnic baskets, opened them, and took out uneaten food. Not having eaten for some time, the stranger gobbled up everything in just a few moments.

"Much obliged, much obliged," he kept repeating as he ate. "I am most grateful. This is delicious. The tea hits the spot!" Tom gulped the rest of the iced tea left in a thermos bottle.

Carter looked over at Jack. "You have a bathtub at your office, don't you, Jack? Let's take Tom there so he may freshen up."

Jack agreed as they both helped the man rise to his feet. Carter took the bedroll and motioned to the two women and

Annie. "Ladies, why don't you return to Lou and Jack's house? We'll come by after a while."

Ellen, Lou, and Annie climbed inside the Morrisons' big, blue Buick, and off they went. Carter, Jack, and Tom loaded into the Young's Dodge for the brief trip to Jack's office.

"Mama, is it okay for Daddy and Uncle Jack to do that?" Annie asked, referring to her parents' good friend with the term "uncle" as most young people of the time did.

"Oh, Annie, of course! Many folks are in a dreadful way during these hard times. Any time we can help someone, we must do it. Do unto others, you know."

Lou concurred and told Annie that on occasion folks knocked on her back door and asked for any spare food. "It's men riding the trains. They are very nice and respectful, just down on their luck. I always give them something. Our back porch provides a shady oasis of sorts to sit and eat. Afterward, they go on their way. I am grateful we can help them with a small token of kindness."

Ellen addressed her daughter. "Remember how people let us camp in their yards and sometimes even gave us something to eat or a bath, Annie? They didn't have to, but they were kind to us. We shall and we must return the favor whenever we can to help someone else."

After a brief time, Carter and Jack returned. They reported Tom had bathed and shaved, and Jack gave him a clean shirt, a spare kept at his office for emergencies.

"Tom is a courteous and well-spoken fellow," Carter said. "He was trying to find work up north but wasn't successful. Now he is attempting to go back to his home in Tennessee to try sharecropping if possible. Jack and I gave him a few dollars we hope will tide him over until he gets home."

Jack shook his head. "Likable chap. Only forty years old. Looks much older. I hope the road he's traveling turns smooth. Rough roads abound right now, and it's a real shame. Things must get better. They can't get much worse."

Turning to Annie, Carter said, "When we can lighten someone's burden, when we can help someone who can never repay us, then we must do so, daughter. As Jack said, our journey through life is the same as traveling a road. Sometimes it's smooth, but sometimes it's rocky. Remember the dirt road we took when we first left for Hillview? Remember that red dirt in the air, and the road so rough you said you didn't think we'd ever get through? You complained that all you saw was choking, blinding dust, and the jostling caused by bumps and 'craters,' as you called them, was painful. I had to stop to let the dust settle just so I could see the road ahead. But we got through, didn't we? Sometimes the road of life is so rough and obstructed we cannot see our way, and the pain seems too much to bear. Other times the road is so smooth and sunny that we forget the struggles of our past and how we got here. As we travel our road, we must help others travel theirs. Remember this always."

They packed their belongings and returned to the peace and comfort of their rented home. Sunday's last hours were bittersweet for Annie because she had just one Thursday with Mittie McCormick remaining before school resumed. Annie despaired at the loss of weekdays with Blink and mornings helping Ellen with chores. No more lazy afternoons reading on the porch. She found herself the rest of Sunday afternoon apprehensive of the new school year. The girl had made no close friends last spring. Her thirteenth birthday in May was a muted family celebration because Annie did not know anyone well enough to invite to a birthday party. Annie's worries centered on what the next term might bring. New friends? What else?

****

Preparations for the coming session filled the last week before school. Ellen purchased notebooks, pencils, and a new dictionary for Annie. She completed two more school dresses

60

for Annie made from the fabric sent by Annie's grandmother. Annie spent one entire day playing hopscotch in the dirt, hide and seek, and two-person baseball with Blink. Thursday arrived, and Ellen gave Annie a plate filled with sugar cookies as a gift for Mrs. McCormick, Susie, and Susie's husband. Neither Annie nor Ellen had ever laid eyes on Mr. Rutledge, but Ellen told Annie she was sure any man liked sugar cookies.

On that last precious Thursday afternoon of summer, Annie and Miss Mittie spent their time on the sun porch convulsed by laughter and conversation. Adorned with ferns and potted plants, the porch with its cool, slate floor illuminated by filtered light and a multicolored rag rug provided the perfect setting for friendship to grow. Miss Mittie offered advice on the upcoming school year. She sensed Annie's apprehensiveness, so she spoke to the opportunity of finding friends in school. Miss Mittie reiterated her support for Annie's friendship with Blink.

"You are one special young lady, dear Annie," the old woman whispered in Annie's ear. "Be friendly to everyone. People will respond in kind. You will be fine!"

Miss Mittie related more snippets of her childhood. Her stories describing what occurred during and after the Civil War interested Annie the most. Annie imagined she lived during the long-ago time herself, visualizing herself in long skirts with many petticoats. She twirled around and around in front of Miss Mittie before she became dizzy on the verge of falling to the floor. Annie even curtsied to her friend before falling victim once again to a case of the giggles. The girl's antics captivated Miss Mittie, and she clapped her hands while throwing her head back. "You bring me such happiness, Annie!" Miss Mittie's lilting laugh was infectious. It appeared to Annie that even the potted plants smiled that afternoon.

When it was time to leave for the day, Annie leaned over the chair where Miss Mittie sat and kissed her on the cheek. A tear appeared on the girl's cheek, swept away by a rosewater perfumed handkerchief held in the old woman's wrinkled, bluish hand.

"I will see you soon, Annie! You come over whenever you wish so we can visit more, do you hear? You are always welcome."

"I will, I will. I promise I will."

Annie bolted from the sun porch and out the front door without stopping to say goodbye to Susie Rutledge. She stood on the sidewalk, tears streaming before the late afternoon sunlight dried them. Her mother drove up and stopped by the curb so Annie could climb inside the car.

"You have been crying, Annie. What is wrong?"

The girl settled into the front seat and gazed at the floor of the car. Annie wiped her eyes and sniffed twice before admitting she was sad for her Thursday visits with Miss Mittie to end.

Ellen reassured Annie that visits after school were still possible and suggested Annie set aside one day of the week for such. Although the lengthy afternoon visits of summer were improbable, she could stay an hour or two before going home.

"Why don't you continue seeing Miss Mittie on Thursdays, Annie? Instead of visiting the library or waiting at Daddy's office, go to the Rutledge home! Goodness, you don't have to stop your visits!"

"Why, Mama! I hadn't thought of that. How foolish of me! She told me to come whenever I can, so I know Thursdays are still fine! Don't you think?"

"Of course, I do."

A quiet ride home followed, with Annie smoothing her dress and remembering bits of the stories Miss Mittie had shared. Her dread of the new school year faded during the ride. Miss Mittie's reassurances took root in the recesses of the girl's brain, calming her fears somewhat and allowing a sliver of self-confidence to take hold.

The last Friday, Saturday, and Sunday before school began were a blur. Delicious food and laughter completed another

Sunday picnic. This time it was just the Youngs because Lou's debilitating headache prevented the Morrisons from taking part. Annie confessed it was nice to be just the three of them sitting under the big tree at Town Park on that last Sunday before the school year began.

"I love it here under this tree," said Annie.

"We are a fine trio, are we not?" her father rejoined. "Here's to Annie! The new school year!" He raised his glass of lemonade in a toast, and the other two joined in, clinking their glasses while laughing out loud.

"Another toast, dear husband! Here's to us! Here's to our new life in Hillview! Here's to this wonderful day!" Ellen was giddy. Glasses clinked, and lemonade sloshed on the quilt, causing the three to laugh more.

The day ended on a high note with a simple supper on the back porch. A colorful patchwork tablecloth Ellen had sewn from more remnants adorned a round wooden table on the porch. Ellen located the table in the home's attic, and Annie helped her bounce it down the stairs and through the kitchen to the porch. A deep scrub with soap and water restored the table's top to a pristine white surface, but the tablecloth added a festive touch. As Bitsy chewed a fresh bone from the butcher, here they enjoyed their last supper together before lazy summer days gave way to schoolwork, schedules, crisp autumn weather, and unexpected discoveries.

FROM THE SOIL

Miss Mittie's advice was correct. Annie took it to heart, reaching out in friendliness to classmates, and in doing so found they responded in kind while at school. Annie was an exceptional student which garnered her teacher's attention and the notice of classmates. She remained right much of a loner, however, and while she engaged in school activities with girls in her class, she did not spend time with them outside the classroom. She still saw herself as somehow different, an outsider. Blink was her weekend compatriot. Bitsy was her treasured, constant companion. Miss Mittie was her kindred spirit, and she continued to be close with her parents.

Annie reserved Thursdays after school for visits with Miss Mittie at the Rutledge home where a cookie and a glass of milk greeted her upon arrival.

Susie's hard shell cracked a bit more. She mustered what one might construe to be a faint smile once in a while. Although Miss Mittie and Annie had less time than during summer, they engaged in conversations and games of dominoes. Miss Mittie discussed the latest book she was reading so Annie could check it out after it returned to the library. The woman related more stories of her childhood, teen years, and adult life. These stories included vivid descriptions of people, places, and every sort of happening. Miss Mittie, often wearing the cameo Annie thought so enchanting, brimmed with enthusiasm during their time together. These visits further cemented the relationship between the girl and the old woman.

By the time weather cooled and leaves turned orange, yellow, or crimson, the rear woods had captivated Annie. A wide swath cleared of brush by Carter Young now exposed a pleasant view of the orchard. Along the rows of apple trees, the pickers were now visible. Men perched on ladders and filled canvas drop-bottom buckets before handing them to the women and children standing on the ground. After they emptied several buckets into a field box, women hoisted the filled box onto horse-drawn wagons that transported the apples away for processing. Annie relished the earthy smell of autumn and listening to songs the workers sang as they brought in the harvest, and those sights, sounds, and aromas painted an indelible picture in the girl's mind. Bitsy accompanied Annie and sniffed, sometimes chasing a rabbit that jumped out of the underbrush before settling into a spot and napping.

Annie gained permission from her mother to carry a small chair to the clearing so she could sit and take in the world surrounding her. There, she balanced schoolwork on one leg and completed many of her assignments while enjoying solitude. Bitsy, after conducting her survey, lay at Annie's feet, ever ready to respond to a smell or sound.

Ellen felt unease with Annie spending time at the rear portion of the property. She worried her daughter might not hear the call to supper, suffer an encounter with a wild animal or unseemly character, or worse. Ellen instructed Annie to stay at the edge of the woods closer to the house, so she was within earshot and Ellen's sight. The woods, though, drew Annie to its tranquility, the rustling of its leaves, the occasional scurry of a squirrel or rabbit, and the soft chatter of birds. Her chair somehow found its way deeper and deeper toward the property's rear boundary, much to her mother's displeasure.

One afternoon, as the sun's rays filtered through the changing foliage, Annie spied what appeared to her a rock formation. She rose from her chair, lay her book on the ground next to Bitsy, and walked to the spot. What the sun and loss of foliage exposed was not a pile of rocks or a natural rock formation. Instead, it was the remnant of a stone wall similar to ones she observed in other places around the county. Scattered stones rested on the ground, obscured by vines and mud. In places, no stones were visible.

To Annie, the wall appeared old and in a sad state of disrepair. The girl meandered along the wall's edge to one end of the clearing and gazed back at the unmistakable outlines. Although vines and fallen tree limbs covered the rubble, Annie judged the wall must run along the entire back boundary of the McCormick property, forming the west boundary of the orchard. She estimated the original wall had been not much over three feet tall and three feet wide. On the far side of the wall's rubble, she saw another stone wall. This one sat at right angles with the rubble wall, overgrowth did not obscure it, and it formed a straight line along the orchard's south boundary. Annie had not noticed the other wall before, but she thought it charming and continued staring at it, taking in the manner by which the stones were stacked and arranged.

"Annnnieeeee! Time to come inside!" Ellen rang the dinner bell on the back porch.

With haste, Annie gathered her schoolwork. The girl and the dog raced the entire distance to the house, Annie brimming with enthusiasm to tell of her discovery.

As the family sat around the dinner table discussing events of each one's day, Annie bubbled over about her discovery of the remains of an old stone wall. Ellen appeared dismissive, but Carter acknowledged he had noticed the wall's remnants when clearing brush and vines.

66

"Many of these stone walls we see date from the 1800s or earlier," said Carter. "When farmers cleared land to plant crops, they used rocks dug out of the ground to show property boundaries. Such a shame this one has deteriorated. I've considered rebuilding it or at least making it more visible by clearing away brush that obscures it."

"Daddy, did you notice another wall alongside the orchard? It looks beautiful to me."

Carter replied in the affirmative and declared the view of the orchard was one reason he was clearing a trail to the back.

"The wall over on the orchard's south boundary is attractive, Annie. You're right. The crumbling one on this property in all likelihood served a purpose to prevent someone from falling off the rocky ledge on its other side. It designates the property boundary, too, and I'm sure it was once as well laid out as the handsome wall on the orchard property."

****

After her first encounter with the rubble of the old stone wall, Annie spent more of her free time at the property's rear boundary. She labored to free debris from the formation. She picked up scattered stones and stacked them on the wall, but some were so heavy that lifting them proved difficult. Sometimes they fell or shifted out of position, which steeled Annie's determination to improve her wall-building skills. She experimented with turning them one way or the other and using ones of different sizes, which yielded better results. Annie used her father's work gloves, but they were much larger than her small hands, which made her work awkward. This obstacle did not frustrate her. To Annie, this was just another challenge.

The clearing and rebuilding process was tedious, and Annie completed a scant fifteen-foot section before the weather turned frigid. After the first hard freeze, she discovered her hands, even with gloves, became icy-cold and miserable. A raw rain settled in for several days, making the surroundings muddy and treacherous, so with reluctance, Annie abandoned the project until spring.

****

That first winter was typical for their part of the country. Several snowfalls, three exceeding one foot in depth, brought joy to the girl whose experience with the white fluffy stuff was limited to a few paltry coverings that melted within a few hours or a day at most. A sled discovered above the rafters of the outdoor shed once again provided thrills and yelps of glee for a young person. Bitsy adored leaping through snowdrifts, and Ellen and Carter relished in their daughter's joy and the silence of falling snow. Such weather made Carter's travel to and from his office difficult, so he remained in town a few evenings, sleeping on a cot to ensure availability to his patients.

Soon after Thanksgiving, Blink's father cut a cedar tree from a hillside on his property and delivered it to the Youngs.

"You have been so kind to Blink and Cora that I want you to have this tree, Dr. Young," Ned announced with a strong sense of pride. "Merry Christmas to you!"

The family made good use of exquisite Christmas decorations stored in the attic after Miss Mittie told Annie where to look. A box containing presents from Ellen's parents arrived in the mail. When viewed under the tree, the gifts made Annie believe they were the luckiest family there could be. Annie received a new sweater knitted by her grandmother and a flowered dress sewn by her mother. Her favorite gift was a pair of sturdy work gloves her dear mother had fashioned from a pair of men's cotton work gloves. Ellen had cut one pair and sewn them back together so they fit Annie's hands.

"I think I shall never convince Annie to stay away from that stone wall, so I made her a pair of gloves to fit her hands," she mentioned to Lou Morrison. "Annie can stack those doggone rocks as much as she wants, I guess!"

As winter progressed, Annie flourished in her studies. She was an outstanding student who enjoyed history and writing, and her teacher often read Annie's compositions aloud as examples of fine writing. This spotlight on the girl did not further school friendships; it aroused jealousy. Oblivious, Annie introduced Blink to the game of dominoes, and the two reveled in sledding on a hill behind the Hill cabin when snow was deep enough.

Carter's base of patients continued to grow, but receiving payment for services was still hit and miss. The Great Depression dragged on and continued to create hardship.

Ellen began accepting commissions to sew an array of clothes and other items. Garden club ladies became her first customers. She resisted accepting payment but did so after the women insisted on paying for her work. They told Ellen her workmanship was exceptional.

"Ellen, your talent should not go to waste," one proclaimed. "You are doing me a great favor by allowing me to give you this cloth I have been saving and make something splendid out of it!"

Because stylish store-bought clothing was often not available or affordable, women perked up their wardrobes by adding feathers and bows to hats, collars, and belts. Ellen had an artistic eye and the talent to add these touches, so word of her talents spread around Hillview. She soon declined work because she could not complete every request she received.

During this bleak year in American history, they had enough to eat, a comfortable, warm, and cozy home, and they had each other. Carter and Ellen Young's hearts were full.

***************_

Late February 1934 brought warmer days along with frigid days. A snowstorm wreaked havoc on tree limbs with a wet, heavy blanket of snow. The family lost electrical power, but a raging fire in the fireplace kept them warm until power resumed two days later.

Annie yearned to retreat to the woods so she could continue on her wall project. She and Bitsy tromped through the mud one afternoon to see if her work survived the winter. It appeared to Annie that the wall remained as she had left it, which pleased her. After she and the dog returned to the house, Annie matter-of-factly told Ellen she planned to resume work soon.

Ellen shook her head. "You are obsessed with those rocks, sweet child!"

After mud dried and temperatures warmed a trace, the girl and the dog were at the wall once again. The gloves she received for Christmas helped her go faster than before, and she was even more grateful for the gift than she was at Christmastime.

Annie told Blink about her new project, and sometimes, if he had completed his chores, he showed up and helped Annie with her task. He pushed a wheelbarrow filled with stones Ned had plucked from his fields to the work site. "My p-pap says

you can have these, Annie. He calls 'em 'mountain potatoes' and doesn't want 'em!"

On one lazy Sunday afternoon in early March as sundown loomed, Annie scavenged for stones scattered on the ground. She almost overlooked a good many obscured ones packed into the ground. Annie raked leaves and vines from the immediate vicinity, then took the spade she had toted from the shed and pried these recent finds from the earth. Excavated ones she tossed into a pile, and she continued finding more and more, making a mess of the ground as she dug. Layers of caked mud coated these chunks of limestone, so sizes and shapes were not discernible.

She complained to Bitsy, "Whew, this work is hard! I'm tired. We should go back to the house since it's getting near suppertime."

As soon as she finished speaking, Bitsy leaped to her feet, each leg stiff, stubby tail straight up into the air. The dog's ears bent forward as she began barking at the wall's remnants. It was as if she saw or sensed something she considered threatening. The ferocious barks and intermittent growls continued for a good couple of minutes before Annie could calm the dog. Annie saw nothing to rile Bitsy. She peered through the trees, but nothing appeared amiss. Since it was getting dark, she turned and began running toward the house. Bitsy followed, glancing backward as she ran.

Annie had always sensed safety and comfort by the wall. She had seen birds, squirrels, and rabbits, but never another human or animal she feared. Quiet and serenity were two features she most coveted, so this notion of unseen danger unnerved her. The girl decided not to tell her mother of this development, for fear Ellen might forbid her from returning to the wall.

****

It was the following Wednesday afternoon that she and Bitsy returned to property's rear. Sun had dried out much of the muck on the stones in Annie's pile, so she began scraping off those stones. She used a paint scraper she had found in the shed, and it was just what she needed for the task at hand.

Bitsy was her usual self, so a relaxed Annie sat on a stool and hummed a tune.

As she scraped and chipped the caked dirt from one unique and uneven stone, something fell from a large clod and struck the ground with a clink. Annie looked at the item, but it was so smeared and stained by the clay she could not identify it. She picked it up for a closer look. At first, she thought it was a smaller stone lodged at one edge of the larger one. As she turned it over and wiped away a piece of the sticky clay, what exposed itself was not a stone, but a piece of gold jewelry. The clasp first caught her eye, and she continued to brush and wipe away on her recent find. When she saw what the piece was, her audible gasp awakened Bitsy from a nap.

"Bitsy, look at this! It's a cameo the same as Miss Mittie's! Except the lady's face turns the other direction!" Bitsy, uninterested in this turn of events, stretched and started walking around in a circle, sniffing the ground as she walked.

A puzzled Annie continued to remove caked dirt from the cameo using her handkerchief dampened with a little spit. The possibility she could knock the face off or otherwise damage the brooch concerned her. Lost in concentration, Bitsy's sudden growl startled her and made her drop the cameo to the ground.

Again, as she had a few days prior, Bitsy stood stiff, stared straight ahead, and quivered as guttural eruptions escaped her furry throat. She began barking, her eyes never wavering from the same spot straight ahead.

Annie scanned the horizon searching for what elicited such a response from the dog, but she saw just the orchard, its apple trees still bare of leaves. Nothing prowled around the ground. Nothing moved except stray clouds high in the azure sky.

"Bitsy, what on earth is wrong with you?" Annie tried to collar the dog, but Bitsy broke free and charged the wall. She barked and growled, and when she reached the broken wall, she stood there barking without pause. This frightened Annie, and she picked up the cameo from the ground where it had fallen. She turned and began running back toward the house, calling the dog as she ran. Bitsy turned and ran after Annie as if to protect her from an unseen threat.

Both were breathless when they reached the back porch. This second episode of Bitsy's peculiar behavior left Annie too discombobulated to remember the tools she left at the wall. She stood on the back porch, removed her shoes, and took several deep breaths as she attempted to regain her composure. Annie slipped the dirty cameo into her coat pocket and stuffed her work gloves on top. Then she opened the back door and assumed a nonchalant air as she entered the kitchen.

"Annie, why was Bitsy barking?" Ellen did not look up as she continued peeling potatoes.

"Um, a squirrel."

"Goodness, the sound of it concerned me. It wasn't her usual barking sound. You've come in earlier than usual. Everything okay back there?"

"Oh, she was, um, she was sleeping, and it woke her. I guess it scared her."

"Such a funny little dog! Go wash up so you can help me. Jack and Lou are coming for supper tonight. I forgot to tell you Daddy invited them, and I didn't think of it until after you went out back."

Annie stared at her mother standing at the kitchen sink. Bitsy was at her water bowl lapping water as if she had drunk none in a month.

"Hurry, honey. Please set the table for me but remember to wash up first and put on your clean clothes." Ellen looked up from the sink as she put the potatoes in the pot and glanced at her daughter. "Annie, are you all right?"

"Sure."

Annie washed her face and hands, ran a comb through her hair, and changed into the dress she wore to school before sprinting downstairs. Careful to arrange knives, forks, and spoons in the way her mother had taught her, she then filled water glasses and set those at each setting. She was fussing with folding napkins when Ellen entered the dining room.

"Why, Annie, this table looks delightful! You will be a marvelous hostess someday."

Annie grimaced at the thought. Hostessing was not something she considered for her future. At that moment, she felt guilty for not telling her mother of today's discovery at the wall or Bitsy's odd behavior. Should she wait until after the Morrisons left to tell her parents? Should she not tell them? Should she tell Miss Mittie what she had found? Annie was one confused young lady.

Mouth-watering fare, pleasant conversation, and frequent laughter punctuated the evening. Ellen's juicy pot roast was a hit. Lou brought green beans she canned the preceding summer along with homemade bread still warm from her oven, but her custard pie was everyone's favorite. Annie forgot her personal dilemma as she listened to the adult conversation at the dining room table. Often, when the two couples were together, talk of hard times permeated the conversations, but that night there was nary a word. Gaiety filled the room.

Annie hurried to help her mother and Lou clean the table, then excused herself to complete her schoolwork. Truth was, she had no schoolwork but wanted to further scrutinize the cameo. Annie could not decide if she should show it to Miss Mittie. To add to her conflicted state, Annie felt uneasy asking her parents for advice or alerting them to Bitsy's weird behavior.

Annie let Bitsy out the front door. Then, ever so discreetly, she opened the hall closet door and took the cameo from her coat pocket, making sure her father and Jack, sitting in the parlor, did not take notice. After tiptoeing up the stairs and putting on her pajamas, she took the wastebasket kept next to her dresser and moved it by her bed. Using a handkerchief, she began brushing more dirt from the brooch, so dirt fell into the basket. The cameo was filthy, but no part appeared broken, not even the delicate face. Its bent pin was all but broken in half, but she saw nothing else out of kilter. She considered washing the cameo in the bathroom sink but thought better of it. Annie was in a quandary. She could not decide how to proceed with this unusual artifact, and Bitsy's strange behavior troubled her.

The front door opened and sounds of pitter-patter of paws on the downstairs floor followed. The adults were saying goodbye for the evening, and Annie smiled at the enjoyment her parents experienced when they were with Jack and Lou. While goodbyes were still being said, Bitsy trotted up the stairs to Annie's room and jumped into the doggy bed on the floor next to Annie's bed. Annie, fearing the arrival of her parents to tell her goodnight as was their custom, scooted the wastebasket to its usual location, tucked the cameo in her book satchel, and climbed under the covers. There she was when Carter and Ellen walked through the door a few moments later. They exchanged kisses, extinguished the light, and Annie found herself in the darkness listening to Bitsy's soft breathing and the wind whistling through the cedar tree outside her window before she drifted off to sleep.

****

Thursday morning dawned bleak and rainy. Winds lulling Annie to sleep the night before ushered in a front bringing near-freezing temperatures. Bitsy did not want to go outside, but she scooted out the door and did her business while Annie held the kitchen door open for her to return. The kitchen stove provided pleasing warmth as Annie wiped the dog's wet paws and dried off her fur.

"Brrrrr . . . it's bitter out there, Annie!" Carter Young's voice boomed as he set his bag next to the front door. "Are you dressed warm enough?"

"Yes, Daddy. I'll wear my heavy coat, too."

"You visiting Mrs. McCormick today?"

"Yes, Daddy."

The three enjoyed hot Cream of Wheat, soft-boiled eggs, and toast for breakfast. Annie's satchel rested on the floor next to her father's medical bag, so when it was time to leave, she picked it up and waited for her parents by the front door. Rain reduced to a drizzle as they made their way to the car.

Annie remained silent during the ride to school. Carter glanced at Ellen and cocked his head toward the back-seat passenger with a quizzical look. Ellen shrugged and shook her head as if to say, "I don't know." It was rare for morning rides to town to be without conversation as Annie was a perpetual chatterbox. That morning, though, she stared out the window at passing scenes, deep in thought.

When they arrived at school, Annie made a quick exit and jaunted into the school building after planting a kiss on each of her parents' cheeks. Ellen and Carter made no mention of their daughter's silence on the drive to Carter's office. He kissed Ellen goodbye and waved as he strode to the door, unlocked it, and began his workday. It promised to be just another Thursday.

NOT JUST ANOTHER THURSDAY

An uncomfortable chill and clouds lingered after school dismissal. Annie sprinted to the Rutledge house and was delighted to find Susie had hot chocolate waiting. Miss Mittie rested on the sun porch as customary, but she had a thick blanket on her lap which extended to the floor, covering her legs and feet. A wool shawl caressed her shoulders. Table lamps brightened the room, giving it an inviting warmth unlike the dreary outdoors.

"Come in here and get warm, Annie! I thought spring was around the corner, but we are freezing again! The gas heater over there doesn't keep this porch warm enough for me."

"Good afternoon, Miss Mittie! This hot chocolate tastes delicious. It's a delicacy. Chocolate is expensive, Mama says."

The old lady leaned in toward the girl and whispered, "Nothing is too expensive for my best friend." She winked at Annie and, sporting an impish grin, leaned back into the chair and adjusted her glasses.

Miss Mittie's manner suggested the time was right for Annie to reveal her discovery.

"You remember that I have been rebuilding the old wall at the back of your property, don't you, Miss Mittie?"

Miss Mittie's blue eyes crinkled, her lilting laugh more of an amused chuckle. "Yes, you have told me over one hundred times!"

Annie scrunched her face. She took a deep breath. "Yesterday I was working at the wall, and I found lots of stones packed into the ground. I think they'd been there for a long time, so I was digging them out of the mud and putting them in a pile. There was so much dirt caked on them I couldn't tell what shapes they were or how big they were."

"I imagine. The wall dates before my time, but it was in good condition when I was young. My husband never tried to do a thing with it, though, after we built our home there. He cut brush away so we could see the property line, but no one has touched the wall for . . ." Her voice trailed.

"Well, I was cleaning the rocks so I could stack them. I couldn't stack them unless I cleaned them, you can imagine, and you will not believe what fell out of one clod of dirt!"

Miss Mittie chuckled again. "A bag of gold? Pirate's treasure?" She scratched her head and made a funny face.

"No! This!" Annie reached in her coat pocket and withdrew the dirty cameo, handing it to the woman with a flourish. "It looks the same as yours, but the lady faces the other direction!"

Miss Mittie's countenance shifted from amusement to horror. A groan escaped her lips as she turned the cameo over and over in her bony, blue-veined hand. Color drained from her face as she looked at Annie. She reached and grabbed the girl's hand.

"You discovered this in rocks from the stone wall, you say?" In a hushed tone, Miss Mittie's voice quaked.

Annie flinched and began to shake. She did not expect this reaction from the woman she cherished.

"Yes, it was, um, it was in a big clod of dirt that fell from a rock. I've cleaned it off somewhat, but I didn't want to damage it. Miss Mittie, what is wrong? Oh, my, I thought you'd think it a coincidence since you have one like it. I'm so sorry! What have I done?"

Mittie McCormick settled back into the chair once again and adjusted the shawl tighter around her shoulders. She closed her eyes for a long moment before replying to Annie's question.

"I never expected to see this again. The cameo has been lost since I was eight years old. I haven't thought of it forever. It belonged to my older sister, Phoebe. Oh, Phoebe was telling the truth. Oh, my . . ." Her voice once again trailed as tears streamed from her eyes.

Annie began crying, too. Miss Mittie's sadness confused her. It upset her. Annie was angry with herself, and she wanted to take the cameo back and pretend she had never found it.

The moment Miss Mittie saw Annie's hurt, she wiped her own tears with her always ready silk handkerchief and then reached out to wipe Annie's face.

"Sweet girl, I must not upset you with my emotional ways. You knew nothing of this cameo! Why, you have done me a favor! You have! Now I know my sister told the truth. It was a dreadful occurrence. Phoebe said she lost this piece by the wall. Nobody believed her because they searched the site high and low. Papa searched, and Phoebe searched, but they never found it. Oh, it was awful! Please don't cry or think you have done something wrong, because you have not!"

Bewildered, Annie tried to comprehend the woman's explanation. Why could the loss of a piece of jewelry create such profound angst among Miss Mittie's family? It made no sense to Annie.

Miss Mittie continued to examine the cameo, turning it over and over, her gentle brushing causing a small volume of dried mud to fall to the floor. She ran her fingers over the surface, murmuring her sister's name again and again. She stopped, stared at the cameo, and held it toward Annie.

"Annie, I want you to keep this. I shall not speak of this discovery to Susie. I do not wish to upset her. Any talk of events or people involving this cameo brings her significant pain. She wants to hear nothing and wants no talk in public discourse. Susie views it as a dreadful secret that must stay buried. This discovery of yours proves to me that something my sister said happened may very well have happened, even though others denied and dismissed what she claimed. Time doesn't permit an explanation today, but I shall explain at our next visit. Please sweep up this dirt from the floor and put it in the wastebasket." Miss Mittie's tone was stern, a tone Annie had never heard, and it concerned the girl.

"Okay, Miss Mittie, I will keep it. I don't understand, but I hope you'll explain it so I do. I don't want to cause any trouble or for Mrs. Rutledge to be angry with me, and I don't want to hurt you, either!"

"No, don't fret, Annie, my dear. It is not a problem. It's a good thing."

Annie began turning the numbers over in her mind. Miss Mittie said Phoebe lost her cameo when Miss Mittie was eight years old. How old was she now? She hesitated before asking the question.

"When was this lost, Miss Mittie?"

"Ha! A clever way to figure out how old I am, Anna Ruth Young!" Her impish grin had returned. "I was eight. Phoebe was fifteen. It was in 1863, my dear, in another age, in another century, during a terrible, terrible time." Miss Mittie shook her head and shivered as she remembered. "Oh, it was a terrible time."

Footsteps startled them both, and Susie stood in the doorway. Annie closed her right hand around the brooch to shield it from Susie's view.

"Berta and I are in the kitchen. Do you need anything, Mother? Annie?"

"No, Susie, we are fine." Miss Mittie's voice rose just above a whisper.

"Annie, your mother telephoned and will be here in ten minutes to gather you." With that proclamation, Susie Rutledge swept out of the room.

Annie raised herself from her chair and put the cameo in her coat pocket. With Miss Mittie's handkerchief, she gathered the dirt on the floor and shook it into the wastebasket. She put on her coat and returned to the chair, sitting on the edge.

Miss Mittie reached again and clasped both of the girl's hands into hers. "Do not worry. A complicated story it is, and I have not considered it for a long time. My sister Phoebe was a sweet girl, but she was rebellious. Papa and Mother struggled with her! After she lost the cameo, there were most difficult times for our family and for Phoebe. She, uh, well, I will explain it next Thursday. You go to the front door and watch for your mother."

Annie stood and leaned over to kiss Miss Mittie on the forehead as was her custom. She asked the woman whether she should tell her parents of the cameo. She explained she had not mentioned it, but did Miss Mittie want her to tell them? Should she keep it a secret?

Miss Mittie remained silent for a few seconds. "You should not keep secrets from your parents, Annie."

Annie nodded, exited the room, and walked toward the front foyer. Ellen pulled to the curb in a few moments, and the girl and her mother left the Rutledge house.

"How was your visit today?"

"Fine."

"Annie, we are going straight home today instead of retrieving Daddy. He and Jack are attending a civic dinner tonight. Jack will bring Daddy home afterward."

"All right."

As she shifted the car into second gear, Ellen's eyes glanced over at her daughter. In a sudden moment, she slammed on the brakes, so she did not hit a gray cat that dashed into the street. The abrupt stop made Annie tilt forward and catch herself on the dashboard.

"Mama, you be careful!"

Annie's stern tone surprised Ellen, but she said nothing except she was pleased she did not hit the now out-of-sight feline.

Ellen related her day's activities. The Piggly Wiggly employed a new checker. She reviewed the proceedings of her garden club meeting. If this was a normal Thursday afternoon, Ellen could not have inserted a word in edgewise, but on this Thursday afternoon, Annie remained quiet. The girl responded to her mother's stories with several "um" comments, but those were the extent of her interactions.

When they reached home, Annie slogged up the steps, and as she opened the front door, Bitsy leaped out and bounced up to greet her. Annie did not react to the dog's enthusiastic greeting. Ellen stood by the car observing the dog and the girl, reflecting upon Annie's odd behavior.

"Annie, please put your books in the house and help me bring in groceries. I have a good many today."

Annie did as directed, and after placing sacks on the kitchen table, she asked permission to retreat upstairs for a brief time.

"Do you not feel well, dear?" Ellen felt Annie's forehead.

"I am fine, just tired. I will let Bitsy inside in a few minutes."

Ellen agreed to Annie's request with the admonishment to take a quick rest. Carter did not plan to be home for dinner, so Ellen did not need help to prepare a simple meal of chipped beef on toast. "I will call you when dinner is ready, dear," she said.

Annie collapsed on her bed, gazing through the rain-spattered window as tree limbs rippled in the wind. Several things troubled her: the cameo and Miss Mittie's reactions to it, Bitsy's behavior at the wall, and that she had shared none of this with her parents. She found herself in a high state of bewilderment. Could it be she should abandon the wall project if its tiny treasure brought her friend heartache? The answer seemed straightforward, and she resolved to stop. With her decision made, she drifted into a fitful nap before being awakened by Bitsy pouncing onto the bed.

"Annie, supper is ready! Come downstairs."

Groggy, she stumbled to the bathroom and splashed cool water on her face before descending the staircase into the kitchen.

"We will eat here at the kitchen table, dear. Do you have schoolwork?"

"No. I completed my assignments in class today, and I've read my book for my book report. We will write our reports in class tomorrow."

"You are a wonder kid, Annie! Whee!" Ellen threw her arms in the air as if to celebrate a victory.

Annie let out a meager laugh and threw her arms into the air, too.

Repartee between the two pushed Annie back to her usual self. They chatted at length and finished supper with two sugar cookies for dessert. Annie helped her mother clean up the kitchen before they retired to the parlor to tackle the jigsaw puzzle already under construction. Ellen built a fire in the fireplace, and they listened to the falling rain while pondering the placement of puzzle pieces. Bitsy curled up in front of the fire and snored, the sound bringing chuckles from Ellen and Annie as they collaborated on their project.

Bedtime arrived in no time. Annie kissed her mother goodnight and stumbled upstairs for a warm bath. After putting on the cotton flannel pajamas her mother had made, she crawled under the covers. She smiled at Bitsy, who settled into her own bed and sighed off to sleep. The day's worries had melted away, so deep sleep arrived in an instant. She did not even awaken when her father came through the front door, and the door banged shut in the wind, shaking the entire house.

When Saturday arrived, Mother Nature decided spring should be in the air, so the day dawned fair and warmer. After breakfast, Carter inquired as to Annie's plans for the day. He suggested helping with her wall-building, saying recent rains should make it much easier to pull vines out by the roots. Wall rebuilding should move forward without difficulty.

"Your mother is planning to drive into town for the church Helping Hands event. I thought I might till her garden while she's gone, but she asked that I wait until she can oversee my work!" Carter Young snickered as he completed the sentence. "So, Anna Ruth, I am free as can be to help you today!"

This unexpected offer took Annie by surprise. She had decided to stop working on the wall, but her enthusiastic father offered assistance. She did not wish to discuss her recent decision, fearing questions, so she accepted his help. In actuality, she loved working alongside her father in any undertaking. She adored him. Carter's practice kept him busy, and times together were not as frequent as either liked. Patients' needs often interrupted evenings at home or weekends, so this turn of events filled Annie's heart with joy.

Ellen drove off to church. Annie and her beloved father donned their work gloves, loaded a hoe, shovel, spade, and lopping shears into a wheelbarrow and together strolled to the back of the property. It pleased Annie that her father was with her because Dr. Young might protect them from any danger if Bitsy behaved in an odd manner. At the very least, he might discover what was upsetting the dog.

Carter pulled vines and dug out small volunteer trees and wild honeysuckle. He cut back low overhanging limbs and cleared a good bit of the space in a couple of hours. His strength and skill allowed him to do more than Annie could, and she appreciated the fruits of his labor. She knew the job she had undertaken was mammoth. The environs of the wall now appeared cleaner and tidier, and with new resolve, Annie decided to resume her restoration efforts. Carter returned to the corner of the property where Annie had stacked those first stones and pulled more vines away. While the wall was just over three feet high, nothing an animal could not hurdle with ease, it gave definition to the property line. It was beginning to be an aesthetically pleasing formation once again.

"I believe it's lunchtime, Annie. Why don't we get a bit of nourishment? When we return, I'll bring my saw to cut these bigger limbs and small trees away. It's looking nice here, is it not?"

"Nice? It looks magical, Daddy!"

Bitsy came running when Carter whistled, and the three returned to the house. Annie breathed a sigh of relief that Bitsy's behavior had been normal.

After lunch, Carter and Annie returned to their toils. Brandishing a pruning saw from the shed, Carter dispensed with larger overhanging limbs and tree sprouts while whistling his version of "Mule Skinner Blues" through his teeth. Annie went to the spot where she unearthed the cameo and positioned stones washed clean by the recent rain in place on top of the wall. She attempted to mimic her father's whistling, which amused him. Bitsy sniffed tree trunks and the ground, to her right and to her left, behind her and straight ahead. It was as if the dog was searching, but she was not perturbed, just doing what curious dogs do. By the end of the afternoon, a brush pile of twigs, vines, limbs, and saplings occupied a sizable space several yards from the wall.

"Annie, we have made genuine progress this afternoon. We should be proud of ourselves, my girl!"

Bitsy sniffed the brush pile and turned to jump up on Carter's leg. She yapped once and scampered toward the house, her way of saying it was quitting time.

Annie and her father gathered the tools, packed them into the wheelbarrow, and headed toward the house. When they

85

opened the back door, a sweet aroma of fried chicken greeted them. Ellen had returned and was cooking supper.

Another blissful day ended with good food and conversation, a roaring fire in the fireplace, and an evening of jigsaw puzzle fun. Annie forgot the mystery of the cameo. She basked in her parents' love and the peacefulness surrounding them in their home at the end of the lane. For one moment, their world appeared solid and serene.

THE CURSE

T he next week brought more rain and chilly weather, so work at the wall was not practical. Annie attended school and, as usual, excelled in her studies, but a deep sense of dread invaded her psyche on Wednesday afternoon. Annie wanted to learn more of the mysterious cameo, but what Miss Mittie might say frightened her. She still had not mentioned this predicament to her parents, which pushed her dread deeper and deeper.

Thursday dawned cloudy but not as raw as earlier in the week. March was soon drawing to a close, yet a late snowstorm always loomed as a possibility. After school, Annie walked to the Rutledge home, expecting she knew not what. Miss Mittie rested on the sun porch as usual, blanket around her lap, shawl around her shoulders. This time she sat in a rocking chair closer to the heater and was completing a crossword puzzle.

Susie retreated to the kitchen to prepare two cups of hot chocolate and two cookies for the now best friends.

"I am relieved to see you, Annie," said Miss Mittie. "The possibility you might be fearful of coming to see me today after my behavior last week concerned me. Did I frighten you with my reaction to your discovery? I am so sorry. Please don't be fearful."

Annie nodded. "I thought I did the wrong thing to show you the cameo. I don't wish to cause you discomfort or sadness."

"Did you bring it with you?"

"Yes. It's in my coat pocket."

Susie entered the room with the drinks and cookies on a tray, situated the tray on the table next to Miss Mittie's chair, and left the room without speaking.

"Bring it to me and sit close," instructed the old woman. "I wish to examine it again."

Annie retrieved the cameo from her coat and scooted her chair close to Miss Mittie. The girl handed the piece of jewelry to her friend and sipped her hot chocolate.

As Miss Mittie examined the cameo in her hands, Annie saw the unmistakable image of sadness and reflection overtake her friend's face. Annie's lip trembled as she set the cup back on the tray with a loud clank.

Miss Mittie cleared her throat. "Annie, I will tell you a story. The story is one I have not spoken of in many years, one I pushed into my mind's recesses and tried to forget. If you know the story, it may help you understand things relating to this town and this county and why a few old-timers are standoffish around me."

Annie was unprepared for what followed.

"When I was a little girl, I had an older sister named Phoebe. I mentioned her to you last week. Phoebe rarely adhered to rules or social conventions. Phoebe had a mind of her own. As to the cameo, our grandmother brought them as gifts for us. Phoebe loved hers and begged Mother to allow her to wear it when she was thirteen years old. Because I was a good bit younger, Mother kept mine for safe-keeping."

Annie tried to digest the timeline. "Oh," she said.

"When Phoebe lost her cameo, it was during that dreadful Civil War some call the War Between the States. We lived in a divided part of the country, consumed with suspicion and hate. That war tore apart families. Families here sympathized with the North, and others sympathized with the South. Times were hard, and food was scarce. Our part of the valley was in Northern hands. Then it switched to Southern. Then it switched back. Soldiers of both sides came and went. I was a child, but I knew times were terrible." Miss Mittie shook her head as her face took on a somber cast. "Terrible times, Annie. Terrible times."

Miss Mittie took a sip of hot chocolate, which by this time was cooling. Then she smiled at the girl sitting in front of her.

"Our father was a physician, you know," Miss Mittie said. "We lived in the house across the big road from your lane."

Annie nodded.

"Papa helped anyone in need. Papa harbored no prejudices toward anyone who needed aid. He did not care whether one was a Union sympathizer or a Confederate sympathizer, and he did not care whether a person was colored, white, free, or slave. Papa ministered to the poor and to the wealthy. Our family received lots of chickens and turnips as payment! Southern sympathizers didn't appreciate his beliefs, so sometimes he . . . and we . . . were not afforded courtesy by those folk. I recall seeing soldiers wearing blue and soldiers wearing gray coming to our home. Mother scooted me to the parlor or to the room Phoebe and I shared when soldiers needing care came to call. Papa tended them in our kitchen or downstairs in the barn underneath the living quarters of our house. Soldiers' wounds could be dreadful, something my mother did not wish me to see. On occasion, Papa asked Phoebe or Mother for help. This occurred if Papa needed more help with surgeries. To be honest, any wounded or sick folk that came to our home frightened me."

Miss Mittie continued her explanation. "There is something else. Papa and Mother despised the practice of holding people in bondage. In fact, they assisted coloreds who were attempting to slip the bonds of slavery and get to freedom even before the war broke out. Few people around

89

here knew. Activities such as those were secret. Such activities *required* secrecy, you understand. Those activities were dangerous."

This news shocked Annie. She knew from history lessons that assisting runaway slaves could bring dire consequences to the person giving aid.

Miss Mittie heaved a sigh, rocking in her chair. "Phoebe disobeyed Papa's order to stay home the day she lost her cameo. My sister's custom was to take her horse for rides. Oh, he was a lovely bay Morgan named Blaze. Had the most stunning white marking on his foot and face, he did! Anyhow, she enjoyed riding Blaze in the afternoons along trails on our property or through the fields. That afternoon, Papa instructed her not to ride. It concerned him soldiers were nearby because of what he heard when he was in town in early morning. He told us we were to stay by the house and not to go outside the fence surrounding it. Phoebe had earlier saddled Blaze, but Papa insisted she unsaddle him and put him in his stall in the barn."

"Where were you, Miss Mittie?"

"I was playing with my dolls on the front veranda. Papa was inside in his office. Mother was in the kitchen. Phoebe, though, rode off on Blaze without making a peep, and none of us saw or heard her leave. Russell, our colored man, knocked on the door and told Papa that neither Blaze nor his saddle were in the barn. Russell had gone into the barn to feed the horses an hour after Papa told Phoebe not to leave and discovered the empty stall. He had overheard Papa's instruction to Phoebe not to go out. Papa was furious."

"Was Russell a slave?" asked Annie.

"Oh, no! Goodness, no!" Miss Mittie stomped a foot and shook one hand in the air. "Russell and his wife were our *employees*. I assume he was a slave at one time, but someone, I suspect Papa, had given him and his wife Thea their freedom. Besides helping Papa with farm chores, Russell was an accomplished wood carver. He honed his craft by carving oak canes for Papa's patients who required them. He carved canes for years, even before the war. It pleased Papa that Russell asked to offer this service, and he paid Russell for each cane besides his wages. Russell tailored his canes to the patient's height, so they were just perfect. During the war, though, he made lots of them, so Papa had a ready supply. This cane I use is one Russell made. Isn't it exquisite?"

"It is." Annie again noted the intricate carvings on the cane leaning against Miss Mittie's chair.

"Thea helped Mother so much," said Miss Mittie. "Both of them were kind and wonderful to Phoebe and me. Thea taught me how to play dominoes. I believe I told you that."

"I'm sorry. I guess I thought . . . they . . . please continue."

"We did not know where Phoebe had gone, Annie, yet Papa and Russell saddled horses hoping to find her. Papa believed he might know what direction she had taken because she had a special spot she liked to visit. Papa told Mother and me to stay inside the house with Thea. Not long after they took off to find Phoebe, she and Blaze came galloping home. Papa and Russell were still within earshot of the dinner bell, so they heard it when Mother rang it to alert them. Phoebe was a dirty mess. She was hysterical and crying. Incoherent. Blaze was in a lather, and we could see he had run the entire way home from wherever they had been. When Papa and Russell arrived in a few moments, my sister was on the ground, weeping uncontrollable tears. She couldn't speak, but after Mother brought her water and washed her face, was she able to mumble a few words."

Susie interrupted the story as she entered the room, casting a quizzical glance at her mother. Miss Mittie had been speaking in hushed tones the entire time. An enthralled Annie, sitting at the edge of her chair and leaning forward, was inches from her dear friend's face. Susie's entrance startled them both.

"Mother, Mrs. Young will be here in a half-hour. I had not heard you talking, so I'm checking on you. Is everything all right here?"

"Everything is hunky-dory, Susie," said the old woman, a slight smile on her lips.

Susie Rutledge wheeled and left the room. The close relationship her mother had forged with Annie Young puzzled Susie and aroused jealousy. She retreated to the kitchen where she and Berta, the housekeeper, continued their dinner planning discussion, leaving Miss Mittie and Annie alone on the sun porch.

"So, what happened next, Miss Mittie?"

"It concerned Papa that Phoebe might be injured, so he began examining her. She protested that she suffered no injuries, that she was dirty because she had fallen off Blaze and crawled through mud. Mother and Papa helped her into our house, and Thea drew a bath, heating several pots of water. Mother and Thea helped Phoebe bathe, washing her hair and soothing an enormous scrape and bruise forming on her leg. Phoebe appeared unhurt otherwise."

Annie breathed a murmur of relief. "Good! I was afraid she was injured."

"Her physical condition was fine, but not her mental condition, Annie. Later in the afternoon, she repeated over and over she had seen something dreadful. She started weeping and shaking again, and we couldn't console her. Both Papa and Mother tried to make her tell them what she had seen, but she did not say. Phoebe stared at the ceiling in silence and then started wailing. It was horrible, horrible, horrible to see her in such a state."

Annie imagined the scene inside Miss Mittie's household that dreadful afternoon. She visualized a hysterical fifteen-year-old girl, adults scurrying back and forth, and an eight-year-old Miss Mittie standing alone, watching in silence. This vision in her mind left Annie speechless.

"My dear sister did not act right after that. She alternated between fits of tears and staring at the ceiling in silence. When Mother told her the cameo was no longer pinned to her dress, her fits became worse. Phoebe screamed things that sounded nonsensical. She was obsessed with finding the cameo. Her behavior continued for a week or more before she told Mother and Papa what she saw. They didn't tell me details then. Remember, I was small, an innocent child, so I am sure they did not want to frighten me. I learned what happened later."

"What did she see, Miss Mittie?"

Susie Rutledge's voice boomed through the hallway, "Annie, your mother is pulling up in front of the house. Hurry, child!"

Miss Mittie sat back, sighed, and took Annie's right hand in both of hers. "Go now, dear. You have heard enough for today. I will tell you the rest at our next visit."

With reluctance, the girl stood and leaned over to kiss her friend on her wrinkled forehead. She donned her coat, checking to make sure the cameo was still in its pocket, waved, and walked out the sun porch door toward the front door. "Goodbye, Mrs. Rutledge!"

"Goodbye," came a curt reply from the kitchen.

Annie plodded toward the car and settled into the back seat as Ellen assisted her daughter with her book satchel.

"Enjoyable visit with Mrs. McCormick today?"

"Yes."

"Mrs. McCormick is such a sweet person. I'm glad you two have become friends. We are lucky to have her in our lives." Ellen glanced over at Annie to see her reaction, which was a slight nod as Annie's eyes turned toward the sky.

When they drove up to Dr. Young's office, he was waiting outside for them, an unusual occurrence. He did not have house calls on the way home, either. The drive home was one of small talk between the adults with a rare brief answer from Annie to a trivial question.

After dinner, Annie asked, "Daddy, have you ever heard of Miss Mittie's sister, Phoebe?"

Carter squinted and looked at the fire blazing in the fireplace. "No, I don't believe so, Annie. Ah, didn't Jack say she had a sister? Maybe that was her name."

"Oh, I just wondered. Her sister was older than Miss Mittie."

"Was Mrs. McCormick speaking of her today?" asked Carter

"Yes."

After the exchange with her father, Annie retreated upstairs for her bath and bedtime. She was tired and fell asleep soon after, with Bitsy snuggled in her bed on the floor. She still had mentioned nothing to her parents of Phoebe's cameo.

****

The next week was a whirlwind until Thursday arrived. It was busy for the family and for Annie in particular, who had a fair volume of schoolwork. No opportunities to spend time at the wall developed, and a quick visit from Blink and his mother bringing a warm loaf of bread provided Annie her only contact with anyone other than schoolmates and her parents. Ellen completed a dress for a prominent lawyer's wife in town, and Carter had a full schedule of patients, making for late evenings three nights in a row.

When Thursday dawned, Carter suggested Annie skip her afternoon visit to the Rutledge house. A patient was in serious condition in the hospital, and Carter needed access to the family car that day and later into the evening so he could check on the patient. This meant Ellen must postpone her market day.

"Oh, Daddy! I just have to go! It's too important! Please, can I go? I must see Miss Mittie today!" She tugged at his arm.

94

Annie's near hysterical reaction to his suggestion was unexpected.

"Why is it imperative you go today?" Ellen asked.

"It just is. It just is. Believe me! I will walk home if I have to, even if it's dark. I must go!"

Carter suggested maybe she could visit the old woman the next day on Friday.

"Dear, I will telephone Susie Rutledge and ask if tomorrow is convenient," Ellen said. "I can do so this minute."

A tearful Annie waited for her mother to make the call while her father paced by the front door.

Susie informed Ellen the next day was inconvenient because she was expecting guests for lunch and games of bridge. If Annie could not come today, her visit must wait until Thursday of the next week.

When he saw the girl's sobbing reaction to this news, Carter sighed and walked to Annie's side. He put both hands on her shoulders and searched her face. "Annie, I will make sure either I or someone will retrieve you from the Rutledge house today. I don't understand why today's visit is so urgent, but tonight I want you to tell your mother and me why. You have not been acting yourself after recent visits there. Do you understand me?"

"Yes, Daddy. I do."

Carter and Annie left the house. A telephone call from Carter to Ellen later in the morning disclosed that his patient was improving. Jack Morrison had agreed to visit the man late in the afternoon so Carter could retrieve Annie from the Rutledge home.

Thus, on a Thursday in March of 1934, Annie learned what Phoebe witnessed so many years ago, and Carter and Ellen learned of the childhood curse that followed Miss Mittie into adulthood.

BLOODY MURDER

Susie Rutledge greeted Annie in a curt voice. "I'm pleased you could come today."

"Yes, so am I, thank you," said Annie.

Miss Mittie sat in her usual spot, blanket around her lap, shawl around her shoulders. The book she had been reading rested in her lap. She looked up and smiled as Annie entered the room and put her coat and satchel on a chair near the door.

"Hello, girl! Come sit, come sit!"

"Miss Mittie, are you up to telling me the rest of Phoebe's story, or is it too painful for you? It is not my business, you know. If I hadn't found her cameo, you wouldn't have to speak of it or worry over it. The cameo belongs to you. Don't you want it back?"

Miss Mittie smiled, winked at Annie, and shook her head.

"No. I will tell you Phoebe's story, but you keep the cameo. Keep it as a reminder of me. Clean it as much as possible. Someday you may be able to wear it. If we had a jeweler in Hillview, he could repair the pin and clasp and polish the gold. With these hard times making everything difficult, it may be a long time before we once again have such a craftsman in our midst, I fear."

96

Annie nodded. "If that's your wish, I'll keep it, but if you want it returned, just tell me, please! Thank you for believing I deserve it."

The old woman's familiar laugh put Annie at ease. At her advanced age, Miss Mittie felt fortunate to have found such a dear friend, and she filled in the blanks remaining after their last meeting. The unfolding story was one Annie deemed tragic and unnerving.

Miss Mittie conveyed to Annie that Phoebe told her parents a disturbing tale of what happened that afternoon in the woods. Phoebe had disobeyed her father, taking Blaze for a ride through cornfields toward the wooded locale where Annie found the cameo. Back then, the stone wall was tidy, straight, and void of any overgrowth. The wall delineated the boundary between Miss Mittie's family farm and the orchard owned by a wealthy Hillview banker, a man by the name of Morse Blanton. Phoebe enjoyed that part of her father's property because it provided a commanding view through the trees overlooking the Blanton land. Miss Mittie and Phoebe's father maintained a trail running through the woods alongside the stone wall so he could keep the boundary free and visible. Phoebe rode the trail often.

"Morse Blanton was loud, coarse, and an overbearing, wealthy bully. Because his family had lived in Hillview since pre-Revolution times, Blanton believed his station in life was above anyone. He was not well-liked, but most folks had no choice but to conduct business with him. He didn't appear to have lost money or power during the war. Instead, he prospered while others struggled. Blanton let it be known he was Secesh, that's a staunch southern sympathizer, Annie, and he owned several slaves. His son Albert worked alongside him in the bank, and Albert's outward manner was the mirror image of his father's. Their physical presence differed, though. Morse Blanton was short in stature, overweight to the point of obesity, and he sported a thick black beard flecked with gray. Albert was tall, thin, and rakish, but a pasty complexion gave him an unhealthy image. People often saw Morse mounted on his big, sorrel gelding named Caesar, waving a long stick of tough hickory whittled into a cane and holding it as if it were a weapon. Rumors circulated that Morse used his hickory stick to whip any person or animal that displeased him. Nasty man he was!"

Miss Mittie observed a chickadee out the window before eyeballing the girl as a spellbound Annie wrinkled her brow.

"Annie, on the afternoon of Phoebe's incident, she was galloping Blaze along the trail by the stone wall when she saw a group of men through the thicket of trees. They were on Blanton property. She heard the men shouting in powerful, angry voices. Phoebe told Mother and Papa she reined in her horse and slipped to the ground to see what was happening. As she peered through the trees, she recognized Morse and Albert Blanton, but she did not recognize the other men except for a young colored man, Russell's nephew, Ben. An older colored man was shouting at Albert, his arms pointing toward Albert. This was shocking to Phoebe because coloreds always deferred to whites. President Lincoln had issued his Emancipation Proclamation, but around here most former slaves remained where they were. Were they free? It was difficult to tell."

Miss Mittie explained that pushing and shoving ensued along with more yelling and cursing. Phoebe could hear only a few words with clarity, and those included crude insults directed toward Ben and the other black man. In an instant, Morse Blanton pulled a handgun from under his coat and fired in quick succession at both black men, knocking them to the ground. Morse and the others, quarreling among themselves, checked the bodies lying on the ground. Phoebe understood nothing they said. She told her parents she began crying and shaking as she watched this scenario unfold, holding Blaze's reins fast. The sound of the gunfire spooked him, and he almost bolted. Phoebe said the men hoisted the two lifeless bodies onto the backs of two horses and rode away.

Rattled and quaking, Phoebe mounted Blaze and jerked on the bit to turn him around. Unaccustomed to such treatment, Blaze lurched to keep his footing, and Phoebe fell from the horse, scraping her leg on the wall before landing hard in the adjacent mud. With a dutiful Blaze standing by, Phoebe remounted and headed home at full gallop.

"Phoebe's story was one my parents had trouble accepting. They knew the Blantons, but Phoebe's story was beyond their comprehension. The horror Phoebe saw did not let her rest. It stayed with her every moment."

Miss Mittie recounted that Phoebe insisted she had seen a murder committed by one of Hillview's most prominent residents. She was relentless in her declarations to her parents, proclaiming it was not a dream or her imagination.

"After a few days, Papa asked Russell as to the whereabouts of his nephew Ben. When Russell told Papa that Ben and his father, Russell's brother Israel, had disappeared, Papa knew in his heart Phoebe spoke the truth. Russell told Papa he thought Israel and Ben had gone up north to get away from Blanton. Ben often said he wanted to join the Union Army. Ben's sister Molly asked Russell and Thea to let her live with them if the men didn't return. Russell could not understand why Israel or Ben never mentioned plans about leaving and just left Molly by herself at Blanton's. That was unlike his brother, he told Papa. Russell found it downright puzzling."

"Where did they live, Miss Mittie? You told me Russell and Thea lived on your family farm, but where did Ben and his family live?"

"Ben, his father Israel, and his sister Molly lived on the Blanton land. They had been Morse Blanton's slaves. Blanton still owned them in his mind, even though Lincoln's Proclamation freed slaves. It was dreadful. For years, even before the war, Morse Blanton and Papa got into terrible arguments over slavery. Papa wanted no part of it. Papa deeded Russell the cabin and surrounding land where Russell and Thea lived, and he paid Russell white man's wages for work they performed. Mother even taught Thea to read and write."

"What happened then? Was Mr. Blanton arrested? What happened to the bodies?" Annie was incredulous.

Miss Mittie continued. "Papa and Phoebe called on the sheriff with Phoebe's information, and the sheriff questioned both Albert and Morse Blanton. The Blanton men were vehement in their denials, and Morse accused Phoebe of lying. News of the accusation leaked, and that's when cover-up machinery got rolling. Morse Blanton threatened the sheriff with foreclosure on his property. He threatened the newspaper owner with the same if the man printed any word of the accusation. In short order, Blanton began spreading the rumor Phoebe was crazy, and because Phoebe was flighty and naughty anyhow, the idea took hold."

Miss Mittie related that countless people disliked the Blantons, but that the sheriff took no action fueled the flames of gossip and in due course destroyed poor Phoebe. Yet Phoebe maintained her story was true, and she had lost her cameo at the exact spot where she observed the murders. An exhaustive search of the ground near the wall never unearthed the cameo, so the Blanton tale of imagination gone wild in a crazy adolescent girl became cemented in the minds of many. Those who might have believed Phoebe's version of events hesitated to offer support because Blanton's bank was the only one in town. His bank held mortgages on properties, and he delighted in foreclosures. He gained wealth and power through those foreclosures.

"What of your father, Miss Mittie? Did Morse Blanton threaten your father?"

Miss Mittie threw her head back and sneered. "No, he did not. Papa did not have a mortgage on our farm. He did not patronize Blanton's bank, and he paid our taxes on time. We were most fortunate. Most fortunate. Papa did not trust Blanton. He never had. Papa hid our money in several places on the farm. Nobody knew where except for Mother. Papa and

Mother even buried silver pieces and other treasures when the war began to keep any from falling into unknown hands, whether Union or Confederate."

"Well, I'm glad to hear that!"

"They did enough damage to my family, though," Miss Mittie said. "The gossip mill rendered Phoebe a troubled soul. Phoebe never recovered from her experience. When she went to school, classmates taunted her. They taunted me. Classmates called me 'Feeble-Minded Phoebe's Ugly Sister' and spat on me. It became difficult for Papa, too. A few people feared coming to Papa for care because Blanton held their mortgages. Papa was the lone physician in the county, so folks traveled a long way for care elsewhere or sneaked out to see Papa."

The story did not end there. Annie learned that not long after the murders, Russell's niece and Ben's sister Molly moved into the cabin with Russell and Thea. Molly began showing signs of being with child. She refused to name the father.

"Morse Blanton contacted Papa when Molly first joined her Uncle Russell and Aunt Thea in their cabin, telling Papa Molly was his property and Papa must return her to him. Papa refused. After Molly started showing evidence of her condition, Blanton told Papa to keep the girl because she was no longer of any use to him. He used words to describe her I will not repeat. Morse Blanton was a horrid man. So, Molly stayed with Russell and Thea. Annie, I do not know whether I should tell you of this. You may be too young to hear of such."

"Oh, my father is a doctor, you know, Miss Mittie. I know these things. Please continue." Annie hesitated. "The name is familiar . . . Blanton. I think Daddy has a patient, a Mrs. Blanton."

"Oh, yes."

Annie urged, "Please go on with the story."

"I believe Phoebe thought she could make the Blantons admit the truth. If she spied old Blanton on the sidewalk, she might stand up on her tiptoes and yell right in his face. Any chance she had, Phoebe confronted Morse and told him he and Albert were murderers. Blanton just ignored her, or called her crazy, and kept walking. Phoebe spent hours looking for her cameo at the wall to no avail. Mother kept telling Phoebe finding the cameo proved nothing, just that she had been by the wall at some point. Poor Phoebe woke in the night, screaming. Sometimes she insisted a boy of around her age was there when the murders occurred and knew the truth. When Mother and Papa asked her who he was, she couldn't name him. She said he appeared to her in dreams. Phoebe said he was no one she had ever seen. He wore dirty and disheveled clothes, and he appeared injured and bleeding. She said the boy told her she was right. Morse Blanton shot the two colored men."

"Did you ever learn who the boy was, Miss Mittie?"

"No, we did not. Phoebe mentioned no one else before she began having those dreams, so we dismissed him as a figment of her imagination."

Annie's heart was heavy after learning of Phoebe's torment. How horrific to witness an event so hideous and shoulder the fear that the guilty might never be brought to justice. To make matters worse, gossip mills ruined Phoebe's reputation, causing most of the town to believe her insane.

Miss Mittie sighed and took a sip of her drink before continuing. "Papa and Mother were beside themselves over Phoebe's plight, you can imagine. The anguish she felt. The war raged. Stress and isolation made our lives more difficult. My parents decided upon a plan that now may sound heartless, but it was what they thought best. Papa arranged for Phoebe to leave us and go stay with Mother's unmarried sister, Aunt Sallie, near Philadelphia. Phoebe could continue her education in a female seminary located there. Philadelphia was safer than here. We had frequent skirmishes around here, and major battles occurred too close. One needed to always be on guard because we never knew when soldiers might appear."

Miss Mittie took another sip and looked at the ceiling. "I believe that because Papa treated wounded soldiers, whether Union or Confederate, word of his kindness spread on both sides of the conflict. Union and Confederate troops burned homes and stole livestock and valuables. We experienced no trouble from any soldiers. Papa and Mother explained to me that taking Phoebe to Aunt Sallie was best for Phoebe, but getting Phoebe there was a formidable undertaking. Papa took a buggy packed with provisions and two extra horses. He left Russell in charge of things at our home and delivered Phoebe by himself. To this day, I do not know how Papa succeeded and returned to us unharmed, considering troops, battles, bandits, and other hazards along the way. I believe in my heart his contacts from years of assisting runaways in their journeys to freedom aided him in his dangerous journey. Papa never spoke of the trip after he returned, other than to say it was challenging."

Annie found this information astonishing. The only words she could muster were, "Oh, my goodness!"

Miss Mittie disclosed that Phoebe stayed with her aunt for the duration of the war and her family near Hillview carried on without recriminations from the Blantons. Miss Mittie's father, known to his patients and friends as Doc Mueller, continued to work the farm and minister to wounded or ill soldiers that passed through, and he tended to anyone needing medical care. Patients once intimidated by the Blantons returned. The farm fed the Mueller family well. Russell and Thea worked as they had before Phoebe's incident, while Molly and her baby boy remained with them in their small cabin. Russell built another room onto the cabin to offer more space. Morse Blanton avoided the Muellers. Gossip aimed at "Feeble-Minded Phoebe" still emanated from his lips, though, if an opportunity presented itself. Neither Ben nor his father ever returned, and after a time no one saw

Molly or her baby. Miss Mittie did not know what happened to them.

"Phoebe and Aunt Sallie cared for hospitalized and wounded soldiers in Philadelphia." Miss Mittie adjusted the collar to her dress and frowned. "Phoebe's experiences assisting Papa were invaluable to her as she trod among the rows of beds, trying to ease suffering. Letters to Phoebe and from her were as frequent as possible, since war was never-ending. We missed her, and she missed us."

Miss Mittie's eyes closed, and she paused before she spoke again, her eyes remaining closed. "By war's end in 1865, Phoebe elected to stay with Aunt Sallie and care for her. Aunt Sallie suffered from consumption, which nowadays we know as tuberculosis. It's an awful, deadly disease. When Aunt Sallie died, Phoebe had to decide. Should she stay where she was or return to us?"

Annie observed her friend's distress as she spoke and reached out to take Miss Mittie's hand, clasping it with a firm grip.

Miss Mittie opened her eyes. "Although in those days it was not known or proven the disease was contagious, Papa believed it was. Consumption was rampant throughout both Union and Confederate hospitals. Could Aunt Sallie have contracted it there? Had Phoebe contracted the disease? If so, returning home might expose us to the disease. The murders she saw still haunted my sister. A return home might reopen the wounds in her heart and once again make her a target of gossip and bigotry. My parents counseled her to stay in Aunt Sallie's home and continue nursing as a career."

Miss Mittie straightened in her chair and wiped her nose with a rosewater perfumed handkerchief as she gazed out one of the sun porch's many windows. Her gaze turned to Annie.

"Phoebe returned home. She should have listened to our parents, yes, she should have. Phoebe made an unwise decision."

Annie listened, and her heart broke for Phoebe.

"The moment she returned, Phoebe faced what she experienced before she left for Aunt Sallie's, even worse. The gossip mill churned, slamming Phoebe with accusations and name-calling. She retaliated by placing handwritten leaflets on lampposts in town proclaiming Morse and Albert Blanton murderers. Again, she accosted them if they happened across each other, Phoebe wagging her finger at either of their faces and screaming they were murderers. Her nightmares returned. Her visits to the stone wall and searches for her lost cameo resumed. Phoebe became irrational, lashing out at our parents and at me. She had crying fits and sat unmoved for hours, staring out the window at the distant mountains."

Annie's beloved friend recounted that Phoebe fell ill. Rib - breaking coughs wracked her body, and fatigue, sweats, and chills overtook her. She coughed up blood. She lost weight.

Phoebe and Miss Mittie's father, Doc Mueller, determined she had contracted consumption. Again, Phoebe's parents made the hard decision to send her away, this time to a modest medical clinic near Philadelphia. Two nurses, sisters who had treated the disease so prevalent among soldiers, ran the establishment. The facility was in the nurses' home, and it accommodated six patients, offering fresh air and isolation from the public. Although the clinic, unique for its time, served only those suffering from consumption, gossip ensured the citizenry in and around Hillview believed Doc Mueller had committed Phoebe to a mental institution.

"I have put much of that time out of my memory, Annie. We missed Phoebe, but her actions after her return threw our household into such disarray that, to be honest, it was better to have her elsewhere. I had grown accustomed to the whispers and learned to ignore the nasty comments tossed at me by schoolmates. I held my head high and walked right past, never acknowledging their taunts. A few times, a larger girl pushed or tripped me, but I got right up, dusted myself off, and continued on my way. If you ever face such circumstances, Annie, remember these words: get up, dust off, and press onward."

"I'm so sorry! How dreadful for you and your family. I'll remember your advice, but I cannot imagine such cruelty nowadays. Daddy says gossip is akin to the poison ivy rash. It spreads fast and creates misery. What happened to Phoebe?"

"Your father is correct, my dear girl. Phoebe remained in what we now call a sanitarium for around two years, I believe. Papa said she wasted away. Both of my parents visited, putting handkerchiefs over their noses and mouths. They did not take me with them. My brothers, much older than I, left this region before the war, and they never visited Phoebe. After Phoebe died, Papa brought her home. We buried her in a small cemetery on the old farm. Papa and Mother are there, too."

"Oh, that is so sad!" Annie wiped tears from her eyes.

"Papa said even as she weakened, she continued to call the Blantons murderers. Phoebe's last words to Papa were, 'I know someday the truth shall be told.' Papa said he just held her hand and promised her it would. Even after I married, there were people in town who whispered as I walked past them. I was still Feeble-Minded Phoebe's sister. Phoebe's story lived long after she did."

Susie swept into the sun porch in a tizzy. Susie had not kept track of time, nor had Annie or Miss Mittie. "Annie, your father is out front! You must go now."

Annie gathered her belongings, leaned over to kiss her friend on the forehead, and sprinted to the front door while an impatient Susie tapped her foot. The girl was breathless as she climbed into the car.

"I'm sorry, Daddy! I didn't know you were here."

Dr. Young searched his daughter's face. "It's not a problem, dear. I arrived but a few moments ago. Let's go home. We have a lot to discuss."

MORE QUESTIONS THAN ANSWERS

That evening was one Annie later recalled to her granddaughter as a most painful experience. With great shame, Annie admitted to her parents she had been dishonest with them by hiding her discovery at the stone wall. She recounted the tale of Miss Mittie's family ordeal years ago. Annie's distress was visible as she spilled out everything. She wiped tears from her eyes several times using her mother's handkerchief.

The three Youngs stayed in the parlor for the story. Annie perched on the edge of the sofa with Bitsy at her feet. Ellen sat at the other end of the sofa, holding a pillow. Carter sat in a chair he pulled closer to his wife and daughter. He held the same stance during the entire time, elbows resting on his lap, hands supporting his chin.

Annie feared the anger and disappointment of her parents, but there was none. They understood her hesitancy to tell of her discovery and Miss Mittie's story. Now they understood Annie's odd behavior, and it relieved Carter and Ellen to know what troubled their daughter. Each reassured the girl she must never hesitate to tell them everything, whether right or wrong. They reiterated their deep love for her.

"We are your champions, Annie," said Carter. "We will always stand behind you. We will love you and be here for you, no matter what."

Torn between a wish to wrap her daughter in her arms or to scold her for not coming forth sooner, Ellen winced. It saddened her that Annie feared to confide in her parents. She took Annie in her arms. "What a burden you have been carrying, sweet."

Bitsy leaped onto the sofa and began licking the girl's arm.

"There is something else, Mama. Bitsy has been peculiar our past few times at the wall. She barks and growls without warning. I don't understand what is bothering her. I see nothing."

Ellen and Carter exchanged glances. Ellen worried that someone was hiding on the other side of the wall, at the bottom of the rocky, overgrown-by-foliage ledge. Carter speculated an animal was living in the brush or searching for food. Carter held confidence in his theory and assured Ellen and Annie he planned to investigate.

Annie extracted the cameo from her pocket and handed it to her mother. "See, Mama, it was once elegant! Just the same as Miss Mittie's."

Ellen turned the piece over and over in her hand and gave it to Carter to examine. He returned it saying, "Ellen, why don't you see if you can clean it up somewhat? Use nothing harsh on it, but wiping it with warm water may help dissolve dirt. It is a shame to let it sit in this condition."

Ellen agreed to clean the cameo but announced it was time for Annie to prepare for bed. Cleaning the cameo must wait. Annie hugged both of her parents and proceeded up the stairs. Carter opened the front door so Bitsy could enjoy one last romp before she retired for the evening with Annie.

After tucking Annie into her bed with Bitsy lying in hers, Carter and Ellen Young closed their daughter's bedroom door and retreated downstairs to the kitchen. There, they knew Annie could not overhear their conversation. Ellen put water in the teakettle and set it on the stove before pulling out a chair from the table and sitting.

Carter spoke first. "Such a tragic story. Mrs. McCormick's poor sister. Isn't it a shame, Ellen?"

"It's dreadful! I am worried this has dredged up horrible memories for Mrs. McCormick. It is upsetting for Annie, too. She feels terrible about this dear woman's story. What grievous events!"

"I know, I know."

"What should we do?" Ellen asked. "Should we visit Mrs. McCormick and offer our apologies? Should we accept this knowledge, clean up this cameo, and put it away? I'm torn."

Carter wiped his forehead with his handkerchief. What had unfolded disturbed him. He was uncertain how they should continue. He shook his head. "I don't know."

Ellen rose and walked to the stove. She scooped tea out of its container on the counter and spooned it into two tea infusers. She then set two cups on the counter, inserted one infuser in each cup, and poured the boiling water over them. Carter reached out and took his cup, setting it on the table in front of him.

"Carter, one concern I have is if we go see Mrs. McCormick, her daughter will want to know what we are doing there. Annie said Susie doesn't know of this, and Mrs. McCormick doesn't want her to know. I'm worried if Susie knows Annie has brought up these unpleasant memories to her mother, she may prohibit more visits. I don't want to cause Annie or Mrs. McCormick more pain. Susie Rutledge is a difficult woman, I fear. One moment she is nice, and the next she borders on rudeness. She tolerates Annie's visits because they mean a great deal to her mother. I believe she is pleasant to me only because I sew for a few of her friends. Susie, I'm afraid, resembles my own mother, concerned more with appearances and social status than for the well-being of others. She could hurt both Annie and Mrs. McCormick."

Carter shook his head and said, "It's unfortunate, but I believe you're correct."

Carter and Ellen Young drank their tea in silence. Carter traced an imaginary circle on the table, while Ellen stared out the kitchen window into the darkness.

In a few minutes, Carter rose and walked to the sink, placing his cup in it. "We need to go to bed, Ellen. It's late, and we need rest."

Restful sleep did not come. Both tossed and turned, mulling over in their minds the best course of action. In the morning, the groggy adults prepared for the upcoming day. Annie appeared rested. She said she felt much better having told her parents of her interactions with Miss Mittie and of Phoebe's story. Off to work and school went Carter and Annie, while Ellen attempted to clean the cameo, hoping to restore it to at least a fragment of its former elegance.

After school, Annie remained behind to speak with a few of the girls in her class. This was a rare occurrence, but to Annie, it was a promising sign of potential friendships. After these interactions, she hiked the short distance to her father's office and waited for him to finish his day.

One patient, an unpleasant-looking woman, sat in the compact waiting room when Annie arrived. The woman glanced up from her book and scoured Annie from top to bottom. Such scrutiny made Annie uneasy. The girl smiled at the woman, but she received no reciprocating gesture, so she pulled a book and her notebook from her satchel. At that moment, Maude Renner, Carter's nurse, entered the waiting room from the door leading to a compact kitchen space and took her seat at the receptionist desk.

"Hello, Annie! How was school today?" asked Maude.

"It was fine, Miss Renner. I have schoolwork I need to complete."

The woman reading the book stopped and stared at Annie. Annie could not determine the woman's age, but her hair was a dirty gray, and her face somewhat wrinkled. Her hat featured a peacock feather and brooch pinned to the brim, and an alligator handbag rested in the chair nestled against her dress. She was nowhere as old as Miss Mittie or as Annie's own grandmother. Stout and staid, the woman returned to her book in silence, glancing up to look at Annie every few minutes.

After a short while, a gentleman Annie recognized as Mr. Berger from the shoe store on Main Street emerged from the examination room. He directed a smile toward Maude and Annie, and he acknowledged the seated woman with a cheery, "Good afternoon, Mrs. Blanton."

The woman nodded her head without looking up from her book and continued reading.

Annie came within an inch of dropping her notebook. Her pencil fell to the floor. She was sitting across from a descendant or relation of Morse and Albert Blanton, and this realization flustered her.

Miss Renner rose and walked through the door leading to the examination room. She returned and, holding the door open, told Mrs. Blanton she could see the doctor. Mrs. Blanton rose, emitted a loud, "Harrumph" and stomped toward the door.

"It's about time, Maude," she hissed.

Annie observed Miss Renner after closing the door and taking her seat once more. Miss Renner glanced over at the girl and smiled.

"She sounds fussy," Annie said in a virtual whisper, looking at the closed door.

Miss Renner leaned over her desk. "She is always fussy! She had no appointment, but she insisted upon coming. We had a busy schedule today, and I told her she might have to wait until after the last patient left. She arrived earlier than expected, so she has been sitting here a good while, to be fair."

Annie returned to her schoolwork. She completed the tasks at hand and stuffed everything inside her book satchel.

112

"There is sunshine cake on the counter in the kitchenette. Why don't you get a piece, Annie? I brought it in this morning. Doctor and I each had a piece with our lunches today. Check in the icebox for milk."

Maude Renner, a spinster who loved to cook, often brought delicious desserts for Carter to share with Ellen and Annie. She was a kind and dignified woman who enjoyed Annie's after school visits and expressed amusement with Annie's tales of the latest episodes of Bitsy's mischievous adventures.

Annie ate a piece of cake and drank a glass of milk in the kitchenette, considering the entire time that Mrs. Blanton sat in the room next to the one where she was eating cake. She finished her cake, took the plate, glass, and fork to the sink, and washed them before placing them on the drainboard. Annie returned to her seat in the waiting room to watch Miss Renner enter information on patients' charts as she hummed a tune and took an occasional sip of coffee.

In a few minutes, Dr. Young emerged from the examination room as he held the door for Mrs. Blanton. "Goodbye, Mrs. Blanton," he said.

"Yes, goodbye." She hurried out of the office, ignoring Miss Renner and Annie as she swished out the door.

Carter handed Miss Renner a chart and told her not to bother with billing. "Just mark this as a courtesy visit, Maude."

The nurse shook her head in disgust. "I will. You are too kind, Doctor. She can afford to pay, you know."

He nodded and turned to Annie. "I will be ready soon, but I need to make one visit before we go home."

Annie understood this was part of her father's job. She did not resent these on-the-way-home visits. She remained in the car while her father attended to his patient. It was common for house calls to be brief, and this one was no exception. Soon they were on their way home.

Ellen prepared a satisfying evening meal, and the family retired to the parlor after Annie and Ellen washed and put

113

away dishes. Bitsy bounced inside as soon as Annie opened the front door, racing to her bowl in the kitchen to lap a big helping of water.

Annie settled into a chair and opened her library book. Ellen, holding the cameo in one hand, walked to the chair where Annie sat. At that moment, Carter retreated to the hallway where the telephone demanded attention.

"Annie, I tried to clean the cameo today. It looks better, but I can't get it to look so handsome as it once did. There are a fair number of scratches on it, a tiny corner piece is missing, and the clasp is broken and bent. For the time being, why don't you put it in your jewelry box and save it?"

Annie held the brooch in her hands and turned it over to examine it front and back. It did look much brighter, but her mother was correct that it was not in pristine condition. "Oh, Mama, you did such a nice job of cleaning it! Thank you! I will put it in the box and keep it. Miss Mittie wants me to keep it."

"Yes, I understand. It is generous of Mrs. McCormick."

Carter returned to the parlor. "That was a patient who is experiencing trouble breathing. I'm headed into town to check on her. Ellen, I'll ring you up if I'll be home late."

Carter collected his bag from its home next to the telephone table, and with a wave of his right hand, walked out the door.

Annie expressed disappointment her father had left. "Mama, I wanted to ask Daddy about one of his patients in the office this afternoon. It was Mrs. Blanton, the lady who had the poison ivy rash once? I guess she is related to the people who killed Russell's nephew and brother. I want to know who she is. She wasn't friendly to Miss Renner or to Mr. Berger from the shoe store."

"Oh, Annie, you shouldn't say such things! You don't know for certain either of the Blanton men killed Russell's brother and nephew. You are just repeating what a girl said years ago, seventy years ago! Please don't repeat that to anyone."

Annie bit her lip and looked at the floor. "I won't repeat the story, Mama, but I believe Phoebe."

As a distraction, Ellen tuned the radio to a comedy show, and the two laughed at the skits until it was Annie's bath and bedtime. Ellen let Bitsy out for her day's last exploit, and Annie snuggled in her bed. When Ellen opened the back door for the dog, Bitsy hopped inside, then up the stairs, making a beeline to her own bed next to Annie's. Annie was already asleep.

Ellen walked downstairs, turned off the radio, and returned to the kitchen where she had left a cup half-filled with tea. She drank the rest, even though it had cooled, and was washing out the cup when she heard the car come up the driveway and saw its headlights through the kitchen window.

"How is your patient, dear?"

Carter set his bag on the floor in the hallway. He shook his head.

"Oh, she's fine. Nothing is wrong with her that losing weight won't cure. Her imagination and medical knowledge gleaned from her imagination are always working overtime. Are any cookies left?"

"Yes, come sit in the kitchen. Tea or milk?"

"Milk will be great." Bags had appeared under his eyes, and his face looked haggard. He addressed Ellen as he munched an oatmeal cookie. "I'm so tired, Ellen. It's been a busy week, and with Annie's plight and dealing with Mrs. Blanton, I'm just beat."

"Mrs. Blanton?"

"Yes, she's a challenge."

"Annie was speaking of her after you left. She said Mrs. Blanton was in your office today and wasn't cordial to either Maude or to Mr. Berger from the shoe store. Annie wants to question you about her. She thinks your patient is a relative of the gentlemen Phoebe saw. I instructed Annie not to repeat the story because we don't know if is true."

Carter nodded. "I'm glad you told her that. I know nothing of the woman except she is the wife of a banker in town and a hypochondriac. Her husband may be of that family. She is the patient I just visited. Nothing is wrong with her. She wants attention. Good Lord, I shouldn't be telling you this. I know you won't repeat what I said to anyone."

"No, I won't. But Annie remembered she had a case of poison ivy rash a while back!"

"The girl has a memory, doesn't she? Let's get to bed ourselves. Tomorrow is Saturday, so maybe we can sleep later. Do we have any plans?"

"No, although I plan to work on the dress I am making for Mrs. Thomas from church."

"Good!"

They strode upstairs arm in arm, glad the week was over and hopeful upcoming ones proved uneventful. Restful sleep came to both.

****

Saturday morning dawned sunny and cool. Signs of spring were in the fresh smelling air. A few daffodils peeked through the earth, and bits of green replaced browns of winter. Annie awoke to find only her mother in the kitchen, drinking a cup of coffee.

"Where's Daddy, Mama?"

"He's still upstairs sleeping! Let's let him rest more. He was exhausted last night when he returned home."

As Ellen prepared eggs and scooped oatmeal from the pot on the stove, the girl opened the back door to let Bitsy outside. The dog romped through the grass, sniffing and searching for whatever curious dogs search for as soon as they go outside on a crisp spring day.

Annie devoured the oatmeal and scrambled eggs served up by her mother, followed by two pieces of buttered toast. Ellen baked bread on Fridays, so the bread was soft and fresh, and Annie savored the buttery goodness.

When Annie finished her breakfast, she retreated upstairs to brush her teeth and put on her Saturday work clothes, taking care not to wake her father. Afterward, she proceeded downstairs and told her mother she was planning to gather her tools and go to the wall to continue her rebuilding project. Ellen nodded her consent and watched as the girl took out for the shed to retrieve her tools. After Annie revealed Bitsy's behavior at the stone wall, Ellen remained concerned regarding her daughter's presence there. Bitsy, who had been sitting on the back porch, trotted along at Annie's heels toward the wall.

Soon, a groggy Carter Young, with tousled hair and still wearing pajamas, descended the stairs and entered the kitchen.

"Are you all right, Carter?" He still looked tired to Ellen.

"I'm good, just sleepy. I was bone-tired last night."

"Let me get your oatmeal and eggs for you. Here's coffee." She poured a cup from the percolator on the stove. He took the cup and sat at the table, observing the blooming African violets in the window over the sink.

"Where did you get those violets?"

Ellen snickered at the fact he had just noticed the plants that had been in the window for several months. "One of my garden club ladies gave me cuttings from hers. These took root and are blooming now."

He smiled. "I suppose I've been too busy to notice. Sorry. Where are our girl and the wonder dog this morning?"

"Annie ate breakfast and raced to the back with Bitsy a while ago. She got the wagon with her tools from the shed. I hope everything is okay back there. I'm concerned Bitsy has acted peculiar at the stone wall."

As he finished his coffee and breakfast, Carter assured Ellen he planned to check out her concerns as soon as he dressed. He reiterated his belief that a squirrel or rabbit was

117

hiding in the rocks on the orchard side of the wall. That rock ledge was steep and provided many places where a small animal could hide unseen, yet a dog's nose could smell any critter.

After Carter dressed and returned downstairs, he stole a glance at Ellen, seated at her sewing machine, in a compact room off the parlor. The space contained a desk, chair, and one wall of shelves filled with books. Carter and Ellen assumed the room had served as Dr. McCormick's home office, but it was now Ellen's sewing room. They had moved the desk against one wall so the sewing machine and a fabric cutting table sat in the middle of the room. Stacks of fabrics and bindings covered the entire top of the desk. A window allowed Ellen a northern view.

"I'm headed to the back!" he shouted as he slammed the back door.

"Okay!" came the response over the sewing machine's whir.

By the time Carter Young reached the stone wall, Annie's project for the day was well underway. She had already stacked several stones and was clearing brush from the next section needing restoration. Bitsy strolled along the completed section, sniffing and eyeing the wall and its surrounding territory.

"Good morning, Daddy! Did you sleep well?"

"I did, thank you! You are moving right along this morning."

"We are. Bitsy isn't nervous this morning. She's just fine, Daddy."

"Good, sweetheart. I'll check that other side of the wall, though. Your mother is a worry-wart."

He scoured the length of the exposed and rebuilt structure and found a spot where the ledge was not steep. As he climbed over the wall, he held onto rocks and tree limbs, letting himself to the level ground, six to eight feet below. He made his way as best he could, pushing brush and vines away.

"Annie, toss the rake to me. I need a tool to push this underbrush out of my way."

With the rake in his hands, he could walk with more ease as he pushed and pulled vegetation from his path. Carter believed no human had been in the vicinity because it was too difficult to navigate. He saw no breaks in the vines or brush and no trampled foliage. Overgrown vegetation hid rocks in the ledge, but a small creature could burrow through with ease. As spring brought more lush foliage, a person or larger animal would experience real trouble climbing up the ledge and over the wall. Convinced no threat existed, he returned to the access point and climbed back up, scratching his arms and hands and catching his trousers on the abundant briers. Annie held out her hand for him to grasp as he shinnied over the wall.

"Annie, I'm convinced whatever has made Bitsy so nervous is just an animal. In all likelihood it's a squirrel or rabbit, something small. Nothing that will hurt you or Bitsy. Everything is okay. I will go to the house and tell your mother. If you wish, I can come back and clear away more brush for you."

Annie agreed, so he returned to the house and assuaged Ellen's fears. Soon he arrived at the work site with a jug of water, two strawberry jam sandwiches, a water bowl for Bitsy, and two small stools.

There they sat and consumed their snacks before continuing with the jobs at hand. By lunchtime, Carter had cleared over ten feet of the rubble, and Annie had restored four feet of the wall.

Annie and Bitsy were the only returnees after lunch. Carter received a telephone call referring to a patient from the hospital, so he drove into town.

Annie worked in silence, humming an occasional tune until Blink and his noisy wheelbarrow appeared on the scene.

"Hi, Annie! Look h-here! Pap sent me w-with rocks! Look here!" Blink's eyelids fluttered in their familiar fashion as he grinned and waved at the girl.

Annie received her visitor with an enormous hug. She was unearthing nowhere near the number of stones she needed and was becoming frustrated with the slow pace of her work. "Oh, Blink! This is wonderful! I am running short and was wondering where to find more usable rocks. Thank you!"

"I can't stay, Annie. Pap says I have to help him ready the new field today. I'll h-have more for ya later." He dumped the contents on the ground, turned, and ran back toward the house, pushing the empty wheelbarrow as fast as he could as it bounced up the sloping yard.

Seated on a stool, Annie sighed and swigged a drink of water from the jug as she patted Bitsy on the head. "Bitsy, Blink and Miss Mittie are my best friends besides you. My only friends. Isn't it odd?"

As Bitsy lapped water from the bowl, Annie started placing the stones Blink had delivered. She had been at this task for twenty minutes or so when Bitsy growled and charged at the wall several feet from where Annie toiled. Legs straight and stiff, the dog's ears pointed toward the wall as she barked in a frenzy.

"What is it, Bitsy?" Confident her father's assessment meant no person or animal could cause harm, an annoyed Annie strode over to the exact spot of Bitsy's attention. She peered over the wall remnants and stared at the ground below the ledge.

The gasp escaping her lips startled the dog so much that it ceased barking and ran to Annie's side where she stood, hands on hips, feet frozen to the ground.

"Who are you, and why are you scaring my dog?"

SOLDIER AT THE WALL

He stood on the opposite side of the stone wall at the bottom of the ledge, a mere ten feet from Annie. The figure shook his outstretched hands and head at the same time as if to show he meant no harm. A slight young man of perhaps fifteen or sixteen years, he was filthy with matted auburn hair. Faint stubble on his face was caked with mud, and a bloodied shirt hung loose on his gaunt frame. His ripped and soiled trousers, attached to a pair of suspenders, were so short the bones of his ankles protruded from beneath. He wore one tattered brown boot on his right foot, but his left foot was shoeless and covered in mud. What appeared to be a canteen was slung around his shoulders, and he held a faded gray cap in his right hand as he spoke.

"Fear not, girl," he implored in a low southern drawl. "I mean you no harm. No harm will come to you or your dog from me. For a good while, I have observed you both, my mind attempting to discern your intentions. Are they good or ill? Please accept my humble apologies for any fright I may have caused." He smiled and stood still, awaiting a response from the startled girl.

"Who are you?" Annie asked, her voice trembling. "You've been watching me? I've never seen you. You look hurt, and you need a bath."

He smiled and shook his head. In a soft and calm voice, he responded, "Noah is my name. No, wounded I am no more, but . . . alas . . . my status allows me the ability to see without being seen. For so long I have been unknown and unseen, that when you first arrived and began disturbing my . . . my . . . I perceived risk. Thus, I engaged in voyeurism. You, I believe, are of good intent. Allowing you to see myself and engaging with you is a most adventurous action for me."

None of Noah's words made sense to Annie. At least Bitsy had stopped barking and was just sniffing toward this person who stood before them among vines and brush on the lower side of the stone wall's remains. The young man climbed up the ledge with ease, and as Annie stepped aside, he leaped over the stones, landing on the ground next to Bitsy. The dog moved closer and sniffed his feet, tail wagging as if she was greeting a friend. Noah crouched and patted her head, roughing her ears.

"She is a fine dog!" He looked up at Annie's incredulous face. "A long time it has been since I possessed a dog. His name was Dash. He was larger by not much than Miss Bitsy here, and his fur was brown with black on his nose and ears."

"I don't understand how you have been watching me, but I haven't seen you, nor has Bitsy until now. Daddy says nobody has been over there. Here you are, though. Have you been hiding in a tree?"

Noah stood and shifted his feet. He appeared resolute as he once again spoke, his drawl fascinating to Annie. "I fear my story is one you may find unbelievable, but true it is. Please know you are safe, Annie. Harm you I will not. Frighten you I hope never to do again."

Annie stared in disbelief at this grimy, half-barefoot figure who had appeared from where she believed nobody could have been. Annie glanced at Bitsy, who was by now sitting on the ground with her head cocked toward Noah, her stubby tail still.

"I am a spirit, a restless one, an apparition if you will. I have inhabited this region for much longer than you have been alive, and I have seen . . . witnessed . . . events . . . which disturbed me to my core, so deep I cannot depart this earthly abode until the . . . events . . . resolve. Resolved they are not, yet you are the force that may bring such resolution."

"What? Are you telling me you are a ghost?" asked the dumbfounded girl. "I do not believe in ghosts, Noah. Tell me the truth! Tell me now!"

The abrupt sound of Blink's wheelbarrow, filled with another load of stones, rumbled toward where Annie and Noah stood.

"Yo, Annie! Back again!"

Startled, Annie turned to see her friend stopping to retrieve stones that had bounced out of his overloaded wheelbarrow. When she turned around, Noah stood in the same spot, smiling. "You will scare my friend," she admonished the boy.

"No, I shall not. See me he cannot."

By the time Blink reached Annie, he was breathless. "P-Pap told me to hurry so we can get more cleared before supper, so here's what I have now. How you doing so far?"

Annie glanced around to find Noah still standing next to her. Blink stooped to adjust a shoelace and stood upright when finished, oblivious to Noah's presence.

"You look f-funny, Annie. What's wrong?"

"I'm okay. Blink, do you see anyone else here?" She once again glanced at Noah, who stood his ground.

Blink scanned the area. "Bitsy, she's sitting over yonder. I got to go. Pap, he'll be m-mad at me for taking so long. See ya!"

Blink turned around the now empty wheelbarrow and started bouncing it toward the front of the property as he trotted away, whistling a tune as he waved back at Annie.

She turned to Noah. "Blink did not see you. He didn't see you."

"No. No, he did not see me. I do not wish to create an uncomfortable state of affairs. You, Miss Annie, are the first person I have allowed to see me since . . ." his voice trailed.

"Since what?"

"Since my demise."

This confused Annie and left her frightened and uncertain of how to continue. The girl did not believe Noah's assertion he was a spirit, but Blink had not seen him. Who was this . . . this *person*? He appeared out of nowhere! Was it possible he was an apparition, a ghost, a spirit of someone who died long ago? Could he harm her? Bitsy, who as a general rule, was nervous around strangers until she felt more comfortable in their presence, was now in Noah's arms licking his face! For a moment, the girl felt faint, and she leaned against a tree to keep her balance and clear her head.

"I don't know what to believe," she said. "My heart is beating so fast I can't think! This is too unbelievable."

She stared at the sight before her: a filthy, dirty, injured boy, not much older than herself. He held her beloved dog in his arms and whispered to Bitsy as the dog continued to lick his face. Blink had not seen him. Annie could see and speak with him. As for Bitsy? Bitsy was in hog heaven in this fellow's arms.

"Are you in pain? Blood is everywhere on your shirt."

Noah chuckled and exhaled with a loud sigh. His countenance then became more serious as he set Bitsy on the ground. "I was injured by a wound that did not end well. This blood is long dried. If you wish, I shall explain to you. My explanation will take time, and soon evening will be upon us. I take my leave now. When you next return, I shall render a full accounting."

With those words, he turned, leaped over the wall, and faded into nothingness. It appeared to Annie he just . . . evaporated.

Nothing before had shocked and shaken Annie so in her young life. Her face flushed. Her heart pounded. She pinched her left arm to confirm if she was awake. Gazing at Bitsy, she saw the dog yawn and stretch her two front feet in front. The dog plopped on the grass and stared into Annie's bewildered eyes.

Annie could not continue, so she called Bitsy and leaving tools, the stools, and her wagon where they were, plodded to the house at a snail's pace. She opened the back door and entered the kitchen where her mother was preparing the evening meal.

"I didn't expect you so soon, Annie." Ellen did not turn from her chores at the kitchen sink. "Are you finished for the day?"

"Yes, Mama. I'm tired." Annie opened the icebox and examined its contents. A bottle of water rested on a shelf; she removed it and set it on the table before taking a glass from the cabinet. "I'm thirsty, too." She poured water into the glass. The bottle remained on the table as she sat in a chair and stared at her mother. With her apron tied into a tidy bow at the back of her waist, Ellen chopped vegetables in her ever-efficient manner.

"Daddy will be home soon," Ellen said while continuing her work. "He stopped off at Jack and Lou's house to consult with Jack. The patient he visited today is of concern. I told him to invite the Morrisons for dinner since we have a good bit of ham Mr. Cole gave Daddy as payment for a visit. Jack and Lou will arrive not long after Daddy gets home. Lou has clothes to take off the clothesline before leaving."

"Oh. I'll freshen up and come back. Do you need any help, Mama?"

"The only help I need is to set the table. I made Jell-O earlier. You'll enjoy it."

Annie finished her glass of water and left the kitchen to retire to her room. Upstairs, she lay on her bed and gazed out the window. Bitsy jumped up and snuggled against her waist.

The afternoon's events had exhausted the girl. Curled into a ball with Bitsy, Annie fell asleep.

****

The mixed sound of voices and laughter floating up the stairs awoke Annie and Bitsy. Bitsy jumped off the bed and raced downstairs to see the cause of the commotion before Annie could rise. When she sat up, she remained drowsy and shook her head. Realizing she had fallen asleep, she rushed to the bathroom to splash water on her face before hurrying downstairs to where the four adults stood, carrying on a lively conversation.

"Hello, Annie!" Jack's cheery voice bellowed from the parlor. "Welcome back from dreamland! Did you have a nice nap?"

Annie nodded in embarrassment. "Hello, Aunt Lou. Hello, Uncle Jack."

"Hello, dear," said Lou. Lou Morrison's plump, ruddy cheeks radiated her warm and amiable nature.

Annie walked to her mother's side and pulled at her apron. "I will set the table, Mama."

"No need, Annie. Lou helped me. You appeared weary, so I didn't want to disturb you. Are you rested?"

"Yes."

The aroma of ham baking in the oven permeated every corner of the house as both families consumed the meal with considerable chatter and laughter emanating from the adults. Annie remained silent.

It was during dessert that Annie blurted, "Do any of you believe in ghosts?"

This outburst shocked Ellen. "Annie, please don't interrupt when adults are talking! You know better."

"Oh, I'm sorry," an embarrassed Annie said. "I'm just curious."

Jack guffawed and in his boisterous voice expounded that he had never seen one, but he heard they existed. Then he snickered and took a bite of custard pie. His laugh and smile were infectious.

"No, I don't," said Ellen, who remained annoyed at her daughter's lapse of manners.

With her usual sweet charm, Lou chimed in, "I have never thought of it, Annie. Never thought of it one bit, honey."

"Daddy?" Annie addressed her father who sat at the head of the table.

Carter Young paused before he answered. "I don't know, Annie. I will say this, though, that I have felt my parents' presence many times in the years since they died. Sometimes I sense they are right there with me, guiding me. Is it their spirit speaking to me?" He shook his head. "I don't know."

The diners were quiet. Jack broke the silence by directing a question toward Annie. "Why do you ask, Annie?"

"Oh, I just wondered."

As the meal concluded, conversation returned to the usual adult matters of the day. Afterward, Annie cleared the table as Lou and Ellen washed dishes. Annie excused herself to go upstairs and prepare for bedtime, which she did before crawling under the covers and falling into a deep sleep.

****

Rain and thunderstorms ushered in the next day. The family attended church services and remained afterward for conversation and refreshments with other congregants in hopes the thunderstorm would roll on by. They returned home in a driving rain and found a fallen tree limb blocking the driveway. Rain soaked Carter as he dragged it to the side of the driveway, and as soon as they entered the house, he charged upstairs to remove wet clothes and hang them in the bathroom to dry. When he reappeared downstairs in fresh clothing, he told Ellen he felt weary and desired a quick nap.

Ellen offered food, but he said he was not hungry after the refreshments at church. So, he retreated upstairs, and after Ellen changed out of her church clothes, she returned to the kitchen to prepare lunch for herself and Annie.

Annie was not hungry, so Ellen set out a few crackers with cheese. As they sat at the kitchen table munching their snacks, Ellen brought up the question Annie raised the preceding night.

"Why did you ask about believing in ghosts last night?"

Annie shrugged and responded that nothing in particular elicited the question she posed at dinner.

"If you say so. Let Bitsy back in the house, please. She has been sitting on the front porch trying to stay out of the rain."

After Bitsy re-entered the house and Annie dried her with a towel, Annie asked permission to go upstairs to read her library book. She and the dog retreated to Annie's room. Once in her room, she walked straight to the east window, the one facing the rear of the property, and stood in silence gazing out toward the wall.

In a few minutes, the girl detected movement at the property's rear woods. She expected a deer to emerge, but it was Noah picking up fallen twigs from the path her father had cleared. She pulled the curtains shut and jumped on her bed, pulling the covers over her head.

"Oh, goodness, I must go to the library tomorrow after school to research ghosts!" she told Bitsy.

Nothing out of the ordinary happened that day, except Carter Young napped, a rare occurrence. Ellen continued her sewing project for Mrs. Thomas. Annie resumed reading her library book. Her east facing bedroom curtains remained closed as rain continued to fall.

"We needed this rain, but it's rained enough." Ellen passed collard greens and ham around the table at suppertime. "I had intended to do laundry and hang it this afternoon since I'm behind in my washing."

"Sunday is a day for rest and relaxation, Ellen, so don't fret."

"No calls from anybody who is sick, either!" Annie said.

Carter smiled. "Yes, it's a treat, isn't it?"

"Daddy, who is Mrs. Blanton?"

Carter glanced at Ellen before answering Annie's query. "A patient, Annie. She was in the office when you were there Friday."

"Yes, she was. She wasn't friendly to Miss Renner or to Mr. Berger from the shoe store. Is she part of the Blanton family that killed Russell's brother and nephew?"

Ellen put her arm across the table to tap Annie's wrist. "I told you not to repeat that, Annie! You don't know if the story is true. Don't repeat it!"

"Oh, okay, Mama. But Daddy, is she a member of the old Blanton family?"

Carter sighed. "Well, I don't know. Her husband is a banker in town. I don't know, Annie. It's best for you to take that assertion of yours and put it to rest."

"The name is the same. The occupation is the same. I thought . . ."

"Annie, quit!" Ellen rarely raised her voice to her daughter, but frustration got the better of her. "Mrs. McCormick's story is tragic, but it doesn't concern anyone here and now. What happened occurred years and years ago. There is no way to know whether the story Mrs. McCormick's sister told was true or her imagination. Please!"

"Ellen, it's all right," said Carter. "Annie won't pursue this line of thought out loud, will you, Annie? You could hurt people. People we do not know."

Annie stared at the floor. "No, Daddy, I won't speak of it to anyone except you and Mama." Speak of it she did not, for the time being.

****

Annie Young raced to the library on Monday after school and headed to the reference section. Her scouring of the shelves and her near frantic pacing along the aisle aroused the interest of librarian Georgia Albright. The woman approached Annie.

"May I be of help, Annie?" she asked the girl who was straining to see titles on the top shelf.

"Oh, thank you, Mrs. Albright. I'm searching for something, but I'm not sure what. If I need help, I'll call you." Annie continued to peer at the spines of books on a tall shelf without looking at Mrs. Albright.

"Have a research paper?"

"Um . . . yes, that's right." Annie liked Georgia Albright, who was pleasant and willing to help library patrons, but she avoided the prudish assistant librarian, Florence Bigler. Once, Annie overheard Miss Bigler speaking to Mrs. Albright, referencing Dr. Young. With a most condescending voice, she questioned aloud what may have brought him to Hillview. To Annie's mind, Florence Bigler embodied the suspicious and resentful prejudice toward outsiders that seemed ingrained among Hillview's old guard.

Mrs. Albright returned to the counter after reminding Annie she was there to help if needed. She continued to study the girl's unusual behavior.

Annie found a slim book titled *Studies of the Supernatural: Experiences Explained.* She thought to herself there weren't many experiences since the book was so thin. She removed the book from the shelf, sat at a desk, and thumbed through, taking copious notes in her notebook as she perused pages. When the clock above the check-out counter chimed once at four-thirty, she flipped through more pages before returning the book to its proper position on the shelf. As she gathered her papers, pencil, satchel, and sweater, she noticed Florence Bigler staring at her through narrow greenish-brown eyes, projecting a cool and disapproving air.

"Goodbye, Miss Bigler," whispered Annie as she walked past the counter. "Please tell Mrs. Albright I found what I needed."

"She has gone home." Miss Bigler then directed her sneer toward an older gentleman approaching her counter with a book.

Annie scratched her head as she navigated the steps to the sidewalk at the library's entrance. "That lady is so unfriendly," she said aloud as she headed to her father's office.

After dinner, Annie retreated to her bedroom where she reviewed her library notes. She had hoped the library might offer answers to her questions, but it did not. She concluded that she must decide for herself. Should she believe the incredible occurrence at the stone wall? Or should she not?

UNWILLING WARRIOR

A telephone call Thursday morning from Susie Rutledge brought the unwelcome news Miss Mittie suffered from a cough and was not well enough for a visit.

Ellen retrieved Annie from school and drove straight home since Carter planned to attend a civic meeting with Jack that evening. Jack would bring Carter home after the meeting.

Bright sun had shone the entire day. The ground was not muddy, so Annie spent her time until supper at the wall. She had left her tools there, and it relieved her to see they were unharmed by rain. She hoped to work with the stones washed clean by the rain and once again receive a visit from Noah who had promised to explain everything at her next calling at the wall. Annie was still uncertain of his claim that he was a spirit. Her gut told her he may be an apparition of sorts but not a spirit in the ghostly sense of the word. Noah had lifted Bitsy up and held her in his arms. Blink did not see him standing next to Annie, and he appeared to evaporate, disappear. Confusion clouded her senses.

The work gloves were damp, so Annie picked up stones with her bare hands and started arranging them on top of the wall. She realized a few had been moved and set into the front face of the wall, providing better support for other stones. Blink had not been in the vicinity, so who moved the stones? There sat Noah on a stool left at the work site.

"I noticed stones needed more support, so I rearranged them. Does it meet with your approval? We . . . Pa, my brothers, and I, built a wall such as this around our house using rocks dug from the ground."

She was neither frightened nor surprised to see him, for she had expected him to appear. She nodded her approval and walked toward him. Holding out her hand, she said, "May I touch you?"

"You may." He held out his arm.

Annie squeezed his forearm. His skin was rough, and the cloth of his shirt was coarse. She stepped nearer and touched his auburn hair, then his face. He felt the same as any person.

"Yes, I guess you are real," she admitted. "Make yourself disappear, please."

Noah stood, walked a scant distance, and faded into thin air. He then reappeared, sitting on the stool once again.

"What are you thinking, Annie? What are your brain and your intuitions revealing to you at this moment?"

"My brain and instincts tell me you are what you say you are, but I don't understand. I should fear you, but for a strange reason I don't. I am sad for you because you haven't gone to Heaven yet. Did you go to Heaven and return? Oh, I don't understand what any of this means, but I'm not afraid."

"A welcome revelation! Yes! I mean you no harm. My simple yearning is that you help me bring forth the truth of a great wrong that occurred long before your time. It is my hope that by relating to you my story, my journey, and what took place here, you shall aid me in my quest."

"I trust you, Noah, and I'll listen." She then parked herself on the second stool. Bitsy stretched out at Noah's feet and closed her eyes.

Noah began his story in a soft, staccato tone. "I hail from western North Carolina. We were ordinary yeoman farmers.

133

My father, my mother, and my three older brothers worked our farm. My oldest sister helped Ma with the house. A young sister, a tyke of ten, did what she could. We were a close-knit clan. Pa, a man in his late sixties, experienced bouts of neuralgia, which meant at times he could not carry out required tasks. These debilitating episodes were increasing when we learned North Carolina had taken leave of the Union. Early on, my state declared its loyalty to the United States, but after Fort Sumter, it left the Union and joined with other southern states in the rebellion."

"I have studied the Civil War in school," Annie said. "That is when you lived?"

Noah stood and stretched. "Yes. I was approaching my sixteenth year. Such distress among my kin the war created. Those who supported the Rebel cause angered Pa because he was Union. Pa's loyalty was to the Federals. Pa's father was a militiaman, a patriot, in the War for Independence. My pa despised slavery. He referred to eastern planters who owned slaves as 'The Silk Stocking Crowd.' Pa believed no man should own another. I heard him express his anger that Mr. Lincoln's name was not on our ballot for President. Pa was a contrarian, but he was a principled man. Discussions at our table devolved into raucous and disagreeable discourse. One of my brothers, Theodore, often left the table in fits of anger. Theodore believed the proper course of action was to stand with our neighbors in South Carolina, Georgia, and Virginia. He believed in the Rebel cause."

"What happened to Theodore? Did he join the Confederacy?"

"Yes. My other brothers, George and Jacob, joined Federal forces. George and Jacob left first, heading into east Tennessee where there was a Federal recruiting station. Other Unionists, such as my older sister Ibby's beau, did the same. I knew not the brothers' whereabouts after they took their leave. Not long after George and Jacob's departure, Theodore joined the Confederates. My brothers' absence from the farm

134

left the four of us tasked with the farm's survival, along with my young sister Mamie who attended school. We toiled each day from sunup until sundown. Sundays often could not be taken for the Lord or for rest. Pa's condition meant his work was sporadic, so Ma, Ibby, and I did the best we could. We planted fewer crops and let fields go. Times were rough. No notification of my three brothers' whereabouts ever came, so Ma and Pa found themselves anxious much of the time."

Noah rubbed his forehead and wiped his face with his left hand. Braced by his right hand on the other stool, he eased himself onto the hard, wooden seat. The boy glanced at Annie to note her reaction to what he had told her and observed a face flushed with fascination, her brow wrinkled with confusion.

"I am just, um . . . amazed by your story, Noah. It's bewildering. I am talking to you and listening to your story of a time long gone!" Annie let out a loud groan. "I don't know what to think, I think."

The teen-aged lad laughed aloud. "You are an amusing young lady, Annie! You do not think you know what to think? Your words befuddle me!"

"Well, I am befuddled, too," she mumbled as she shook her head and touched a forefinger to her lips. "How did you get here? Did you come here before you died? Are you appearing now to confuse me?"

"Allow me to continue so you will understand."

"Well, I'd be much obliged!" Her voice betrayed her impatience. She regretted her tone as soon as she spoke. "I'm sorry. I didn't mean to be rude." She reached over and touched his sleeve. "Go on, Noah."

Noah continued with his story, a story hundreds if not thousands of soldiers during that time could have told. It was a time when brothers fought against brothers, fathers and sons became enemies, and women held on to survive without menfolk.

135

"We continued as best we could. Pa was much distressed with my brother Theodore's decision. It pained him. Ma anguished over my three brothers. Our farm was a few miles from Leaksville, yet we stayed to ourselves and rarely went to town because neighbors were Confederate while others were Union. Pa wanted no part of arguing with old friends. Pa, he did as he was able, but often he was much exhausted from the work. My sister Ibby toiled in the fields with us. Little Mamie worked hard whenever she could."

Noah stopped speaking and put his face into his hands. When he raised his head, his eyes were red and swelled with tears.

"One day when it was boiling hot, Pa was plowing behind our mule. Pa's head had been painin' him something fierce, but he pressed on. He screamed this awful shriek and held his head in his hands. Ma ran to him, as did I, but when we reached him, he had fallen to the ground and was gone. Pa was dead, Annie, dead there lyin' in the dirt."

Noah moaned and trembled with the memory. Annie, speechless, knew not how to comfort him.

Noah continued, "We buried Pa in the fenced plot where he and Ma had buried the baby girl who passed before my birth. We kept working the farm as best we could. The red clay where we lived made it difficult. That soil can be hard to work. Ma and Ibby canned and put the goods in the root cellar. There was not as much food as we needed, but we were careful with portions. The neighbor who farmed next to us butchered an aging ox and a hog. He gave us a good bit of cured meat and salt pork. He feared Yankees coming through and stealing his livestock, so he wanted to beat them to the draw by helping us. When our milk cow went fresh, we had milk, butter, and cheese. Chickens provided eggs. Stories circulated of Yankees marauding and stealing items of value. They thieved horses, livestock, and they burned homes of southern sympathizers. We heard Confederates did the same to Yankee sympathizers. Ma and Ibby stuffed jewelry and other items of value and meaning to us in a box and buried it in our cemetery plot. Ma even removed her wedding band and buried it. We did not have much, but Ma refused to lose the few valuable items we possessed. She and Ibby put a wooden cross where they buried the box so they could extricate it after war's end. Ibby carved the words *Baby B* on the cross!" Noah chortled and slapped his knee as he remembered his mother and sister's handiwork.

Annie remembered Miss Mittie's account of hiding valuables, and she told Noah she understood the practice was common. Annie's escape from the Dust Bowl helped her understand hardship, yet the cruelties of the Civil War were beyond compare during Noah's mortal time on earth.

"Noah, please tell me more. Mama will call me to supper soon."

"Confederates conscripted me in 1863. Rebels rode up to the house, guided there by someone in town. They were searching for me. Ma had wrought a scheme in case of such an occurrence. She planned to explain I was a boy much younger than my actual years and could not engage in battle because of a physical condition limiting my mobility. She attempted to carry out this scheme when the soldiers appeared, but her pleas fell to cruel ears. The soldiers forced me to remove a horse from our barn, mount it, and ride away with them from our farm. Such means had earlier extracted four other young fellows from the vicinity, and the soldiers forced us within their midst to prevent escape. I can still hear Ma's screams as we rode away that day. The horses kicked up a right smart cloud of red dust as we made our departure, so I could see nothing behind me. Ibby tried to chase after, but the pace of our egress was too rapid. At that moment, I knew I was now a slave facing a future of violence and uncertainty, the likes of which I could not have imagined even in my most disturbing dreams."

The sound of Ellen's voice and the ringing of the back porch dinner bell startled the two. It was getting late, and the bell summoned Annie to the house.

"Noah, you must tell me the rest when I come again. Please! I must go now!"

"I shall do so!" He tipped his cap and vanished.

Annie grabbed her tools and stools, tossed them in the wagon, and she and Bitsy returned to the house as if nothing was out of the ordinary. Annie contemplated the tale this spirit had told her, and thoughts of his life after conscription filled her brain until their next meeting.

NOAH'S JOURNEY

A nnie did not return to the wall until Saturday. After helping Ellen clear breakfast dishes from the table and promising to dust downstairs rooms in the afternoon, Annie took her wagon filled with tools and headed toward the old stone wall. Eager to grasp more of the story her recent acquaintance promised to tell, she walked as fast as she dared so her tools and stools did not bounce out of the wagon. Bitsy loped along, sniffing the wind.

She did not wait long for Noah to appear. Bitsy ran to him, and he scratched behind the dog's ears as Annie set up the two stools.

"Good morning, Annie!"

Noah's quiet drawl comforted her. That he was no longer a disheveled stranger boosted Annie's confidence, and she responded with a wave and simple, "Hello, Noah."

"I have been awaiting your arrival. Shall we continue with my story or press on with work? I am desirous of giving you the knowledge of my story, but your tenacity to complete your project is strong, I realize."

"Please. I want to know your story, Noah. Everything. Shall we work while you talk?"

"Certainly."

Noah took a sharp breath and began excavating rocks hidden beneath the soil. Annie took others from the pile Blink had deposited and began placing those on the wall while Noah worked.

"You left off when the Rebel soldiers took you away from home," she reminded him. "What happened after that?"

"So much, so much." His chin dropped to his chest as he plunked a hefty rock into the pile he had been creating.

"First, they took us boys to somewhere in Virginia, but I do not know the exact whereabouts. They gave me a broken-down flintlock with a bayonet affixed, a canteen, and a knife. My uniform included these trousers, this shirt, this cap, and a most uncomfortable wool jacket. No boots, shoes, or gloves. We practiced shooting at targets, but we farm boys could shoot just fine. Each of us hunted squirrel, rabbit, deer, and turkey to feed our families. Officers instructed us in various ways to kill Federals using our bayonets for hand-to-hand combat. Rations were scarce, and those we received were often foul and of dreadful taste. I missed Ma's ability to turn a meager meal into a fine tasting repast. Weather was frigid. Snow showers made our conditions even more miserable. A few blankets were available to those of higher rank, but we privates just huddled together to stay warm."

Annie stopped work and stared at her brand-new friend who was recounting history from a firsthand perspective. The books she read detailed none of what Noah conveyed. She plopped onto the seat of a stool and absorbed his words, hungry to learn more of his experience.

Noah continued working and speaking, not realizing she had abandoned her efforts.

"Time was fleeting, Annie Young, so I cannot recall how long we were at this encampment. After a time, they ordered us to march, and march we did. Officers reminded me with regularity that I was now a private in the Army of Northern Virginia, a fact that as a North Carolinian, I resented. I had no recourse, so I and my fellow fresh fish, I prefer the term abductees, did as instructed. We marched, prepared for battle, and camped again near Fredericksburg, awaiting orders from a General Early."

Noah stopped and inspected the wall's height before continuing. "Orders received the next morning were to hold Marye's Heights near the city. I knew not what that meant. There was a stone wall taller than this one, and they positioned us behind it. I laid there, still as can be, and awaited my fate. A fellow who had befriended me earlier instructed me to keep my head low. I recall inquiring of him the date, and he responded he believed it was the third day of May. If I were to die, I desired to know the date. March the twentieth was the day they took me from our farm."

Noah's tortuous saga mesmerized Annie Young. She cradled her head in her hands and leaned forward so she missed no detail of what followed. Bitsy moved in closer and rested her head on Annie's feet.

"The commotion and smoke were nothing I could have ever imagined, Annie. Gunfire thundered in a relentless fashion, worse than the most violent thunderstorm, and the smell of gunpowder saturated the air, burning my eyes and nostrils. A cloud formed by munitions overtook us, making vision impossible beyond a few feet. I stumbled upon a fallen Federal still clutching his muzzle loading Enfield Pattern rifle, a weapon far superior to the crude rifle given me, so I pried it from his hands. With skill and practice, this Enfield could fire up to two shots per minute. I did the best I could and fired into the cloud ahead of me. As men continued to fall, we pressed closer to that rock wall, climbing over bodies, pieces of bodies, and blood-soaked earth. It was kill or be killed. I wretched as I moved through the horror. I was so frightened that my entire body shook with violence to the extent I could no longer load or aim my rifle."

Noah stopped speaking and scrutinized the stone wall before continuing. "Screams of pain and anguish were as distinct as the gunfire. How long this fighting continued I know not, but it suggested eternity to me. The fellow who had told me the date fell at my feet, a hole in his gut the size of my fist. I attempted to stop his bleeding, but I could not. At that point, Federals began climbing over the wall. They swarmed as ants coming after spilt honey. I hoisted my rifle and wielded its bayonet into the air at a blue body coming toward me. Instead of shooting me or thrusting his bayonet into my gut, he kicked me hard in the head, knocking me backward off my feet."

Noah paused and stopped extricating rocks from the mud. He turned to discover Annie perched on the stool, enraptured. He joined her and sat on the other stool next to her as her eyes followed his every movement.

"Have I upset you, Annie?"

Annie hesitated. She replied that his story upset her, but she desired him to continue. Annie tried to imagine the horror he had endured.

"I knew nothing until much later. In my first consciousness, I sat upright, my head swimming, and scanned the sights surrounding me. At that exact moment, two Federals yanked me by both arms and examined me with haste to determine my injuries. I experienced difficulty walking, but they half dragged and half carried me as we stepped over numerous bodies and body parts. After a time, we reached a cordoned off area. Inside, Federals guarded Confederate prisoners, of which I was one. After a day or more, they loaded us on a raft sort of contraption and guided it across the Rappahannock River to Federal territory. I felt a sense of relief, which I am confident was not the reaction my superiors desired if they had known. I lived with the fervent desire to return home."

Noah continued to relate what happened after his capture. He devised escape plans, but he realized his ideas were not workable at that juncture. Because of his aching head, occasional dizziness, and nausea, he lost track of time. He could not tell Annie how soon the soldiers rounded up prisoners and moved them from this encampment.

"A guard informed us the battle we engaged in at Marye's Heights occurred just before another battle at a site known as Chancellorsville, which Confederates won. This Confederate victory required Federal troops and we prisoners to retreat north with haste."

Noah and his fellow prisoners marched to a departure point on the Potomac River where they boarded a steamboat bound for Old Capitol Prison in Washington, D.C. The complex, former temporary home of the United States Capitol, had served as a private school and boarding house before its use as a prison for captured Confederates during the Civil War.

Noah realized he could be shot or drown in the fast-moving waters if he jumped overboard, so he did not try an escape. As a result, he and the other prisoners endured cramped quarters and vermin infestations during a near month-long stay in Old Capitol Prison. The accommodation was a temporary stop before transfer elsewhere for long-term confinement.

Federals loaded Noah and his fellow prisoners into a railroad passenger car dispatched from Washington to Fort Delaware, which Noah learned was on an island. As the train steamed toward its ultimate destination, Noah devised an escape plan. He feared incarceration at Fort Delaware would render nil any chance of escaping and returning home. Trouser and jacket pockets stuffed with bread, he watched and plotted. He soon implemented a course of action that might offer his only chance of escape.

Noah recounted to his captivated audience of one that the locomotive stopped at a relay house. Once it pulled away and got under full steam, he planned to jump through the window next to his seat. Noah reasoned if he leaped while the train ran at a slow pace, guards could jump off in pursuit. Guards might shoot or bayonet him where he landed, so he felt his chances of survival were better if he jumped while traveling at full speed.

Night had fallen by the time they departed the relay station. As the speeding train approached a bridge over a fast-running creek, he poised himself on the sill, looked both ways with a hasty glance, and jumped from the window. He heard gunshots and the whiz of bullets hitting the surrounding water. Noah was neither hit by a bullet nor injured in the fall, except for a bloody hand received when it grazed a boulder. He was, however, left with acute soreness in the muscles of his shoulders and chest and a bruised and twisted left knee. He broke no bones. His extrication from the creek took him through a thicket of honey locusts, resulting in painful arm lacerations received while protecting his face. Soaked and dazed, yet conscious, he retreated to nearby woods to await either daylight or capture. Noah fell asleep after expressing his gratitude to a higher being for his good fortune to still be alive and not so injured he could not travel.

At sunup, he began his grueling trek back to his home in western North Carolina. Guided by the sun's position in the sky, he headed west, taking care to avoid being spotted by Union patrols. He traveled along a creek bank for several hours, stopping to drink as needed and cool off in the water. When he realized the stream turned northwest, he abandoned the route and tried a more due west approach.

After two days, Noah headed south. He was ravenous since his pockets were empty, but blackberries and whortleberries he scavenged along the way sustained him. He soon arrived at the Potomac River and realized this could be the barrier that ended his escape. Noah determined he was unfit to swim across, so he turned toward a train whistle heard in the distance. He hoped the track ran north/south enabling him to cross the river by running across the trestle.

As he headed in a more eastern direction, he stumbled upon a shanty nestled among a grove of trees with a path leading to the river. Peering from behind an enormous cottonwood tree, he saw two row boats tied at the river's edge and three boys casting fishing poles into the water. Weak with hunger and thirst, he took a chance and approached the three. Such action could cost him his life, return him to Federal custody, or cause him to be handed over to Confederates. Noah took the gamble, smiling and waving at them in as genial a manner as he could muster.

"Yo, there! Catching any fish this fine morning?"

Startled, the boys closed around each other as if to offer protection from the intruder.

"I am lost, and I am curious if you may be so kind as to guide me as to a satisfactory crossing point on the river. I am desirous of returning to my home on the other side."

The boys observed Noah was not much older than themselves and he did not appear armed. They responded that they knew a suitable crossing point. The boys questioned Noah. Who was he? Why was he lost? Where had he been? Where was he going? They did not display alarm at his presence, though. The three listened with intent interest as Noah concocted a tale.

"Annie, I gave them a false name, saying I had fallen off a train headed to stay with family members at a destination deemed safer by my parents. I claimed I was trying to avoid both Federal and Confederate armies for fear of being captured and conscripted by either one. My responses satisfied the boys' curiosity, and one who appeared the oldest stated that he, for the same reason, was fearful of soldiers from both sides. He told me they had seen Federal and Confederate troops, Confederates headed north, and Federals headed south. The boys' parents were not home but were in the nearest town getting supplies. They offered me food, which I devoured along with several cups of water. I was not confident they believed my story, but I reckoned they were not faithful to either side of the conflict. When the oldest offered to deliver me across the river in a boat, I accepted his offer with quiet joy."

Before entering the vessel, Noah said he could use a map. The boy replied he had no map, but Virginia lay on the south side of the river. Noah climbed aboard with a canteen of water given him by the youngest boy and a small haversack containing peaches, half a loaf of bread, and hardtack from the others. Upon reaching the opposite shore, the boy assisted Noah out of the boat. Noah slung the haversack over his left shoulder and extended his right hand to his new acquaintance.

"Here, you may need this on your travels, friend." The boy handed Noah a Bowie knife. "Take it. My pop took it off a dead Reb over to Sharpsburg. Awful battle there last year, and my pop is right much the scavenger. He picked up a good many rifles and knives off'n the dead after the fight. He won't miss no knife. Watch where you go. Rebs and Federals are everywhere."

After this exchange, Noah tucked the knife into his pocket and made his way up a hill toward a thick grove of trees. The sound of oars splashing in the water faded in the distance as Noah took in a heavy breath and resolved to face whatever came next.

****

Days passed as Noah traveled unknown territory, always on the lookout for soldiers of either army. He avoided civilization. Without map or compass, his reliance on the sun's position led him in roundabout directions on cloudy days. Noah came across a road and followed it, eyes and ears vigilant for signs of troops. Rations held out for several days because he was careful in his consumption.

At one point, he abandoned the road he had been traveling after he heard horses' hooves and rolling wagons in the distance behind him. Fearful of detection, he raced into a thicket and remained hidden as the procession approached.

146

Soldiers in blue stopped for relief near where he lay among rocks, and he overheard them theorizing another detachment was several miles behind, advancing as this bunch was toward Winchester. An hour's long respite enabled the troops to start back up again, refreshed. When they had passed, Noah retreated farther into the woods, attempting to keep the road in sight, but he could not. In spots, woods gave way to farm fields, so he ended up several miles west, dodging open pasture, tended crops, barking dogs, and people. He followed deer paths through the most rugged terrain and cut his way through vines and thickets with the knife given him by the boy who transported him across the river.

It was as he advanced toward yet another open region one morning at sunrise, he encountered a Federal picket post of a dozen soldiers. The soldiers spotted Noah at the same time he saw them and dashed after him firing and calling out for him to name himself. He plunged into a dense thicket of sumac bushes. Bullets whizzed by, slicing through foliage, and as he thrashed through the thicket, one bullet found its mark, slicing into the back of his left shoulder, shooting into his chest. Noah fell and lay still trying not to writhe in pain, create movement in the bushes, or cry out, which could reveal his location to his pursuers. No attempts to enter the thicket occurred, and the soldiers stopped firing. Noah heard someone call out, "Save yer powder! He's dead!"

Annie's hand flew to her mouth in horror. Tears streamed along her cheeks as she realized he was relating to her the facts of his own death. As she wiped her eyes on her sleeve, she looked over at him and saw his face was expressionless.

In an emotionless tone, he responded to her tears by explaining he did not die there in the sumac thicket. "It was later, Annie, and I have more to tell you. I know what occurred here. I was here."

Noah continued. "The soldiers left. The sun became disagreeably hot, and I spied a stand of trees across the field at the bottom of a ledge with a stone wall at the top. This wall.

I determined the trees offered shade. Feeble from exposure, hunger, and loss of blood, I could not walk, so I dragged myself across the field to the trees. This task was endless in my mind, yet I persisted in halting spurts until I reached the trees."

Noah recalled that he hid among the trees and underbrush at the bottom of the ledge for a good while. Leaning against a large basswood tree, he attempted to plug his wound with the tree's large leaves and torn pieces of his shirt. He lost consciousness but regained it upon hearing a commotion in the field near where he hid from danger.

"Loud and angry voices from men in the field shocked me back to consciousness, Annie. In my dazed state, I considered running to them, grabbing the reins of a horse, mounting it, and riding off before they shot me. Then I remembered my dire condition and that such thoughts were foolish. I remained in my hidden position and observed their conduct from my vantage point."

It was obvious to Noah, even in his dazed state, this congregation of men, two black and four white, were engaged in an antagonistic encounter. The older black fellow shouted while pointing toward two of the white men. Noah had never seen such behavior from any black person. The black man appeared to accuse one he called Albert of violating his daughter. He mentioned the name Molly several times, and Albert's response to the accusations was arrogance and indifference. Language spoken by the white men was vile, some words familiar, others unfamiliar to Noah. All the words, he was certain, were words his own father would have slapped his face for uttering. He told Annie that in the flash of an instant, one white man, a portly one with a beard, withdrew a revolver from under his coat and shot the older black man. In immediate succession, he shot the younger one. Both fell dead. Albert admonished the shooter with the words, "Damn you, Father!"

Another white man, an older one, addressed the shooter, screaming, "You are a man of evil impulse, Morse! Look at what you have wrought!"

Annie cried out, "That's what Phoebe saw, Noah! Miss Mittie's sister saw that!"

"The girl with the horse? Yes, she was above me behind this wall. They could not see her, nor could they see me due to denseness of foliage."

"I speculate I was in such a shocked state because of what I witnessed, I believed I was hallucinating, but I was not. I observed the men drape the bodies of the fallen over two horses. They held a discussion as to disposal of the dead before they rode off, two of them doubling up on horses. The girl left. I attempted to rouse myself enough so I could speak to her, but I could not. I was too weak."

Realization of the truth of Phoebe's story stunned Annie. The girl sat mute on the stool, staring at Noah the entire time, mulling the information over and over in her head. Neither spoke any words for several minutes.

Annie broke the silence. "What happened to the murdered men? Do you know?"

"Yes."

"Well?"

"My wound continued to bleed, leaking the life from me, and within moments after the incident my body was lifeless. I reckon the nature of what I had seen was so abhorrent, my spirit froze and found itself unable to move on."

Annie spoke through her tears. "Oh, Noah, how awful! How sad! I'm sorry! What happened to you is horrible. I am so sorry!"

Noah shrugged and continued, undeterred by her tears. "Not long after my demise, the lanky fellow named Albert and the paunchy man Morse returned. They searched the ground near where the murders occurred. Because many hoofprints and footprints littered the region, they scoured a larger part of the field near where my body lay. The older fellow spotted my

149

body in the grove of trees, and they both rushed to it. I must relate to you, Annie, it was a most peculiar scene to witness!"

Annie's brown eyes grew wide. "I imagine so."

"My deceased condition was obvious, and their consternation with this unexpected development was real. The men scanned the vicinity, the entire time engaged in disagreement. They loaded my corpse upon one horse and transported me to a clearing among a grove of trees near a creek. There, they tossed my body into a trench dug with great haste. It was next to other freshly dug and covered over spaces in which I believed lay the bodies of the two Negro men. It was an unceremonious burial, I must say to you."

Noah told Annie he returned to the spot where the murders and his death had occurred. His curiosity as to what the two men searched for before they spotted his body led him to root about the vicinity. Noah found the item, a gold pocket watch engraved with the initials *MB* and an engraving inside reading *Morse Blanton*. Noah took the watch from its place in the dirt and traveled to the burial site near the creek where he removed a good many rocks from the creek. He heaped rocks on top of the makeshift graves to mark their location and buried the watch under one set of rocks. Noah confessed his optimism to Annie that someday the man who killed the two individuals could be held accountable for his crime. By placing the watch with the graves, perhaps truth might come to light and justice result. Noah recalled that he observed the man named Morse searching where the crime occurred several times after the incident. Blanton's visits did not coincide with Phoebe's search for her cameo at the stone wall, which Noah surmised was a blessing for Phoebe's safety.

"Until someone holds them accountable for their crime, my spirit will not leave. I must see that justice prevails, and you, Annie, are the force to achieve that." Noah was matter-of-fact in this assertion.

"But, but Noah, they are dead! It happened in 1863. It's 1934! They are . . . dead!"

"Yes, those men are dead, and I am dead, but the consequences of their crime affected others. Do you not believe the truth must come to light?" Noah gazed into her eyes, penetrating her soul. "Do you not?"

Annie's eyes surveyed remnants of the wall, once a silent witness to tragedy. Her gaze reached beyond into the neighboring apple orchard. A sense of duty struck her, a sense of resignation. The truth *should* come out, and it was she, as Noah asserted, who was the vehicle to deliver the truth to light. She stared into Noah's eyes, her heart racing, her mouth dry.

"Yes, I suppose I do, Noah. How can that happen? Miss Mittie was a child younger than I, and she has no way to prove what Phoebe said was true. Nobody will believe me if I say a *ghost* told me what happened! I mean, don't you understand nobody will believe my story? You're a *ghost,* for goodness' sake! How on earth can I bring the truth to light? Tell me!"

Annie's reluctance exasperated the spirit who sat next to her. He had put his hope in Annie to expose the truth of the awful crime and hasten his passage to the world beyond the one in which he was trapped. A dejected Noah stared at Bitsy, still sleeping at Annie's feet.

"I must trust you, Annie Young. I have provided information unknown to others and desire you to follow those clues to the truth. And . . . Annie, I prefer the term *spirit* to the most disagreeable moniker of *ghost.* The latter sounds shallow and contrived. I am a spirit. Yes, I am a restless and impatient one. I am weary, and the truth has waited too long."

The girl acquiesced and without further words began gathering her tools and placing them in the wagon. Noah assisted her, and as she turned to pull the wagon up to the house, he tapped her on the shoulder.

"Please, Annie, do not be disheartened. Do not show fear. The task ahead is righteous."

She nodded, straightened her shoulders, and with resolution continued her trek to the house as Bitsy trotted beside the wagon, stubby tail vibrating.

I BELIEVE

"**I** wondered when you'd return! Did you forget that you were to dust the downstairs this afternoon?" Ellen greeted Annie and Bitsy as they came through the kitchen door.

The task had slipped the girl's mind, yet she pretended it had not. Annie washed her hands in the kitchen sink and removed a dust cloth from a drawer across the room. She walked into the parlor and began dusting the furniture.

"No, Mama, I didn't forget. I just let time get by me. It won't take too long, I promise!"

She rushed to dust the furniture in the downstairs rooms, but her mind wandered to the events Noah relayed to her. His tale overwhelmed her. As she mulled over the details, this preoccupation caused her to complete her chore in a haphazard manner.

A subdued Annie dawdled over her food while her parents conversed during the evening meal. Carter and Ellen exchanged glances and observed Annie as they ate, but they did not press their daughter to answer questions or to take part in conversations. After dinner, Annie and her mother cleaned the table and washed dishes while Carter retreated to the parlor to read the local newspaper he had purchased in town. Once kitchen chores were complete, Ellen and Annie joined Carter in the parlor. There the three listened to Jack Benny on the radio while completing a jigsaw puzzle. Annie spoke but a few sentences the entire evening.

****

Uneventful days brought Annie to her usual Thursday visit at the Rutledge house. She did not return to the wall beforehand. The girl had been mulling over Noah's many revelations, and she could not decide whether to divulge Noah's existence to Miss Mittie. Might Miss Mittie consider her crazy, much as townspeople had considered Phoebe? Concentration on her schoolwork suffered, and her teacher kept Annie after school one day to ask what troubled her. After assuring her teacher everything was normal, Annie attempted to better keep up appearances to her parents and her teacher.

On Thursday afternoon, none other than Miss Mittie met Annie at the Rutledge front door. She gave Annie a hug. The tiny woman's bun bobbed side to side as they walked to the sun porch, Miss Mittie's wooden cane tapping on the floor as they went.

"I have been strolling around the lawn this afternoon, Annie! It's a lovely day, so I felt the need to soak in sunshine and inspect flowers that may soon bloom. Just daffodils so far, but they are delicate and colorful." She settled into her chair. "Is it too warm for hot chocolate?"

Annie eyes lit. "No. Hot chocolate is always good!"

"Well, then! Please run into the kitchen and ask Berta if she will make two cups for us. Susie's suffering with a headache and is upstairs. Berta will be happy to make us hot chocolate."

Annie walked to the kitchen, swung the door open, and entered to see Berta, the Rutledge housekeeper, standing over the stove, stirring something in a large pot.

Berta was a thin, olive-skinned woman in her early 40s with brownish hair cut in a stylish bob. She turned to Annie

154

when she heard the kitchen door open. Deep dimples in her cheeks displayed her delight at seeing Annie.

"Hello, Berta," Annie said. "Miss Mittie asked if you could please make us two cups of hot chocolate."

Berta replaced the lid on the pot and walked to the icebox to get milk. "I will! Miz M is so glad to have you as her little friend. You make her happy. Go on, now, and I'll bring it to you when it's ready."

Annie went back to the sun porch and sat at the game table with Miss Mittie.

"My back feels stronger when I sit at the table today, Annie, so should we play dominoes or just chat?"

Annie was pensive. "Well, today could be a chatting day, Miss Mittie."

"Do you have a specific topic in mind, dear?"

Annie's demeanor took a serious turn. Confusion engulfed her, and she hesitated in her nervousness. What course of action should she take? Should she discuss Noah? Miss Mittie radiated a spunky and spry mood this day, so Annie feared turning her toward a darker path.

"Well, well . . . Miss Mittie, do you believe in g-gho . . . spirits?"

"Ghosts?"

"Spirits."

"What is the distinction, Annie?"

Annie looked at the floor and shook her head. "I suppose I don't know. I guess they are the same. The word *ghost* sounds shallow and contrived, don't you think?"

Annie's statement puzzled Miss Mittie. "Where did you get those ideas, dear girl?"

"I prefer the term *spirit* because it sounds . . . um . . . more friendly."

"To answer your question, Annie, I am uncertain whether whatever you want to call them exists. Can it be? It sounds possible. Why could they exist? I cannot answer. I don't

155

believe I ever had an experience with one, so I don't know. That doesn't answer your question, though, does it?"

Berta entered the room with two hot chocolates on a tray.

Miss Mittie smiled and reached out her hand to touch Berta's arm. "Thank you, Berta. When you leave to go home, please be sure to leave the kitchen light burning. I may fix myself a light supper with the soup you made. Mr. Rutledge will be late, and Susie stays in bed for a good while with her headaches."

Berta agreed and waved at Annie as she left the room. As Annie raised the cup to her lips, she watched her friend's face for a clue. Should she expose Noah's existence? Miss Mittie drank hot chocolate and murmured, "Ummmm, good! Yum, yum, yum!"

Cradling her hot chocolate in both hands, Annie took a profound breath and moved forward with her story. Between sips, she related Noah's entire tale, one that validated Phoebe's revelations.

With her hands folded together, Miss Mittie sat on the edge of her chair, drinking in the story, her face expressionless, her demeanor calm and unruffled. Annie searched her friend's eyes and mouth for clues as to the woman's reaction as words poured from Annie's tongue. The girl found none until the story ended. Then, Annie saw a furrowed brow and Miss Mittie's mouth drawn into a thin line.

"I'm sorry if I have upset you, Miss Mittie," Annie said as tears formed in her eyes. "You believe this account one a . . ."

"Crazy person might have made up?" snickered the little lady as her hair bun gave a scant wobble.

Annie dropped her head. "Yes."

Miss Mittie leaned across the table and took Annie's hands into hers. She looked into Annie's tear-filled eyes as she spoke.

"I have seen and experienced many things in my long life, Annie girl. Happy and unhappy. Several I have not comprehended. I understand nothing of the supernatural, or ghosts, or spirits as you call them, but I trust what you are

156

telling me. Not for one moment do I believe you fabricated such a story. You have a vivid imagination, but you did not make up a false narrative and try to pass it off as the truth. I know for sure. I know you that well."

Wrinkled, bony hands squeezed Annie's youthful, supple ones, and a warm, sweet smile took form in her eyes and on her mouth directed at the forlorn girl

"Well, your tale is one I never expected to hear, Annie. Never, never, never. Could your Noah be the boy in Phoebe's dreams? Gracious! I see how you believe this development vindicates Phoebe and indicts the Blantons, yet much time has passed. Folks have moved on with their lives. Morse and Albert are both long dead. Albert's son Clay still lives, but he wasn't even born when these events occurred. Molly? Who knows what happened to her and her baby? I realize this spirit wants to reopen everything, but what might such accomplish? Shall we just let this go? This makes me relieved for Phoebe's memory, but we cannot bring justice to anyone. Those times were different, terrible, frightening. Ordinary people and those in power threw much injustice at Negroes, and whites accepted the injustices, the many horrible things. Even now I fear, if you tell Noah's story, the response from countless people will be, 'Who cares?' This is awful, but it's true, too true. Why even my Susie will say this."

Her friend's reaction shocked Annie. Annie believed as soon as Miss Mittie heard Noah's story, she would insist Annie bring the revelation to light.

"It isn't right people considered Phoebe crazy, and those Blantons lived as if nothing happened! Who were the other men? They should have spoken up! They should have told what happened! That Morse Blanton was a dreadful man, Miss Mittie!" Annie's voice rose.

Miss Mittie nodded in agreement as she adjusted her spectacles. "Yes, Morse Blanton was a monstrous man. Albert was not as cutthroat as his father, I do not believe, but for sure Old Morse Blanton was not an upstanding citizen. I cannot know the other men's identities, but they hid the truth. They are dead, too. It was a different time, Annie Young. I must tell you, though, if such happened today, the same outcome is probable. We must let this go. Forget it. Shove it into the recesses of your mind and do not speak of it. That's what I have done. Tell Noah you have told me everything, and I say he may cross over now."

Annie sighed and responded with a meek, "Okay" as she squinted at the clock on the wall. It was time for Ellen to arrive, so she rose from her chair and took the tray with the empty cups back to the kitchen. After returning to the sun porch, she gathered her books and jacket, kissed her dear friend on the forehead, and exited the house to wait on the porch. Within a few minutes, the Youngs' black Dodge pulled up to the curb.

The moment Annie climbed in, Ellen perceived something was not right. She asked in a soft voice, "How was your visit today?"

"All right."

"Just all right? Is Mrs. McCormick not feeling well today?"

"No, she's fine. Mrs. Rutledge has a headache and went to bed."

"I'm sorry to hear she felt ill. Mrs. McCormick was in good spirits, though?"

"Yes."

"We aren't getting Daddy today. He and Jack are attending a meeting at the hospital, so Jack will bring him home later."

"That's fine."

Annie spoke no further on the ride home. Ellen hummed a Ruth Etting tune, attempting to break the awkward silence as they bumped along the road from Hillview out to their lane west of town. When they arrived at the house, Ellen asked Annie to help bring grocery sacks into the kitchen. After unloading groceries and letting Bitsy outside for a run, she retrieved her satchel and jacket from the car and lumbered up the stairs to her room. As she flung her things onto the bed, she burst into tears. Sobbing, she crawled under the covers, soaking her pillow as tears continued to flow.

"What have I done? I've hurt Miss Mittie, and now I must hurt Noah, and I hate what I've learned! I wish I'd never gone back to that stupid wall!"

In a short while, a soft knock on her bedroom door roused Annie as she wiped her eyes.

"Annie? Annie? Are you okay?" Ellen stood outside the door, and Annie could hear Bitsy's paws scratching at the door.

"Yes, Mama. I'm okay. Let Bitsy in, please."

As soon as the door opened, the little dog rushed in and jumped on Annie's bed. It stunned Ellen to see her daughter's red face and mussed hair as the girl sat upright. She rushed over to the bed and sat beside her weeping daughter.

"Annie, I knew something was wrong. What is it? Did something happen to Mrs. McCormick, or did something happen there that upset you? Please tell me!"

Annie grabbed her mother's shoulders and brought her close, sobbing into Ellen's bosom. "Oh, Mama! I've done something terrible! I don't know how to fix it," she cried as her mother held her close. Ellen reached into her pocket and brought forth a handkerchief to wipe the girl's tears.

"You couldn't have done something terrible, I'm sure, Annie," reassured Ellen. "Tell me what you think you have done. It can't be that awful."

As Annie struggled to gather her composure, she sat back and blew her nose into the handkerchief Ellen provided. She took several deep breaths. Keeping her composure proved difficult. She began to cry again, burrowing her head into Ellen's shoulder as her mother stroked her hair. Bitsy lay on the bed and rested her head on Annie's leg.

"Oh, Mama, you won't believe me if I tell you. It's too crazy and peculiar and awful. I told Miss Mittie today, and she didn't care, and it's so strange. Nobody will believe me."

159

The clanging telephone in the downstairs foyer required Ellen's attention. When she returned to Annie, she advised the girl that someone canceled the meeting Jack and Carter were to attend, and Jack's Buick, parked at the hospital, did not start.

"Daddy needs me to come to get him, Annie. Mr. Glenn who owns the Buick agency is coming to tow Jack's car, so I must take Jack home before returning. Wipe your face and come with me. I won't leave you here alone when you are so upset. We'll speak more of what has upset you this evening."

A dutiful Annie washed her face and tried to press the wrinkles from her dress. "May I bring Bitsy, Mama?"

"Yes. Hold her so she doesn't jump around, though."

They spoke no words on the ride into town where they retrieved Carter and Jack from the hospital. It perturbed both men that someone had canceled the meeting without notice, so they were not in the best of moods. Ellen, Carter, and Annie dropped off Jack at his house. Although a gracious Lou welcomed the Youngs for supper, they declined. As their car rounded a corner where Olivia Watson's Diner stood, Ellen blurted, "Let's stop here and have supper!"

"What?" asked Carter. "Is she open?"

Ellen parked the Dodge in front, and they stared at the window to determine whether Olivia was open for business.

Ellen pointed toward the restaurant. "Yes! Lights are on, and Olivia is standing by a table. Annie, it will be fine to leave Bitsy in the car while we eat. Bitsy can watch us through the windows. Come on, y'all!"

A reluctant Annie climbed out of the car, patting Bitsy on the head as she closed the door. The three entered the diner, one of three restaurants in Hillview still open in 1934. Olivia Watson's food was appetizing, and although she had cut back on her menu because of difficulties getting produce and supplies, what she served was satisfying and well prepared. The restaurant sported bright tablecloths, each a different color, at every table. It provided a cheery spot for Hillview's

160

residents to gather, engage in conversation, and enjoy a reasonably priced meal. Carter sometimes ate lunch there, so when he walked in, Olivia Watson greeted the threesome with a wave and a hearty, "Hi, Doc!"

"Good evening, Olivia," Carter said. "Are you still open tonight?"

"You bet I am, Doctor! I don't close until seven o'clock. Once upon a time, I stayed open later and had more help, but I've made adjustments with these hard times. I keep my prices low so people can afford to let me cook for 'em. Come in and have a sit."

They chose an emerald green-clad table near the window, so they were in Bitsy's sight. Three other patrons sat at a cherry red-clad table across the room, and they acknowledged the Youngs as they took their seats. Two more diners entered a few moments later and seated themselves at another table, this one covered with a yellow cloth. The menu offered tasty dinner fare, but Annie elected to have breakfast for supper. She pushed the afternoon's ordeal at the Rutledge house out of her mind and ordered scrambled eggs, bacon, and pancakes with Log Cabin Syrup. Ellen and Carter both opted for the meatloaf special with mashed potatoes and green beans. The three enjoyed the rare treat of a restaurant meal. Carter's grumpiness vanished, and Annie engaged in conversation. Ellen monitored the girl for any clue as to Annie's earlier episode following her visit with Miss Mittie.

When they returned home, Ellen instructed Annie to bathe and ready herself for bed. She was eager to tell Carter what had occurred that afternoon, which she did while the girl bathed. Carter could fathom no explanation for Annie's behavior unless it had something to do with Phoebe and the Blanton men. As soon as Annie came downstairs in her pajamas, Ellen asked if Annie had schoolwork to complete. A spelling test was on the schedule for the next day, but Annie was confident she knew how to spell the words. Carter asked his daughter to please tell them what had upset her.

161

Annie crawled onto the sofa and drew Bitsy close. She took a long, deep breath. The girl resolved to keep her composure and began telling them everything. She unveiled Noah, his story, that he saw Morse Blanton shoot Molly's brother and father, and that Noah needed the truth revealed. At several points, Annie insisted her parents may think her insane after hearing her story, but she was not, and she was not making up the tale.

These revelations took a good while, and it was long past Annie's bedtime when she finished speaking. By the time she had told them everything, including Mrs. McCormick's reaction, the ordeal left her exhausted and filled with guilt. Tears flowed again, and Carter and Ellen both held her close, attempting to soothe her. Words of reassurance were fruitless as the girl sobbed and sputtered through her tears. After a time, she went limp in her father's arms as they sat on the sofa. Carter hoisted her into his arms and carried her up the stairs, tucking her in her bed and covering her with a blanket. The girl was asleep as soon as her head hit the pillow. Ellen let Bitsy out for a quick run, and the dog zipped up the stairs as soon as she re-entered the house, jumping into her bed next to Annie's.

"Oh, my gracious, Carter!" Ellen grasped Carter's arm. "So, this explains the ghost questions! Where has she dreamed this?"

"Annie didn't dream it, Ellen. It's not her imagination. Something happened back at that wall. We've seen evidence in her behavior. It's real. The places and the time frame of which she speaks are real, Ellen. The story is too intricate and factual from a historical perspective. Our daughter did not invent this or imagine it. She couldn't have done that! I believe her. As strange as it sounds, I believe her."

They sat in the kitchen and drank tea in silence as the grandfather clock in the hallway struck midnight.

"Let's go to bed, Ellen." Arm in arm, they trudged up the stairs. "Ellen, we must sort this out soon . . . tomorrow or Saturday. Oh, boy, this development is something, is it not?"

DELIVERANCE

Friday morning ushered in another nippy March rain. When Ellen entered Annie's room to arouse her for school, she found her girl in deep slumber. Under the circumstances, Ellen and Carter agreed to keep Annie home from school. Carter grabbed his bag and left to see a patient on the way into his office.

As Ellen drank her coffee, she contemplated what had happened the preceding night. Annie's story of a ghost, or spirit, as the girl called him, appearing to her and corroborating a tale of murder told years ago sounded surreal to Ellen. Ellen dismissed stories of spirits. She had never considered the subject with any seriousness. Ellen knew her daughter, though, and she knew Annie told the truth. The mystic tale of Noah's existence worried and confounded Ellen as did Annie's welfare and her relationship with Miss Mittie. As she sipped her coffee and watched the rain, Ellen heard Annie descending the stairs.

"Mama, I'm late for school!" A dazed Annie held onto the banister as she navigated the stairs. "Has Daddy left?"

"You were in such a sound sleep that Daddy and I felt it best to let you sleep more. It was late when you went to bed last night. Your teacher will allow you to make up your spelling test, I'm sure. Come into the kitchen and have breakfast."

Annie sat at the table while her mother prepared oatmeal and soft-boiled eggs. Bitsy pranced into the room and licked Annie's leg before returning to the parlor and settling into her favorite chair near the window, resting her head on the chair's arm.

"Mama, what I told you last night is true. Noah is real. I didn't make up the story."

Ellen set Annie's breakfast on the table. "I know you didn't, Annie. You must understand this is strange and bewildering to us. I have never believed in ghosts . . . uh, spirits. Your story is an extraordinary tale. I have never heard such, but Daddy and I believe in you. We know you."

While Annie spooned at her oatmeal, Ellen reached across the table and took Annie's hand into hers.

"Annie, Daddy is not home, but I believe he agrees with what I will say. Mrs. McCormick is correct. We should let this go. The horrible events happened long ago, and although it was terrible, you can achieve nothing now by dredging up an awful history. This story can harm people. Mrs. McCormick! Mrs. McCormick endured so much as a child and young woman, and you don't want her to endure more gossip. She is old. It could be cruel, Annie. Nobody knows where Molly and her baby went or what happened to them. To repeat the story is not fair to the Blanton family, either. Why, they may know nothing of it. Nothing! The story is sad and horrific, but it's 1934. You can prove nothing. Nothing good can result from bringing it into the open. Nobody will believe a story a . . . *spirit* told you! You can believe it. We can believe it. But leave it alone. Leave it alone."

"Mama, I know what you say may be true, but . . ."

"It *is* true! For now, it's best you stop rebuilding the wall. If you want to continue, you may do so only if Daddy is with you. I'm concerned for you being back there alone. This talk of murderers and ghosts needs to stop!"

The conversation stopped with a violent flash of lightning and a deafening clap of thunder. Bitsy barked, zipped into the kitchen, and stood between Ellen's legs, the dog's frantic eyes looking up in fright.

"Goodness, I wasn't expecting that!" Ellen began wiping up coffee she spilled on the table with the first crash of thunder. "I thought we were having a quiet rainy day!"

Another flash and thunderclap followed, and lights flickered twice before they went out. In a moment, torrential rain fell, and the sound of large drops hitting the tin roof drowned out any attempts at conversation. Ellen rose and took a hurricane lamp from a shelf, lit it, and parked it on the table. She then retreated to the parlor where she lit another lamp kept for times when there was no electricity.

"Annie, go upstairs and get dressed. The storm shouldn't last long."

Annie did as her mother directed, putting on a new yellow and blue calico dress Ellen had sewn. As she smoothed out wrinkles in the fabric, she looked out the window toward the back of the property. There, standing in the midst of the cleared trail to the stone wall, stood Noah, rain pouring around him. A shudder went through her body as she raced to the window and closed the curtains.

Ellen was correct that the storm was short-lived. Rain stopped after twenty minutes, but they still had no electricity. When Annie returned to the kitchen, she found her mother kneading bread dough. Wiping her hands on her apron, Ellen glanced over at her daughter and sighed. To keep the girl busy, she suggested Annie sweep the front porch.

Annie completed the task in short order. When she returned and hung the broom on its hook, she addressed her mother. "Do you have anything else you want me to do, Mama?"

"You may go to Cora's and buy eggs. Let Bitsy outside while I get the dough ready for the oven. Then I'll get you money for the eggs."

166

A dejected Annie whistled to the dog, opened the back door, and Bitsy scurried off the porch. Recent events and the reactions of her parents and Miss Mittie put a heavy weight on the adolescent girl's shoulders. She pulled a chair out from the table and slipped into it without a word as she observed her mother placing dough into two greased and floured bread pans. Ellen patted them into shape, set the pans on top of the stove, and covered each with a towel so the dough could rise. Annie considered her mother exquisite in every way. Ellen's warm voice and bright eyes radiated at all times, and a scowl was rare. That Annie's revelations upset her dear mother saddened the girl. Annie never wished to disappoint her parents, yet Ellen's responses convinced her she had done so.

"Here is money for Cora." Ellen's voice was flat. "I need a dozen eggs if Cora has a dozen. If not, get what she can spare. Don't get muddy as you walk there."

Annie took the cash and started toward the front door.

"Put on your coat!"

"Okay, Mama. I'll put Bitsy back inside, too." Annie opened the front door to find the dog sitting on the porch. The girl took a towel kept in the hall closet and wiped Bitsy's feet before allowing Bitsy to enter the house. Annie draped the towel over one of the front porch's chairs, then struck off on her errand. Annie hiked along the driveway and turned left on the narrow dirt lane toward the Hill cabin, avoiding puddles. Ellen, tears streaming, watched Annie through the kitchen window as she left, her heart aching for her tormented daughter.

****

"Why, Annie Young! Hello!" A surprised Cora Hill opened her front door. "Why aren't you at school today? Everything okay with your family?"

"Hello, Miss Cora. Everything is fine. Electricity is out, but we are fine. Mama kept me home today because I didn't sleep well last night. Mama wants eggs if you have any."

"Oh, come in, come! I gathered eggs this morning before the storm hit. Look now! The sun is shining. This spring weather is something!"

When Annie entered the house, the aroma of baking bread engulfed her senses. She loved the smell of bread in the oven. As she followed Cora Hill into the kitchen, she took deep breaths.

"Miss Cora, your bread smells wonderful!"

"Oh, Annie, aren't you sweet! There's just something about bread baking that smells grand, you know. It always does! These loaves are ready. Sit and I'll cut you a piece after I put the eggs in your basket. How many eggs does your mama want?"

"She can use one dozen, but as many as you can spare is fine."

"Oh, I got more than that! My laying hens are laying! I'll get your dozen easy. These are ones I gathered this morning."

Annie observed Cora as she positioned eggs in Ellen's basket, making sure none broke. Blink's mother was always pleasant and smiling. Cora's pep amazed Ellen; she had remarked to Annie about Cora's vivaciousness several times.

Once the eggs rested in the basket, she opened the oven and brought out three browned-to-perfection loaves, which she set on top of the stove. She took one pan and turned it upside down on a towel sitting on the kitchen counter next to the stove. Cora turned the loaf over, took out a knife, and cut two big slices, one for herself and one for Annie.

"How 'bout butter on this bread, Annie?"

"Oh, yes! The best way to eat it!"

"I churned this butter yesterday, so it's good and fresh. Here you go!" Cora spread the yellow goodness on top of both slices. After handing Annie her slice, Cora took the other and sat across the table from Annie.

Cora and Annie munched on the hot bread with butter running along the sides. As Cora rose and retrieved two napkins from a drawer, Annie blurted a question she had never considered asking.

"Miss Cora, how did you and Mr. Ned get your place here? I'm just wondering since it's on the property Mrs. McCormick says used to belong to her family."

Cora returned to the table and handed Annie a napkin. A puzzled look came over her face.

"Well, Annie, my Ned's daddy, his name was Billy, left it to us. His daddy, Ned's granddaddy, gave it to Billy. Miz McCormick's daddy, his name was Doc Mueller, gave this log cabin and twenty acres to Ned's granddaddy. Ned's granddaddy and grandma worked on the Mueller farm and lived in this cabin. After they died, Billy fixed it up a good bit and added onto the kitchen to make it bigger. Ned and I covered the logs with the wood boards that's on here now. Looks more modern, you know! Warmer in winter, too!"

"Oh? This is interesting, Miss Cora!" a startled Annie said.

Cora chuckled. "Well, I don't know if it's interesting, but it's what the truth is! Before Billy added this bigger kitchen, it was just four rooms. One of those rooms, it's Blink's bedroom, looked as if Ned's granddaddy had built it onto the original part of the cabin. Ned added the indoor bathroom five years ago. What hard work that bathroom was! It's the best improvement we ever made! It sure is!"

"I bet it was! Umm, Miss Cora, when did Mr. Ned's daddy give you the property?"

"Well, Billy passed on in 1921, I believe. He left it to us in his will. Ned and I lived here and took care of him until he passed. Ned's mama died a long time before Ned's daddy. Ned has three sisters, but they live far away."

Cora rose from her chair and set their plates in the kitchen sink. Annie rose and put her hand around the handle of the egg basket. She summoned the courage to ask Cora one more question.

"Miss Cora, was Mr. Ned's grandfather's name Russell?"

Cora turned toward the girl. "Why, yes! His given name was Russell. His last name was the same as ours, Hill. Granddaddy Russell chose the last name Hill since he lived on this little ole' tiny hill! Former slaves did that, you know. They picked out last names because many didn't have one. Some took former masters' last names, but Granddaddy Russell picked Hill. How did you learn of Ned's Granddaddy Russell?"

"Uh, Mrs. McCormick told me. She was telling stories of when she was a girl, and she said Russell and his wife Thea worked for her family. Mrs. McCormick thought so much of them. She loved them."

"Oh, my, yes they did. They weren't slaves any longer, you know. No, sir! Doc Mueller, he didn't own slaves. He was Quaker, you know. He sent Ned's daddy Billy away before the Civil War broke out. Sent him up north to a school so he could learn to read and write and get a trade. Billy said Doc Mueller helped lots of Negro folk get up north before that war broke out. Helped 'em run away to freedom. Doc Mueller paid Ned's granddaddy Russell for his work, and he gave him this land for his very own as I told you. Doc Mueller was a fine man, Billy always said."

Annie headed toward the front door. When she reached the door, lights flickered, and electricity resumed.

"Goody! Light's back! I can do my ironing now!" Cora opened the door for Annie. "Tell Ellen 'hello' for me!"

"I will, Miss Cora. Tell Blink the same from me, too!"

Annie caressed the egg basket as she navigated the lane back to her house. She intended to go to her room and take out a notebook where she could jot the information Cora had given her. Annie believed she was on the trail of determining what happened to Molly and her baby and did not want to forget any details. Did Morse Blanton re-claim Molly as his property and take her back to his farm? What happened to Molly's baby? Did Molly know who murdered her father and brother? Could Molly have moved away? Was Molly dead?

Did Russell know Morse Blanton murdered his brother and nephew? Who else knew Blanton murdered the men? These questions and more raced through her mind as she made her way home. When she entered the house, Ellen was standing in the doorway.

"Goodness, girl! What took you so long?"

"Oh, Mama, Miss Cora had just taken bread from the oven, and we ate a piece with butter on top. It was delicious!"

Ellen took the basket. "Cora's bread is delicious. I'm sure you enjoyed it."

"Yes, we were talking while we ate. She was glad the lights came on so she can iron." Annie followed Ellen into the kitchen. Ellen put the egg basket on the kitchen counter and began placing eggs into the container she kept in the icebox.

"Do you have any chores for me, Mama?"

"Go to the cellar and bring up two jars of beans, please. We'll have those for dinner tonight. I am planning to fix the roast I bought at the market yesterday. You can peel potatoes after you bring up the beans."

Even though Annie wanted to run upstairs and write her notes on Cora's conversation, she fetched the beans, plopped herself in a chair, and began peeling potatoes. Soon, she was humming her mother's favorite tune, "I've Got the World on a String."

It surprised Ellen to see such pep in the girl after the preceding day's events, but it pleased her. Could it be, she thought, Annie might forget the story and secrets she had learned?

After completing her potato peeling chore, Annie requested permission to retreat to her room. Ellen agreed, and the girl bounded up the stairs two steps at a time. Bitsy followed and jumped on the bed the moment they arrived.

Annie took out her notebook and, sitting on the bed next to Bitsy, wrote everything Cora had told her. Cora's mention that Doc Mueller was Quaker puzzled her. Annie had never heard the word and was unsure of its meaning.

Annie tiptoed downstairs and slipped into the parlor where a set of *Encyclopedia Britannica* sat on a shelf. She sat in Bitsy's favorite chair and turned to the volume containing the term *Quaker*, where she learned of the Christian religion called Society of Friends. Quakers opposed war and slavery. As she shoved the book back on the shelf, she realized Doc Mueller's religious beliefs led him to not hold slaves. The story told by Miss Mittie and Cora of Doc Mueller assisting slaves in their quests for freedom painted a picture of a kind and courageous man.

"I wonder why Miss Mittie's father sent Ned's father up north?" she asked Bitsy. "Was he trying to get Ned's father away from slavery? It must have been the reason."

She returned to her bedroom. There she removed from her notebook the page of notes from her conversation with Cora Hill and stuffed them in the bottom drawer of her nightstand. The drawer contained other notes relating to Miss Mittie's stories of her childhood and of Phoebe. Annie responded to her mother's call to lunch with a quick, "Coming, Mama" and trotted downstairs to the kitchen.

Ellen told Annie she planned to continue sewing a skirt for a lady in town, and since she had no more chores for the girl, Annie was free for the remainder of the afternoon.

"No wall building, Annie."

Annie dropped her head. "I understand." She believed her parents might not permit wall-building any longer. She pondered for several minutes and announced she could clean the flower beds surrounding the house. Annie knew this chore was one her mother did not enjoy. Readying the flower beds for spring was a task Annie could complete with pleasure.

Annie's offer delighted Ellen. "Oh, thank you, dear! Put on your overalls and wear your galoshes. It's still muddy."

Annie did as her mother instructed. She hung her dress in her wardrobe, donned an old shirt and her overalls, and pulled on her big, rubber galoshes before heading to the shed. There, she retrieved her wagon, pruners, and rake. She and Bitsy then proceeded to the flower bed bordering the front porch. As she gathered leaves and spent flowers, she could hear the radio in the parlor playing a popular show for homemakers.

A familiar voice interrupted her efforts. It was Noah, demanding to know why she was not at the stone wall. Startled, Annie looked up, and there he was in the yard, leaning against the dogwood tree.

"Noah, I'm sorry," she whispered. "I may not go back there any longer by myself. I told Mama and Daddy about you, and they don't believe it's good for me to continue alone. They said I need to forget everything because telling the truth could hurt Miss Mittie and other people. The murders happened too long ago. Miss Mittie says we know the truth now, and you are free to pass over to the next world. Miss Mittie says it will do no good to bring up the whole affair."

Dejected, he knelt on one knee. His despair was palpable. "I see. Annie, my heart told me you were the teller of truths and that you will not give way to the directions of others. This turn of events is troubling. It is disappointing beyond my deepest dread."

"I'm sorry, so sorry. I hate to disappoint you, but now that Miss Mittie knows the truth, can't you pass over? Um, by the way, um, Noah, did you know what happened to Molly or her baby?"

The spirit shook his head. "I know not who Molly might be. One of the murdered men mentioned the name." He rose to his feet and walked away, shoulders bent. "I shall remain available to you should you regain the strength to seek the truth. I wish you had not revealed my existence. Darkness and despair have overcome me."

Annie tried to respond, but he left in an instant. This confrontation upset Annie. Annie had feelings for Noah and wished to help set him free. She abandoned her flower bed project and sat on the front step, wiping tears from her face as Bitsy rested her furry head on Annie's lap. This was the scene greeting Carter Young when he drove up the driveway earlier than expected.

"Annie, are you all right?"

Annie wiped her tears. "Yes, Daddy. I was thinking. The murders, you understand, and not wanting to hurt Miss Mittie."

"Been sitting here long?"

"No. I'm not sure. Just a little while, I guess. I was cleaning out the flower bed for Mama when . . . uh . . . I . . . just . . . got to thinking."

Carter Young sat on the step next to Annie and pulled her close, giving her a kiss on her cheek. As he patted Bitsy's head with his other hand, he hugged Annie tight.

"I'm sorry these developments have upset you so," Carter told her. "Too much to comprehend. You are a girl who shouldn't bear such a burden. The troubling things you learned and your meeting with this . . . um . . . ."

"Spirit?"

"Yes. These developments baffle me, dear Annie. I know not how to advise you. This also confounds your mother. Our primary concern is not to hurt you or Mrs. McCormick . . . or anyone."

Annie buried her head in his shoulder. She always felt safe in her father's arms, and even in her confused and conflicted state, in his arms she felt comforted. Both remained on the porch step embracing for several minutes until the girl pulled away and declared she was "fine" and wanted to complete her flower bed job.

As Annie resumed her work, Carter observed her behavior and noted how determined and detail-oriented she was. She pulled each spent flower and weed from the soil with meticulous precision, shook them off, and dropped them in the wheelbarrow. As Annie returned to raking leaves covering the soil, Carter wiped his brow, rose, and walked into the house.

"Ellen, I'm home early!" he called out so she could hear him over the radio and the hum of the sewing machine.

"What? My gracious! This is a surprise!" Ellen stopped sewing and entered the parlor to see Carter placing his medical bag next to the telephone table before heading into the kitchen.

Ellen followed him to the kitchen and saw the day's mail in his hands. With a mischievous grin, he handed her a letter from her mother as he asked her to sit at the table and not open the letter yet.

"We received good news today, Ellen."

Ellen's quizzical look amused him, and he laughed out loud. Impatient, she pounded her palm on the table. "What?"

"Do you recall the letter about the ranch I received a good while back from an oil company? It was a drilling contract, and I signed it and returned it in the mail. Do you recall?"

Ellen nodded, puzzled.

"Well, they struck oil on the home place, Ellen! Look at this check that came today!"

Carter handed the check to Ellen, who turned it over several times, her eyes widening each time she read the number. While not an enormous sum of money, it was a most welcome addition to their bank account. She laid it on the table and looked up at her husband.

"Carter, I'm flabbergasted! I thought oil companies weren't drilling now. Have you not read the newspaper? Drilling stopped because of the economy! It's been on the radio, too."

"They're still drilling in a few places, and it looks as if we have a piece of what they're searching for under the ground back there. This surprised me, too, but it's marvelous news, isn't it?"

Ellen's head swam with astonishment. This unexpected news eased her financial worries. Although monies brought in by her sewing provided a meager cushion to their finances, this added income held the promise of fattening that cushion.

Shaking her head again in disbelief, Ellen got up, wrapped her arms around Carter, and kissed him right on the mouth.

"This is splendid news! Oh, my goodness, Carter, what a surprise!" Ellen brought both hands to her mouth and shook her head again. "It's a godsend. What wonderful news the postman delivered today. This lifts a worry from our shoulders, does it not?"

"It does, my dear." Carter folded the check, returned it to the envelope in which it had arrived, and placed it in his medical case in the hall. He returned to the kitchen where Ellen, sitting at the table, read her mother's letter.

"Everything okay back there?"

"Fine. Mother's letters always include pleas for us to return. She repeats her complaint she is 'lonesome and blue.' Brother is fine. Mother says people are still experiencing difficulties. The drug store is surviving, though."

Bitsy's barking cut into their conversation, and the sounds of voices coming through the front door rang through the downstairs.

"Mama, Daddy! Blink and Miss Cora are here!"

Ellen and Carter rushed to the door to greet the visitors. Cora Hill was holding a steaming mock apple pie in her hands protected by several towels.

"Ellen, I tried this new recipe, and it made more than enough for us. It's supposed to taste the same as a real apple pie made with fresh fall apples."

Ellen took the pie from Cora, and they marched into the kitchen, giggling much the same as schoolgirls.

Annie and Blink remained with Carter in the parlor. Bitsy sat in eager anticipation of the attention she knew was coming from the boy.

"Annie, how you doing?" Blink asked as he rubbed Bitsy's ears. "How you doing, Doctor?"

Annie and Carter responded they were well. Annie and Blink then began a conversation pertaining to their respective schools as Carter joined the women in the kitchen.

After more pleasantries, Cora announced she and Blink must leave. "I'm glad I had the eggs you needed, Ellen. It was nice to sit a spell and visit with Annie this morning. She was interested in learning about Ned's family."

As she retrieved Blink from the parlor, Cora addressed Annie. "Annie, my Ned has lots of stories. Whenever you want to learn more, just catch him when he's resting."

After a short round of goodbyes, Ellen, Carter, and Annie retreated into the house. The couple exchanged concerned glances as they observed Annie climb the stairs to change out of her overalls and wash up for dinner. Lingering apprehension offset the relief they felt because of the news received in the mail that day. It was obvious from Cora's comments the girl was not abandoning her search for the truth.

THE MANUSCRIPT

March surrendered its chilly rains and blustery days to April. Spring enveloped the entire county with blossoms: the whites of apple trees and dogwoods, the purple pinks of redbuds. Virginia bluebells and wild violets sprouted throughout woodlands, giving the woods a purplish hue, and gentle winds drifted Lily of the Valley's sweet aroma through the air. Winter's brown transformed to lush green as birds fluttered around potential nesting sites and scurried for earthworms, early seeds, and emerging insects.

As April turned toward May, Annie longed to resume work on the stone wall. She kept the curtains on her bedroom window facing the property's rear boundary closed so she could not see Noah should he reappear. When Blink arrived at the wall to deposit a wheelbarrow load of rocks, he could tell there had been no recent work. A puzzled Blink dropped his load and returned home, telling Ned he did not think Annie was continuing with her project. Faithful to her parents' wishes, Annie had abandoned the wall.

Thursday afternoon visits with Miss Mittie continued, but mentions of Noah or long-ago events did not ensue. Games of dominoes were the primary pursuit. Miss Mittie asked Annie what books she was reading, but Annie told her she had no time for reading.

"That's odd," said Miss Mittie. "When Susie took me to the library yesterday, Georgia Albright said you were there every day after school."

"Um, yes. I'm doing research for a paper," Annie fibbed.

"What paper?"

"Um, a history paper. I'll finish soon."

Annie *had* been researching history at the library. Her research, however, was not for a required school project, but for her own information. Annie hoped to glean insights into what became of Molly and her baby. Had the truth of the murders of Molly's father and brother ever emerged from the deep well of secrets held within the hearts of those involved?

She hoped a glimmer of information could lead her to a rightful resolution, one that might enable Noah to leave his earthly prison.

When Annie's search of the reference section yielded nothing of value, she asked Mrs. Albright if the library contained a book relating to Hillview in another section of the library.

"Well, Annie, we have a handwritten manuscript an old gentleman wrote many years ago," Georgia Albright said. "The fellow wrote a history of the town and this part of the valley, but he never finished. When he died, his children gave us his papers. We don't display his manuscript on any shelf because the pages are fragile and unbound. It isn't a published volume, either. To be honest, I have read little of it. I am not sure it's even factual, so I hesitated to tell you of its existence. We never promote it to anyone. If you care to read it, I will get it, but you must be careful with it. It's fragile. Will you promise?"

This news thrilled Annie.

When Mrs. Albright set the papers in front of Annie, Annie saw worn and yellowed pages. The title page included a pen and ink drawing of the town square, and the handwritten title read "A History of Hillview and its Surrounds" by William

Walker Brown. The author had penned the history starting with pre-Revolution times. With caution, Annie thumbed through the manuscript and found pages numbered at the bottom. Her glance at the last page affirmed the volume ended around 1900. A newspaper clipping, the obituary of William Walker Brown, was tucked after the title page. It read:

William Walker Brown, Esq, age 78, departed this world for his heavenly home on September 26, 1921. Born in Hillview, death claimed the lawyer and well-known historian after two months of a lingering illness which his advanced years could not overcome. He resided at 153 East Thomas Street. Funeral services will be held on Thursday at 10:30 in the morning at the Methodist Church. Mr. Brown's parents were H.G. and Lollie Brown, descendants of Hillview's earliest residents. He is predeceased by his wife Mae. Mr. Brown is survived by his son W.W. of the home residence on Thomas Street, daughters Mrs. Dora Lancaster of Richmond, Virginia, Mrs. Aida Rogers of Chicago, Illinois, and Mrs. Berta Simmons of Hillview.

One name in the obituary gave her a start—Berta Simmons. Could that be the Rutledge housekeeper, Berta?

Annie found William Walker Brown's handwriting difficult to decipher, but she worked her way through the pages, absorbing each detail. Brown confirmed the name of the town's founder, his unsavory life, and circumstances of his death. The manuscript discussed Quaker families settling the region in the early 1700s, and Annie learned a Quaker settlement occupied a location along the macadam road between her home and downtown Hillview.

Mrs. Albright observed Annie as the girl read the manuscript. The librarian found it unusual that the precocious youngster showed such interest in an old man's recollections and research. When Mrs. Albright mentioned this to her colleague, Florence Bigler scowled and shook her head in a most disapproving manner.

"Why is that girl so snoopy?" Miss Bigler asked.

"Snoopy? I think it's nice she is interested in our region's history. Unique for sure, but nice. Annie is bright and loves to learn. I understand she is an excellent student."

"Learn what?" shot back Miss Bigler with a snarl. "She's nosy. She's looking for something. Trying to get dirt on someone, I'll wager you."

"Oh, Flo! Too suspicious you are. You suspect anyone who hasn't lived around here since Adam and Eve! Lighten up, why don't you?"

When Annie reached the Civil War period in the manuscript, she found descriptions of events and people fascinating. William Walker Brown detailed how the Hillview region changed hands several times, going from Union to Confederate and back, just as Miss Mittie remembered. Homes and other buildings served as hospitals. Several surnames mentioned were ones Annie recognized as those of current Hillview citizens.

When she reached page 148, she discovered a gap. Pages 149 through 167 were missing. Annie assumed at least a section of the missing pages applied to 1863 because the preceding ones described events of that year. Page 168 picked up in 1868. Where were the missing nineteen pages? She thumbed through the rest of the manuscript but discovered everything in perfect numerical order. This gap perplexed Annie, and that it covered the period of most interest to her, annoyed her.

"For goodness' sake, Mr. William Walker Brown! Where are those pages?"

The girl glanced at the clock over the check-out counter. It was nearing five o'clock. She gathered the papers, made a notation in her notebook where she had left off, and returned the document to Mrs. Albright.

"Learning interesting information, Annie?"

"Oh, yes. It is interesting. But, uh . . . Mrs. Albright, are you aware pages are missing from this manuscript?"

Georgia Albright shook her head. "No. But as I told you, I haven't read it. I glanced at a few pages at the beginning and thumbed through the rest."

Annie showed the librarian where the gap occurred. "He's describing events in 1863 on page 148. There are nineteen pages missing. Mr. Brown numbered his pages. Plus, when I started reading page 168, it made little sense, so it's plain those pages are missing and it's not a numbering problem. I looked for the pages throughout the rest of the manuscript."

"Annie, I'm sorry. I don't know. When Mr. Brown's daughter brought it to me, she didn't mention missing pages that I recall. She brought it in several years ago."

Annie thanked the librarian and left the library. Georgia Albright returned the manuscript to the back room where she returned it to a box marked "William Walker Brown History."

****

The next Thursday at the Rutledge home started as usual. As soon as Annie took her seat in the sun porch, she popped a question to Miss Mittie. "Where is Berta today?"

"Berta is here on Mondays and Thursdays, but she has a dentist appointment this afternoon. Bad toothache. Why do you ask?"

"I've been reading a history manuscript at the library. Mr. William Walker Brown wrote it, and Hillview's history is the theme. Mr. Brown's obituary is tucked inside, and it says one of his daughters is Berta Simmons. Could that be Mrs. Rutledge's Berta? Berta is an unusual name."

"Oh, yes, Annie! Berta was his youngest child. Mr. Brown was an attorney who considered himself a historian."

Annie's responded with a hushed, "Oh."

"The book speaks of Hillview, did you say?"

"It's a history of Hillview and the entire region. It starts way back."

"Ah, around the time of Hillview's founding, I suppose?"

"Yes, Miss Mittie. Before that time. The manuscript isn't complete, and it's not in a proper binding. It's handwritten, and it stops as if he just quit writing. Mrs. Albright said his children brought it to her after he died because they thought it should be in the library. Mrs. Albright doesn't put it on the shelf because it's very fragile and not a bound and published book."

"Mr. Brown died several years ago," Miss Mittie said. "His children sold the building where his law office was to Art Haverton, who operates a drug store there now. It is nice Georgia has kept his book safe."

"Well, Miss Mittie, I discovered yesterday that pages are missing. While I read it, I found a big gap. Nineteen pages. I showed it to Mrs. Albright, but she knew nothing. Mrs. Albright told me she has never read the manuscript."

Miss Mittie adjusted her bun. She smoothed the blanket around her feet and cleared her throat before speaking again, "What was happening when the gap occurred? Perhaps he made a mistake or thought those pages not important or incorrect and removed them."

Annie shook her head. "No, he numbered the pages, Miss Mittie. There are nineteen pages missing; pages 149 through 167 aren't there. Mr. Brown was describing events in 1863, and then it skips to something happening late in 1868 that has nothing to do with what he was describing. It makes no sense. It's as if somebody removed those pages on purpose."

"1863? What events, Annie?"

Annie hesitated before responding, "A church or meeting house burned. He . . . um . . . he . . . had earlier mentioned his friend . . . Albert . . . Blanton. That's when it stops, and pages are missing."

Miss Mittie's face took on a concerned countenance as she glanced at the blanket in her lap. Taking her handkerchief from the pocket of her sweater, she removed her glasses and wiped what appeared to Annie to be a tear from one eye. The petite woman addressed the girl seated in front of her.

"Annie, you are trying to uncover more on what Phoebe saw, are you not?"

Annie's head drooped. With hesitation, she raised her head and looked her friend in the eye. "Yes, I am, Miss Mittie. I didn't know this manuscript existed, but when I asked Mrs. Albright if there were any history books relating to Hillview, she showed it to me. Believe me, I don't want to hurt anyone. I just want to learn more. What happened to Molly and her baby? They worry me. I'm worried Morse Blanton might have taken Molly back and hurt her baby."

"I understand your curiosity. Yes, I recall that William Walker Brown and Albert Blanton were friends. They were near the same age. To be honest, I wondered in later years if Brown was with the Blantons the day Phoebe saw the terrible event. People knew William Walker Brown as Will Brown. His father, H.G., and Morse Blanton were close friends at one time, I believe. Will Brown is referring to the Quaker meeting house on the road from town leading out toward my childhood home. The meeting house burned not long before Phoebe's incident. It's difficult to see the remains from the road. During winter, you can see a chimney in the distance on the south side of the road. It's just this side of the big cornfield. Can't see it in summer because leaves are on trees next to the road, and corn is high. Mother and Papa were of the Quaker faith, the Society of Friends. Did I ever tell you that?"

Annie nodded as if her friend had been the first to report the information, although Annie learned it earlier from Cora Hill.

Miss Mittie acknowledged the nod. "Rumors circulated that southern sympathizers who could not abide Quaker belief that slavery was immoral set the fire. Quakers were pacifists, which means they didn't believe in war. Quakers settled here before the Revolutionary War, but more than a few considered

Quakers *different* if you will. Outsiders. Papa and Mother were not regular at meetings during the war, though. Papa tended to patients much of the time and kept the farm operating. Mother did not go without Papa for fear of running into soldiers. People said soldiers even hid in trees! Mother felt unsafe. One never knew when soldiers could appear. Both sides even came into Hillview and brought their war with them, sometimes injuring innocent residents. It was tragic when the meeting house burned. I must tell you my parents suspected Blanton or his friends may have done the deed. Morse Blanton was a malicious, Yankee-hating southerner. He was a cruel slave owner. He was not an exemplary man."

"Oh, Miss Mittie, I am sorry! Was this William Walker Brown a southern sympathizer, too?"

"I recall nothing specific concerning him or his father, but maybe they were. Who knows? One needed to be cautious when speaking back then. Hate and suspicion infected everything. As a child, I wasn't privy to much of that discourse."

"I see," said Annie. "Miss Mittie, I don't want to upset you. It must have been terrible. I want to know, though. Do you think Berta might know what happened to the missing pages?"

Miss Mittie shrugged. "I have no way of knowing, but I will ask her when she comes Monday if you wish. I'll tell her you are reading her father's manuscript at the library and you noticed several pages missing. Berta is dear, and she will tell me if she knows. I will let you know what she says next Thursday. How is that?"

"Yes! Wonderful!"

No mention of past events marred the rest of the afternoon. They began a game of dominoes, and in what felt an instant, it was time for Annie to leave. A quick peck on her friend's cheek followed by a cheery, "Goodbye, Mrs. Rutledge!" aimed in Susie's direction, and Annie was out the front door. She skipped along the sidewalk to the waiting Dodge with Ellen at the wheel.

After picking up Dr. Young at his office, the family headed home. As they passed the ruins now concealed by foliage, Annie told her parents it had once been a Quaker meeting house. "Someone burned it during the Civil War."

"I didn't know that," Ellen said. "Those ruins have aroused my curiosity before. Last winter, I noticed the chimney. I thought it was once someone's home. How terrible."

Annie disclosed that Mrs. McCormick said rumors circulated indicating southern sympathizers had set the fire. "They burned it because Quakers didn't believe in slavery or war. Isn't that awful?"

Ellen agreed it was awful.

"Those were sad and dangerous times," Carter agreed. He changed the topic by addressing Annie. "Annie, if weather permits and I don't have patient visits, why don't you and I continue rebuilding the stone wall? I know your heart is set on it, and, to be honest, I'd enjoy that, too. I'd find pleasure in seeing it as it once looked, and I'd appreciate a view of the apple orchard. The blooms on those trees are splendid right now."

This suggestion startled Ellen, but she remained silent. She desired the wall-building project stopped. Annie's reaction, however, was one of astonishment and glee because she feared a permanent prohibition on visits to the stone wall.

"Okay, Daddy!"

****

So, on a Saturday when sun shone bright and a deep blue sky held not one solitary cloud, Carter and Annie Young hiked to the wall and continued reconstructing the once well-defined and visible formation. They chatted of school and insignificant matters as they worked, stopping once in a while to rest on a stool, take a drink of water, and munch on crackers. Ellen surprised them at lunchtime with a basket of goodies she had prepared. Included were peanut butter and pickle sandwiches, hard-boiled eggs, cottage cheese, and one oatmeal cookie each. Carter offered Ellen his stool upon which to sit, where she perched and surveyed the wooded surroundings and the stone wall.

"Ellen, have you had lunch?"

"Yes, I have. I brought you two something to eat so you won't waste any of this perfect weather. I haven't ventured here before, and I thought it best for me to see firsthand what is so important to our daughter and my husband."

As she nibbled at her sandwich, Annie gazed at her mother. It was a pleasant surprise to see Ellen at the work site as she had never expressed interest in or support of the project and appeared adamant Annie not resume her work.

"Look, Mama, see how nice it looks!" Rising from her stool, Annie walked over to the wall and pointed out how the stones fit together. "Daddy and I have taken a good bit of time to arrange the stones so they will stay put. He helped me and showed me how to do it in the correct way. Look over there at the orchard. The apple trees are blooming and are just as lovely as they can be!" Annie pointed over the wall toward the neighboring property.

There he was. Noah stood on the other side of the wall, tipping his cap. Attempting to hide her astonishment, Annie feigned a cough and turned back toward her parents. Bitsy, happy to see Noah, began barking and jumping at the wall, tail in motion in its always quivering manner.

"I believe Bitsy likes the view too, Annie," said Ellen. "That dog is so funny sometimes."

"Um, she is," Annie responded with hesitation as she observed Noah reaching across the wall to pat Bitsy's head. "Uh, I . . . I . . . uh, I don't know why she acts the way she does."

Carter noted his daughter's behavior and that of the dog. He observed Ellen who was taking a sip of coffee from the thermos she had brought as she looked along the length of the completed wall. Carter's gaze turned back to Bitsy who was acting as if someone was patting her head. Dr. Carter Young acknowledged the scene as if he knew someone was, indeed, patting her head.

Ellen soon gathered the remains of lunch and dropped them in her basket. Strolling over to her husband, she gave him a quick kiss and turned to Annie.

"Enjoy your day, Annie. Don't work too hard! You, too, Carter!"

As Ellen strolled back to the house, she stopped, turned, and observed Carter and Annie as they resumed their work. She had voiced concerns regarding Annie working alone on the project, but with Carter on the scene, everything was fine. This arrangement satisfied Ellen because she understood her husband and daughter enjoyed the work and time together. She even came to appreciate the view of the orchard with its ocean of cotton white blossoms.

Neither Carter nor Ellen could see the figure overseeing their efforts—the ragtag youth of a different time chasing little Bitsy around the trees as Carter studied placement of stones.

Ellen stole one last glance at her daughter and husband together at the wall as she closed the back door and reflected on the scene.

"Our life is good."

THAT'S WHY, AND THAT'S WRONG

"Good afternoon, Annie! How are you this exquisite spring day?" Berta Simmons flung the door open to welcome Annie to the Rutledge home.

The sight of Berta delighted Annie. She was eager to learn what the woman knew of the missing pages to William Walker Brown's manuscript and could hardly contain herself. "I'm fine, thank you!"

As Berta ushered Annie onto the sun porch for her weekly visit, she stopped in the hallway and addressed the girl with a soft smile. "Miz M tells me you are reading my father's manuscript at the library."

"Yes, I'm interested in learning more about this part of the country. It's very interesting."

"Dad considered himself a historian, you know. He wrote of things he researched and heard from old-timers. I vaguely remember the piece you're reading. I must tell you; I had forgotten one of my sisters took it there."

Annie then asked the question to which she wanted an affirmative answer. "Did you know pages are missing, Miss Berta?"

"Annie, I did not. Dad tossed things around his desk and his study. Tidy he was not. My father added pages to his works, and he took pages out. He had a box at one time that contained his discards and other items, and he kept it in a special compartment in his study at our house. The compartment wasn't small. It was spacious and concealed inside the wall behind a shelf on his bookcase. Dad called it his cubbyhole. I thought it odd he had such a thing, but he was eccentric. Do you know what that means?"

Annie nodded. "Somewhat odd?"

Berta cackled. "That's right! That was Dad! Annie, I'm uncertain my siblings even knew his cubbyhole existed. I was the youngest by several years, and I spent a fair chunk of time with him in his study. I played with items he kept on his desk and on his bookshelf. The smell of his pipe was strong in the room, and I liked the smell! Children can be funny, sometimes, you know."

Annie chuckled. She did not share Berta's appreciation of a pipe's aroma, but she could imagine a little girl playing with desk accessories just to be near her father. Annie remembered doing the same thing as a young child before the family's move.

Berta continued. "You've piqued my curiosity, Annie. I'll check the cubbyhole as soon as I go home. I live in our old family home now. My brother lived there until he died six years ago. When my husband died a couple years back, my sisters and I decided I should live there so things wouldn't deteriorate. Sisters live too far from here to check on it, and they are getting along in years. It sat empty after my brother died. The house is too big for just me, but I close off rooms I don't use, so it's fine. Dad's study is one of those rooms. I haven't been in it in months and months. My brother never used it either, so it looks just as it did when Dad died. I cover the furniture to keep the dust off everything. Next week, when you come for your visit, I will let you know what I uncover. The cubbyhole is empty, I imagine, so I doubt if I will find any pages to his manuscript."

"Oh, that's nice of you, Miss Berta! I appreciate it. Maybe we can solve the mystery of the missing pages!"

Berta hooted once again. Berta was a gentle soul with a hearty cackle that could make any person smile. Right before Annie walked through the door to the sun porch, Berta patted the girl on her back and snickered, "We're just two detectives, aren't we?"

Berta returned to the kitchen. Miss Mittie flashed an enormous smile as Annie entered and sat across from her at the table where they played dominoes.

"Berta told me she will search for your missing pages, Annie. She's a sweetheart, is she not?"

"She is. I hope she finds them!"

Annie's beloved Miss Mittie smiled and began placing dominoes on the table. They mentioned nothing more of missing pages or the whereabouts of Molly. Miss Mittie's lilting laughter and discussions of plans for the coming summer were the only sounds coming from the sun porch that afternoon.

****

When Annie arrived at the Rutledge home the following Thursday afternoon, Susie Rutledge met her at the door. Susie informed the girl in her usual monotone voice that three boxes waited for her on the sun porch. Berta had received a telegram from her ailing sister in Chicago who needed Berta's help. So, Berta dropped off the boxes before leaving on the train for Chicago. Susie ushered Annie to the sun porch where Miss Mittie and three boxes awaited.

The grande dame of the sun porch was sipping tea when the girl arrived, and she set her cup on the table as soon as Annie entered the room. "Well, I bet you did not expect this!" Miss Mittie pointed to the boxes sitting in a corner.

Annie's eyes grew large as she stared at the boxes. They were so large she was not sure she could even get them into the car when her mother came to retrieve her. She rushed over and stared at the one on top. When she opened a flap, she saw it filled with yellowed and musty smelling papers and more papers, crumpled, smooth, and torn. Annie turned to her confidante and shook her head, her mouth open in amazement.

"Berta said everything in her father's cubbyhole is in those boxes, Annie. She had no clue the cubbyhole contained so much. Berta apologized for their condition, but she had no time to examine any of the items before she left. I have instructions from her that you may look at *everything* to see if your missing pages are there. Berta said you may find the contents informative."

"Oh, my goodness, Miss Mittie! I don't believe it! That cubbyhole must be enormous!"

"I reckon so! Here's a note Berta left. Read it."

Annie opened the envelope and removed the note it contained. She read it aloud:

Dear Annie,

I am sorry I had no time to organize or examine this mess. It may be awhile before I return from my sister's home, so please go through everything.

What a surprise it was for me to find Dad's cubbyhole crammed with these papers! I was completely unaware. Dad kept his things in no order or fashion, so I packed everything from the cubbyhole into these boxes. Maybe you'll find something of interest. They smell musty from being locked in the wall. You might wish to air out the papers.

Berta

"Well, Annie, I believe you have something to occupy your time when school is out!" Miss Mittie said. "I wish to offer you the opportunity to keep the boxes here and sort through everything, but Susie doesn't appreciate disorder. Take them to your home, please."

"It will be fine, I'm sure. We don't use one bedroom, so I can spread things out on the beds in there."

Impatient Annie wanted to search the boxes' contents, but she played a game of dominoes with her friend. They had no time to complete the game before Susie Rutledge entered the room and directed Annie to ready the boxes for transport before Ellen arrived. Annie could see Susie's authoritarian manner annoyed Miss Mittie, but the woman could do nothing other than toss her daughter a disapproving glance, which Susie either did not see or ignored.

Annie took the boxes and set them on the front stoop before she returned and gathered her satchel. When she leaned to give her friend a quick kiss, Miss Mittie brought out another box, a small one she had concealed in the chair under her blanket.

"A little birdie told me Saturday is your birthday, Annie! Here is something for you. Don't open it now! Wait until Saturday! It holds good wishes and lots of love from me."

Annie was speechless. She could only muster a weak, "Oh, thank you, Miss Mittie!"

A car horn tooted out front, so Annie tucked the box into her satchel, ran to the front door, opened it and waved at her mother. To Ellen's surprise, the girl hauled a box from the porch to the waiting vehicle, setting it on the grass. She returned to the porch and brought the other two boxes out, setting them on top of each other. Ellen exited the Dodge and walked around to the side where the boxes sat.

"What is this?" Ellen stared as Annie offered an impish grin.

"Oh, Mama, let's get them in the car, and I'll explain. Will they fit in the back seat?"

With much effort, the two situated the boxes so they could shut the door before they climbed into the car.

"Okay, Mama, let's go!"

"Yes, we will. So, what are these boxes, daughter!" Ellen asked as they drove away.

Annie answered with a coy smile. "Well, I don't know. I will tell you and Daddy what I know when we pick him up at his office. And Mama, Miss Mittie gave me a birthday gift." She pulled the small box from the satchel's inner pocket and showed it to her mother, who acknowledged it was a sweet gesture for Mrs. McCormick to remember Annie's birthday.

A puzzled Ellen and an overjoyed Annie rounded the corner to Carter's office where Ellen parked at the curb and sounded the horn. Maude Renner opened the office door, waved at Ellen and Annie, and shouted, "Doctor will be out in a flash!"

When Carter started toward the car, Annie crawled into the back seat and wedged herself next to the boxes. Her father peered into the car as he eased into the front passenger seat. There was no room for his physician's bag in the back, so he held it on his lap.

"What on earth do we have here, girls?"

Ellen replied that Annie had brought the boxes from the Rutledge house and promised to explain why they occupied the back seat as soon as Carter sat in the front seat.

"All right, Miss Anna Ruth Young, you almost fourteen-year-old, you. What's in those boxes?" Carter asked.

As they rolled along toward their home, Annie related the story of William Walker Brown's manuscript, the missing pages, and the cubbyhole at Berta's house. Ellen and Carter listened, each with varying degrees of concern over the obvious fact Annie was investigating the murders despite their warnings. As she chattered on describing what she had learned so far from the manuscript, Ellen's concern deepened. A darkness overtook her face, which she attempted to hide from Annie. Carter showed no outward concern. He just listened, nodding at intervals to show he was soaking up the information.

By the time they reached home, Annie had completed her story and scrutinized her parents' faces for indications as to their thoughts. She knew her research was worrisome and uppermost in their thinking. Approval from her parents was not optional to Annie. She adored them both and never wished to disappoint.

No one spoke. Carter deposited his medical bag on the front porch and returned to retrieve a box. Ellen opened the front door of the house, and Bitsy buzzed past, leaping off the porch.

"Let's set the boxes here for now, Ellen." He put the first box on the parlor floor. Annie then set her box on top of the first one. When they returned to the car, Carter brought in the remaining box while Annie retrieved her satchel.

"Daddy, are you disappointed in me?"

"Disappointed, Annie?"

"Because I have been investigating local history?"

Carter Young shook his head. "Oh, sweet girl, knowing your disposition, it would disappoint me if you were not. Your mother and I just hope you do nothing to hurt Mrs. McCormick or anyone else. I think it's healthy for you, though, to learn of that time in history. Does Mr. Brown's book tell you a good bit?"

Annie nodded as she set her box in the parlor. "The manuscript is interesting, Daddy. I hope the missing pages are in these boxes."

Dinner conversation included nothing on Annie's research. Instead, Ellen asked if Annie wanted to have a birthday party to celebrate her upcoming fourteenth birthday. "Invite friends to come here or treat them to a movie in town. I understand a comedy is playing called *We're Not Dressing*. It stars Bing Crosby, Carole Lombard, George Burns, and Gracie Allen. What are your thoughts?"

Annie sat motionless for a few moments as she considered the opportunity. With a sip of her milk, she exhaled and replied, "No, Mama. I might enjoy the movie, but to be truthful, I am not close friends with anyone at school. Besides Miss Mittie, my best friend is Blink, and he tells me he can't sit in the regular seats at the movie theater. He must sit in the balcony where Negroes are required to sit. I don't want a party."

The realization that Annie still considered herself an outsider plus the grim reminder of Hillview's racial attitudes distressed Ellen. She winced, and her shoulders sagged.

Annie said, "Maybe we can eat a special dinner in town? At Olivia Watson's Diner? Her food is a treat, and Mama won't need to cook! Maybe we can go see the movie? Just we three?"

Ellen hid her disappointment as she slid her napkin on the table. "Carter, how is that idea?" She rose from her seat, picked up a bowl of leftover mashed turnips, and started back into the kitchen.

"Fine idea, Annie!" Carter slapped the table with his hand. "What time is the Saturday matinee, Ellen? We can get delirious at the theater and devour a delicious dinner at the diner!"

Annie started giggling at Carter Young's alliterative comment. She, too, rose from the table and started assisting her mother with clearing the table.

"Daddy, did you decide during the delectable dinner we just devoured that a delicious and delightful dinner at the diner will be dazzlingly decadent?"

"Why, Annie, indeed I did!"

Ellen threw back her head as she balanced dishes in her arms. "You two are so silly!"

****

Saturday morning promised a perfect spring day of few clouds and cool temperatures. The family started Annie's birthday with a breakfast of flapjacks, and Annie opened her parents' gift after the meal. She received a new flowered jumper Ellen had sewn, which delighted the birthday girl. In addition, she received three dollars tucked in an envelope mailed from her grandparents. Annie remembered the box given her by Miss Mittie and raced up the stairs to retrieve it from her satchel. When she came downstairs and opened it, she found a small gold locket inside with a note written in an old woman's scrawl.

Dear Annie,
   Phoebe gave me this little locket right before Papa took her to the sanitarium. Phoebe is the girl in the photograph. I hope you will treasure the locket.
I love you, dear Annie,
Miss Mittie

"Oh, Mama here is Phoebe! Does she not have a delicate face? Look, Daddy! What a special gift from Miss Mittie!" Annie was so touched by the present, that tears welled up in her big brown eyes and streamed along her freckled cheeks.

Ellen turned the locket over in her hand and peered at the girl inside the piece. A sadness swept over her as she remembered the story of Phoebe's tragic life. "Yes, she is exquisite." The countenance in the locket projected a haunting feature that affected Ellen. She wiped a tear as she handed the locket to Carter.

Carter's response was a tender admonishment to Annie to care for the locket because it was precious. It was precious to Mrs. McCormick, so precious that she had given it to Annie to keep forever. It was now Annie's responsibility to take care of it. Annie made a solemn promise to her father to always treasure the locket as Ellen hung it around her daughter's neck.

"What an extraordinary birthday!" the girl announced. "I have a new jumper, three whole dollars, and this locket. Plus, Mama made a wonderful breakfast, and we are going to a movie and dine at the diner for dinner! I think fourteen is a grand birthday! Thank you, Mama and Daddy!"

The three laughed and hugged each other. Bitsy jumped into Carter's arms and licked each one's face.

"We have chores to complete before we go into town, though," Carter said. "I must do repairs in the bathroom. Ellen has clothes to hang out, and even the birthday girl must do her Saturday chores. Let's get going!"

Each proceeded to their awaiting tasks. As Ellen hung laundry on the clothesline, Bitsy grabbed a shirt from the laundry basket and headed toward the rear woods with the shirt trailing from her mouth.

Flabbergasted, Ellen yelled to the dog in as loud a voice as she could muster, but the pesky pup ignored her pleas to drop the shirt. Annie bounded to the kitchen door to ascertain the cause of the commotion. The tone in her mother's voice alarmed her, and she worried Bitsy might be in danger.

"Annie, Bitsy stole a shirt from the wash basket and ran toward the backwoods! She won't stop, and I can't see her. Go get her!" Ellen's annoyance was unmistakable as she continued hanging the rest of the wash.

Annie raced to the back where Bitsy dragged the shirt through the grass and dirt until it snagged on tree stubble, causing the dog to lose her grip.

"Bitsy, what on earth got into you?" Annie stopped where the torn shirt clung to the small stump. "Oh, no! Look at Daddy's shirt! It's ruined, you naughty dog!" Her exasperation at the dog's antics turned to tears as she examined what remained of Carter's shirt. Bitsy continued to the wall and barked in the direction of a tree. As if on cue, Noah, appeared, bent over, and patted Bitsy on her head. He then picked her up in his arms and strolled to where Annie stood, holding the torn shirt in her hands.

"The absence of your company has left me despondent, Annie," Noah said in his gentle drawl.

"I told you I'm not allowed to come back here unless my father is with me, Noah."

"Yes, you explained this to me, but still I have missed your company and that of little Miss Bitsy here. Your investigation?

Progress? You may find it necessary to go across lots to force the truth to light."

Annie took a profound breath. She told Noah of William Walker Brown's manuscript, the missing pages, and of Berta's discovery. His eyes lit at once, and he urged her to scour the papers Berta had found for any additional information. "Please, Annie," he implored.

Annie reached for the locket hanging around her neck and opened it. "Miss Mittie gave me this locket, Noah. This is Phoebe!"

Noah leaned closer and took the locket in his hand. His brow deepened as he studied the tiny image. "This is the girl." His tone was sober. He closed the locket and stepped back, once again imploring Annie to right the wrong from many years ago.

Annie winced, pondered for a moment, then sprinted back to the house where Ellen waited. Noah put Bitsy at his feet and instructed the dog to "go home," and without hesitation, the dog obeyed.

A breathless Anna Ruth Young arrived in the kitchen, clutching the torn shirt. The screen door banged behind her, startling Ellen who had just gone inside the house.

"Oh, Bitsy! What have you done?" Ellen grasped the shirt in her hands and held it up to the light to survey the damage. "It's a dirty mess, and it's ripped from one end to the other. It's ruined!"

"Mama, I don't know what got into Bitsy. She acted as if she was playing a game." In her own mind, Annie was certain the dog pulled the shirt from the basket knowing Annie would chase her to the stone wall where Noah waited.

Carter entered the kitchen carrying his hammer. He had been upstairs in the bathroom nailing window trim around a drafty window.

"What's the commotion?"

Ellen shook her head and told him what Bitsy had done. "It was one of your good shirts she dragged through the yard! It caught on something and tore so much I can't mend it. Oh, that dog!"

Carter's response was a simple shrug. The ruined shirt did not unsettle him.

Lunchtime approached, so Ellen fixed a light meal, and the three prepared to attend the comedy matinee playing at the town's one movie theater.

Motion pictures during the Great Depression provided afternoons and evenings of fantasy and escape from the somber realities of the day. Comedies lifted spirits and brought joy into people's hearts, while westerns brought excitement and suspense. Even in desperate times, people paid the fifteen-cent admission price with no hesitation. The afternoon of Annie's fourteenth birthday was no exception, and moviegoers filled the theater.

Before the feature film started, a newsreel provided a window into world events, and after the newsreel, posters advertising coming attractions splashed on the screen. The theater's owner took to the stage and promoted an upcoming talent show. Then, as the movie clicked along, the entire theater erupted into gales of laughter with each absurdity. Annie and her parents enjoyed themselves that pleasant Saturday afternoon.

As throngs of patrons were leaving the theater, Annie heard her name called. "Annie, hey, Annie!" It was Blink who was exiting the theater's side door with his parents.

"Hello, Blink!" she shouted toward her friend. Ellen

waved at Cora as Ned turned to see to whom his son was speaking.

Blink, grinning and jumping with excitement, stopped and waited for Annie's family to catch up to him and his parents.

"Wasn't it a f-funny show, Annie?" Blink's eyes flickered in quick succession. "I l-loved it!"

Carter tipped his hat to Ned and Cora and addressed Blink. "You bet it was, Blink!"

Annie and Blink engaged in animated chatter, and Annie repeated her adoration for Carole Lombard. There on the sidewalk next to the theater, the four adults exchanged brief pleasantries as other theatergoers passed them by.

Annie heard her name called again. This time, four girls from her class at school beckoned to her. The group headed toward Annie. The girls stopped in front of Annie and asked if she had enjoyed the show.

"Oh, yes, I did! I love Carole Lombard, don't you?"

Annie noticed the girls were not looking at her as she spoke, but were instead staring at Blink and his parents, then back at Annie's parents. They did not respond to her remark referring to the blonde actress.

Ellen interjected, "Annie, please introduce us to your friends!" She understood the curious stares and was attempting to defray the disdain radiating from the girls' faces.

Annie did as her mother instructed, introducing the girls to her parents and then to Blink and his parents. Each adult responded with a "pleased to meet you," and Blink nodded his head several times, his nervousness preventing him from uttering a sound.

Annie's classmates acknowledged her parents but ignored Blink, Cora, and Ned before they continued along the sidewalk. "See you at school, Annie," shouted one as they merged into the crowd.

Annie did not respond to the four girls. Instead, she turned to the Hill family. "I'm sorry they were rude. They're not good friends of mine."

Cora brushed off the girl's remark with a wave of her hand and a generous smile. "Immature girls can be that way. Think nothing of it."

"We are going to Olivia Watson's Diner for supper! Today is my birthday, and this movie and the diner are part of my birthday celebration. Do you want to come? Please do!" Annie asked with anticipation as she focused back and forth between Cora, Blink, and Ned.

Ned stepped in before anyone else could say a word. "Thank you much, Annie, but we can't today. Happy Birthday to you, though! We must get on our way now."

His father's response disappointed Blink. Blink attempted to engage Ned with a plea to join the Youngs at the diner. Annie, too, frowned but said nothing. Ned tipped his hat to Ellen and Carter, said, "Good to see you," took Cora's arm, and crossed the street. They turned left into the alley running perpendicular to the street.

Blink lingered with Annie, watching his parents walk away, hoping they might leave without him so he could go with Annie and her parents.

"Tobias!" Ned stomped back to the sidewalk and barked, "Come now!"

Blink started running toward Ned, looking back and waving. Carter and Ellen continued walking to their car parked along the street. Annie shrugged her shoulders, shook her head, and quickened her step to catch up with her parents.

The three piled into the Dodge, and Annie sighed and stared out the window as they drove away. When Carter rounded the corner on the next block, Annie waved to the four girls from her class who congregated on the sidewalk, laughing and flirting with two boys. The girls spotted Annie in the back seat of the vehicle, and instead of waving in response, they glared at Annie as the car rolled by the group.

Carter was oblivious to the girls on the corner, but Ellen observed their behavior with concealed sadness. Turning to Annie, she said, "What do you wish to eat at Olivia's tonight, birthday girl?"

As she shook her head, Annie responded with a quiet, "I don't know" and sank into the seat.

A joyous, celebratory dinner did not ensue. The experience with Annie's classmates and Ned's sudden departure cast a pall over the Youngs' pale green-clad table. Ellen and Carter attempted to introduce topics of conversation, but Annie responded with simple nods and an occasional, "Uh, huh."

Carter repeated how flavorful his dinner was and was starting yet another, "My, this dish is tasty" when Annie interrupted him.

"I wish Blink's family could have come with us."

Ellen cleared her throat. "Annie, your invitation was thoughtful, but . . . uh . . . the Hills could not eat here. Only, uh . . . white people can eat here, I am afraid to say."

"What? Why is that?" Annie was incredulous.

Ellen looked at Carter as if to implore him to answer the question. She realized he was wavering, trying to think how to answer, so she reluctantly proceeded.

"It's the same reason Blink told you he is required to sit in the balcony at the theater. Negroes may not eat in restaurants here. It's a rule in Hillview. I'm afraid you need to know that Hillview is what's known as a Sundown Town. That means colored people may not be in town after sundown. It's not fair nor right, but those are the rules. I don't understand it, and I hate it, but it's the way things are here and in other regions, the South in particular. Ned didn't want to make you uncomfortable by explaining. That's the reason he left so fast."

"Those are stupid and ugly rules! They're unfair!" Annie's indignant exclamation generated disapproving glances from the next table. "Who made up those rules?" In a muffled voice to her father, she said, "But Olivia Watson is a nice lady. Why does she have that rule?"

Carter cleared his throat before giving her an answer, an answer he knew could not satisfy her curiosity and an answer he knew was not a moral one.

"Annie, these types of, uh, traditions have carried over since after the Civil War. A segment of society believes colored people are inferior to white people. It is unfortunate that white folks in various places have these rules and laws. Is it right? No, it's not. It is *not* right. Your mother and I treat each person with dignity. We do not believe anyone is inferior to another, and we want you to always be respectful of others, black or white, brown or . . . *whatever* and believe the same as we believe. I'm sorry this situation exists in Hillview. I hope one day it will be different, I sure do, but it's best not to cause trouble for Blink and his family. We don't want to put them into a position where they could be embarrassed."

The dejected birthday girl hung her head. As she lifted her head to study her parents and other patrons at Olivia Watson's Diner, she saw only white faces. Her innocence had collided with ugly reality. Of course! That was why Blink and his family exited the theater through a side entrance. The side entrance led to the balcony where they were required to sit. That was why Blink attended another school away from town. That was why it surprised Blink when they first met that she thought he attended her school. That was why her classmates glared at the gathering of two families, one black and one white, on the sidewalk. That was why she saw no black faces in the Hillview Presbyterian Church. That was why no black faces expressed delight at the lighting of the town Christmas tree. That was why. It dated back to the time Phoebe Mueller saw two black men murdered and nobody cared.

"Oh, I see now. That's why." She shook her head as she spoke. "And that's wrong."

NINETEEN PAGES

S unday morning after Annie's birthday, a clanging telephone in the downstairs hallway disrupted the subdued atmosphere at breakfast. It was the hospital calling to tell Carter they had admitted one of his patients who suffered from an undetermined illness and was in dire condition. Carter dressed in a hurry and grabbed his doctor's bag as he dashed out the front door.

"I suppose there will be no church for us this morning, Annie." Ellen's tone was one of resignation as she watched him drive away.

This development relieved Annie. The opportunity to open the boxes from Berta had not presented itself since she left them in the unused bedroom upstairs.

"I want to examine the boxes Berta gave me, Mama. Unless you have chores for me?"

Ellen understood her daughter was eager to see what mysteries she might solve. She shook her head in reluctant capitulation and gave Annie permission to delve into the boxes once breakfast was over and she was dressed.

Thus began a new phase of Annie's search for the truth. She entered the bedroom where three boxes rested on a bed, heaved a sigh, and opened one. Berta had crammed an enormous volume of stuff into it, and Annie could discern no order to the material. The musty smell of papers long forgotten in the cubbyhole rose from the carton as soon as she opened it.

"Oh, phew! What an awful smell! I suppose I will have to look at one page at a time and try to organize them," she told Bitsy who was lying on the other bed. "Even if I find nothing relating to Molly or the murders, I can help Berta by getting things in order and airing out this mess. This box is a disaster!"

In a systematic fashion, Annie scanned each scrap, card, and sheet of paper, sorting each into stacks according to what they appeared to be. She emptied the first box in just over one hour. When she opened the second box, she found several legal documents folded inside envelopes. These she arranged in a separate stack to examine later. Toward the bottom of the box, she uncovered several papers bound with string. Those were letters addressed to William Walker Brown. She tossed those in yet another stack with plans to read them later.

In what appeared to Annie a brief period, Ellen called her to lunch. At first bite, Ellen wasted no time inquiring as to Annie's progress. Annie explained her method of organization and told her mother she was near the bottom of the second box.

"My goodness, I thought it might take you days and days to go through everything!"

"I've read nothing in depth. The mess needs organization so I can read everything. I see lots of things aren't of interest to me. Lots of invoices and such. I'm not sure what these papers relate to, but I haven't found the missing pages from his manuscript yet."

When Annie returned upstairs to the scene of her detective work, she laughed out loud at the disarray. She launched into the remains of the second box and finished organizing in under thirty minutes. There appeared to be no explicit reason William Walker Brown hid so much in his cubbyhole.

"Mr. Brown, you messy man!" Annie said. "Here we go again." She opened the third box with a sigh.

Near the top of the third box's contents rested another set of smooth and unwrinkled papers, handwritten and bound with string. When she glanced at the first page, she saw the number 149 at the bottom. As she thumbed through the remaining pages, it astonished her to see they ranged from 149 to 167!

Her heart pounded as she pored over each page. The pages detailed events of a day in 1863. Morse and Albert Blanton and, yes, William Walker (Will) Brown and his father, H.G. Brown, had an encounter in an orchard that resulted in the murder of two black men.

The documents revealed that Molly's father Israel and brother Ben had followed the two Blantons and two Browns to the field beyond Annie's stone wall. The Blanton and Brown men planned a day of turkey hunting. Brown's account confirmed that Israel and Ben were former slaves once owned by Morse Blanton. Israel accused Albert Blanton of inappropriate conduct with his daughter Molly, resulting in her being with child. A livid Israel continued his tirade against Albert. Ben tried to restrain his father, but Albert's insolence, denials, and scoffing at the accusation escalated hostilities. William Walker Brown detailed the shooting of both Israel and Ben as sudden and shocking, just as Phoebe and Noah had described.

Morse Blanton's violence left the other three stunned. Albert Blanton and Will Brown remained mute, but H.G. Brown chastised Morse in a harsh and unrelenting manner until Morse Blanton's meanest, bullying nature reared its ugly head. He seized the elder Brown by the shoulder, throwing him to the ground and striking him with brutal kicks to his midsection and buttocks while wielding his hickory stick. Morse then pulled his Colt six-shooter and aimed it at the elder Brown's head, uttering obscenities as he did so.

207

Albert held Will Brown back when he attempted to protect his father from further harm. In an instant, Morse holstered his gun and slammed his hickory whipping stick across Will Brown's arm, ripping open the flesh and causing significant pain. Old Blanton then ordered the others to load the bodies onto the horses and exit the vicinity, which they did. William Walker Brown described their trek to a site near a creek on Blanton's property, well beyond view of any neighbors, dwellings, or travelers. The manuscript detailed the burial of two bodies in shallow graves dug with haste using shovels Albert had fetched from the Blanton barn.

It became plain to Annie that William Walker Brown was attempting to free his conscience with this part of his manuscript. In his writing, Brown asserted that Morse Blanton blackmailed his father, H.G. Brown, by threatening to say young Will Brown shot the men in an insane rage and tried to kill Morse Blanton. Again and again, Blanton threatened to bring charges of attempted murder against William Walker Brown. Any injuries inflicted upon the Brown men by Morse Blanton was justifiable self-defense, he planned to claim. Fear

of such threats and incrimination bought the everlasting silence Morse Blanton desired from Will Brown, H.G. Brown, and his own son, Albert.

"Morse Blanton was a horrible man, Bitsy! What a cruel, rotten person he was!"

The missing pages mentioned Phoebe, too. William Walker Brown expressed regret that she became the object of ridicule and malicious gossip. He did not mention her by name, but his descriptions left no doubt as to whom he referred. As to the friendship between Morse Blanton and H.G. Brown, it ended that day in the field, according to the author.

The plot then took an extraordinary turn. As Annie read the remaining pages, she gasped and grabbed her face in disbelief. From Brown's words, she learned Albert Blanton and Molly were lovers. Albert planned to take Molly and leave the locale to start a life together farther north where a multi-racial couple might experience less hate and exclusion. Albert confided this to his best friend, Will Brown, who then conveyed the tale to anyone who read his manuscript. Albert's father knew of the relationship but thought it was only Albert sowing his wild oats. Molly had been Morse Blanton's property, and Albert was welcome to do what he wished with such. Although Albert maintained his aloof and superior manner to curry his father's favor, Brown's missing pages revealed he was in actuality a gentle fellow who cherished Molly in secret.

The nineteen pages further detailed that Albert and Molly did not go north as planned. Brown gave no reason for this, but Albert stayed in Hillview and joined his father in the bank.

No further mention of Molly appeared in the remaining pages. It was as if Molly had evaporated into thin air.

A frantic Annie thumbed through the remaining papers in the third box, attempting to find any answers to the mystery of Molly and her baby. None could she find, and as she flung the last paper to the floor, she heard her father's voice calling from downstairs.

"Ellen! Annie! I'm home now!"

Bitsy leaped to her feet and bounded down the stairs, sliding on the hardwood floor as Annie raced behind.

"Hello, Daddy! How is your patient?" Annie gave him a tight hug.

"Mr. Graham was in a perilous state. I performed an appendectomy, and he should recover just fine. The nurses on duty at the hospital are diligent. I'll return after supper to check on him, though. Smells good, Ellen!"

Annie had lost track of time. She, too, could smell something inviting in the oven.

"It will soon be ready, so come help get the table set, will you, Annie?" called Ellen.

During the meal, Ellen informed Carter of Annie's detective work. Both queried the girl as to her findings, and Annie could not contain her enthusiasm as she relayed the information she had found the missing pages. She shocked her parents with the news that Albert Blanton had planned to leave the region with Molly to begin a life together elsewhere. By the time Annie finished speaking, she was breathless.

Carter was first to respond. "That's amazing, Annie! It's impressive that you turned up Mr. Brown's missing pages, and it's astonishing that young Albert was in a serious romantic relationship with Molly. So unusual for that time in history. Dangerous, even. I find this information . . . it's . . . it's *miraculous*. Lord, what a shock!" He rubbed his chin with his hand and turned to Ellen, his mouth open in disbelief.

Ellen agreed. She voiced the opinion that it was obvious Albert was not the unsavory person they and others believed him to be. "I agree with your father that you've made a remarkable discovery. This Morse Blanton fellow was loathsome, a repugnant man. I'm saddened to learn this. It's tragic."

Annie informed them she had not yet examined several stacks of what appeared to be letters. "I still am wondering what happened to Molly and to her baby. This makes the mystery more, uh, strange, don't you think?"

"It does, it does," said Ellen as she began gathering the dinner dishes.

While Ellen and Annie washed dishes, Carter sat in the kitchen sipping at a cup of coffee, observing his beloved wife and daughter. He rose and planted a light kiss on each of their cheeks, then placed his cup on the kitchen counter. As he walked to the hall and picked up his medical bag, he called back to the kitchen. "I'm off to the hospital to check on Mr. Graham. I'll be back before long."

After mother and daughter put away the dishes, Ellen suggested tuning into a radio program while they awaited Carter's return. But tonight, radio was an unwelcome distraction to Annie. She explained to her mother that she could not pay attention to a radio show while her mind raced through the possibilities lingering in the boxes upstairs. It was obvious to Ellen this was true, so she relented and urged the girl to look at everything.

"Examine every paper, Annie. Every single piece of paper."

Annie scanned paper after musky paper, bundle after bundle. When she untied yet another bundle, she was expecting to find more random letters or notes of little importance. The contents of this stack astounded her much the same as her discovery of the missing pages. Letters addressed to William Walker Brown from one Albert Blanton made up much of the contents. Those contained instructions from Blanton concerning Molly and her baby, a boy named James.

"Oh, my! Gosh!" she cried to Bitsy as she read through the following letter:

Willy,

Such tragic developments have transpired in recent months that I cannot consider how I may proceed without your assistance. We are two witnesses to a dreadful occurrence, and neither of us may disclose knowledge of such else we reap the wrath of my elder and wound beyond comprehension a sweet soul. I wish to cause no distress to others due to my cowardice.

The continued denials devour my soul. My plans, until now unknown by anyone other than my dear Molly and yourself, shall not be workable. I fear for her and for the future of the small one we conceived. He is now a robust eleven months of age and grows stronger and more amiable with each passing day. James is his name. When one looks upon his visage, it is apparent he is of mixed heritage. His complexion is not dark but is more white. To rear him in these environs will be most difficult.

I have made arrangements for Molly and James to be delivered to a respectable family in the Philadelphia region. They will accept Molly as a housemaid, giving her and the boy shelter and comfort. I shall convey funds with regularity to cover expenses for the two.

Is it conceivable that you may draw up necessary papers to guarantee these funds shall always be at the ready and transmitted? Such arrangements should be completed soon as Molly's uncle plans to deliver them in a few weeks' time, thus, I wish arrangements to be in place.

Danger abounds on every front. I fear for the safety of the travelers, yet I fear for them more if they remain close. The Mueller girl's accusations incense the old man. I fear he may retaliate in an unspecified fashion against the two who own my heart.

Bert

This letter hurt Annie's heart. Poor Molly. Poor Albert. Poor baby James. It was obvious from this letter that Russell knew the truth of Albert and Molly's plight but perhaps not of Israel and Ben's demise. Such dreadful secrets Albert and Will Brown held, and such pain the secrets caused!

Annie devoured the remaining pages. There she found more notes from Albert to his friend, simple notes of thanks for clandestine meetings in Brown's law office and for Brown's attention to detail in drafting legal documents. The final paragraph of one grabbed her attention.

Now that arrangements are completed and recorded, thanks to your precise work, departure is this upcoming Wednesday. Russell will deliver our cargo at the behest of Doc Mueller. Such a noble man Doc Mueller is that despite his daughter's travails he aids in this journey to safety. Russell will carry freedom papers in case of confrontation with troops. You have my undying gratitude. Pray for safe travels.

Annie now knew at least a few details which she had been intent upon discovering, yet there were more questions. Did they arrive without incident at their destination? Did they stay in Pennsylvania? Did Albert continue to send money? Did Albert see Molly and James again? What happened to James?

Annie held the letters in one hand and carried them downstairs to share with her mother. Seated in the parlor, Ellen muted the radio's volume when Annie entered the room.

"Mama, you just will not believe what I have learned!"

Ellen read the letters and looked at her daughter. "Why, Annie, I believe you have answered many of your questions, have you not?"

"Yes! But I want to know more!"

"Yes. I understand. My goodness!"

"I will read everything else, Mama. I wanted you to see what I've learned so far." Annie started back up the stairs. "Tell Daddy when he comes home!"

Returning to the bedroom, Annie's eyes focused upon another stack of papers bound with string. As she thumbed through the papers, most appeared to be legal documents, but she scrutinized each page so as not to miss any reference to those of importance to her quest. She picked up a folded stack of papers tucked inside another bundle. When she unfolded them, she discovered to her amazement that they comprised a directive from Albert Blanton relating to Molly Hill and one minor child, James Hill. The directive laid out in explicit terms when and how to handle payments for Molly from Blanton's bank to one in Philadelphia. They were to continue until James reached the age of majority, a term unfamiliar to Annie. She assumed it meant when James became a recognized adult. She examined more papers and, in a few minutes, opened one entitled The Last Will and Testament of Albert Blanton, dated February 4, 1889. Before she could read it, the robust voice of Carter Young boomed from downstairs. He had returned from the hospital.

She left the will on the bed and ran to greet her father. Without taking a breath, she reeled through her findings as they both walked into the kitchen. Annie continued her non-stop monologue while Carter snatched an oatmeal cookie from the jar on the counter and took a seat at the kitchen table.

"Gracious, daughter! I should say you've uncovered quite a chunk of startling information. I am . . . amazed such important papers were stuffed inside a wall! Was your Mr. Brown attempting to hide them, or was he a poor organizer? Maybe he had no other way to keep them safe when he retired? It's curious, isn't it, Ellen?" Ellen had entered the kitchen and was standing, arms folded, listening.

"And, Daddy, Mama, right when Daddy came home, I had just opened Albert Blanton's Last Will and Testament! I didn't read it yet. May I bring it, and we can read it together?"

Ellen sighed and nodded as Annie leaped up the stairs two at a time. When she returned, she laid the folded musty folio containing Albert James Blanton's will on the kitchen table. There at the table, the three sat and digested the legal document drafted on behalf of Albert Blanton and witnessed by William Walker and H.G. Brown.

Most of the language concerned ownership of the Blanton bank. Morse Blanton had died ten years earlier, and Albert inherited total ownership. Albert's will designated his shares of the bank go to his son Clay. In addition, Albert named a manager of the bank until such time Clay Blanton *obtains experience and education to direct the business with competence.* The will mentioned Clay Blanton's age of nineteen years as of February 4, 1889. The document did address personal property and real estate holdings, including the orchard beyond the stone wall. Albert's will bequeathed that orchard to Albert's wife, a woman named Nancy, with the stipulation that upon Nancy Blanton's death, the referenced property shall go to one James Hill of Philadelphia.

Annie grabbed her father's arm and gripped it hard. "Oh, my goodness! James! That is Molly's baby! Do you believe it?"

Both Ellen and Carter were agog. Albert Blanton knew where his son lived and wanted to acknowledge him in his will!

Ellen ran her hand through her chestnut hair. "I must admit I am astounded, Annie!"

"Who owns that property now, Carter? Do you know?"

"No, I don't."

"Could this James Hill still be alive?" Ellen asked. "Let's see, he was born in 1863 or 1864? He could be alive now. Around 70 years old? I'm curious. Could Ned and Cora Hill be related to Molly and James?"

Annie disclosed the relationship between Blink's family and Molly and James. She explained that Miss Mittie's father, Doc Mueller, gave the cabin and land where Blink's family lived to Ned's grandfather, Russell. Russell worked for Doc Mueller. Annie further spelled out that Doc Mueller had sent Ned's father, Billy, to a school in Philadelphia before the outbreak of the Civil War.

"May I ask Miss Cora about any of this recent information?" Annie asked.

Carter and Ellen responded with an emphatic, "No!" in unison. They admonished Annie to not question anyone at that point. This material was of such a sensitive nature they feared their daughter could insert herself into a position that could damage and hurt others. They instructed her to keep everything to herself until she spoke with Miss Mittie on Thursday of the following week.

Annie agreed. She advised her parents she was sleepy and wanted to bathe and go to bed. As she ascended the stairs to bathe before retiring, she called back to Carter and Ellen.

"Thank you, thank you for understanding how important this mystery is to me!"

They both acknowledged her gratitude with blown kisses toward their daughter as they returned to the kitchen.

"Coffee, Carter?"

"Yes, ma'am! We both can use coffee right now. Clear our heads, maybe." He shuddered. "Oh, my word, Ellen. How will this turn out?"

POWER OF THE WILL

On Monday, Annie found it difficult to concentrate at school. Thoughts of the papers she had found swarmed in her head, and she longed to share what she had read with Miss Mittie, Berta, and the Hills. The wish to tell Noah what she had learned also consumed her.

So, on Tuesday afternoon when she returned home from school, she opened the curtain covering her bedroom window facing the stone wall. Surveying the horizon, she hoped to see Noah there, but at first glance, she did not. She opened the window and waved her arms, hoping to elicit a response from the spirit who inhabited the back section of the property. She dared not call out to him, for fear of alerting her mother. Within a few moments, her hope was rewarded as Noah emerged near the stone wall. Annie beckoned him to come closer until he was standing in the yard under her window.

She whispered through the open window. "I've learned things! Can you come up here?"

In an instant, he appeared beside her, assessing his whereabouts. He was ill-at-ease and fidgeting as he bent to pat Bitsy's head. The quizzical look on his face led Annie to relate recent revelations in hushed tones. She implored him to follow her to the next room where she had strewn contents of the cubbyhole around the room. Annie showed Noah the letters and the will she had found. Next, she presented the missing pages from the manuscript. While Noah examined the treasure trove of information, Annie returned to the stack of papers she had not yet inspected. Her heart pounded faster as she read a letter from Albert to his friend and attorney. It disclosed Albert Blanton was ill and disillusioned.

Willy,

Circumstances prevent me from calling on you at your home or practice for counsel. I appear unable to recover from a most disagreeable illness that is worsening. Doc Kendall is unclear as to what I may have contracted or whether I suffer from a condition my body may not combat.

Please call at the house at your earliest convenience. You are in possession of my Last Will and Testament. You may need to present it forthwith if I do not recover.

You are aware of my life's failures. I have created a dreadful state of affairs by allowing the old man to force devotion to his bank and even to a wife with whom I share no mutual affection.

Yet I desire that Nancy shall receive ample funds and real estate to support the life she desires after my demise.

The old man groomed Clay for the short eight years they shared on earth to be as ruthless and filled with greed as was he.

My hope is James shall have the ability to remedy the legacy I leave. My appreciation to you for serving as intermediary for my correspondence with my sweet Molly these years can never be adequately expressed. The burden I bear, that you and I bear, involving the fate of her father and brother weighs heavy upon us. She must never know the truth for it would turn her heart against me.

Please hurry.

Bert

The contents of this letter tore at Annie's heart. Turning toward Noah, she observed his face as he read the papers she had given him. She saw puzzlement and asked what was troubling him.

"I did not have the opportunity of advanced schooling, Annie Young. Words are written here I do not comprehend. The phrases. I believe I see here that the events troubled the Albert fellow. He does not appear to be evil. Is my reckoning correct, do you agree?"

"I agree! Oh, Noah, he was in love with Molly! His father was a terrible person, wasn't he? You must read this letter." She rested the letter she had just read on top of the others.

Annie continued to sift through the remaining papers. None of them concerned the Blantons, so she began placing papers back into the boxes. She smoothed them and re-tied strings binding the stacks. Papers unrelated to the Blantons filled two of the boxes with ample space left at the top. The third box she saved for Blanton-related materials.

"Annie, I am well pleased with what you have learned. You now know that I and the girl Phoebe were truthful. Now we know the man called Albert was not, as he appeared, a person of low character. Now we hold proof that the other three men present when Morse Blanton did his killing were unwilling participants. What plans are you contemplating?" Noah's gaze unsettled her.

Annie's cheeks grew hot. Her breath quickened. She was unsure what she planned to do. But Annie knew for sure that when she visited her friend on Thursday next, Miss Mittie would question what she discovered in the boxes. She hoped Berta had returned from her sister's because Berta was likewise curious. Truths of a time past now belonged to Annie, and this presented a dilemma. Annie felt a responsibility she had never experienced. Revealing the secrets hidden in William Walker Brown's cubbyhole could harm the reputations of deceased people and their descendants. Those secrets presented more questions. The whereabouts of James and future ownership of the orchard behind the McCormick home where Annie lived were two unanswered ones. Why had Brown hidden nineteen pages of his manuscript?

"I don't know, I don't know!" She turned toward Noah, but he had left.

"Bitsy, what will I do?" The dog was scratching her ear.

Annie plodded back to her bedroom where she stared in silence at the photos of movie stars adorning one wall. They no longer held her interest; she thought them irrelevant and superficial. She crumpled and crammed the photos into her wastebasket before plopping herself on her bed, caressing Bitsy.

That night at dinner, Carter posed the same question Noah had asked of her. "What now, Annie?"

She replied with profound uncertainty how to go forward, then showed her parents the last letter from the cubbyhole. The three discussed consequences of revealing the information but agreed Berta and Miss Mittie must review each piece. They resolved that Ellen should collect Annie at school on Thursday and deliver her with the boxes to Miss Mittie. Ellen agreed to stay with Annie for the duration of her visit.

****

Thursday, they awoke to a foreboding, monotonous drizzle. Happy, exuberant chatter filled the schoolyard after dismissal, but Annie exhibited a somber face as she walked in silence to the waiting car.

"Hello, Mama," she said as she climbed into the Dodge. "Are you ready?"

Ellen patted Annie's knee. "I am ready, Annie, and you shouldn't worry. You have answered questions Mrs. McCormick has asked for years. It will be fine."

Miss Mittie herself answered the door. She was perky, smiling, and surprised to see Ellen. "Oh, Ellen! It's delightful to see you! Annie, I want to know what you found in Berta's boxes! Come in, please. Susie and a friend drove over to Roundtree to visit a woman they know, so she won't return for a good long while. Berta has not returned, so I am alone today!"

"We have Berta's boxes in the car, Mrs. McCormick," said Ellen. "But if she has not returned yet, do you prefer we keep them until she does? One box contains a fair quantity of information Annie and I know you want to see." Ellen waited for a response before going through the front door.

The little lady paused. "Bring in the one of interest to me but leave the others. Susie doesn't appreciate clutter. She'd object to boxes left here, and the time of Berta's return is unclear."

Annie retrieved the pertinent box from the car and took it to the sun porch where the two women stood. Miss Mittie offered Ellen a seat as she sat in her usual chair. She smoothed her dress and clapped her hands in anticipation as Annie set the box on the floor next to the chair.

Miss Mittie apologized for not having any cookies to offer. "I'm afraid Susie left before breakfast this morning, and I discovered our cookie jar is empty. Ellen, hot water is on the stove. Please make two cups of tea for us if you don't mind. I was preparing to make some when you knocked! Annie, a glass of milk?"

"No, thank you," said Annie as she showed Ellen to the kitchen and returned to sit across from her treasured friend. Annie retrieved papers from the box and set them on the table in front of Miss Mittie. The box of dominoes on the table's corner remained idle.

"Miss Mittie, this box holds several, uh, secrets. The missing pages from Mr. Brown's manuscript are here! So much is here. I don't know where to begin!"

Ellen entered the sun porch and set Miss Mittie's tea on the table as she took her seat in the chair next to the old woman.

"Mama, where should we start?"

Ellen took a sip and began. "I . . . we . . . hope that what Annie discovered will not upset you, Mrs. McCormick. We think it possible Mr. Brown attempted to hide these papers, but we cannot be sure. First, the missing pages to his manuscript show that your sister's observations were correct. Mr. William Walker Brown, or Will, his father H.G. Brown, Albert Blanton, and his father Morse Blanton were in the field with two black men, Israel and Ben Hill. Albert's father, Morse Blanton, shot Israel and Ben dead. These missing pages further tell, in a surprising twist, that Albert Blanton and Israel's daughter Molly were in love and planned to leave here for a life together up north."

As Ellen disclosed what the missing pages documented and what other papers from the cubbyhole revealed, Miss Mittie locked her eyes on Mrs. Young and took in everything. With hands clasped and lips pursed, she nodded as Ellen spoke and released a gentle sigh as each revelation came forth. Her tea remained untouched.

Annie interjected now and then, but Ellen spoke the most. Annie brought forth letters from Albert to his confidant, William Walker Brown, as well as Albert's will for Miss Mittie to examine. When the woman had read everything, she looked up at Annie and Ellen, her mouth open in amazement.

"Gracious, I never ever thought this! This proves Phoebe was truthful, yes, but the knowledge that Albert Blanton and Molly were in love with each other is astonishing. Miraculous! I thought he was such a . . . haughty and . . . pompous, snobbish person of poor quality. I suppose his demeanor was a front. He acted as his father expected him to act. The poor fellow. He lived under his father's heavy thumb and never crawled out from under it. This news leaves me speechless! I don't know what to say!"

"Miss Mittie, did you know your father helped Russell take Molly and baby James away?"

Miss Mittie shook her head so hard her bun tossed from side to side. "No, Annie. Remember, I was a mere child. Papa and Mother protected me from much. They sheltered me. I'm shocked!"

Silence prevailed for several moments. Miss Mittie fidgeted with the cameo at her neck, the twin to the one Annie dug out of the dirt. With a sudden heave, she extended her palm forward and wrapped it over Annie's slender hand. She declared circumstances had changed since she told Annie not to pursue the truth of what happened in the field beyond the stone wall.

"When Berta returns, we must show her this, every piece of this, Annie!" She flung her arms in the air and came within an inch of striking Annie's shoulder. "I do not recall the name James Hill. Oh, there is too much I can't remember! I'm uncertain. I hate being old!" A frown of despair crossed her face.

The three mulled the circumstances. Ellen reiterated her belief the past should stay in the past and no good could come from making public the information found in the papers. People, including Miss Mittie and her family, could be hurt, she insisted.

Annie theorized that because Miss Mittie knew and Berta would soon know the truth, Noah's torturous, restless existence may end, and he could be free to pass to the next world. Yet, whatever happened to James and Molly continued to haunt her. Did James inherit the orchard as his father had directed? Miss Mittie, too, desired to learn the fate of Molly and James, since her father played an essential role in their departure. The three concluded that Annie and Ellen should return the box to their home and not speak of its contents until Berta returned.

"My Susie does not appreciate clutter, you know. She does not appreciate a single thing reminding her of my sister Phoebe and the difficult times we experienced. Susie assigns great importance to her standing in society. I, myself, do not care, but . . . she does. I do not care one whit. Best we do not keep the box here. Berta can take it home when she returns from her sister's."

So, Ellen and Annie returned the box to the car and bade the sweet lady goodbye.

Ellen and Annie headed to Carter's office and updated him with the developments. After reflection, Carter expressed his belief that Berta held the keys to whether any of the information should become public. The papers were, he stated with great clarity, hers and hers alone. Ellen and Annie concurred.

****

School dismissed for summer recess the next day. Annie bade classmates farewell as they set out in different directions when the final bell rang. Instead of heading to the library or her father's office, she walked four blocks to the courthouse. Upon entering, she asked the woman at the receptionist desk how to research deeds. Carter mentioned the prior evening a deed search could tell whether, as dictated by Albert's will, James Hill had inherited the property behind their home.

The receptionist directed Annie to another room and instructed her to ask the women there for what she was searching. Annie proceeded to a room with a mid-size wooden desk just inside the door.

"What is the address, dear?" The plump, bespectacled brunette peered at Annie over her thick, rimless glasses.

"I don't think it has a street address. It's not in town. It's out on the ridge running road past a big red barn, I believe. On the west side of the road. Does that help?" Annie feared she lacked enough information to get answers to her question.

"Hmmmm. Not altogether. Can you tell me the name of a former owner? We have more than a few ridge-running roads with red barns around here." The woman looked toward the ceiling as she spoke in a most dismissive manner.

"I know who owned it a long time ago. Part of it comprises an orchard behind our house, and . . . it's . . . oh, it's so beautiful! If I ever find who owns it, I want to tell them how I enjoy looking at the trees. They were beautiful when they bloomed!" Annie did not wish to divulge the true reason for her search, so she babbled about the orchard's beauty.

The woman behind the desk chuckled. "How sweet, dear! Who owned it a long time ago? I can find the current owner if I know that information. How long ago?"

"In 1889."

"My goodness! Well, who owned it back then?"

"Mr. Albert Blanton."

The woman sighed, rose from her desk, and proceeded to a shelf containing rows of enormous books. She brought one back to her desk and opened it, thumbing through pages until she stopped on one page. Laying a ruler on the page, she glided it along the page until she found something of interest. The woman grabbed a pencil and wrote numbers and letters on a piece of paper before closing the book.

"I can find it, dear. Sit. I'll be back in a moment."

Annie sat. The woman returned in a few minutes with another book and plunked it on her desk. She adjusted her glasses, opened the book, and thumbed through more pages. When she stopped, she once again took the ruler and glided it along the page.

"Ah, here we go, dear! Yes, Mr. Albert Blanton owned it in 1889. He passed the next year, leaving ownership to his wife, Mrs. Nancy Blanton. Now, his widow passed in . . . let me see here . . . in . . . oh, is she still living? Ah, here is a notation. Oh, she passed earlier this year! The estate is not settled yet, I don't believe. We still show her as the owner. Let me check something else."

The clerk rose and scurried to more shelves. A woman seated behind a second desk next to a wall glared at Annie. Annie smiled at her before diverting her eyes, searching the room. She observed rows of books, potted plants on

225

windowsills, and moisture stained window shades covering half of the room's windows. The room smelled musty, doubtless because of leather-bound volumes and a leaky roof, betrayed by water stains on the ceiling.

When the clerk assisting Annie returned, she held papers in her left hand. "The estate of Mrs. Blanton has not settled as yet, dear. I searched to discover what the property's disposition may be once it's settled. Here is Mrs. Blanton's Last Will and Testament in our awaiting settlement file! Now, she designated the property in question go to her only heir, Mr. Clay Blanton. Mr. Clay Blanton, you may know, owns the Citizens Savings Bank on this block. So, dear, once the estate is settled, Mr. Clay Blanton will own the property. I should think it shall stay an orchard for a long time, and you may enjoy the view. Have I answered your question?"

Annie was incredulous. "Yes! Thank you very much! I suppose I didn't consider Mrs. Blanton could have still been alive in such recent times. It's surprising."

"Yes, dear. I didn't recall she had passed. Here is her obituary. We cut these out of the newspaper and keep them in the files. Do you want to read it?"

"Oh, yes! Thank you!" Annie took the clipping, concealing any hint of emotion.

Death claimed Mrs. Nancy Yeager Blanton, widow of the late Albert James Blanton and daughter of the late Clayton and Abigail Yeager, Tuesday a week. Mrs. Blanton's health had deteriorated for several years, rendering her an invalid; thus, her peaceful passing was a blessing for her and family. She was 83 years of age. She is survived by her only son, Clayton Blanton of Hillview, his wife Esther, and three grandchildren: Edward J. Blanton of Macon, Georgia, Yeager M. Blanton of Columbus, Ohio, and Mrs. Sue Esther Noland of Richmond, Virginia. Two great-grandchildren survive. Funeral services will be Friday afternoon at three o'clock at Illinois Street Methodist Church. Burial at Green Acres Cemetery.

"Thank you very much for your help, ma'am. I appreciate it. Um, when do you think they will settle the estate?"

"Oh, two or three months, no longer than six."

"Thank you," Annie mumbled as she left the office. Acknowledging the receptionist, she exited the courthouse and raced to her father's office a few blocks away. She was out of breath when she arrived and greeted Maude Renner, who was turning off lights in the examination room.

"Hello, Annie! Doctor is at Haverton's Drug Store. He'll be back in a jiffy. Are you glad school is over for the year?"

"Oh, I guess so. Uh, Miss Renner, is Daddy's patient Mrs. Blanton named Esther?"

"Why, yes, that's her first name."

Annie perched on a chair in the waiting room. Carter returned from the drugstore just as Ellen parked the family sedan in front of the office. Annie and her father walked out together as Maude switched off the lights and locked the door. Carter and Annie climbed into the Dodge, and off they went as Maude took off in the other direction, sauntering toward her house.

"Annie, how does it feel to be free for the summer?" her father asked. "I hope this will be a most pleasant and relaxing summer for us!"

The summer of 1934 proved to be anything but relaxing.

THE BROWN BOX CONNECTION

The summer of 1934 was carefree for most Hillview girls. Books, radio, the nighttime sky, or an occasional movie fueled innocent imaginations. Sounds of laughter, bicycles, and ballgames rang through town, but Annie Young remained a solitary soul. She had just three close friends other than her parents and Bitsy: Blink, her easygoing and untroubled neighbor, Noah, the spirit no other person could see, and Miss Mittie, her cherished companion of another era. Annie's fourteenth summer soon became one of suspicion, disillusion, and more revelation.

Miss Mittie telephoned with news Berta had returned and suggested Annie bring the boxes to her next Thursday visit. Together, Annie and Miss Mittie could divulge what the boxes revealed regarding "the incident" as the old woman called those tragic events of 1863.

Divulge they did. The three huddled on the sun porch while Berta listened and read papers Annie placed before her. An incredulous Berta learned her father had been involved in two murders and old Morse Blanton had blackmailed her father and grandfather to keep them quiet. The forbidden love between Albert and Molly elicited soft groans and tears from

Berta as she read Albert's poignant letters to her father, William Walker Brown.

Annie briefed both women on her visit to the courthouse. That Nancy Blanton's will referring to the land beyond the stone wall was in direct conflict with her husband's wishes was disconcerting.

Berta grabbed her head in both hands. "I am dumbfounded by this! Never in my wildest dreams have I thought such, such a . . . oh, such a terrible occurrence involved Dad. This Albert Blanton is unknown to me because I was born after he died. Dad never spoke of him. Did my sisters and brother know of him? I don't know. My brother W.W. has passed, and sisters are not in good health. My sisters are much older than I. I was an afterthought, an accident!" she cackled, her raucous laugh penetrating the room. A moment later, her serious disposition returned.

"My parents told me they named me after a dear friend of Dad's. Good Lord, his friend must have been Albert Blanton. Bert. Oh, my word." Her lips quivered as she spoke in a hushed voice.

To know with certainty that Phoebe had been truthful relieved Miss Mittie of a significant burden. The cruel deaths of Ben and Israel saddened her, yet the notion Molly and son James appeared to have vanished brought on the deepest sense of despair. She questioned aloud if they could trace their whereabouts. Molly, she speculated, must have died, but James might be alive. James Hill was the rightful heir to the tract beyond the stone wall, but it appeared from Annie's research that Nancy Blanton's will denied her husband's final directive.

Miss Mittie pounded her hand on the table. "How nice for that fine orchard to be in someone's hands besides another Blanton."

Berta agreed. Her eyes flashed as she proclaimed the missing pages belonged in the library with the rest of her father's manuscript. Berta said a search for Molly and James should start as soon as possible. Her passion grew as she recalled how honorable people in the Hillview area had lost their homes because of ruthless foreclosures by Clay Blanton and the Citizens Savings Bank.

"Clay Blanton does his dirty deeds with glee. My late husband's brother, Frank Simmons and his wife, were victims of his bank. Poor Frank's law practice suffered so when these terrible hard times began. Frank couldn't pay the mortgage on their home. Clay denied requests for extensions and grabbed the little bungalow as quick as he could. Frank and his wife moved in with family, and it was just several months ago that they could move out and rent a small house. He tries to practice his profession, but few people can pay a lawyer nowadays. My sister-in-law got a ticket-agent position at the train station, which gives them financial stability."

Annie pounced on Berta's words. Her eyes lit up, and she gasped aloud.

"Miss Berta, your brother-in-law is a lawyer, you say? Could he find out what happened to Molly and James? Could he make sure the orchard goes to James? Could he do that?"

Miss Mittie sat straighter in her chair as she turned to Berta. "Could he, Berta?"

Discussion continued until disrupted by the slamming of the kitchen door as Susie Rutledge made her arrival. Berta scurried toward the kitchen to shove the evening's dinner in the oven and set the dining room table for the evening meal. It was obvious from Susie's puckered lips and wrinkled brow that it displeased her these chores remained undone, but she said nothing. She poked her head through the door to the sun porch and addressed her mother and Annie with a quick, "You fine here?" before heading upstairs.

When Berta returned, she informed the other two she planned to inquire if her brother-in-law may help solve the mystery. She enlisted Annie's help to carry the boxes to her old Model A parked in front of the house and drove away.

"Miss Mittie, I hope Berta's brother-in-law will find Molly and James and fix the problem with the wills," Annie confided to her friend after Berta had gone.

"I do, too, Annie. I do, too."

Thus began the quest for which Annie longed and upon which Noah insisted. It pleased Noah that the truth may soon become known, and he pledged to aid Annie in any way possible. The spirit and the girl had grown close since he first appeared. Although Annie's wall-building became less frequent as she could work on the project only if her father was present, the two continued to visit often.

Annie and Noah conversed at the clothesline, on the porch, or in Annie's room. They discussed countless matters, not just the Blanton affair. Noah's stories of life during his mortal time mesmerized Annie. Annie gained insights she never forgot from their conversations. She learned from the boy how people lived and spoke, how they spent free time, and how they perceived events of the day. Noah was a treasure trove of knowledge that an eager, voracious Annie consumed. She took copious notes of their conversations and kept them in her nightstand's bottom drawer. From Annie, Noah learned of modern life, automobiles, movies, the Depression, and that the Union had won the war in which he was an unwilling participant. He lamented that he never saw his family again and expressed the hope each of his brothers survived, returned home, and enjoyed full and happy lives. Noah regretted the sorrow that must have overcome his mother, not knowing what happened to him.

"I long to see Ma to assure her of my strong devotion. I long to know if she survived the war with no more hardships and achieved peace in her soul. Annie, my only hankering as I traveled after my escape was to return home to Ma. How I wish I could have made it and not witnessed what I saw here." Noah's eyes filled with tears as he spoke of his family.

****

231

On the Saturday afternoon after Annie's visit with Berta and Miss Mittie, Blink appeared at the front door. He toted stones and a pair of work gloves in his wheelbarrow. Ellen invited him inside the house, but Blink stood on the porch and spoke.

"Miss Ellen, D-Doctor Young stopped in the road this m-morning while I was picking up twigs, and I told him Pap had a few more r-rocks for Annie. He told me to bring 'em to her. He told me I could help Annie if she wanted help!"

"Oh, how nice, Blink! Annie just completed her chores, so if she wants to work back there, I suppose it will be okay if you are with her. She's on the back porch. Come on inside, Blink!"

When Blink opened the screen door to the back porch, it appeared to him as though Annie was speaking to someone, but nobody else was present. Puzzled, he called to her that Ned had a few unwanted stones he had unearthed and shared the excellent news that Annie's parents consented for the two friends to work together at the stone wall. An elated Annie gathered her tools. Together, the pals made their way to the wall, leaving Bitsy inside the house.

Blink and Annie relished the company of each other, and on that fine afternoon they spoke of happenings around Hillview and of their dreams for the future. Blink loved to sing and whistle when they were together. When with Annie, his nervousness disappeared, and his stutter abated. As they worked that day, Annie inserted questions relating to Ned's family into their conversation which elicited a shake of the head or an "I don't know" response. If she wished to learn more of Ned's kin, she needed to speak with Ned herself. They toiled at the wall for an hour, and suppertime for both approached. As they strolled back to the house together, Ellen called out to Annie as soon as they were within earshot.

"Annie, come get money and run ask Cora if she has a half dozen eggs! I tripped over Bitsy and dropped my eggs on the kitchen floor! We don't have enough for breakfast tomorrow!"

Annie gripped the coins in her fist as she and Blink headed toward his home. The girl was eager to get there. Might Ned be available to answer questions?

"Mam, Annie needs eggs!" Blink bounded up the steps to the red front door with Annie right behind him.

Cora and Ned were in the kitchen. Cora was preparing the evening meal as Ned sipped a cup of coffee. Both turned and greeted Annie with a warm welcome. Cora said she had a half dozen eggs she could spare, laughing as Annie told her of Ellen's accident.

"Glad we don't have a dog here! I'd be tripping over it every time I took a step!"

Blink addressed his father. "Pap, Annie's been asking me questions about people. Ask Pap, Annie. Bet ya he knows!"

"What you want to know, Annie?" Ned took a sip from his cup.

Questions rolled off her tongue in quick succession as she attempted to gain any information relating to Molly and James.

Ned's answers were succinct and to the point. No, he did not recall hearing of Molly or James Hill. Yes, Doc Mueller sent Ned's father, Billy, up north for schooling before the Civil War erupted. There, Billy learned to read and write, learned history, science, and mathematics and trained as a blacksmith. He took courses in bookkeeping. When he returned after the war, he worked his blacksmith trade in town. Billy forged metal into useful pieces people purchased for their homes and farms. People considered him a talented artist, too, because his metal sculptures decorated both interiors and exteriors of homes. One Hillview businessman even put his bookkeeping skills to use. Billy Hill's reputation was that of a trustworthy man. He married, and he and his family moved into the cabin with his parents, Russell and Thea, to care for them in their declining years.

"I remember little of my grandparents, Annie," Ned told her in response to a question relating to Russell and Thea.

"They died when I was a squirt. Pap told me they were fine folk. Pap sure held Doc Mueller in high regard, too. Said he could never have been a success without Doc Mueller's help. You sure are making me consider things, girl! Pap said Grandpappy Russell built on to the cabin for kin. Never knew who, though. You say this Molly is that kin?"

"Yes," Annie said, but she did not communicate the full story, just that Molly was Russell's niece and that she and her baby James had lived in their cabin for a time.

After a lengthy pause, Ned eyed Cora. "Cora, where's the box we found in Pap's chest?"

"Up in the attic. Want me to get it?"

"Please." Turning to Annie, he said, "Cora and I found a box with a few things in it years ago. I don't remember what was in it. Cora found it under a blanket in a small chest my pap kept by his bed. Maybe we will learn something."

Cora brought a brown wooden box and stationed it in the middle of the kitchen table. Ned and Cora removed its items and spread them on the table. Medals, coins, and folded papers made up the contents. Ned unfolded the yellowed pages, several of which had water stains making deciphering them difficult. Cora took a few and began to read. She found letters from Ned's father Billy to Russell and Thea, written from The Institute in Philadelphia. Others were letters from Thea to Billy.

Ned shook his head. "I don't think Grandpappy Russell could read or write."

Annie responded, "Maybe he couldn't, but Miss Mittie's mother taught your grandmother Thea to do both."

Curious, Annie asked what The Institute was, so Ned explained that was the school to which Doc Mueller had sent his father.

"The Institute for Colored Youth. Quakers founded it way back when. Doc Mueller was Quaker, so he knew folks there."

Annie stopped with a start. "Oh, I must go home! Mama was fixing supper when I left! Please tell me if you learn any information on Molly or James!"

"Sure will!" Ned said. "We've never read these letters, Annie, so we'll see what we learn!" He patted Annie on the back as she headed for the front door. "I'm grateful you told us this, Annie!"

When Annie arrived home, her father had returned, and supper was ready. Conversation revolved around the knowledge that Ned knew nothing of his distant kin, but the contents of a brown box might yield clues.

****

As Annie and her parents left for church the next morning, Blink was waiting for them in front of his house. The boy jumped with glee in the lane when he saw the black Dodge headed in his direction.

"Annie, w-we found something about Molly! Come after church!"

Annie could not concentrate on the minister's sermon or on words to hymns sung. As soon as the service ended, she bounded the steps two at a time, double timing it to the car to wait for her parents. They took far too long speaking with other churchgoers, impatient Annie noted. When Carter and Ellen at long last got to the car, Annie urged her father to hurry straight home. He obliged her request to get out at the Hills' driveway, admonishing her to not overstay her welcome and to "get on home for lunch" soon.

Annie Young raced up the dusty driveway to the Hill cabin and found Ned headed toward Cora's flower garden, toting a wheelbarrow filled with dirt.

"Yo, Annie! Blink told us you'd be coming soon! Come inside, and we'll show you what we found."

Blink and his mother were in the kitchen, and Cora reached out to hug Annie when she entered. The four sat at the kitchen table as Cora brought forth the contents of the brown box. She handed four letters to Annie, who read them aloud with mounting astonishment.

Ned's father Billy saved several letters between him and his parents, and the four Cora gave to Annie contained information of significant interest. A letter from Billy, written in late 1864, relayed information soon after he met up in Philadelphia with his father, Russell, and *the precious cargo, Molly and her boy.* Billy wrote in his letter that *both are well settled with Hinshaw family and doing fine. Boy is walking everywhere he can get to and makes sounds resembling words.* Billy's letter continued with *I will look in from time to time* and reiterated his admiration for Doc Mueller, requesting his parents to communicate his best wishes to the man. Billy had completed his courses and worked in a blacksmith shop in Philadelphia for the war's duration. He yearned to return home, a longing that could not be satisfied as long as war raged.

A letter from Thea to Billy included gratitude for Billy's attentions to *the sweet Molly and her babe.* She questioned whether Billy had any news of Ben or Israel. *Our hope is they made it to freedom,* she wrote. Thea implored her son to be cautious in his dealings and to come home as soon as he deemed safe. Mentions of everyday life and hope of war's end were frequent.

Billy wrote in another letter that *Cousin Molly has learned to read from Mrs. Hinshaw. She cares for Hinshaw children and little James. Cousin is desirous of ability to write so she may send letters to Hillview. I offer aid, but it is not accepted. The correspondence is from her heart, and she says she does not wish me to see in her heart. Molly practices when time allows. Soon will be proficient.* Toward the end of Billy's letter, he inserted: *James grows big. He's more white skin not dark as we are. Smart tyke.*

The fourth letter Ned and Cora found was dated late 1867. The letter from Billy to his parents detailed his departure date and route from Philadelphia back home. He addressed Molly's position in a lengthy paragraph:

Hinshaws shall keep our kin in their home. Cousin's work and inclinations are pleasing and cause them to wish her remain in their employ. Young James is a delight. The boy speaks and laughs much. Hinshaws plan to school him with their boy of same age. He looks to Hinshaw as a father. Calls him Papa. Molly say it is agreeable. Mrs. Hinshaw remains in bed with sickness and does not improve. She tells Molly boy's name should be Hinshaw. Molly say his name is Hill. Those in Hinshaw home give thanks for Molly. I am in receipt of a locked box of correspondence and photographs from Molly to transport to Will Brown the lawyer when I return. Hinshaw delivered Molly and James to a man who made pictures of their likenesses. Molly gave me one to give to you so you will receive it upon my arrival. I am hopeful of future visits here because of friends I value and to see our kin. It is less challenging since war no longer prevents travel.

The letter disclosed Billy's pending employment with the Hillview blacksmith.

"Oh, my!" Annie clapped her hands when she finished reading the four letters. "This is wonderful!"

Cora reached into the box and withdrew a faint photograph, a tintype. Handing it to Annie, she said, "Annie Young, meet Molly and James Hill."

Annie gasped and stared at the fragile photo. A young black woman stared back at her, braided hair pulled back, a lace collar circling her thin neck, her lips turned upward into what Annie thought to be a faint smile. A toddler whose complexion was lighter than the woman's, perched on her lap as her left arm held him tight. He stared at the camera with eyes wide open and his mouth rounded as if he was determining whether the camera and the man behind it were friend or foe.

"Oh, goodness, look at them, Miss Cora! Oh, my!"

237

Cora reiterated that neither she nor Ned had read the letters before the preceding night. These four were the only ones containing any reference to Molly.

"Ned and I are thrilled to learn of your curiosity about these people we did not know, Annie," Cora said. "We have learned so much from reading these letters. The medals came from the school Ned's daddy attended up there in Philadelphia. The coins are from a business. They aren't actual money, but they look like pennies."

Annie did not acknowledge more recent discoveries since she did not have permission to do so from Miss Mittie or Berta. She thanked Ned and Cora, hugging them and Blink as she exited the front door.

Annie's heart raced as she darted toward home. Opening the front screen door, she bolted inside and called to Carter and Ellen. "Mama, Daddy, I've seen a picture of Molly and James!"

Annie's description of the letters and the photo she had viewed intrigued Carter and Ellen. Both stated that Annie should tell Berta and Miss Mittie what Ned and Cora had discovered.

Carter mused, "Ned and Cora should know the truth, as painful as it may be. You have opened a Pandora's box, Annie, but secrets are not good. Secrets fester and cause pain. Your mother and I have been concerned these developments might hurt Mrs. McCormick. In due course, though, secrets come to the surface. Talk this over with Mrs. McCormick and Berta. They will want the Hills to know."

"I will!" Annie shouted. "May I telephone Miss Mittie tomorrow morning to ask if I may come? Berta is there on Mondays, too."

Carter and Ellen agreed as the girl turned on her heel and skipped into the parlor where Bitsy napped. After patting the dog on its head, she leaped up the stairs to her room, where she signaled Noah to appear, and appear he did.

Annie observed his reactions as she whispered what she had learned. It was satisfying for her to see his smile and to know he was pleased.

"Excellent," said Noah. "If Blanton had not murdered Molly's father and brother, events would have taken a different turn, you are aware. Albert and Molly could have forged a life together with their little one. William Walker Brown's father would not have been in such a precarious position. And . . . alas . . . I would not still be in this painful quest for everlasting peace."

"Yes, Noah, I know." She touched his arm. In a moment, he disappeared.

PANDORA'S BOX

"**G**ood morning, Mrs. Rutledge. This is Annie Young. May I speak with Miss Mittie, please?" Annie tried to keep her voice from betraying her excitement on that Monday morning.

Annie's eagerness to share information intrigued Miss Mittie, and she told Annie to come as soon as possible. She advised Annie that Berta had just arrived at the Rutledge home. Carter had left for his office earlier than usual, so Annie Young kissed her mother, gave Bitsy a pat, and headed to town on foot. She wore a large-brimmed straw hat and carried her notebook under her arm as she covered the four miles to the Rutledge home. A few cars passed her along the way, two offering rides, but she declined.

By the time she arrived, she was sweaty and flushed. Susie answered the front door and remarked, "You look . . . goodness, Annie!" She invited the girl inside and offered a glass of water as she led Annie to the kitchen where Miss Mittie and Berta were perusing recipes at the kitchen table.

"Good morning, Annie!" sang Miss Mittie. "I was attempting to help Berta find Mother's recipe for spoon bread. I cannot recall the measurements for every ingredient. Sit and cool off!"

Susie withdrew and retreated upstairs as Annie gulped her drink and flung her hat and notebook on an empty chair. She then disclosed what she had learned and described the photograph of Molly and James. These developments astonished both women, and it thrilled Berta to learn more of the people referenced in her father's papers.

"Wonderful!" Miss Mittie clapped her hands as she spoke. Her blue eyes sparkled.

"I came as soon as I could. My question to you both, though, is whether I may tell the Hills what we know. They know nothing, just that Molly and James lived in the cabin and were kin. What do you think?"

Berta replied first, announcing she had discussed the matter of the two conflicting wills with her brother-in-law, attorney Frank Simmons. She disclosed Frank planned to visit the courthouse to review the status of both wills. He speculated Albert's will was the determining document as to the orchard property's disposition, but he needed to examine the records on file before forming a professional opinion.

"None of this once secret information is a secret anymore, is it?" Berta asked. It was a rhetorical question. In a moment, she answered her own question. "If James Hill is still alive, he should become the rightful owner of the orchard behind your property, Miz M. The truth must come out. It is time."

Miss Mittie agreed. She acknowledged her earlier belief that no more should be mentioned of the murders or other sordid details of the past, but circumstances had changed. She had changed her mind. The occurrences of the past now pertained to "current happenings," as she called the recent turn of events.

"Annie, I believe your Noah may rest now, don't you?"

"Who is Noah?" Berta asked.

This exchange startled Annie and embarrassed Miss Mittie. The old woman had not intended to divulge Noah's existence, but the words flowed before she could catch herself.

Annie feared telling Berta of her secret friend, but she was on the spot and had no choice but to respond.

Before Annie could utter more than a few words, Susie re-entered the kitchen. Displeasure at the sight of her employee socializing with Miss Mittie and Annie produced a scowl. Susie sensed that she had interrupted secretive whispering, which further irritated her.

Annie grabbed her hat and notebook and pushed the chair back from the table. "I should go now! Miss Mittie, can you explain my friend to Berta, please?"

The old woman nodded, smiled, and winked at the girl. Annie bade the three women goodbye and hurried out the front door. At the corner, she leaned against the lamppost, looked up at the cloudless sky, and breathed out a quiet, nervous laugh.

"Oh, my goodness! Now someone else will know about Noah and think I'm crazy!" she said to the lamppost. With resolve, she straightened her hat, tied its crimson ribbon under her chin, drew a deep breath, and began her long trek home.

****

Annie found Ellen in her sewing room stitching a skirt while she listened to the radio.

"Hello, Sweetie! Did you see Mrs. McCormick and Berta?"

"Yes. They want me to tell Ned and Cora everything. I didn't stop there on my way home, though, because I'm hot and tired from walking! It's a long walk from town! I'll go have a drink of water and rest for a while before I do my chores."

"Lunch is waiting for you on the kitchen table, sweet. I thought the walk and your visit might tire you, so I dusted this morning after you left. Dusting was your only Monday chore. After you rest, go over to Cora and Ned's. Tell them what you know. I'm happy to go with you if you wish."

Annie shook her head, gave her mother a tight hug, and went to the kitchen where she savored her lunch and two glasses of milk from the icebox. She basked in the breeze coming through the window where Ellen's blooming African violets perched on the sill. For a few quiet moments, she contemplated the unfolding events, then she carted her plate and glass to the sink and informed Ellen she was on her way.

Cora was hanging clothes on the clothesline as Annie shooed a flock of clucking hens out of her path and approached the cabin.

"Good afternoon, Annie Young! What you need today, girl?"

"Nothing today. I want to talk to you and Mr. Ned, though. Is this a convenient time?"

"Oh, Ned and Blink just got home minutes ago. They're having lunch. It's a perfect time!"

Seated at the kitchen table with Cora, Ned, and Blink, Annie detailed facts surrounding Ben and Israel's murders. She related the unimaginable tragedy of Albert and Molly. She spoke of the directive in Albert Blanton's will dealing with the property beyond the stone wall. The revelations astonished each member of the Hill family. Each remained speechless the entire time Annie spoke, sitting in complete silence for several minutes after she stopped speaking. They stared at Annie, stunned by what they had just learned.

Ned was first to speak. "I'm trying to understand this, Annie. Israel Hill was my grandfather's brother, and Ben was Israel's son? So, Israel was Molly's father, and Ben was her brother? That's something, isn't it? I've never heard their names. Nobody knew what happened to them except for poor Mrs. McCormick's sister? Everybody thought she was crazy? I'll bet you Grandpappy Russell didn't think she was crazy. Not for one bit. I'll wager you he knew in his heart she was right."

Cora confessed her heart ached for both Molly and Albert. "I've heard of the Blanton men. My people said they were not upstanding, but you say Albert was. My word! Grandpappy Russell was sure good to add on to this cabin for Molly and her baby, too."

Blink asked about James Hill. "Is he an old m-man? Do you know where he is, Annie?"

Annie could not speculate whether James still lived or where he could be if he was still alive. She surmised he grew up around Philadelphia since that was where he and Molly were at the outcome of the Civil War. She told the Hills Berta's brother-in-law, lawyer Frank Simmons, was investigating the two wills. Annie expressed hope Mr. Simmons might uncover more information regarding James. Before leaving for home, Annie promised to keep the Hills apprised of any developments.

Ellen greeted Annie's arrival at the front door with the news Berta telephoned and wished Annie to return her call. "I wrote her number on the pad by the telephone, Annie. She is at her home."

An anxious Annie returned the call and learned from Berta that Frank Simmons had researched Albert Blanton's estate settlement at the courthouse. Albert's will filed at the courthouse was the same as the one found in William Walker Brown's cubbyhole. Mr. Simmons told Berta he planned to contact the attorney handling Nancy Blanton's estate. His purpose? To inquire why Nancy Blanton did not mention James Hill in her will and to confirm whether anyone had attempted to locate James Hill. Berta and Mr. Simmons both theorized that neither the Blantons nor their attorney knew who James Hill was, since his parentage was a secret. It was possible they ignored Albert's directive because they could not locate James Hill, or maybe James Hill was dead, or maybe they did not care to investigate.

After retiring early, Annie greeted the next day with new vigor. The hope of learning more from Frank Simmons's conversation with the Blanton attorney buoyed her. After breakfast, Ellen dispatched Annie outside to hang laundry. As

244

she affixed wet clothes on the clothesline, Noah leaned against the clothesline post, absorbing every additional detail Annie provided. Noah was pleased, which thrilled Annie. No distance of time existed when she was with Noah. An invisible cocoon of sorts caressed them, and their bond grew deeper with each communication.

****

No news came of any dialogue between the two attorneys. By Thursday's arrival, Annie's impatience turned to exasperation as the dutiful daughter accompanied her mother to town in the morning. Ellen's errands, which seemed endless to the girl, lasted until lunchtime, so they stopped at Olivia Watson's Diner for lunch. After sharing a special treat of Olivia's grilled hot dogs, Ellen dropped Annie at the Rutledge home.

"I will pick you up later, dear. I am headed to the market and will return for you and Daddy later. Lou and Jack are coming for dinner tonight."

Annie nodded as she stepped off the running board of the trusty Dodge and dashed to the front door where Berta waited to welcome her.

"Frank has spoken with Ralph Bennett, who is handling the Blanton estate. Bennett says he never saw Albert's will, which my brother-in-law says is ridiculous. Nancy and Clay Blanton knew what Albert's will dictated, just as Ralph Bennett knew. Frank knows Bennett isn't truthful." Berta continued in near tirade fashion as she accompanied Annie to the sun porch where Miss Mittie waited.

Miss Mittie's face betrayed her alarm. "What do you think, Annie? Frank told Berta that unless we find James, Clay Blanton will inherit the orchard." Eyes flashing, and her voice quivering, she blurted, "We must find James Hill!"

"Oh, my! I don't know! Miss Mittie, James might be dead! Maybe he moved far away! Berta, does Mr. Simmons have any ideas?"

The housekeeper leaned forward, and in a hushed voice confided that Frank Simmons was now looking into what happened to James. She added that barrister Bennett's reputation was not an ethical one by any measure.

"Frank says Ralph Bennett is a weasel who takes advantage of those in most need. He has been Clay Blanton's attorney for years and handles the bank's foreclosures and other legal matters. I gave Frank the papers from Dad's cubbyhole, and he informed Bennett what he had in his possession. Frank says time is short, but he will try everything he can to find James Hill or at least learn what happened to him. He may have died years ago." Berta's eyes darted from one to the other as she spoke, anticipating their reactions.

Annie offered to seek permission from Ned and Cora to turn over their letters in case they may help Frank Simmons in his quest. She wondered aloud if tracing the Hinshaw family in Philadelphia might give them answers to the puzzle. Both women agreed it was an excellent idea and urged Annie to speak with the Hills as soon as possible.

Miss Mittie snapped a question. "Annie, do you believe Noah could be of help? Might he help solve the mystery of the boy's whereabouts?" Her lilting laugh filled the room. "The boy! Why, if he is still alive, he's seventy years old!"

Annie hesitated and glanced at Berta before answering. Berta appeared curious, not alarmed or dismissive as Annie had feared. It was obvious Miss Mittie had familiarized Berta with Noah's existence. "I don't think so," said Annie with a trace of uncertainty in her voice. "He knew nothing of Molly or James."

Berta soon left the room to complete her chores. Before retreating to the kitchen, she implored Annie to speak with Cora and Ned as soon as possible. "We must, we *must* find James Hill!"

Annie spent what was left of the afternoon with Miss Mittie, much of the time dedicated to James Hill. Where was he? Was he still alive? Was he an honorable person? Was he a kind man? Did he have a content life? Did he know who his father was? In the South, a person of mixed heritage was likely to be treated with contempt, shunned, abused, even brutalized. It was fortunate, Miss Mittie counseled Annie, that it appeared James grew up elsewhere, near Philadelphia or farther north. If true, he may have been spared the hostility Hillview would have offered.

Before heading for the front door to await her mother's arrival, Annie gave Miss Mittie a soft kiss on the forehead. "I believe Mr. Simmons will discover the truth, Miss Mittie." Annie's voice held a distinct tone of wistfulness.

Carter was waiting on the sidewalk when Ellen and Annie drove up to his office. His glance toward Ellen betrayed a developing concern as he slid into the passenger seat next to Ellen, but he greeted them with a hearty, "Hello, girls!" He and Ellen discussed the evening ahead with Lou and Jack. It was when he turned to Annie, sitting in the back seat, the conversation took a dark turn.

"Esther Blanton came to the office today. She claimed you, Annie, are spreading gossip, rumors concerning her husband and his father. Mrs. Blanton was angry and said I better make you stop. She ranted on and on, saying a lawyer in town called their lawyer and insinuated her mother-in-law's will wasn't proper, and he planned to challenge it. The Blantons' attorney felt threatened, according to her. I told her I knew you were not spreading information around town as she accused. She was threatening to me in her accusation, yelling at the top of her lungs and creating a scene in the waiting room. I feared Maude might faint."

"Carter, no!" Ellen jerked the steering wheel to avoid hitting a curb.

"Oh, Daddy, how awful! I have said nothing to anybody except Berta, Miss Mittie, and the Hills. Berta asked her brother-in-law who's a lawyer to check on the wills, and he spoke to the Blanton lawyer. I can't imagine he threatened anyone! What a terrible thing to happen! I am so sorry!" Annie's lips trembled, and tears flowed.

Carter offered a faint smile and instructed Annie not to worry. He reached over the seat to pat her leg and give her his handkerchief. "Before Mrs. Blanton left the office, she ordered Maude to pack up her records and deliver them to Jack. She said she will become his patient now. I'll be straight with you both. It's fine with me, but poor Jack! A Pandora's box is now open for sure, but we will handle it. We will handle it together."

An uneasy dinner followed. Jack and Carter retreated to Ellen's sewing room after the meal to discuss Jack's new patient in private. Ellen, Lou, and Annie remained in the kitchen washing dishes as Ellen filled in Lou on the genuine cause of Esther Blanton's rage. The details stunned Lou, but she remained unfazed and responded with warm assurances.

"Ellen! Annie! Don't you worry. If anyone will spread rumors or ugliness on anyone or everything, the person is Esther Blanton! You did the right thing, Annie. Don't let it hurt you. You unearthed an awful secret hidden for too long. I am sad to learn of the murders. Those poor men! I'm sure more incidents such as these happened. I'm sure they happened around here. People accepted it. After slavery, many whites valued Negroes even less than before. They didn't care if a colored person went missing. The most brutal atrocities imaginable never got reported. Oh, I hope it turns out well for this James Hill if he's still alive. Gracious!"

Carter and Ellen discussed the day's events and potential recriminations after Annie retired for the evening. Concern for their daughter and the effect recent events could have on her were utmost in their minds. Well known and influential, Clay and Esther Blanton wielded power in Hillview. The Blanton bank was the largest in town because of its long-standing practice of financing mortgages for those on the lower end of the economic scale. When a customer missed one or two payments, the bank foreclosed. After foreclosure, the bank often rented these foreclosed properties to their prior owners and evicted them when rent went into arrears. The bank was heartless. As for Esther Blanton, she considered herself the grande dame of Hillview society. She gained a smug satisfaction when women curried her favor to become part of the town's social *elite*. With trepidation, Carter and Ellen pondered consequences of an entanglement with the Blantons.

****

The next morning, Annie gobbled her breakfast and raced to the Hill cabin. Ned and Cora were quick to loan her the letters and tokens that might be of use to Mr. Simmons, and Annie responded with profuse gratitude before heading back to her house. She telephoned Berta to tell her what she possessed. With no hesitation, Berta jumped in her car and drove to Annie's house to retrieve the items. Berta was eager for Frank Simmons to have every piece of information possible as he delved further into the mystery of James Hill.

Ellen invited Berta inside and offered coffee, but Berta declined. "I must deliver these to Frank this minute. I feel terrible that for lo these many years, my father's cubbyhole concealed so much truth and tragedy. If Frank can set things straight, then I want Frank to do it as soon as possible."

Annie handed over the letters and tokens. She had examined the tokens and discovered each of them came from one business in Philadelphia, HMH Cannery.

"Berta, Hinshaw was the name of the family Molly and James lived with in Philadelphia. The initials are HMH. Could they stand for Hinshaw? What do you think?"

Berta shook her head. "I don't know." She promised to relay every question and possibility to Frank. Before leaving, Berta gave Ellen and Annie enormous hugs and blew a kiss as she climbed into her old flivver. Ellen and Annie waved as she bounced along the driveway and turned onto the dirt lane leading to the main road back to town.

"Well, we'll see what happens," Ellen said. She hugged Annie and took the girl's face in her hands. "I love you, sweets!"

Arm in arm, they traipsed back into the house, Bitsy at their heels.

JAMES WHO?

The search for James Hill began, and Frank Simmons wasted no time. The short, rotund, and rumpled lawyer scurried to and from the courthouse, chewing a soggy unlit cigar as he walked and talked. Already, he had reached out to a former colleague in Philadelphia who had many contacts with old Quaker families, hoping the friend might throw light on James Hill and the Hinshaw family.

Annie continued her visits to the library, poring over the Brown manuscript line by line in search of any missed clue.

Berta Simmons scoured every crevice of her father's study, searching for any shred of additional evidence that may prove fruitful. She removed drawers and searched the desk. She paged through each book on every shelf. Berta scrutinized the walls behind each of the shelves, hunting for another hidden door to no avail.

Ned and Cora searched each crack and cranny of their attic for any new clue. They found nothing.

Miss Mittie's brain turned over and over as she tried to recall any relevant detail from her childhood, but her efforts were for naught.

Ellen Young fretted over how these efforts could cause harm to her daughter and others.

Carter Young did not allow his concerns to affect his work. He attended to his patients, and his office appointment calendar remained full. His family finances solidified, thanks to a gradual improvement of economic conditions, Ellen's sewing commissions, and income from oil royalties.

And Noah? Well, he remained impatient, trapped in his earthly prison pining for release. More restless and frustrated than before, his attentions turned to rebuilding the stone wall, often at a frantic pace. Whenever Bitsy ventured near the wall, she had a calming effect on the spirit. Noah halted his work to reward her with pats and belly rubs, always speaking in an inaudible voice, his southern drawl soothing to the ever-nervous terrier.

****

One morning at the Young home, the telephone rang with its usual clatter. When Ellen picked up the receiver, she dropped it to the floor. As she retrieved it from the floor, she heard Berta shouting through the device.

"Ellen! Ellen! Frank has found him! Frank has found James Hill! And he is alive! You must tell Annie! I have called Miz M, and she is ecstatic. Does Ned have a telephone?"

Ellen replied that the Hills did not have a telephone, but Annie would go to their house posthaste to inform them.

"Where is he?" Ellen asked. "Where does he live? Does he know of his father? Does he know about the will? Does he know anything?"

Berta responded that Frank Simmons wanted to meet with everyone in his office so he could explain what he had learned before he began proceedings to challenge Nancy Blanton's will. Was the following afternoon at one o'clock convenient?

Because the following afternoon was Thursday, Ellen acknowledged the day, time, and location were convenient. She promised to tell Berta whether the Hills could attend.

252

The cramped law office of Frank Simmons took on an air of anticipation and apprehension that Thursday afternoon. Berta and Miss Mittie entered first, with Berta assisting her companion into a chair. Annie and Ellen came next, followed by Ned, Cora, and a fidgeting Blink. Annie spotted Noah standing in the corner, leaning against a bookcase, fingering his cap as his eyes scanned the scene.

Frank Simmons chomped his cigar, then picked a small bit of tobacco from his tongue before speaking. "Welcome, folks! What a story we have here!"

The lawyer then recounted the story of Molly and James. They lived with a Quaker family named Hinshaw in Philadelphia where Molly served as the housemaid. Mr. Hinshaw, his brother, and a Mr. Morris had owned a medium-sized business, HMH Cannery. The cannery processed fruits and vegetables and provided products not just to Philadelphia citizens but to the United States Army during the Civil War. The tokens Ned and Cora discovered were from that enterprise. Mr. Hinshaw and his wife had five children born of their marriage, the youngest of whom was a boy a year older than James. Because Mrs. Hinshaw was in poor health, Molly's presence was of great value. She cared for the Hinshaw children and young James, and each Hinshaw came to accept her and James as part of their family.

In 1869, tragedy struck. Mrs. Hinshaw died. It fell to Molly to assume full responsibility for child-rearing and overall management of the household which she did with extreme efficiency. James attended the same school as the Hinshaw brood, and he and the youngest son Samuel were close. Molly never told James of his paternal parentage, and to Molly's displeasure, upon coming of age, young James assumed the surname Hinshaw. Mr. Hinshaw, as had his late wife, encouraged this decision. The Hinshaw children considered James a brother.

Berta brought her hand to her cheek. "No wonder nobody could find James Hill! He changed his name!"

Frank Simmons responded, "Could be, Berta, but I doubt if any Blanton or their lawyer attempted to find him. It's possible your father tried to contact him through Molly when Albert died, but who knows?" His voice trailed off as he shook his head.

Simmons continued, explaining that Mr. Hinshaw's two oldest sons took over running HMH Cannery when their father died. The other Hinshaw and Mr. Morris had died earlier. Both James and Samuel worked in the business, Samuel as bookkeeper and James as chief foreman. The four men prospered into the start of the century. They expanded the business into other areas besides fruits and vegetables, which enhanced the financial standing of each Hinshaw man, bringing them considerable stature and prestige in their community.

Molly remained at the Hinshaw home after Samuel and James reached adulthood, with the large dwelling empty except for her and Mr. Hinshaw. She cared for the home and for him in his later years, acting as his nurse and caretaker. The Hinshaw offspring revered Molly as a maternal figure, never as a servant. James, who remained unmarried, moved his mother into his own home after Mr. Hinshaw's death, where she remained until her passing in 1917. The Hinshaw children insisted she be buried in the Hinshaw family plot, where her tombstone read:

Molly Hill
1845-1917
Forever in our Hearts

Frank Simmons removed his eyeglasses and wiped sweat from the top of his balding head after describing the tombstone. His gaze turned toward Ned, and his voice broke.

"Ned, James told me his mother did not talk of her past, other than to speak of your grandparents and her devotion to them. Molly never revealed names or locations, even though James pressed her for the information."

Simmons turned to Miss Mittie. "James further mentioned a physician. We are aware, of course, the physician was your father, Doc Mueller. Molly told James he was a man whose principles were uncommon for his time. She credited him with arranging her position with the Hinshaw family and thus, giving her and James their lives, lives they could not have otherwise experienced."

The attorney took a deep breath. "Molly told James his father was a white man from a prominent family. She said they were deeply in love during a time when such relationships were unthinkable. Molly explained their relationship could not have been accepted and that James's own life would have been a living hell if she and James remained where they lived. As I said, he requested the identity of his father, but she never divulged it. She did tell James his father had died but provided no more information."

Frank Simmons chewed his cigar and scanned the group to see their reactions. "James recalls that not long before Molly died, he came home to find her tossing papers into the fireplace. He thought it dangerous because of her frantic and reckless manner. As sparks flew onto the floor, James said he rushed to stop his mother just as she collapsed in tears on the floor. He saved the remaining papers, which she pleaded with him to destroy, but he did not. James escorted Molly to her bed, which she did not leave until she passed a week later. James stayed by her side until the end."

Annie interrupted. "What were the papers?"

"Hold your horses! I'm getting to that part!"

The attorney disclosed that James gathered the remaining papers and discovered they were letters addressed to Molly. Each was signed with an *A*. It was obvious to James the letters were from his father, but they offered no identifying information. James told Frank the letters were tender and filled with questions, concern for James, and included comments concerning the author's own life. Most likely, correspondence between his mother and father continued throughout the years, but the letters James saved from the fire were dated 1888-1890.

"Albert Blanton died in 1890," Berta reminded the others.

"Yes," Simmons said. "The final letter indicated Albert was ill, and he believed his recovery was in doubt."

Simmons told the group it astonished James to learn of his heritage and appalled him to learn of the murders. The fact Albert directed the orchard behind the Youngs' rented property go to James upon Nancy Blanton's death was another surprise. He told Frank he desired to come to Hillview to see where his father and his mother had lived and to learn more of their history. In fact, he was scheduled to arrive in two days. Seventy-year-old James held the opinion that if he did not journey to Hillview soon, he never would.

"I must inform you," Simmons said, "James does not appear interested in the property. He said he doesn't wish to cause trouble, so he instructed me to hold off on any legal proceeding until after he arrived. He'll decide then if he wants to contest Nancy Blanton's will."

Annie clapped her hands and looked at her mother in anticipation. Every bit of color had drained from Ellen's face. Ned and Cora, squeezed each other's hand, thrilled to know that meeting their kin was imminent. Miss Mittie clasped Berta's hand and patted it as they beamed at each other. When Annie glanced over at Noah, she caught him in a peaceful smile.

Berta asked more questions. "We understand my father arranged for Albert to contribute monies for Molly and James's upkeep. How was that done? Was James aware of this?"

Simmons replied he had questioned James concerning payments. James knew his mother had a bank account, but he

256

assumed funds came only from her salary at the Hinshaw residence. He closed the account after her death and told Simmons a mere two dollars were in the account.

"I have arranged for him to meet each of you after he arrives by train this Sunday afternoon," Simmons advised. "Instead of meeting here in my office, my wife and I are pleased to welcome him and you to our home. We have invited him to stay with us while he is in Hillview. It is not a sizable house, but we have an extra room upstairs. I'm sure, Ned and Cora, that he will want to visit with you at your home."

Cora's hands flung into the air. "Wonderful! We will welcome him with open arms!"

The group carried on brief conversations before they departed the law office. A sense of victory filled the air with the realization that James Hill, or James Hinshaw, was alive and was returning to the place of his birth. James knew a history existed of which he was unaware. After years of conjecture, he now had answers to a number of his questions. He was eager to meet at least a handful of his blood kin.

****

The two days until Sunday dragged by with considerable apprehension. The Hillview contingent was eager, yet unnerved, to meet the person who until the week prior could have remained just a theory or a figment of their collective imaginations. When Frank Simmons telephoned to say James had arrived and settled in at the Simmons home, each proceeded there with haste. Carter, Ellen, and Annie arrived first with everyone else following in quick succession. Frank and his wife greeted each person with a warm handshake as they entered. Miss Mittie was accompanied not by Berta, but by a sullen Susie Rutledge.

"Mr. and Mrs. Simmons, I am uncertain whether you know my daughter, Susie Rutledge. Susie is familiar with my history and what we have learned, and I felt she needed to see for herself how this has played out. I hope you don't mind her presence here today."

The lawyer extended his hand to Susie and welcomed her with enthusiasm, as did Mrs. Simmons. Susie's response was unintelligible, and she nodded at the others with no hint of emotion. The entire group moved into the cozy parlor where each took a seat and waited in uneasy silence. The uneasiness one feels when an unknown outcome is on the horizon was palpable. Annie scanned the room and located Noah standing in a corner behind a large potted fern that rested on a marble stand. He tilted his cap toward her, his boyish grin the most handsome she had ever seen.

****

James Hinshaw, original name Hill, strode the length of the stairs and entered the room without affectation. A tall and willowy gentleman with high cheekbones and piercing brown eyes, his smile projected a kind and thoughtful temperament. White strands peppered pitch-black, wavy hair, and his skin was smooth. He wore a gray suit with a darker gray checkered tie. The collar and French cuffs of his starched white shirt against his caramel-colored skin presented a picture of elegance in the sunlit room.

As Frank Simmons introduced him, James shook hands with each person, bowing forth when shaking a feminine hand. He asked each to address him by his first name. James gave Ned a hearty hug, and he hugged Blink, too. Blink's head bobbed as he reciprocated with a nervous squeeze of James's torso. This eased tension in the room by eliciting laughs from everyone, even a chuckle from Susie. When James reached the seated Miss Mittie, he knelt on one knee and took her hands into his.

"From what Mr. Simmons tells me, ma'am, your dear father was responsible for the life my mother and I were given with a most extraordinary family. Your father has my undying

258

appreciation. I am grateful beyond words to tell you this in person, and I am heartsick to learn of your dear sister's experience."

Tears filled the old woman's eyes, which he whisked away with his handkerchief. No words came from her trembling lips. She could only squeeze his hands and offer a feeble smile.

James's reaction to Annie was one of amazement.

"This brave girl is responsible for this meeting and for unearthing the truth regarding my kin! Thank you, thank you, thank you! You are an exceptional young lady!" James squeezed her hand and gave it a lingering kiss.

Embarrassed, Annie hung her head but beamed as her father placed a gentle hand around her shoulder and pulled her close.

James sat in the chair provided and addressed everyone by once again expressing gratitude. To learn of his heritage and receive the opportunity to meet those gathered was the most satisfying experience of his life, he declared. He spoke of his distress to learn his paternal grandfather, Morse Blanton, had murdered his maternal grandfather and uncle. He acknowledged circumstances were conflicted and in turmoil at the time of the murders.

"I am sure Morse Blanton was bitter about emancipation and felt it robbed him of his slaves," James stated. "No hate in my heart will I hold toward the man. I am thankful my mother never knew the truth. She was such a gentle soul, and this knowledge would have troubled her in grievous ways. From what Mr. Simmons told me, those events and separation from my mother must have eaten at my father's soul. I am thankful my father, Albert Blanton, had such an excellent friend as your father," he said as he nodded toward Berta.

Dialogue between James and the others centered on locations and people, questions, and answers. He arranged to go with Frank Simmons to the Hill cabin the following morning, followed by a visit to the Youngs to peek at the orchard. James and the attorney reserved the afternoon for a meeting at the office of Ralph Bennett, where Frank planned to discuss the issue of two conflicting wills.

"I have not yet made an ultimate decision on my actions going forward," James told the group. "My inclination is to leave it be. I am soon to be seventy-one years of age. What will I do with an orchard full of apple trees? We sold the Hinshaw business before these hard times hit, and my brothers and I—we think of each other as brothers—received a fair price. With no family to support, I have lived a frugal life with enough to serve my basic needs. I am a fortunate and grateful man. I am not wealthy, but I have enough."

The afternoon, one of retrospection and speculation, came to a close. The Youngs spoke with the Hills on the front porch, and each person waved at Miss Mittie and Susie Rutledge as they drove away. Although Susie did not acknowledge the gestures, the smile on Miss Mittie's face and the wave of her handkerchief elicited another enthusiastic wave from Annie. The girl's innocent countenance belied the ramifications to come the following day.

PEACE WITHOUT JUSTICE

E vents hurtled forward after the get-together with James Hinshaw at the Simmons home. The next day, before Frank Simmons and James came to call at the Young residence, Noah sat on the edge of Annie's bed, where the two exchanged whispers of hope and encouragement.

Earlier in the day, James and Frank had enjoyed a delightful visit at Ned, Cora, and Blink's cabin before proceeding to the Youngs' home. After short pleasantries on the front porch, Carter and Annie escorted the two men to the property's rear boundary, where Noah stood as a sentinel, observing the scene with keen interest. James scanned the horizon, the orchard, and the stone wall, noting that in his mind the site was sacred. He stood solemn and silent for a long while, imagining the scene Phoebe Mueller beheld.

James questioned Frank as to the big house at the end of the lane, the one where Miss Mittie lived as a child and where her father ministered to the needs of Union and Confederate soldiers. "Who lives there now?"

"It sits empty, James. Mrs. McCormick and her brothers sold it years ago to a rich fellow from Washington who wanted to become a country farmer. He possessed no knowledge of farming, and when the stock market crashed, he lost everything. It's too bad because the house has been there since Revolution times and was once grand. They didn't sell their family cemetery on the property, though. The cemetery isn't visible from the road. It's on the far side of that rise over a way, accessed by a dirt driveway of sorts."

James acknowledged these words with a sigh before he and Frank Simmons left for their appointment with Ralph Bennett at the Bennett Law Office above the Citizens Savings Bank.

****

The meeting turned confrontational in no time. Besides Ralph Bennett, Clay Blanton and his wife Esther were present. Frank Simmons offered evidence proving James Hinshaw was Albert Blanton's son and Clay Blanton's half-brother. Thus, James was the rightful inheritor of the orchard property as stipulated in Albert's will. This evidence ignited a firestorm. In most hostile terms, the Blantons denied the truth of each fact and piece of evidence. When confronted with details of Israel and Ben's bloody murders, ear-splitting insults, more denials, and accusations erupted. Clay Blanton addressed James as an impostor and fraud, saying Albert Blanton never consorted with a slave, "a God damn niggerrr." His disgusting emphasis on the slur's consonants so startled the eavesdropping secretary in the next room, that the glass she held to the door to listen better slipped from her hand and crashed to the floor.

A sanctimonious Esther Blanton lunged at James, screeching the vilest bar room obscenities while flailing her fists in circles around her head. Ralph Bennett took to his feet and attempted to calm the Blantons to no avail. The Blantons' tirade continued, threatening Frank Simmons and James with bodily harm and lawsuits for slander. James remained calm and silent, allowing Simmons to speak for him. Clay and Esther Blanton stormed out the office door, but not before Clay turned over a chair and kicked it against the wall.

James rose and addressed Ralph Bennett in a hushed tone. "Mr. Bennett, I am not here to contest the will of Clay Blanton's mother. Please tell your clients. I need no orchard or other inheritance. I do not want it. I desire nothing but to know the truth of my family and the locality from which my dear mother hailed. Much of what has come to light is difficult for Mr. and Mrs. Blanton to swallow, as we have seen, but I hope their angst and anger will lessen with time."

Ralph Bennett acknowledged James's words with a glare and turned to Frank Simmons. "If he wants nothing, why have you brought this into the open? What's the point?"

Simmons, stabbing the air with his unlit cigar, glared back at Bennett. "Because it's truth. It's always been about truth. Albert Blanton wanted the orchard to go to his son James. Ralph, did you even try to determine who James Hill was or where he was when Albert died? Weren't you or Nancy Blanton curious? Did you even speak with Will Brown? You knew Will. Will Brown wrote Albert's will. He knew everything. Why did we bring it in the open now? Because it's the truth, Ralph. And without truth, this poor earth is no more than a big, stinking mess of wild apple butter!"

Frank Simmons thrust papers into his briefcase before motioning to James that they should leave. They exited the office, each acknowledging the embarrassed secretary still sweeping up shards from the shattered glass.

Standing on the sidewalk, Simmons addressed James with a groan, "That did not go well, James. I must tell you that if we contest Nancy's will, it's probable no judge in these parts will rule in our favor. Shall I drop it?"

James nodded in agreement. With thoughtful humility, he restated his wish to not make trouble for the Blanton family or for anyone else, and he regretted if he had done so.

"Ned and Cora have invited me to sup with them tonight," James said. "If acceptable to you, Ned has offered to pick me up at five o'clock and return me to your house later this evening. He says we will drive around tomorrow to see landmarks and share the history of people and points of potential interest. I shall return to Philadelphia the next day unless you suggest I should stay longer."

Simmons responded that he saw little need for a longer stay since no legal work was required, but James was welcome as a house guest for as long as he desired. The men returned to the home of Frank Simmons and his wife.

The moment Ned arrived at the Simmons residence, James conveyed the dreadful details of the afternoon's uncivil meeting. Over supper, Ned, Cora, and James continued to discuss the complete state of affairs as Blink absorbed each word. It was well after Blink's bedtime before plans were set for the next day of touring, and Ned returned James to the Simmons home in his trusty Speed Wagon.

****

The excursion took several hours before Ned and James returned to the Hills for an early supper of ham, green beans, and pan-cooked cornbread. Warm conversation among the four filled the cabin, and by meal's end, each felt they had known each other a lifetime.

Ellen Young had issued an invitation to come for dessert afterward, and the short trek along the dusty lane led to even more conversation and bonding. As everyone sat around the Youngs' dining room table savoring each bite of Ellen's chocolate cake, James announced his plans to return to Philadelphia the following day. He expressed regret that there were no graves of his grandfather Israel or his Uncle Ben to visit. He wished to have placed flowers before leaving.

"I visit my mother's grave with great frequency and leave flowers there when they are in bloom. Such visits bring me solace. She loved flowers."

Ned said, "Yes, I understand. My parents and grandparents rest in the graveyard on the old Mueller farm, there with Doc and Mrs. Mueller. Phoebe, too, I reckon."

With complete absence of forethought, Annie blurted forth a statement that would soon generate even more gossip and turmoil among Hillview's residents. She realized the minute she stopped speaking the consequences of her words.

"Oh, graves exist, Mr. James! I know where they are, uh, well, I don't know. But I know someone who does. Know. Where they are. I think I do."

An astonished Carter Young stared at his daughter. "What did you say?"

A hushed, "What?" emerged from James's lips as Cora choked on her coffee.

Unnerved, Annie's eyes widened and darted back and forth between the others while her face lost all color. Her mouth opened, but no words came.

Ellen tapped her daughter's arm with a gentle touch. "Annie, honey, please explain."

Anna Ruth Young took a deep breath, and the words poured. "I know you may think I'm crazy or imagining things, but there was a boy wounded by Union soldiers who was lying under a tree on the Blanton side of the stone wall. He saw the murders of Ben and Israel, and he saw Phoebe, too. He died there, but his soul couldn't leave, and Morse Blanton came back and found him when he was looking for something, a watch. And the boy, uh, his name is Noah. Well, Morse and Albert Blanton took Noah's body and buried him next to Israel and Ben's graves. And then, since Noah's soul couldn't leave, he found the watch and took it and hid it in one grave. Noah's spirit has never left. He is still here. Noah confides in me, and he told me everything, and he knows where the graves are. He can't leave . . . his soul . . . or his spirit . . . can't leave until he knows the truth has come out. Now that it has, he can leave soon. Truly, I am not telling a lie. Noah exists. Noah is *real*."

Silence descended upon the dining room as its occupants digested Annie's words. The faces of those unaware of Noah's existence radiated astonishment, disbelief, and confusion. A hesitant Blink broke the protracted silence.

"Ah . . . I . . . b-believe you, Annie. I've seen you. I've seen you talking to somebody out b-back. There wasn't anybody there but you and Bitsy. And Bitsy? A few times she was hanging up in the air as if somebody was holding her. But nobody was! Bitsy was up dangling in the air! All of a s-sudden, she was sitting on the g-ground. It was the strangest thing!"

Annie turned to Blink. "Yes! Noah holds her and pets her, Blink! You can't see him because he doesn't let anyone see him except Bitsy and me!"

More silence.

James cleared his throat and addressed Annie. "Young lady, I do not think you crazy or that you have imagined Noah. Do you believe he could tell us how to find this spot where my kin rest?"

"I think he will tell me."

"I must delay my return home," James declared. "Will you telephone me at the Simmons home tomorrow morning? Is morning too soon, Annie?"

"I'll speak with him tonight, Mr. James."

James Hinshaw rose from the table and strolled over to the girl. Laying his hands on her shoulders, he addressed the group. "Please do not think this inconceivable. I am not a wagering man, but I wager today that this dear girl can lead me to the resting sites of my grandfather and uncle. It sounds genuine to me. Ned, may I trouble you to return me to town now?"

"Certainly." Ned scooted his chair back from the table. "Blink does not fabricate, so I hope this ghost . . ."

Annie interrupted Ned. "Spirit! Noah prefers being called a spirit, Mr. Ned."

Ellen shook her head and glanced over at Carter to measure his reaction, which was a simple, proud grin directed toward his daughter.

Everyone exited the dining room to the front hallway where they exchanged hugs and handshakes, and tears welled up in Annie's eyes as their guests departed for the Hill cabin. There, Ned and James climbed into Ned's old truck, and it delivered James to the Simmons home for a good night's rest.

As Carter and Ellen cleared the table and washed the evening's dishes, Annie was given permission to retire to her bedroom. Darkness had fallen, so she opened the curtains covering her room's rear window and waved the lamp from the dresser, hoping Noah appeared. Appear he did, and he responded with profound enthusiasm to her queries concerning the gravesites.

"The location is not far, Annie. Provide me pen and ink, please. I shall draw a map for you."

Upon receipt of the girl's notebook and pencil, and without use of an eraser, he drew a crude map of the route to the clearing where three graves lay. He drew three trees forming a triangular space.

"The graves lie between these trees, Annie. They are up from the creek. The creek runs a distance from there, but if it flooded, bones may have washed away. Of this I am uncertain. I shall not reveal myself to your friends. You must be the one who leads them. I wish you had not divulged my existence, but your reasons are pure and true."

"Oh, Noah! Nobody would believe me if I just said I knew where the graves were!"

Noah's solemn nod showed he concurred. He tipped his cap toward her and disappeared, just as Bitsy bounded up the stairs.

"Annie! Bitsy is excited and is heading upstairs!" Carter shouted from the foot of the staircase. "Are you all right?"

She opened her bedroom door to the hallway and rushed to the top of the stairs. As Bitsy raced into her room searching for Noah, she shouted, "Daddy! I know the way to the graves! I must ring up Mr. James first thing in the morning!"

"Yes, darling. Good night and sweet dreams."

****

The next day brought forth the dawn of Annie Young's new existence as a target of suspicion, gossip, and disdain . . . and a sense of closure for James Hinshaw.

After telephoning James, Berta, and Miss Mittie, Annie sprinted to the Hill cabin to announce her newfound knowledge as to the site of Israel and Ben's graves. Because it was Saturday and not an office day for Carter Young and Frank Simmons, both joined the group as they traveled to the site. The property where the graves were located had once belonged to Morse Blanton, but he sold it to Old Man Taylor, a farmer who used it as a pasture for his cattle. A call from Frank Simmons to the old farmer's surviving son requesting permission to access the property was well received. The group converged at the Young home and then drove the scant distance to a dirt path whose width accommodated the vehicles by the narrowest of margins. After bumping along at a tedious pace, they soon spotted three trees to the left of the path. A dilapidated bridge that traversed the creek ahead appeared washed out.

"Gracious!" Ellen said as she climbed from their dusty Dodge. "I'm glad Mrs. McCormick isn't with us. This terrain is much too rugged for her to navigate."

"It is for sure," said Berta, who made the trek with her brother-in-law in eager anticipation.

Carter scanned the horizon. "There are no fences here, Frank. I thought you told us the owner ran cattle here."

Simmons shook his head. "The old man had cattle, Carter. The fencing is gone, but see those old, rotten fence posts? His boy, Charlie Taylor, told me Blanton sold this strip of land to his father not long after John Wilkes Booth assassinated Lincoln. Land on the opposite side of the creek already belonged to Old Man Taylor. Blanton offered this parcel to Taylor for next to nothing. Charlie told me this morning his father never understood why Blanton was so eager to sell a strip only two hundred feet deep and four hundred feet wide. The price was ridiculously low."

"I think we know why he sold it," James lamented.

The group trudged through dried stalks of tall grass and patches of lush, fresh grass that June morning before reaching a triangle between three enormous sycamores. The creek, several yards away, carried a tiny trickle of water. Steep creek banks showed no signs of recent or past flooding.

"The graves should line up in a row centered in this triangle formed by these trees," directed Annie as she headed toward the spot. "Noah said he piled rocks from the creek on the graves and buried the watch under one of the rock piles."

Ned brought three rakes and a scythe to the clearing. He handed the rakes to the other men but kept the scythe himself. Swinging and flinging grass and weeds in the air, he mowed the space clean between the three sycamores while the others raked debris produced by his labor. Soon everyone heard a shout from Carter Young.

"Rocks are here! Come look!"

Each rushed to Carter's side, and with great delight, beheld several stones in one spot. Soon they discovered more a few feet away. Cattle had toppled and trampled the rocks, encased by mud and grass, but there they were, arranged with care by a spirit long ago.

Tears flowed from Ellen and Cora as they clung to one another. Berta stood with Frank, holding his arm for support as he offered his handkerchief. Ned knelt on one knee. Carter and James leaned on their rakes, staring at the scene before them, while Annie and Blink stood in silence.

Annie heard a rustle behind her and felt Noah's presence.

"I take my leave now, Annie Young," he whispered in her ear. "Thank you for being the lass I hoped you to be. Please pat Miss Bitsy for me. Goodbye, my champion. The remainder of your gracious life awaits."

She turned fast enough to see his figure disappearing, but not before he tipped his ragged cap to her and lifted his hand in a gentle wave.

"What's wrong, Annie?" asked Blink, standing a mere foot away.

"Nothing. Nothing, Blink." Tears streamed from her soft brown eyes, leaving wet trails along her freckled cheeks that glistened in the morning sun. "It's good. It's good."

****

James began digging stones from one of the rock piles. Frank Simmons started on the other. In a few moments, James retrieved a filthy pocket watch and hoisted it into the air, its chain broken but still attached. With great care, he peeled caked dirt away from the piece. With the help of Ned's pocketknife, James pried open the watch, and there, engraved inside the cover, Morse Blanton's name glared forth for everyone to see.

"Hallelujah," Frank shouted. "Praise the Lord!"

As James rubbed the watch, a gold luster shone through the dirt as the others gathered round to witness the uncovering in silent reverence. A breeze rustling through the trees and the song of a lone mockingbird were the only sounds heard for several moments before James spoke.

"This is hallowed ground. My people are here, and it turns out a fine southern boy, an unwilling Confederate, rests here. Mr. Simmons, is there any possibility I could buy this piece of ground, surround it with a fence, and memorialize these graves?"

Frank Simmons paused before he spoke. "The owner, as I told you, is Charlie Taylor. He's getting on in years. Maybe he's interested in selling. Times are hard. Maybe he could use a bit of cash. Let's return to town, and I will telephone him. I'm confident he wants to know what we found."

Before the group adjourned to their vehicles, a somber James Hinshaw, with a quiver in his voice, offered these parting words. "We have discovered something today most will not believe. I am questioning my own beliefs, and I

270

venture you are as well. Whether a spirit led us here today, I cannot be sure, but here we are. Let us go forth knowing what we have discovered and knowing the truth of it. I cannot put into words my deep appreciation for each one of you. Thank you. Thank you. God bless you all."

Blink rushed to James, locking him in a bear hug. More hugs followed before the group returned to the dusty and rutted path they had traversed to reach this hallowed soil. Everyone except for Frank Simmons and James returned to their own homes. Simmons and James drove to the Simmons Law Office on a quiet street in downtown Hillview where Simmons placed two telephone calls.

****

The call to Charlie Taylor produced an unexpected result. When he learned graves had been found, who was buried in the graves, and circumstances of the burials, Mr. Taylor expressed his desire for James to own the strange strip of property Morse Blanton had sold to Mr. Taylor's father. What had transpired on his father's land disgusted Charlie Taylor, and he refused any payment. He reiterated that his father held no respect for Morse Blanton and always remained puzzled why old Blanton insisted on selling the parcel for so little money. Mr. Taylor requested Frank to draw up a deed transferring ownership to James as soon as possible so he could rid himself of such a dreadful piece of history.

Simmons drew up the deed that afternoon. As soon as the document was completed, Mr. Simmons and James drove the few miles out to Charlie Taylor's modest home.

Just in his sixties, Taylor appeared much older than his age because of years of outside work. His weathered face broke into a wide grin as he extended a large and calloused hand to the callers at his door. "Come in, come in! Frank, I haven't seen you in ages. Reckon it's good I haven't needed a lawyer!"

The three seated themselves at the dining room table where Taylor examined the deed and affixed his signature on the document without hesitation. James signed as recipient of the property, and Frank Simmons signed as a witness. When Taylor questioned how they knew of the graves' location, Frank and James told Taylor about Annie's revelations that led them to the graves. This explanation elicited the expected reaction from the old farmer.

"You tell me a ghost told this girl where the graves were? Ridiculous!"

"Mr. Taylor, that's what she said," asserted James in his soft, affirming voice. "It sounds impossible, but everything she told us panned out, even that Morse Blanton's gold watch was hidden beneath stones marking one grave. She told us that. How could she know? Is the information coming from the beyond? Is she clairvoyant? I don't know, but who are we to question?"

Taylor acknowledged James's account and shrugged his shoulders. "I've lived a long time. I never imagined this. How, why did the truth become known? I don't understand. I'm glad the truth is out. As I told you, Frank, Pa never trusted Morse Blanton. I knew that for years. I was a child when old Blanton died, and after his death Pa told me of this strange transaction. It made no sense for Blanton to unload an 'old piece of worthless dirt' my pa said. He said Blanton insisted, insisted mind you, that Pa buy the property for his cattle. Our farm was . . . is . . . not big, and Pa didn't have that many head, but Pa bought it and fenced it. Pa called it 'Blanton's Strip.' We accessed it from that bridge. Bridge washed out a long time ago. I have an ole' Jersey for milking and a dozen Angus yearling for market, and I keep 'em near the house. Haven't gone to that spot in close to ten years. You do whatever you want with the property, James. If these rough times don't get better soon, I may quit and let this whole dang farm go to seed. Good luck to you."

Frank Simmons made his second telephone call of the day to Ralph Bennett, Clay Blanton's attorney. In a short and clipped conversation, he relayed the information Morse Blanton's gold watch had been uncovered on a grave discovered that morning. Simmons requested Bennett to ask if his client wanted the watch as a memento of his father. The call ended when Bennett offered colorful crudities and slammed the receiver.

Frank Simmons and James Hinshaw left the office and started making the rounds, stopping first at Ned and Cora's with the news James now owned the Taylor property, and he planned to make sure the graves received markers.

Next, they stopped by Annie's home to relay the same news and then drove to the Rutledge home to tell Miss Mittie. The news delighted and relieved her, yet the men could see Susie did not share her mother's enthusiasm. In her aloof and abrupt manner, Susie said, "Thank you for coming," as she escorted the men from the house.

The last stop was to the home of Berta Simmons. She wept tears of joy. "Dad would be so pleased," she proclaimed between sobs, and she repeated her regret at not finding her father's papers earlier. "I plan to carry the missing pages of Dad's manuscript to the library and put them in their proper place myself."

Frank invited James to stay a few days longer at the Simmons home so he could handle personal matters at the gravesites. James Hinshaw accepted the invitation with gratitude.

****

Because Monday was a workday, and he wanted to file the deed at once, Frank was unavailable to furnish transportation for James Hinshaw. So, Ned picked up James and drove him to a local stonemason where James ordered three tombstones, one for Israel Hill, one for Ben Hill, and one for Noah whose surname was unknown. No dates of birth could be engraved since that information was unknown, but James instructed the death year of 1863 engraved on the three monuments. The mason was agreeable to the assignment and charged a reasonable fee. James instructed the man to notify Ned when work was complete, so Ned could go with the mason to help set the stones.

The next stop was to the sawmill just outside town where the mill owner agreed to accompany the men to the site. The efficient sawyer measured the space inside the triangle formed by the three sycamore trees, made calculations on his order form, and presented James with an estimate for a fence. It was to be a picket fence four feet tall, and the man could install it within one week. A Hillview resident had ordered the enclosure for his home, but when it was ready, there was no money with which to pay.

"My customer wants me to hold everything until he can pay," the man told James, "but you are here with money. So, I will use what I had made for him. Times are hard. One in the hand is worth two in the bush, you understand! I built a nice gate with an arbor for him. It's perfect for this little cemetery. How many graves are here?"

"Three," James said. "Markers will be installed soon."

"Family?"

"Yes. Indeed, they are."

Ned and James next stopped by Frank Simmons's office and found him in consultation with Ralph Bennett. As they waited in the anterior office, they heard enraged voices coming from behind the closed door where Simmons and Bennett were in engaged in heated discourse.

When the door to the private office opened, Bennett stalked out, ignoring James and Ned who were seated in plain sight. Simmons appeared at the door of his office and motioned James and Ned inside his office. He informed James and Ned that Bennett threatened legal action against James, Ned, Berta, and Carter Young for slandering the good name of the Blanton family. Bennett even hinted he might consider such action against Miss Mittie. Simmons suggested they should not take seriously such threats, as it was rare for Bennett to follow through with lawsuits except for foreclosures. Threats, bullying, and intimidation paid off when directed against the weak and helpless. Word of the graves' discovery had leaked into the town's gossip mill, though, and to say it upset the Blantons was too mild a description.

"I hoped we had a few days before this became common knowledge," Simmons sighed. "I suspect Charlie Taylor talked. Charlie's pappy didn't admire Morse one whit, and Charlie knows a bunch of folks, so . . . it's likely to get ugly around here."

****

Bennett never advanced the threats he made in the office of Frank Simmons, Esquire, but the entire story spread throughout Hillview as fast as fatback through a goose. The graves, the watch, James's parentage, the interracial love story, the murders, and the spirit that led Annie Young to the graves became main topics of gossip throughout the valley. In time, it was doubtful anyone within the region escaped some version of the details.

James remained in Hillview for two more days before boarding the train back to Philadelphia. As promised, the fence was installed around the graves within the week. Ned and Blink whitewashed the pickets and posts, making it dazzle in sunlight, and they planted fragrant lilacs on either side of the gate. The stonemason and Ned set markers on the graves within a month, and the little cemetery was whole.

On one cloudless morning at summer's end, Berta, Ned, Cora, and Blink along with Carter, Ellen, and Annie stood together bearing flowers to place on the graves inside the white picket fence. Each reflected in silence upon murders witnessed so long ago by an innocent young girl. Some seventy years later, another innocent girl ushered a true account of those murders into the glare of light, aided by a restless and impatient spirit who inspired her quest for truth. The spirit, a witness to truth, had been biding his time waiting, always waiting, hoping the stone wall would surrender the key, a broken cameo dropped in the dirt. He had waited for someone, someone like Annie Young, to use the key to unlock the truth. The invisible threads binding the secrets were now severed. Noah's spirit could rest, and Phoebe's last wish was granted.

Annie turned to Blink, repeating what she said the morning they discovered the graves. "It's good. It's good."

EPILOGUE

"**T**here you have it, granddaughter," Anna Ruth declares. "No one knows of this story other than you. Do you think your grandmother crazy?"

KT shakes her head. "No, Nonnie, I don't, but I want to know what happened afterward."

The old woman gulps her water and continues, "The time afterward wasn't altogether happy. We remained here approaching three more years." An index finger points to the decrepit dwelling they passed on their way to the stone wall.

"Suspicion and ridicule made me a target. Hate, too. Because I didn't have friends at school anyhow, nothing changed other than barbs and isolation from my classmates. It never stopped. What Miss Mittie told me, to hold my head high, walk right past, and never acknowledge taunts, gave me strength. Daddy's practice suffered because friends of the Blantons switched to Jack Morrison or the other doctor in town. Others quit seeing Daddy, too, those who thought he had a crazy daughter! Daddy did receive new patients, most of whom been taken advantage of by Clay Blanton, but many couldn't pay. Mama didn't get as many requests for sewing as before, and she resigned from the garden club. Thank goodness oil money continued to come in! It kept us afloat."

"Why did you move away? Was it just too difficult here?"

"Oh, difficulties were part of it, but my grandparents were both experiencing severe health issues. Mama and Daddy returned to where we came from to be of help to them, and I imagine to escape the always churning gossip mill here. Another doctor arrived in Hillview, so it was easy for Daddy to turn over his practice. As for me, my marks were such that I graduated high school early and enrolled at university. It was perfect timing for us to leave."

KT still has more questions. "What happened to Blink? And Miss Mittie?"

Anna Ruth fingers the locket hanging around her neck, the one containing Phoebe's picture, as she answers. "Our Thursday visits continued, but we never spoke of what had happened. We discussed books and played dominoes. When her eyesight became poor, I read to her. Miss Mittie died two years after the revelations. The last time I saw her, she told me she loved me and was glad I had come into her life and proven Phoebe right. Miss Mittie told me something else I have not forgotten, either. I wrote it in my notebook so I could never forget."

Anna Ruth fumbles in a pocket, pulls forth a folded and yellowed piece of paper, and reads aloud:

The pursuit of truth is a restless endeavor, yet with it comes understanding. It is this hard-earned understanding that has rewarded me the most. This gift provided me with a strong and sustaining sense of purpose and the loyal companionship of an everlasting kindred spirit.

Anna Ruth hands the paper to KT. "Maybe you will think of me whenever you read this, dear granddaughter."

KT stuffs the paper in her sweater pocket and looks to her grandmother, scanning her face.

"Susie Rutledge allowed us to continue renting the house, but as soon as we moved away, she put it up for sale. Nobody bought it, so she left it to me in her will! The gesture was one of spite, not generosity! The sign out front has hung there ever since I inherited the place. Someday it will be your albatross, I fear!"

KT winces at the thought of owning a decrepit old house perceived as haunted by locals.

"As for Blink, we remained the best of friends. Our interracial friendship was another reason for disdain directed toward me. Blink overcame his stuttering and nervousness through music. He sang and played mandolin with a local bluegrass band for years, and he became a remarkable landscaper, operating a successful nursery on the Hill property down the way. He was an esteemed naturalist and even had a popular garden show on Hillview's radio station. We regularly corresponded until his death. Blink tended this property, the little cemetery where Israel, Ben, and Noah are buried, and even the cemetery on the old Mueller farm where Miss Mittie rests. I sent him money for the upkeep, but he never cashed a single check. Never. Blink was a good and true friend."

KT hesitates before inquiring about Noah.

"Noah I never saw after the day we discovered the graves. Besides Blink and Miss Mittie, Noah was my best friend. Oh, the discussions of countless things we shared! Beliefs! Dreams! Noah taught me more of day-to-day life and attitudes of average people during the time he lived in the flesh than one could ever learn from books. By his words, his deeds, his sweetness, he taught me the value of life and death, of truth and perseverance. Noah is the reason I found my calling as a history professor of the Civil War period. His stories and Miss Mittie's gave me such insights. My students told me my lectures were powerful and vivid, often asking if I had known someone who lived back then. I told them I had."

These revelations cause KT to view her grandmother in a far richer light. KT had thought the woman somewhat peculiar, but now she understands her Nonnie is extraordinary. She reaches over and takes her grandmother's hand, giving it a kiss.

"Now, I don't want you to think we were unhappy, KT. Oh, we had joyful times, but there were tough times. Mama and Daddy supported me. They were my rock, my strength. The Morrisons remained devoted friends. Ned and Cora, too. Not long before this place became a memory, my Bitsy died. Bitsy was old, and she just got sick and died. Daddy buried her here, near where I found the cameo. Bitsy's death devastated me, but my parents pulled me through my grief. The last thing we did before they put me on the train for Chapel Hill was to visit her grave here. It's over yonder there." Anna Ruth points to a spot next to the stone wall several feet from where KT sits.

"I'm so sorry, Nonnie," KT murmurs.

"Mama and Daddy left town the next day to return to the plains. They retraced the exact route we had taken in 1933. Toward the end of their journey, they observed the red dirt road was no longer shrouded in choking dust and misery as before. Winds had calmed, and the drought had broken. The vision of a sunny blue sky, grazing cattle, the occasional field of tall corn, and that first sweet smell of red dirt so moved my parents that they pulled off the road and wept with joy. Our trials and tribulations had endowed them with a fresh sense of purpose and direction, they said. Daddy counseled me again that the ole' red dirt road was just like life; sometimes it's rough and we can't see how we will get through, and then without warning it's unobstructed and straightforward."

KT acknowledges Anna Ruth's comparison with a grimace.

"They kept in touch with the Morrisons and the Hills, but none of us ever returned to Hillview. Your grandfather and I met and married right before he left for World War II. He was killed near war's end, at Okinawa you know, which forced your mother and me to create a life for ourselves. That your mother never knew her father left my heart heavy. After I left here and embarked on the next chapter of my life, he was the only person besides my parents to call me Annie. Anna Ruth was my name after I left. I left Annie behind, right here." She jabs her bent, arthritic finger toward the ground where she sits.

KT stands and leaves her grandmother to make her way through the brush to Bitsy's grave. Under careful examination, a rock outline is visible. The remains of a rotted wooden cross lie on top, covered in vines and leaves. She clears a few leaves from around the grave and scans the landscape for several moments. KT imagines it so long ago, with Blaze galloping along the trail beside the wall, Phoebe's wind-tossed hair flowing, a carefree smile on her innocent face. KT imagines Phoebe's terror. She pictures her grandmother as a determined girl rebuilding a crumbled stone wall, often with help from a loving father, a loyal friend named Blink, and a restless spirit who at long last found his peace. KT's heart aches. She glances at the sky and realizes the sun will soon set. It's been a long afternoon.

"Nonnie, we must go," she calls. "It will get dark soon. We must return to the hotel."

After getting no response, KT quickens her pace to the picnic site. As it comes into view, she catches sight of the silhouette of the old woman slumped in her chair.

"Nonnie! Nonnie!" KT grabs her grandmother's arm, searching for a pulse. Nothing! She fumbles with her cell phone and punches 911. KT pulls the green and black plaid blanket from Anna Ruth's lap, spreads it on the ground, and positions Anna Ruth upon it. KT tries and tries to resuscitate to no avail. Collapsing into the chair across from her grandmother's body, uncontrollable and body-wracking sobs overtake her.

"No, no, no, no! Not now! Not when I finally know you! Not when I understand!" Her trembling hands embrace her hot, tear-streaked face.

A distraught KT flinches as a furry something brushes her left leg, whirling past in a frenzy. Startled, KT bounds from the chair as a small black, white, and tan terrier settles next to Anna Ruth, gently licking the back of her lifeless hand. No

281

sooner does the little dog appear, but a grimy, auburn-haired young man in tattered pants and shirt comes into view just beyond the wall. Moving with uncommon ease, he leaps over the rubble and strolls toward Anna Ruth. With a gentle smile, he removes his old gray cap and extends his other hand.

"You're here!" beams a freckled, teen-aged girl as she accepts his hand and rises to her feet from the stilled form lying on a blanket. Hand in hand, the girl and the boy stride off at a brisk pace, leaving Anna Ruth's vacant form on the blanket next to the camp chair. Its stubby tail in constant motion, the little terrier tags behind as the three fade into the woods.

The sun is setting. KT and the earthly remains of Anna Ruth are alone. Too soon, the woods' peaceful silence gives way to the sound of a high-pitched siren wailing in the distance, coming closer, ever closer . . . back to where it all began.

ABOUT THE AUTHOR

I was born in Kansas City, Missouri and grew up in Norman, Oklahoma. Good public schools and access to the University of Oklahoma drew my grandparents to Norman in 1920. They viewed education as the key to better opportunity. By the time of my birth, those hard times that defined Oklahoma during Great Depression had been replaced by considerable optimism and prosperity, at  least in Norman. I grew up within a few blocks of the main campus. Like most of my friends and family, I was a diligent student and predestined to attend college at OU.

Upon graduation, with a major in English and a minor in Journalism, I struck out on my own to accept a teaching position in Houston. Despite the miserable heat and humidity, Houston expanded my horizons. Here, I met my husband, gave birth to our child, and spent several rewarding years teaching 8th grade English before co-founding a group of travel agencies with my husband. Those travel agency years were always interesting, and thanks to our dedicated employees, the business grew and was respected for its attention to customer service. After seventeen years in Houston, we were exhausted. We were hungry for a four-season climate, fewer seven-day work weeks, and a more family-friendly lifestyle. We sold the business, and in 1987 it's off to Kansas City.

If Houston was hard, Kansas City was delightful. Over the course of thirteen years, I enjoyed a career in the field of educational publishing, we raised our son, became involved in civic activities, and forged some lasting friendships. My career ended abruptly, due to a series of mergers and acquisitions. We were empty nesters now, and my husband was offered a nice promotion that required us to relocate to the D.C. area.

Our new home was in the historic Eastern Panhandle of West Virginia, about an hour west of Washington. This spot of heaven in the upper Shenandoah Valley was to be our home for the remainder of our years. It offered natural beauty, cultural opportunities, good friendships, civic involvement, retirement, and easy access to our grandchildren in Washington. What could go wrong?

Our son and daughter-in-law did exactly what my grandparents did so long ago. They sought a community with better schools for their kids and better opportunities for themselves. The place—Overland Park, Kansas. After a couple of years, we followed and are happy to be back in the Midwest. Once again, we are close to our dearest ones and their pets, projects, and shenanigans.

My new home office looks out on what was an old farm with a primitive grass runway. Occasionally, the sweet lady who owns the place will taxi her small airplane to the end of the runway, finish her coffee, and go up for a spin around the countryside. I am inspired by my new setting and am more than ready to share a few tales.

SPECIAL RESOURCES

REVIEWS:
I hope you enjoyed this story as much as I enjoyed telling it.
If you'd like to encourage others to read it, please go to my
book's listing on **AMAZON**, scroll down to the *Customer
Review* button and give it a nice rating. The Comments
section there is a great place to leave feedback for me and
other readers. Another great place for reviews is on the
GOODREADS.COM website. Thank you!

FACEBOOK:
Please come to visit at **Jane Yearout, Author**!

I'd really like to know how my tale may relate to you or
someone you know. Although it is just a story, it is based on
things I have learned over time on the red dirt road. Along the
way, I've tried to pack in a few life lessons that may be worthy
of passing forward. If this aspect of my novel touched you in
some way, I'd love to hear your story.

I will use my Facebook page to post any news relating to my
novel, such as events, billion-dollar movie deals, the Pulitzer
Prize, or whether Aunt Pug loved or hated my book.

WEBSITE: www.ashfoard.com
Events. Updates. About author. About novel. Music Page.

WHAT'S WITH THE MUSIC?

Along the Red Dirt Road was inspired by an assorted lot of people, places and circumstances that I've encountered (or imagined) since childhood. After my novel was well underway, I began to realize how beautifully certain music resonated with the narrative. To me, the music made the story fuller, more meaningful than ever, and vice versa. Could it be the same for the people, places and circumstances I was writing about?

For years, I have been a fan of Kathy Mattea and Tim O'Brien. They inspire me on many levels. More recently, I have come to love the work of First Aid Kit, Kacey Musgraves, Mumford & Sons, the Henry Girls, and the Tennessee Mafia Jug Band. Although Cowboy Jack Clements, Al Bowlly, and Ozzie Nelson are no longer among the living, their songs, like those of all the others, blend beautifully with the story line.

Should you listen to the eleven songs in my playlist **BEFORE** reading Along the Red Dirt Road, you may pick up a few juicy clues and find yourself humming as you read. If you listen **AFTERWARD**, I'm betting you'll gain a richer understanding of the story, the characters, and each of the songs. My book and I share a special bond with this music, and I hope you enjoy the artists, their recordings, the lyrics, and the songwriters as much as I do.

To hear the playlist, read the lyrics, or learn about the artists/ songwriters, please visit my website at **www.ashfoard.com**

Made in the USA
Monee, IL
20 January 2023

25757541R00173